Trapped. She was trapped.

Trapped. She was trapped. She thrust her elbow back into the hollow of his belly, and he grunted in pain as she swooped out from under his arm.

"You must calm yourself, Katherine," he said, his tone soothing as he followed her to the bed.

Slipping a hand beneath the pillow, she grasped the butt of the pistol and withdrew it from its hiding place. Cocking it, she thrust it squarely into his groin.

He froze.

"We are not doing this." Her voice sounded husky around the knot of smothering rage lodged in her throat. "How long have you known we could not annul the marriage?"

His gaze slid downward to the gun then moved back up to her face. With studied care, he eased back from her. "I suspected it from the beginning."

Resolve hardened within her. She would not be his wife. She would not be anyone's wife. She kept the gun steady in its position. "Move back."

"My father always told me never to point a loaded pistol at anyone lest you were prepared to fire it." He stepped back, his movements slow and measured, his hands palm out.

"My brother once told me so as well." She struggled not to allow her gaze to waver. "Back up." When he hesitated she added, "I should hate to give you a lead ball for a wedding gift."

Captive Hearts

by

Teresa J Reasor

Captive Hearts

Cover Art by *Kim Mendoza*

The Wild Rose Press
PO Box 706
Adams Basin, NY 14410-0706
Visit us at www.thewildrosepress.com

Publishing History
First English Tea Rose Edition, July 2007
Print ISBN 1-60154-075-2

Published in the United States of America

Dedication

To my Dad, because he thought there was nothing I couldn't do. And to my friend, Jean Lawson, who read this book in its first incarnation and said, "You can make it better." I miss you both.

CHAPTER 1

London, England 1796

"I do not know why you feel you must accompany me." Edward's peevish whine sounded as annoying as a rusty gate.

Katherine braced her hand on the leather seat as the coach turned a steep curve. "You are arranging my marriage, Uncle. Do you not think I should take an interest in the man to whom you are going to promise me?"

"Lord Willingham has assured me his nephew is an honorable man, Katherine."

"A man of honor imprisoned for smuggling. Forgive me if I have some reservations."

Edward drew a deep breath, his long beaked nose contracting. "It was a misunderstanding between him and Lord Rudman. His release has been arranged for tomorrow."

"If he agrees."

"Living for two months in such conditions is enough to test any man's mettle. He will agree."

She pushed aside the leather shade covering the coach window and looked out at the rain-washed London streets. She took care to control her expression and her voice so he would see none of the fury seething within her. How could he be so callous? "Does it not trouble you that in order to get a man to wed me, you must threaten him with prison?"

Edward's gray brows drew together in a frown, his thin face hardening with displeasure. "A husband who will be regaining his freedom, his ship, and his profits, because of you, will have sufficient reason to pledge his loyalty."

She straightened her shoulders. A loyalty thrust down his throat by threats would mean little once they were at sea on his ship. She shuddered at the possible mistreatment she might suffer at the hands of such a man.

"A marriage was to be arranged for you sooner or later, Katherine." He stretched his thin legs out and appeared to study the careful alignment of knee breeches, stockings, and shoes. He pulled a lace-trimmed handkerchief from his sleeve and bent to rub away a muddy smudge from the toe of his expensive leather footwear. "Had your father lived he would have seen to it himself."

"Your eagerness to fulfill your duty as my guardian is touching, Uncle." Her sarcasm earned an exasperated snort.

"I am doing what I think best. I am eager for you to leave all this unpleasantness behind you. If seeing you wed to a Yankee will insure that, so be it."

Unpleasantness! Her entire family lay dead and he resented the inconvenience their demise had caused him.

Lowering his brows into a scowl, he avoided her gaze as he fidgeted with the lacy sleeve draped about his hand. "I know you had hoped to see the men responsible captured." He stuffed the handkerchief back into place. "I am certain justice will be done, but it will be left to others to see to it, not you. Once you are wed, you will have other responsibilities."

He thought to distract her with a husband and all the demands one would entail. Rage clogged her throat and made it difficult for her to breathe. It took several moments for her to beat back the emotion.

Pretending calmness she didn't feel, she settled back into the corner of the seat and brushed away a small piece of lint from the skirt of her black gown. She would bide her time. Once Edward was lulled into complacency, she would do as she pleased.

The coach rolled to a stop, and within moments, the door opened. A footman lowered the steps.

Edward donned his tricorn and alighted from the coach. Adjusting the hood of her cloak over her hair, Katherine paused in the open door, her attention focused on the large flat-roofed building before her. Wet stone mirrored the gray of the clouds overhead. Barred windows and heavy wooden doors gave the impression of brooding malevolence. Rust stained the stone facings around the bars as though the walls wept tears of blood.

She shivered at the thoughts, and at her uncle's impatient gesture, grasped his hand and stepped down from the conveyance. He guided her around the large puddles blocking their path to the side entrance. At his knock, a small square opening appeared in the heavy wooden portal.

"Open, man," he ordered. "It is raining."

"Aye, yer Lordship."

The door swung inward and the guard's rotund figure stepped back to allow them to enter. The dreary light touched on a round bloated face surrounded by greasy hair before the man closed the door and secured it. The dull flickering glow of an oil lamp suspended from the wall illuminated the stained corridor walls and crept across the dirt clogged floors.

The guard's small close-set eyes focused on her. "Ye said nothin' about bringin' a woman with ye."

"This is Captain Hamilton's betrothed, Mr. Hicks. Surely you understand her eagerness to see him."

"This be no place for a woman, yer Lordship."

"After all the trouble he has caused you, I am sure you wish to be done with the man. Her presence may inspire him to be reasonable."

Hicks grimaced. "The Yank be more than trouble. 'E near 'ad a revolt planned amongst the others." A sneer curled his lip. "We should 'ave done away with the whole lot of them colonials a score a years ago."

"I believe we tried that and failed, Mr. Hicks," she said.

A scowl creased his piggish features as he pointed at her with the end of his small wooden club. "Keep yer distance from the bloke. Should the tricky bastard try anythin' whilst yer here, I'll be obliged to knock 'is head for 'im."

He strode down the passageway ahead of them, leaving the smells of stale sweat and garlic in his wake.

Fanning his face with his hand, Edward grasped her arm and hurried her forward. The farther they traversed along the narrow corridor, the more overpowering became the stench of unwashed bodies and human waste. Some poor wretch's cries of pain drifted from within the bowels of the jail.

The walls closed in on Katherine, making it difficult for her to inhale the stagnant air into her lungs. She focused on the dim light offered by the torches hung at intervals along the way and fought the stifling feeling of being buried. She refused to give Edward the satisfaction of knowing how frightening she found the place. To show him weakness would encourage him to exploit her frailty.

Hicks halted before one of the doors. "Lord Willing'am be inside with 'amilton." The large ring of keys he gripped in his beefy hand jingled as he unlocked the door.

"I would ask you to stay here, Katherine, until I have had an opportunity to speak with Captain Hamilton," Edward urged.

She suppressed a shudder at being left in the dark passageway with Mr. Hicks. "Why can I not join you, Edward?"

"He may be more reasonable about the situation if I smooth the way. You do not wish to appear overly eager, do you?"

She bit back the bubble of hysterical laughter threatening to erupt. "Yes, I am most eager to wed a stranger. As eager, I am sure, as he will be."

He thrust his thin features, tight with anger, close to hers, his gray eyes glassy and cold in the dull light. "You will remain here or I will have Mr. Hicks escort you back to the coach." He underlined each word with the stabbing movement of his rain spotted tricorn.

"You have only a moment; then I am coming in."

Her uncle jerked himself erect and puffed out his chest. His thin frame remained stiff with displeasure as he stood back to allow Hicks to open the cell door.

****

"You can't be serious." Matthew Hamilton shook his head in amazement. "If I'd wanted another wife, I'd be wed already."

"What do you mean another wife?" his visitor demanded, his eyes wide with surprise.

"My nephew's wife, Caroline, died in childbirth four years ago, Edward," Talbot Willingham explained.

4

"Good—ah," Edward faltered.

The man's callousness caught Matthew by surprise and he focused on him through narrowed eyes.

Edward's cheeks turned a ruddy color. "I mean—it is good there is no obstacle to the union between you and my niece, Captain Hamilton."

Matthew suppressed a sneer. "There is, Leighton. I don't wish to remarry. I'd say that was obstacle enough."

"You do not seem to understand, sir. Either you agree to the marriage, or you remain here in this place-- indefinitely."

Matthew looked to Talbot. His uncle's nod gave him pause. The marks on the wall just behind the straw cot where he slept caught his eye. He had no need to count them. He had spent two months and one week in this hellish place.

"On completion of the marriage ceremony, your ship and the proceeds from the sale of the cargo will be released to you. You will be free to return to America, with my niece of course."

"Free, but not free." Bitterness rose in him. First they imprisoned him for a crime he didn't commit and now they wished to foist a wife on him. "What is wrong with this woman that you must go to such lengths to find her a husband?"

Edward straightened his skinny frame, his long nose flaring with indignation. "Why there is nothing wrong with Katherine, unless you count being quick of wit and strong of will as faults."

She was probably a harridan. "How old would this-- maid be?"

"She will be ten and nine the first of December, Captain Hamilton. Young enough to provide you many children, yet old enough to allay the boredom of having wed a child right out of the school room."

Leighton had missed his calling. He would have made a gifted auctioneer or perhaps a slave trader.

"Perhaps you would care to meet her?" The foppish Lord moved to the door and opened it.

Matthew had only a moment to wonder what kind of man would bring a lady to such a place when he spied Hicks just outside the portal. His resentment flared. He would not be humbled before the man who had tormented him these last two months.

He folded his arms before him in a relaxed pose, knowing his lack of fear in the guard's presence infuriated the man. "I thought I smelled your stench close by, Hicks."

"Ye don't smell like no flower garden yerself, Yankee," Hicks returned.

"After two months of your stinginess with water and soap, I at least have an excuse. There's no jailer intent on depriving you of such comforts."

The guard grimaced and shook the club at him. "I'll deprive ye of a few teeth if ye don't keep a civil tongue in yer head."

"You may try, my friend."

Hicks's cheeks flushed and he started forward, his club raised. He stumbled and fell like a stone, his head thumping the dirt floor.

"Oh, Mr. Hicks, do forgive me!" A breathless feminine voice exclaimed. "I did not mean to trip you. Here, you must allow me to help you up." The deep blue hood of her cloak partially covered the woman's face as she bent to assist the man on the ground. Once on his knees, Hicks extended an arm to retrieve the club. She stepped to the side, her heel grinding down on his outstretched hand.

The guard yelped and jerked the abused digit back.

"Oh how clumsy of me, Mr. Hicks." She grasped the man's arm just above the elbow and at the same time scooped up the club in the other hand. "Here is your stick," she offered. As he regained his feet, she raised the weapon butt first hitting him just beneath the chin. His jaws snapped shut with a click, and with a muffled cry of pain, he clapped a hand over his mouth.

"Whatever is wrong now, Mr. Hicks?" she asked, her tone laced with concern.

"I bit me bloody tongue!" he groaned and dodged the wooden cudgel as she raised it once again.

"Give me that," Edward demanded, jerking the weapon out of her hand. "Before you kill the man." He turned his attention to the guard. "Hicks, wait outside for us." He thrust the club at the injured man, missing his nose by an inch.

The guard jerked back in reaction, still holding his mouth. He grasped the staff and held it away as though he thought it might set itself on him. As the door slammed shut behind him, Katherine bent to retrieve something from the cell floor.

"He dropped his keys," she announced.

Matthew laughed aloud. She brushed back the hood of the cloak from her hair to reveal glossy burnished curls, deep chestnut in color. The heavy locks cascaded over her shoulder as she turned toward him.

He controlled his expression with an effort, for the beauty standing before him was not what he had expected.

Edward hastened to make the introductions. "Lord Willingham, allow me to introduce my niece, Katherine Leighton."

"It is a pleasure, Lady Katherine." A hint of suppressed laughter played about his uncle's lips as he bent with courtly grace over the hand she offered him.

"Perhaps you should have these." She offered Talbot the ring of keys.

With a chuckle, he accepted them. "Allow me to introduce you to my nephew." Talbot urged her toward him.

Dark, almond shaped eyes the color of wild violets rose to fasten on him. The mass of auburn curls framed one side of her small oval face emphasizing her clear, creamy complexion. Color rose in her cheeks.

A polite smile curved her lips, showing small, even pearl-white teeth. "'Twould seem Mr. Hicks has derived great pleasure in denying you as many comforts as possible, Captain Hamilton." As she surveyed the sparse appointments of the cell, anger flitted across her face. "From what I observed while in the corridor, he seems to enjoy overstepping his duties in regard to disciplining the prisoners as well."

"You could say that," he agreed. The soft clean scent of soap and woman wafted up to Matthew, stirring to life a hunger he tried hard to ignore. Two months aboard ship and two long months of confinement had honed his desire for a woman to a razor sharp edge. "The other prisoners would've relished seeing him get some of his own."

7

"What was it you did to cause Lord Rudman to send you to this place?" she asked without preamble.

"Katherine," Edward objected.

Matthew ignored the man, sensing his freedom rested in the hands of the young woman before him and not her uncle. "It wasn't so much what I did, but what his wife had in mind for me to do. When I refused, she told her husband I had taken liberties. The next morning my ship was put under guard, and I was brought here." Edward broke in, "It matters little what you did or did not do, Hamilton. You can be released as early as tomorrow morning. All you need do is agree to the terms."

Irritation flickered across Lady Katherine's face as she turned her attention to her uncle.

So she wasn't as resigned to being wed to a colonial criminal as she pretended.

"Edward, I would ask for a few moments alone with Captain Hamilton," she said.

The man's gaze traveled from his niece, to Matthew, then back again. "That would not be proper, Katherine."

One wing-like auburn brow rose and a brief beat of time passed before she spoke in a slow measured tone. One fist clenched at her side. "You left me in the hall unchaperoned with Mr. Hicks, Uncle. Are you saying you trust the guard more than the man to whom you hope to wed me?"

Edward compressed his lips, his displeasure at the censor in her tone evident.

"You and Lord Willingham will be just outside the door should I need you. I am sure Captain Hamilton will conduct himself like a gentleman. After all, I do not believe he would wish to do anything that would lengthen his stay here." Her gaze swung to Matthew, "Is that not right, Captain?"

"For certain, Lady Katherine." He inclined his head.

His uncle grasped Edward by the elbow and guided him from the cell. "Your niece will be perfectly safe with Matthew, Edward. She will be alone with him soon enough if they wed, will she not?" The metal door slammed shut behind them.

Her chin rose and her violet eyes took on a flinty hue as she surveyed him from head to toe. She stepped close.

"Do you wish to leave this place?"

"Yes, I do."

"Good." She shed her cloak and folded it over her arm. The square neckline of the black dress she wore was modest enough, but the high empire waistline cupped the generous swell of her bosom like a lover's hands.

Matthew tensed. He wondered if she knew what her beauty did to a man who had been immured for so long. With an effort, he dragged his gaze back up to her face, watching the lush curve of her lips as she spoke.

"I no more wish to wed than you, but I must, and so must you if you wish to be free again."

He braced his feet and clasped his hands behind him, suppressing the quick smile tempting his lips. No sweet natured, tractable miss here, but no harridan either. "Why must you wed?"

For a moment, she remained silent, her long auburn lashes obscuring her gaze. She turned a graceful profile to him as her attention moved to the window set high in the wall. "My uncle is my guardian, and I am at the mercy of his generosity. With my marriage, I will receive a small allowance from the estate. It will not be much, but will be enough on which to live."

He'd warrant there was more to the situation than that. Otherwise, she wouldn't be avoiding his gaze so diligently. "You'll not need it if you're wed."

Her violet eyes returned to him. "I do not intend to remain married long. You will only be allowing me the use of your name for as long as it takes to settle my father's estate and secure my legacy. We can have the marriage annulled as soon as that transpires."

He raised his brows. "And on what grounds do you hope to have the marriage annulled?"

"With my testimony and your uncles, we can prove you were unlawfully coerced into the union. Surely, the courts will grant you—us—an annulment on those grounds."

Resentful of the temptations she presented, he couldn't resist toying with her a little, just to test her resolve.

"As long as the marriage isn't consummated."

Her jaw grew taut and her dark gaze focused on him

intently. "That indeed would be a requirement of both the marriage and the annulment, sir. I would require your word of honor you will respect my wishes."

He was amazed at the trust she extended so easily. "The honorable word of a Yankee prisoner wouldn't hold a great deal of value for most, Lady Katherine."

"The honorable word of Lord Willingham's nephew would. Even I know of your uncle's reputation, Captain. Were you not worthy of his concern, he would not be here." She shifted nearer and tipped her head back to look up at him, her fragile, feminine form only a foot away. Her skin smooth and flawless looked warm and soft. The sweet scent of violets teased his nostrils, making him aware of his unsightly appearance and the rancid smell emanating from his unwashed body. Never had he hated Hicks any more than he did in this moment.

"You would be placing your name, and through association, your uncle's in my trust, Captain Hamilton."

"You'd be marrying down, for though my uncle holds a title, my father didn't," he countered.

Her chin rose. "I have always believed that a man's worth is measured by how he conducts himself rather than the title he holds."

Her earnest sincerity triggered a smile. "The same could be said of a woman, Lady Katherine."

An unexpected flicker of pain crossed her features. He frowned at her reaction, his well-honed instinct for self-preservation sending prickles of alarm racing up the back of his neck.

The cell door swung inward and Talbot Willingham stepped through the portal. His expression grave, his white brows puckered in a frown, his gaze swung from one to the other then settled on Matthew. "Lord Leighton is anxious to know if you have come to a decision."

Matthew ignored Talbot's presence as he sought to delve into her carefully composed features. Even if they were able to annul the marriage, the process could take years and by then her reputation would be compromised. There would be no annulment, and he would be stuck with a wife he didn't want.

Why was she willing to go to such extremes? What trouble would he be accepting if he consented to her proposal? "It would seem a little trust is required to stretch a fair distance, for us both."

"Yes," she said, her voice breathy and soft.

Damn! He didn't like placing his future, his life, in her hands, any more than he cared for Hicks's control. He liked even less having no choice. "Aye, we have come to an agreement."

Conscious of the layer of grime staining his skin, he offered her his hand. Surprising him, she accepted it without hesitation. Though her hand felt small and cold within his, her grasp was firm.

She must be in desperate straits indeed to agree to wed him in his present condition, but not as desperate as he. By morning, he'd be free!

CHAPTER 2

"Scrub harder, Bradley." Matthew leaned forward as the man ran the brush down between his shoulder blades.

"Should I scrub any harder, Captain Hamilton, I should be taking your skin off with the brush. Perhaps a change of water might be in order now, sir. Next we will do your hair and beard." The valet straightened and mopped his forehead with his shirtsleeve.

"I believe I have lice." Matthew smiled at the man to soften the blow. "I'll buy you a bottle of your favorite scotch, Bradley."

The man blanched, but to his credit, his stiff upper lip remained firm.

Matthew smiled. "Shall I send for the scotch now?"

"Nay, I would not wish to share it with the little buggers. If you will rise now, I will send down for more water and we will go after the beasts."

Two hours and many scrubbings later, Matthew viewed his image in the large dressing room mirror. His hair, having been trimmed and deloused, had a healthy bluish sheen, and was tied back with a black cord. His clean-shaven jaw appeared thinner, his cheekbones more pronounced, the cleft in his chin deeper. He would regain the weight he had lost now he was free to eat whatever and whenever he liked. Free. Even thinking the word inspired so many emotions it was difficult to suppress the shout of pure joy that thrust upward and expanded in his chest. He had never given a thought to how precious his freedom was until it had been taken from him.

"Is something wrong, sir?" The valet held a dark blue long coat for him to don.

"No. You've done a fine job, Bradley. I've become human once more." He slid his arms into the coat. It felt good to be clean. More than good. He had been ashamed of his own smell, and had itched, and picked bugs like an animal. He wouldn't soon forget the experience, or the man responsible for it.

"Lord Willingham has invited guests for the wedding, Captain Hamilton. It is not known you were imprisoned these last few months. Lady Willingham thought it best just to say you've been away in the country."

His imprisonment would be an embarrassment to Talbot and Clarisse should anyone learn of it. Though he had done nothing to merit such treatment, he couldn't prove the charges false. His reputation would be blemished and he would be branded a smuggler. The realization stung his pride and prodded alive a cold, dark, frustrated anger it took several moments to control.

He tried to lighten the harsh expression he viewed in the mirror. "You understand why I was held there?"

"Aye, sir." The man's gray brows drew together in a frown. "It's shameful Lord Rudman saw fit to abuse his power in such a way. You may depend on my discretion, Captain."

The man's loyalty brought a smile to Matthew's lips. "That goes without saying, Bradley." He pulled the cuffs of his sleeves free from the arms of the coat.

"The wedding guests wouldn't include Lord Rudman and his wife, by any chance?" He turned to face the valet.

"Aye, Sir. I believe they have been invited by Lord Leighton."

Edward Leighton had broken his word, letting him stew inside the cell another two weeks before releasing him. Had Katherine known of his continued imprisonment? Surely, she had. Wouldn't she have found it strange she hadn't heard from him since their meeting? That morning, en route from the jail, Talbot had spoken of her but had said nothing of her making any attempt to see him.

Resentment bubbled inside him at how the lady had caught and held his attention. He had been tormented by the memory of her smell, like flowers and sunshine. The sweet curve of her lips, the delicate structure of her high cheekbones and stubborn chin had played on his imagination to taunt and entertain him. He had believed in the determination and innocence he read in those large violet eyes.

Aye, she had played him well.

Within the hour he would wed that bit of fluff and would find out to what sort of woman he had bound himself. The agreement he had made with her came to mind. He no more believed in the possibility of an annulment than he did her word. Once wed, he would be stuck with her for better or for worse."

"Are the guards still outside the door, Bradley?"

"Aye, sir." Bradley offered him a look of apology. "It would seem they will be accompanying you to the church and staying until the ceremony is over, as will Mr. St.John."

Matthew gave a brief nod. Anger flowed through him like hot pitch. Unlike *Lady Katherine* and her uncle, he meant to keep his word--as difficult as it might be.

The sheer impossibility of the situation had a wry smile twisting his lips. Checking his stock was properly tied, he stared at his reflection for a moment. He no longer resembled the filthy downtrodden wretch Katherine had tempted with her beauty and her promises of freedom. He wondered if she would even recognize him--probably not.

He turned away from the mirror. "The bottle of scotch I promised shall be delivered to you early tomorrow, Bradley."

The valet grinned, for once losing his well-disciplined dignity. "Thank you, sir."

"Should you hear anything about Lord Rudman or his wife I might find of interest--"

"I will keep you apprised, sir."

Matthew nodded. "Thank you, Bradley."

* * *

Katherine braced one hand on the coach seat against the swaying movement of the vehicle. She clenched the other in her lap as panic struck her. Dear God, she had promised herself to a great bear of a man. Beneath all the grime and unkempt hair, she didn't even know what he looked like! She wondered how she would recognize him at the church. She remembered the pale blue clarity of his eyes. Would eye color alone offer her some way of recognizing her groom?

Why had he not attempted to see her before the wedding? Why had he not answered her messages? If he wouldn't spare her the courtesy of an answer to a note, what could she expect of him? To what kind of man had she pledged herself?

Hannah, her maid, began to toy with the heavy cascade of curls gathered at the back of her head. Katherine shook her head and shot her a glance, nerves making her irritable. The elder woman patted her arm in commiseration and subsided to her own corner of the seat, though she continued to watch her charge, her expression worried.

Katherine's attention swung to the coach window as the vehicle turned between two brick posts, then traveled up a curved drive to the church. When the conveyance pulled to a jerky halt, two footmen appeared to lower the steps and open the door. Edward disembarked, offering his hand as she stepped down. He tucked Katherine's fingers in the bend of his arm and guided her up the circular steps to the front entrance, leaving one of the footmen to assist Hannah.

"I know I have been ill suited as your guardian, Katherine. It is better you have a mate to provide for you and guide you. I am certain Captain Hamilton will prove an able husband."

Able! She wanted no part of able husbands or any other kind.

"Perhaps marriage would offer you a different understanding of family, Uncle," she suggested. "Having children of your own might as well."

"I fear I am too set in my ways to consider such a change in circumstances, my dear."

"Too selfish" would better describe his reasons for avoiding marriage. He wanted her out of his house so he would not be tainted by what had happened to her mother, as she had been.

Her gaze moved about the vestibule in restless dread. Gleaming marble floors and dark scrolled woodwork adorned the space. The moment was at hand. She would be taking a sacred vow, knowing she would later break it. Guilt warred with her need. Fear warred with her determination.

The doors of the chapel parted and Lord Willingham appeared. Katherine found it difficult to draw a full breath as the racing of her heart increased.

"Everyone is seated and waiting, Lord Leighton." Talbot spoke in a hushed tone. His square-jawed features set in grave lines, softened somewhat as his gaze swung to her.

Her anxiety rose to a feverish peak. "Is the Capt—is Matthew here?" Her voice came out breathy and weak.

"Of course. He is waiting for you to join him, Katherine. I will tell them you are ready to begin." He paused, focusing on her with more attention. "You look beautiful, my dear."

A painful knot of emotion constricted her throat. If only her family were still alive, there would be no need for any of this. "Thank you, Lord Willingham."

Hannah drew the lace scarf up to cover Katherine's hair while Edward straightened the ruffled cuff of his sleeve. He handed his black tricorn to the woman.

Reluctantly, Katherine accepted her uncle's arm. Hannah held the door open for them to proceed. Katherine paused just inside the chapel, halting Edward's forward momentum. The long aisle of the church stretched before them, an intimidating length. At its end, stood a man and an enrobed minister. Too distant for her to identify his features, Katherine found some recognition in the breadth of his shoulders and his height. The jittery feeling built in the pit of her stomach.

Edward's determined grip on her arm propelled her forward as the beginning strains of organ music echoed within the sanctuary. The few guests present turned to watch as they progressed up the aisle.

Her groom's rugged features appeared more and more defined as the distance between them lessened. Without the heavy beard obscuring the lower half of his face, the angular shape of his jaw and chin appeared strong and masculine. His nose, well shaped and narrow had an arrogant tilt. His mouth, curved in a sardonic smile of greeting, underlined the fullness of his lips and set to light their sensuality. Resentment burnt in his pale blue eyes as they settled first upon Edward, then on her.

Confronted by his enmity, she grew wary. She had done nothing to anger him. What had Edward done?

Edward released her then stepped aside and found a

seat on one of the pews.

Matthew grasped her arm above the elbow and drew her to his side before the minister.

"Begin."

That one word spoken with such authority gained the minister's immediate attention, and without delay, he opened the bible he held.

As the priest began extolling the virtues of marriage, Matthew grasped her left hand. His fingers long, his nails clean and trimmed, his hand had an elegance about it that drew her eye. He appeared so different from the maltreated prisoner with whom she'd bargained, that she found it difficult to reconcile the two images. Her gaze rose once again to study his face. One well-arched black brow rose in mocking inquiry, his gaze bold as it raked downward to settle on her breasts. The look of appraisal in his expression as he raised one dark brow sent such a rush of outrage through her she almost choked.

He knew! Temper brought heat to her cheeks. Someone had told him about what had happened to her mother, and he believed the rumors. She shifted her weight, intent on ending the ceremony. He grasped her arm his grip tight, holding her at his side.

"I, Matthew David Hamilton, take thee, Katherine Elizabeth Leighton as my wife—" His deep voice steady, he repeated the vows the minister recited.

She clenched her teeth, setting her jaw. She would not wed a man who judged others by the gossip spread about them. He knew nothing of what had happened. Not even she could attest to all the events of that night.

The minister shifted in her direction. "Repeat after me, Katherine Leighton."

Her violet gaze warred with Matthew's pale blue one for several silent moments.

"Will you not honor your word any better than your uncle did?" Matthew's voice, though soft, seemed to fill every nook and cranny of the sanctuary.

She half turned to look over her shoulder at her uncle. What had he done? Beneath her accusing stare, his long thin face flushed red.

If she ended the ceremony, Edward would once again be on the hunt for some unsuspecting man to wed her.

The next man could have less to lose and thus be less eager to agree to her terms. Her gaze rose to Matthew's face. She would be confining him to prison once again and to Mr. Hicks's care.

Damn all men. Damn their untrustworthy, manipulative, uncaring hearts. If she never saw or spoke to another one, it would be too soon.

"I, Katherine Elizabeth Leighton, take thee Matthew David Hamilton as my husband." Rage made her voice shake as she recited her vows without benefit of the clergyman's prompting. Matthew slid the plain gold band on her left ring finger.

"You may kiss—" the minister began.

She stiffened as Matthew's arm slipped about her waist drawing her close against his tall, lean frame. His fingers grasped her jaw bringing her face up for his perusal. Pale blue eyes traced her features one by one, the look in their depths bringing an airless feeling beneath her ribs and a weakness to her limbs. A feeling of panic set her heart to flight as his lips neared hers. She placed a restraining hand against his chest to no avail.

The fierce possession of his lips parted hers and without preamble, he tasted the interior of her mouth with the tip of his tongue as he curved her body into his. Shock held Katherine immobile. He tasted of brandy, sweet and smoky. He smelled of sandalwood soap and man, clean and natural. The movement of his tongue at first startled her then brought a titillating heat to life in the most intimate areas of her body. A desire to move her tongue against his in response tempted her.

The minister clearing his throat reminded her they stood before a company of strangers. She pushed with greater strength against Matthew's broad chest and attempted to wiggle free of his grasp.

He raised his head at his leisure, his blue gaze holding a warmth she found disconcerting. Her face felt hot, as did the rest of her. Her heartbeat raged against her ribs.

"You must sign the marriage contract or the bond will not be legal." The minister fixed them both with a stern, disapproving look. "Please follow me."

CHAPTER 3

Talbot Willingham allowed the leather shade to fall closed over the coach window. "St. John and his guards have broken away finally." He covered his wife's hand in the bend of his arm, his head bent protectively close to hers.

Katherine thought them a couple in contrasts, yet they seemed to fit together like two pieces of a puzzle. Talbot's stocky frame off set his wife's slenderness, his white hair provided the perfect backdrop for her raven dark locks.

"It is only a small reception, Matthew," Matthew's aunt, Clarisse Willingham, spoke from the coach seat facing them. Her pale blue eyes, so similar to her nephew's, moved from Matthew to Katherine then back again.

Talbot cleared his throat. "Lord Rudman insisted he and Lady Rudman attend the ceremony and the reception."

"I wouldn't have expected anything else." Matthew made a dismissive gesture with his hand. His attention swung to Katherine. "We're going to be thrust into a social quagmire before the ink is dry on the marriage contract, Katherine. How do you feel about that?"

She fought to keep the surprise from her expression. Her feelings had never been taken into account before. "I do not suppose it matters how I feel about it, Captain. It seems to be an unavoidable situation. But they cannot make you part of the entertainment, if you refuse to allow them to."

One well-arched black brow rose and a speculative light leaped into his eyes. Katherine looked away. For all the confidence she tried to portray, fear ran in ever tightening circles in the pit of her stomach. She folded her arms against her waist as nerves danced along her skin intensifying the chill inside the coach.

Matthew frowned. "Where is your cloak?"

"I left it behind in Edward's coach. Hannah, my maid, will bring it along."

"It's cold, come share mine."

She turned to look at him. He held the folds of the heavy wool garment open. His long coat edged in black satin piping hung open. His dark blue satin waistcoat clung to his lean torso, accentuating the breadth of his chest and flatness of his abdomen. With something akin to awe, she took in the long line of his body slouched against the seat, his legs spread before him, his feet planted firmly upon the floor. A melting heat spread low in her belly. Her heart fluttered like a bird attempting to take flight. The foot wide span between them seemed too short a distance—and too long. She became aware of Talbot and Clarisse watching the exchange, and her cheeks grew hot.

Matthew slid over closing the distance between them. His arm went around her waist drawing her firmly against him. He draped the fabric of his cloak around her. The heat of his body clung to the garment, enveloping her in warmth. The defined musculature of his chest lay beneath the hand she placed against his waistcoat. Her breast pressed into the curvature of his ribs and the rest of her body from waist to knee aligned with the length of his. His musky manly fragrance overrode the heady scents of soap, leather and wood smoke. He smelled of vanilla and spice and heat. She swallowed against a tide of emotion she had never experienced before. She felt safe yet threatened. She wanted to burrow against him, yet wanted to break free and run. When he grasped her hand and held it against his chest, she felt too addled to protest. The gentle sway of the coach rocked them against one another. She pressed her thighs together mortified by the empty ache that twisted between them. Dear God, was everything she felt written on her face for Lord and Lady Willingham to read?

"As angry as you are with him, I would urge you to be careful when dealing with Lord Rudman, Matthew." Clarisse's brows puckered with worry. "Until you are aboard your ship and on your way home he will be waiting for any excuse to imprison you again. To have his wife prefer another man must surely be a blow to his pride, if not his heart. He has a reputation for holding a grudge to the death."

The soft womanly feel of Katherine's breast against Matthew's ribs distracted him. She smelled of sun warmed violets and woman. Her narrow waist exaggerated the full thrust of her breasts, or from the feel of her against him, perhaps not. He rubbed his thumb against the calluses on the pad of her palm. It surprised him that her hands were marred. Only physical labor of some kind could have created the thickened areas. And he had never seen any lady do more than raise a teacup.

"Being able to hold a grudge is something Lord Rudman and I have in common."

He felt Katherine's stillness. He looked down at her, but couldn't see her expression.

"Revenge is a double-edged sword, Matthew." Talbot shifted, his white brows drawn together in a fierce frown. "The possibility of losing as much as you gain is too great."

"I don't have any plans to do anything rash, Talbot." He struggled to relax the taut muscles of his jaw and shoulders. "I don't want to cause you and Clarisse any more distress than I already have."

"But—" Talbot added.

Matthew remained silent. He couldn't promise not to pursue some form of pay back if the opportunity presented itself. What Lord Rudman had done to him, out of misplaced jealousy, was inexcusable.

He had never understood the nefarious thrill that some men got when carrying on a dalliance with a married woman. There were too many others available.

Virgins were another difficulty to be avoided like a plague. Eagle-eyed mothers hovered near, awaiting an opportunity to help their untarnished offspring capture a mate. The girls, usually part women-part children, dangled their purity like a lure beneath the noses of eligible bachelors as though that alone would make them a suitable wife.

His attention rested on Katherine's profile as she attempted to straighten away from him. With his hand resting possessively against her waist, and her thigh pressed against his, he felt the jaws of the trap pinching closed. The fact that she already wore a ring he had only an hour before placed upon her finger did nothing to alleviate the feeling.

He'd never believed he would marry again, had often insisted he'd never do so. He drew a deep breath. She was beautiful, well spoken, and a liar. This was going to be an interesting adjustment for both of them.

The coach pulled to a stop before the entrance to Willingham's. Talbot rose as soon as the door opened and stepped down to assist Clarisse. Matthew unfastened the frog at his throat and released the cloak from around his shoulders. He turned and draped the garment around Katherine and caught her attention fastened on his face.

"Are you always so solicitous of women of your acquaintance, Captain?"

He smiled at the wary expression he read in her eyes and couldn't resist deviling her a little. "Only the ones that I'm obliged to marry. Remember to call me Matthew now."

Lowering her lashes to shield her expression, she nodded.

He stepped down from the coach and turned to offer her a hand. The cloak nearly dragged the floor, and she gathered the extra fabric with one hand while she took his hand with the other. The grace in which she accomplished the task drew his attention.

He found her a study in contradictions, one moment exuding self-confidence, the next biting her lip in uncertainty; one moment acting the debutante, the next a shy young thing with a blush on her cheeks. Her sage advice about not allowing the reception guests to make him part of their entertainment hinted at experience. What social trials might she have experienced that she exhibited such cynicism? And why would such a beauty have to go to such lengths to marry?

Once the reception was finished, they would be having a long conversation.

****

Katherine focused her attention on Matthew's stock as he smoothed back a stray curl from her cheek and tucked it behind her ear. She tried to relax beneath his

22

touch, to appear normal when he focused his attention on her, but it was difficult when the experience was so new.

At the prison, his lack of fear in the face of the Hicks's enmity had made her doubt the wisdom of a partnership with him, but at the time, she had not had any other choice. Now faced with the strong, self-assured, devastatingly handsome man he had become, she knew she had made a mistake. If he held a grudge to the death, how would he respond when he discovered a woman had once more betrayed him? How would he react to sharing his name with a woman whose reputation had been sullied? How would he feel when he discovered he had married a woman no longer a virgin?

She shuddered. Betrayed by Lady Rudman, he had lost his freedom for nearly three months. Married to a woman who had lied by omission, he would feel even more trapped—if they could not dissolve the marriage.

No matter what happened, she would not hold him to the contract. She had struck a bargain; her reputation might be in tatters, but her honor was still intact. When his supplies were loaded aboard his ship, and he had assembled his crew, she would wish him on his way—if she were around to do so.

First, she had to get through this reception. As they congregated in the dining room for a meal, she skimmed the faces of the twelve couples who made up the party. Some she had met at her uncle's house, others were strangers. All seemed to view the marriage with—for lack of a better word, shock.

Matthew held her chair for her and slid it forward when she was seated. She caught the sullen expression on Lady Rudman's face from across the table. The woman's blond, tightly curled locks hung against her shoulder like fat caterpillars crawling across the deep emerald gown she wore. Her green eyes held an arrogance that hinted at challenge whenever she looked at Katherine.

In her opinion, Matthew's rejection of the woman showed good judgment, but his continued gestures of affection toward his new bride lacked wisdom. "You are courting disaster, Captain," she said in a hushed tone as he ran his thumb over the back of the hand he held. "You are encouraging her to make a scene."

He smiled. "That will be her husband's problem, not mine."

"No, it shan't, it will be mine. It will be I who will be trapped in the parlor with her while you gentlemen are smoking your cigars and drinking your brandy after the meal."

He studied her, something in his gaze sharp and probing. "If it comes to a contest of wills, I'll place my money on you. Any woman who would brave a prison in search of a groom is made of much sterner stuff than Jacqueline Rudman."

She drew a deep breath. "The point is not whether or not I can handle her jibes, Captain. It's whether or not I am willing to. It is not very complimentary to either of us that you are showering me with attention only to pique her jealousy."

He cocked his head his expression intent. "Would you rather I ignored you and caused a wave of speculation among your friends?"

"These are not my friends," she said with more fierceness than she intended.

"Are they Edward's then?"

"Yes."

He nodded, his black brows drawn into a frown.

For months, she had endured public speculation, rumor, and innuendo. She had ignored the men's insults, deflected the women's attempts to divine information, and learned to show a calm immobile face in numerous socially uncomfortable situations. He would invite all those things if he continued and Jacqueline Rudman caused a scene.

He would soon discover he had taken on more than he bargained for when he became aware of her situation. She owed him something in return for that at least.

She leaned close as though to whisper in his ear, her cheek nearly brushing his. "I understand your desire for revenge, but what are you willing to risk to gain it?" She drew back to look into his face.

He rested a forearm on the table at the same time he caught her hand. He toyed with her fingers as he studied her features. As the pale blue intensity of his gaze settled on her face, an airless feeling filled her chest, and it became difficult for her to draw a full breath.

"Certainly not my freedom again or my family." His voice sounded husky alerting her to the fact that he too felt the tug of attraction between them.

She looked across the table at Lord Rudman in conversation with her uncle. "Then leave it. Go back to America and try to forget the past three months. As horrible and humiliating as it has been, it was just a temporary inconvenience. You will have your ship and the money and you will have your life back."

If she could go back to what had been before, she might forget her own quest for justice. But as much as she wished it otherwise, nothing would ever be the same. She no longer had a reputation or a family to lose. The advice she offered him could not apply to her.

"When do you plan to return to America, Captain Hamilton?" Jacqueline Rudman jumped into the lull. Katherine was grateful, for her groom was looking at her with more and more interest as their conversation progressed.

"Within the month," Lord Rudman answered for him.

Matthew's expression hardened instantly and Katherine placed a hand upon his sleeve in warning.

Jacqueline's light brown brows rose. "That leaves little time for you and your bride to enjoy being entertained as a couple."

The thought of dealing with the normal social situations their marriage might encourage brought a knot of anxiety to her stomach. "Less than you know, Lady Rudman. We must travel to Summerhaven to retrieve my clothing and a few other possessions before the voyage."

Edward, sitting at the opposite end of the table, flipped his hand in a prissy, dismissive gesture. "A servant could do that. There is really no need for you to travel to Birmingham to an empty house."

She tensed, surprised. "What do you mean by empty, Edward?"

"I have let the servants go and closed the house. There was no need for it to remain open when no one was there."

Anger, like molten lead, began to simmer inside her. "Why would you do that?"

25

His beaky nose rose, his expression smug. "I had every right, my dear. It is after all part of my inheritance."

Fighting back the emotion threatening to choke her, she kept her features under taut control.

"You do not have any use for my apparel, Uncle." She leaned forward to study him with a purposely speculative light in her gaze. "Do you?"

Edward's face turned red, and he answered in an indignant tone. "Of course not. If it is so important to you, you may send someone to fetch your things from Summerhaven."

She held her tongue with an effort. She would be going to Summerhaven if she had to walk. No one would be going in her stead.

She turned to find Matthew watching the exchange. He leaned back in his chair, his long lean frame settling into a relaxed slouch, his arm resting on the back of the Chippendale chair in which she sat.

"I don't mind accompanying Katherine if she wishes to go. There may be things a servant would find difficult to locate."

A smile leaped to her lips as quickly as Edward's smirk died from his.

"If you are to leave within a month, Captain Hamilton, you have precious little time to spend collecting Katherine's possessions," Edward said.

"I think I can spare the few days that the trip there and back will take."

Containing her relief and satisfaction with an effort, Katherine nodded. "Thank you, Matthew. I appreciate your consideration."

Edward set his wine glass aside. "Suit yourself, but the servants will not be there to see to your comfort."

"I am sure we will manage, Uncle."

His sour look said he hoped they did not.

"Though I have servants in my home in Charleston, living on board ship six months out of the year has insured that I can manage my own care sufficiently." Matthew toyed with loose curl on her shoulder. "I think I'll even be able to assist Katherine in that as well."

Her cheeks burnt. The images that his suggestion

brought to mind stole her breath and made it impossible for her to meet his gaze.

"Matthew, you must not tease Katherine so." Clarisse flashed him an admonishing frown from down the table.

He offered Katherine a smile. "My apologies, sweetheart." He raised her hand to his lips to brush her knuckles with a kiss.

She wished the warm moist heat of his lips did not inspire her limbs to go weak as warm butter.

"Will Mrs. Hamilton be traveling with you on board your ship?" one of the other women asked from down the table.

"No. This will be my last voyage as a sea captain. Now that I'm wed, I'll be settling into married life and concentrating on being a husband and father."

Her lips parted in surprise. She wondered if he truly intended to give up his ship after all he had gone through to get it back.

"Would it please you to have me underfoot and at your disposal, Katherine?"

She had been toyed with enough. She pretended to straighten his immaculately tied stock and offered him a smile. "It is a relief to know that you will be settling down. No woman wishes to think her husband enjoys being away from her for nearly half a year at a time."

"You seem such an adventurer, Captain Hamilton." Jacqueline Rudman's attention focused on Matthew, her expression projecting polite concern. "I hope life in America will not seem boring after life at sea."

"I'm looking for challenges in other places now, Lady Rudman. I believe I'll find it in marriage and fatherhood. I'm sure Lord Rudman feels the same way."

Avery Rudman frowned, making his jowly bulldog features appear even less attractive. "Indeed, Hamilton. Marriage is a challenge, but fatherhood sounds an equally worthy endeavor."

Katherine bit the inside of her lip to contain a smile. Lady Rudman appeared less than enamored with the idea.

Clarisse commented from her place at the foot of the table. "You and Lady Rudman have been married a reasonable amount of time, Avery. I am sure you would both find it rewarding. With a family to see to, women look within their household for fulfillment and place less importance on the adventures of the exterior world."

Katherine met Lady Willingham's gaze. When the woman winked at her, she bit her lip again. Some of the tension eased from her shoulders as she realized she had an ally in the room.

"Being unmarried I know precious little about parenthood, but I do know about the adventurous spirit."

At his words, she turned her attention to the man at her right and searched her memory for a name as she studied his square-jawed features. He appeared to be in his mid forties. His brows were heavy, his hair thick and wavy and barely contained within the black lace at the nape of his neck. His beard grew so dark a shadow colored the lower half of his face. She had earlier experienced a moment of recognition when introduced to him at the chapel, but she hadn't been able to place where or when she had seen him before.

"I have made investments in America both before and after the war, Captain Hamilton. Profitable ventures. You are a lucky man to have captured one of our English beauties so easily, especially one with so illustrious a blood line who is willing to leave England for America."

She caught Edward's satisfied smile and his attempt to straighten his posture.

The man continued. "I knew your uncle many years ago, Mrs. Hamilton. Lord John Wesley Pemberton was a fine soldier."

She almost laughed aloud as Edward stiffened then frowned. "Thank you, sir. My mother was very proud of her brother."

"He and my sister's husband, Lord Ardsley, served together before his death. You have obviously inherited some of your uncle's adventurous spirit if you are eager to leave England for climes unknown."

Something in the man's smile caught and held Katherine's attention.He seemed so familiar. "A woman must follow where her husband, and her heart, leads, Mr. Drake." she said, finally remembering his name. As his green eyes focused on her, anxiety knotted her belly. She reached out a hand and her fingers came to rest on her groom's long muscular thigh. Mortified, she started to jerk her hand away, but Matthew captured and held it in place with his own. He shot her a warning look and laced her fingers with his.

"You must call me Garrett, with your husband's permission of course," Drake bent his head in Matthew's direction.

Matthew returned the gesture.

"It is a shame you are retiring from the sea, Captain Hamilton. We could have done business together. I have holdings in several export companies here in London."

"Unfortunately, this will be my last trip, Mr. Drake. I have several business ventures of my own to run once I get home."

"That is my loss then, I have heard you hold several records for your crossings between England and America."

"That was in my first years of captaincy, not recently."

Katherine studied her groom with renewed interest. She had learned very early in life that a man's desires, his drive to succeed, to control or possess, often lent an understanding to his character. As she studied the hard masculine planes of his face, a shiver of both heat and fear raced down her spine. The more she learned about her temporary husband, the more she wondered if perhaps she had made a bigger mistake than she realized.

CHAPTER 4

"Shall we retire to my study for brandy and cigars, gentlemen?" Talbot rose from his seat at the head of the table.

Matthew followed suit with more haste than was probably polite. The reception had run on endlessly. Now the Rudmans and Edward lingered. He'd had more than enough of their company and wished them gone.

He observed his uncle's guarded expression as Talbot closed the library door behind them. Matthew shifted his attention to Lord Rudman's bullish features. A dark, powerful anger twisted inside him tightening his facial muscles and bringing knots of tension to his neck and shoulders. He drew a deep breath to ease the feeling and gain control of the emotion. Folding his hands behind him, he turned to the fire, and braced a foot on the hearth.

"Shall we get on with it," Talbot suggested.

"There are some specific conditions I must place upon the receipt of your ship and the proceeds of the cargo, Hamilton." Lord Rudman lowered his considerable bulk into one of the sturdy chairs pulled close to the fire. He produced a handkerchief from his sleeve and wiped the sweat from his sparsely covered pate. His attention focused on Matthew as he lowered his hand. "You must have no contact with my wife, nor shall you mention to her you have been detained, and you must leave England within a month, or I will reinstate the charges against you."

"That will be no hardship." He kept his voice even with an effort as he accepted a glass of brandy from Talbot, and then acknowledged his uncle's warning frown with a tip of his glass.

"I must say you are being very civil about all this." Edward cupped the bowl of the brandy snifter within his hand with dainty grace and took a seat.

Matthew sipped his brandy. He didn't want to be civil. A savage desire to lash out at both Lord Rudman and Edward Leighton tormented him. He moved to the French doors to look out into the garden, hoping to find some calming distraction there.

The French doors across the courtyard opened, and Katherine exited the house. She crossed the raised stone patio, her movements decisive as she descended the steps and followed the path to the back of the garden.

So she too felt the need to escape the confines of their guest's presence. He wondered what Jacqueline Rudman might have said to her. The woman had shown her claws more than once over the course of dinner. Fresh anger sparked his resentment anew.

He turned to address both the men behind him, determined to have an end to it all. "I'll leave it to you to find a way to keep your wife from seeking me out, Rudman. I won't be held accountable for her behavior."

Unprepared for the attack, Lord Rudman's cheeks grew flushed and his lips opened and closed like a beached carp as he sought a reply.

Matthew stepped close to Edward's chair, forcing the other man to bend his head back to look up at him. "You left me in that pit for two weeks after we reached our agreement. Your actions are proof enough to me that you have no honor, nor can you be trusted. If you were more a man, I would settle this in a physical manner, but for Katherine's sake, I'll forego that pleasure." He poked the man's bony chest with a forefinger. "For the remainder of my time here in England though, you would do well to stay out of my way."

Edward sputtered in outrage. "The bans had to be posted, and I had no way of knowing whether or not you would remain in England should you be released. I thought it wise to keep you secured until the wedding."

"You thought me as lacking in honor as you and he are." He thrust a thumb at Lord Rudman in a backhanded movement. "In America, we settle our disputes one man to another. There's no need for such underhanded backbiting."

He glared at Avery Rudman. His contempt for both men stewed inside him, sickening, ferocious. "We have other means of managing our women without lowering our morals to do it."

His expression stony with control, Lord Rudman offered no reply to Matthew's diatribe.

Matthew turned to his uncle. "I need some fresh air. I'm sure you'll understand if I don't return until our guests have taken their leave."

Talbot nodded, his expression grave.

Matthew stepped from the room and closed the French doors behind him. He drew a deep breath as he sought to leash his temper, his stomach muscles contracting painfully. The possibility of being returned to prison because of his lack of control preyed on his mind. They would have to kill him. He wouldn't be put back into that hellish place.

He strode down the steps and followed the path Katherine had taken. Her presence at the table had acted as a buffer between him and their guests. Her dark violet eyes, copper streaked hair, and clear creamy skin had drawn his attention again and again. The rise of color in her cheeks each time he showed her attention fascinated him. He wondered what experience, if any, she might have garnered at court, for her response to his kiss had been hesitant and uncertain. He found it hard to align the self-assured young woman who had faced him with such determination in the prison with the innocent who blushed at his every glance.

The late afternoon sun did little to alleviate the nip in the air as he circled the fountain. He paused beside the decorative structure to enjoy the bubbling dance of water springing from the center of an unfurled flower held within the hand of a scantily clad maiden.

He breathed in deeply the fresh breeze wafting against his face. The air of liberation smelled of damp ground tinged with the evergreen scent of freshly trimmed shrubs.

He found himself facing several paths running in spokes to the back of the garden. Not knowing which Katherine might have taken, he continued on the one leading straight forward.

The indistinct sound of a voice behind him caught his attention. He turned to see Jacqueline Rudman bearing down on him. Alarm displaced his calm and his gaze swept the garden for any threat accompanying her. "Your husband will miss you, Jacqueline, and I came out here for a moment's quiet."

The woman's bottom lip protruded in a pout. "How can you be so cold to me, Matthew? You barely spoke to me at dinner or even afterwards, though you had plenty of opportunity."

He braced his feet apart and folded his arms in a stance he hoped she would find less than welcoming. "Did you expect me to ignore my bride at our wedding reception?"

Her elaborately coifed blond hair gleamed as she stood before him. She brushed a nonexistent piece of lint from his coat in a proprietary gesture, her fingers curling around the open lapels of the garment. "No, but I did not expect you would ignore me so completely either." Her lips curled downward into a pout. "Especially after all we have shared in the past. Our having wed other people doesn't have to mean we cannot enjoy one another again."

This woman had cost him his freedom for nearly three months and, at her husband's insistence, remained completely oblivious to it. Repugnance washed over him, and he controlled his expression with an effort. "You approached me when I first arrived months ago, Jacqueline. I told you then I don't sleep with married women. I haven't changed my mind."

Anger flashed across her features. "I gave myself to you without reserve, Matthew. I deserve better from you than a few trinkets."

He shut down the small niggling of guilt before his conscience guided him to say something he would regret. "I was not your first lover, Jacqueline and your persistence leads me to believe that your husband will not be your last."

"You have no right to sit in judgment on me." Her green eyes narrowed. "You did not hesitate to enjoy my favors before."

"As I remember it, I wasn't the only one who experienced pleasure. I accepted nothing that you didn't offer with complete freedom, Lady Rudman. But now I'm married, as are you. I'll be occupied with spending time with my wife, Jacqueline. We are, after all, newlyweds."

Her green eyes fastened on him with open hunger. Leaning against him, her ample breasts pressing against his arm, she stroked the front of his waistcoat. "You forget how well I know you, Matthew. One woman will never be enough for you."

"He shall just have to learn to endure the affections of only one from now on, Lady Rudman. I do not intend to share him."

Jacqueline started and turned at the challenge. Katherine stepped from around a bend in the path and crossed the distance between them. Though her cheeks took on a rosy hue, Jacqueline stood her ground.

Katherine flashed him a look of disgust before leveling her attention on the woman. "Whatever your past understanding with Matthew might have been, he will no longer need your attentions now we are wed."

Jacqueline gasped in outrage. "How dare you speak to me in that manner?"

Katherine stepped close, her violet eyes burning with a dark smoldering heat. "How dare you behave in such a manner? You have approached my husband on our wedding night intent on weaning his affections from me. How else would you have me speak to you?"

A spiteful look flashed across Jacqueline's thin patrician features. "Had he remained in England last year, he would have wed me."

"No, Jacqueline." he shook his head. "Such was never my intent, as you well know. There were never any promises spoken between us." He grasped Katherine's hand and drew her to his side. "I suggest you return to the house and your husband."

Sullen lines of frustration marred the woman's face. Jacqueline raised her chin and returned her attention to Katherine. "We both know why you wed him so quickly."

Katherine grew completely still, and though her expression remained calm and purposeful, there was a contained violence in her stance that caught his attention and had him stepping closer should he need to intervene.

"Take care what you say, Lady Rudman, and to whom. Unlike Matthew, I do not have to play the gentleman and be discreet in expressing my displeasure.

Your husband has obviously accepted your past indiscretions as being in the past. I would think very carefully on what you have to lose should he discover you are openly pursuing another woman's husband. "

Jacqueline retreated a step then seemed to recover her composure and raised her chin. "What makes you think he will believe you?"

She shrugged. "He does not have to. The gossip and speculation that can be started will do the damage. I no longer have anything to lose with my family gone and a new home awaiting me in America. Just what are you willing to forfeit?"

Some of the color receded from Jacqueline's cheeks and with a growl, she wheeled about and stalked away.

Lady Rudman had just disappeared around a clump of brush when Katherine jerked her hand free and rounded on him. Her eyes smoldering with emotion, she thumped his chest with a doubled fist. "You fool! If you are witless enough to come out into the garden with her, you deserve to rot in jail." She stomped off in the direction Jacqueline had just traversed.

Matthew watched the saucy sway of her hips as she stormed up the garden path. Outraged anger at her accusation warred with the interest piqued by her passionate flare of temper. He touched the spot her fist had struck. She had actually raised her hand to him.

He strode after her. He caught her arm before she reached the house and swung her around to face him. "I didn't come out with her. She must have followed me. Do you really believe I'd risk my freedom again over a bit of fluff?"

With a jerk, she attempted to twist away from him. He grasped both arms above the elbow and held her.

She glared up at him, her cheeks flushed from her exertions. "I do not know what you would do. I do not know you."

The weight of those words momentarily cooled his anger. She was right. They were strangers to one another. But not for long. Her eagerness to act the outraged wife surprised him, especially since she had allowed her perspective bridegroom to languish in jail an extra two weeks "so the bans could be posted". His temper fired anew. He would be happy to oblige her by behaving the besotted husband in return for such consideration. His gaze fastened upon the luscious curve of her bottom lip. The woman had the most delectable mouth he had ever seen. He could almost taste it beneath his.

"Matthew, our guests are taking their leave. Katherine will wish to say goodbye to her uncle," Talbot called to them from the steps of the study, breaking the angry awareness that tugged and pulled between them.

He straightened and released her arms. "We shall have time to become more intimately acquainted this evening, Madame, once we have wished our guests on their way." Ignoring the wariness that immediately crept into her expression, he tucked her hand into the bend of his arm and drew her down the stone walk to the steps.

CHAPTER 5

Katherine drew a deep breath of relief as Hannah and Clarisse Willingham finally closed the door behind them. Their womanly wisdom and advice still echoed in her head making her face burn and her stomach to twist tight with knots.

Though her memories of that night, three months past, were incomplete, she thought she understood what men did to women. She couldn't believe there could be any pleasure in such an act. Surely, women only endured it in order to have children. A shudder shook her.

Matthew would behave himself. She had to believe he would.

But the changes in their circumstances made it difficult for her to feel at ease with him. And she did not trust the bold way he handled her as though she belonged to him. The balance of power had shifted in his favor and would remain unchanged as long as they stayed married. In short, he could do as he pleased with her, and there would be nothing she could do about it.

That thought brought with it a fresh wave of anxiety making it difficult for her to breathe. She rose and donned her robe and retrieved a flintlock pistol from the chest in the dressing room. She cocked it to check the priming of the weapon then eased the firing pin back down.

The barrel too long to fit into the pocket of her robe, her gaze moved about the room seeking a convenient hiding place for the firearm. The reasoning behind her need for some form of protection struck her, and tears threatened. Men could not be trusted. Her father had proven that with his treatment of her mother. Her uncle had proven it with the lack of regard he had shown for her and her family. Matthew Hamilton would prove it as well. When he did, she would be ready. She thrust the firearm beneath a pillow on the bed.

Matthew's knock came all too soon. She took several

calming breaths before opening the bedroom door. Her attention rested on the tails of his lace-trimmed stock that was even with her vision before she tilted her head back to look up into his face. The devilish smile he offered her had her stomach turning end over end. Was this all some hideous jest to him?

His gaze swept her features then traveled over her hair, released from its fashionable confines. His well-arched brows rose as his eyes raked down the length of the heavy woolen robe covering her from neck to ankle.

"Come in, Captain." It seemed prudent to address him formally under the circumstances.

As he stepped into the room, he paused to smooth back a stray curl from her face, the tips of his fingers lingering against her skin and following the contour of her cheekbone.

Tendrils of heat trailed beneath his touch, and her legs grew weak. Katherine stepped away from him to close the door, wary of her response to him.

"You must grow used to my touching you if we are to convince your uncle all is well between us, Katherine."

"My uncle is not here hiding beneath the bed, Captain, nor are your aunt and uncle. There is no need for you to show me such attention."

His lips twitched as though he found it hard to suppress a smile. "People newly wed find it hard to resist touching one another. It's a natural part of being lovers." He set aside the book he held beneath his arm to drape his coat over the back of a chair then began unbuttoning his waistcoat.

His attempts to bate her sparked her anger, and she sidled away from him. "We are not lovers, nor shall we ever be."

One black brow rose as he shrugged free of the garment. His long fingers worked the knot of his stock. "Pour us a glass of wine please."

Watching him, a pulse beat at her wrists and throat. She turned to do as he asked. Did he intend to strip completely? "I can step into the hall if you wish privacy to undress, Captain. Or perhaps you could step into the dressing room."

He unwrapped the length of fabric from around his

throat and tossed it aside. "I've finished for the moment. For now I intend to enjoy a glass of wine and a quiet moment before the fire."

She returned to him, a single glass of wine in her hand. Her gaze rose to his face as she extended it.

Offering her a smile laced with mischief, he unbuttoned the neck of his shirt exposing his throat and at its base a dark V of hair. "Will you not join me?"

"I do not care for wine." She wandered to the small dressing table to pick up her brush and began to run it through her hair. She watched surreptitiously as he settled in a chair before the fire and, stretching out his long legs, propped his feet on a small padded stool. A flash of memory came unbidden of how he had looked trapped in that dark, dank chamber beneath the gray stone of the prison. She remembered the marks upon the wall above the bed tallying the days he spent there and her throat grew suddenly tight with emotion. How he must have hated it.

"Clarisse had the dressing table moved in this afternoon. Do you like it?"

She nodded, touched by the other woman's thoughtfulness. "Yes, I do."

"What do you care to drink, Katherine? A husband must know his wife's taste in all things from clothing to her choice of drinks."

A husband, a wife. Those words alone brought a jittery feeling to the pit of her stomach. "I prefer tea to most everything else. On occasion, I drink a glass of sherry before dinner." She fought the compulsion to stare at him. His masculine features held an appeal she couldn't hope to deny. "And you?" Her tongue felt thick and clumsy.

"I prefer coffee at the morning meal, water, if it's pure, a fine wine at dinner, as well as brandy, and port on occasion."

Worried, she bit her lip. Her father had been violent on occasion when drinking. She did not relish being subjected to the same treatment by her temporary husband. The clearness of his pale blue eyes and the strength of his jaw eased her anxiety. The light flirted with the cleft in his chin and she wondered if the tip of her finger would fit the indentation.

"Won't you sit before the fire with me?" He indicated the empty chair before the fire.

She had been running scared ever since he had entered the room and he had done nothing to inspire her behavior. Her own thoughts had done that. Chiding herself on her cowardice, she set aside the brush and crossed the space between them to take the offered seat.

He placed the wine glass on the small table between them and lacing his fingers, rested his hands atop his flat stomach. His blue gaze settled on her. "Thus far, no one knows of my imprisonment because Lord Rudman doesn't wish his wife to know of it. That could change. It will affect you adversely as well should it happen."

His concern for her social standing had guilt tweaking her conscience, and she looked away with a shrug. "I am not overly concerned it will happen, Captain. One whisper to Lady Rudman of the truth, and she'll make Lord Rudman's life a misery. Besides, he will eventually receive whatever punishment he deserves for his actions."

A slow smile tilted his lips. "It's certain he'll more than once rue the day he met her, if he hasn't already."

She couldn't resist probing his feelings for Jacqueline Rudman. "As much as you have?"

"More. It's he, who must live with her for the rest of his days. My sentence lasted less than three months." His gaze followed the movement of her fingers as she manipulated the thick strands of hair braiding it. "It's a comfort knowing I have a possessive wife who doesn't wish to share my attentions."

Remembering the woman's bold behavior brought a quick flash of anger. She had behaved as a common trollop and still retained her social standing unscathed, while Katherine, who had been attacked, was branded a social pariah.

When she remained silent he said, "Jacqueline is used to getting what she wants. I didn't encourage her."

"Perhaps not today, but it was obvious you had been — acquainted before. You did not warn me of that when last we spoke."

"I had little opportunity to send greetings from my

cell in the last fortnight."

Her fingers stilled at the bitterness that tinged his words. Why had Edward done that? Surely, he knew it would only cause more strife between her and Matthew. Or had that been his intention? "I was not aware you had not been released until just after the wedding. Had I known, I would have tried to persuade Edward to make it so." She held the end of the braid then pulled a ribbon from her pocket.

He dropped his feet from the stool and rose from his seat in one swift, graceful movement. Her heart skipped a beat, and she shrank back as he braced his hands upon the arms of her chair and loomed over her, his face close to hers. "I didn't appreciate having the promise of freedom dangled before me then, without warning or explanation, having it jerked away." He plucked the ribbon from between her fingers, but didn't withdraw immediately.

Slowly, deliberately, he studied each feature of her face, brow, cheek, nose, and mouth. Her stomach did a long slow roll at the look on his face. His attention settled on her lips for such a long moment of contemplation, she struggled to suppress the nervous desire to moisten them. His wine laced breath feathered warm against her face to mingle with his musky male scent. For a moment, she thought he might kiss her again. When he straightened and took a step back, she didn't know whether to feel relief or disappointment

A long silent moment passed as she struggled to recover. She wondered at how easily he inspired such a jumble of feelings. "It was needlessly cruel." Her voice came out husky, and she cleared her throat. "But I did not have anything to do with your remaining in jail." It would do no good to mention the letters she had sent since he obviously had not received them. That too was probably her uncle's doing.

A scowl darkened his features as he lowered his tall frame back into the chair, his movements impatient.

"Bradley won't be coming this evening. You'll have to act as my valet and help me remove my boots."

Her legs weak as jelly, she rose and stood before him and waited for him to extend his foot. Divesting him of his boots took only a moment, and she set the shoes beside his chair.

"Bradley couldn't do better." The smile that tilted his lips displaced the frown that lingered about his features. He caught the loosened braid dangling over her shoulder to hold her where she stood. "You're very tempting in your wool robe, Mrs. Hamilton." He caught the sash of her robe and with a jerk pulled her down into his lap.

Startled by the intimate feel of his hard muscular chest against her breasts and his thigh beneath her buttocks, she froze. The warmth he exuded through the linen of his shirt seeped into her hand. She fought the compulsion to lay her head against his shoulder. Would he put his arms around her and just hold her for a moment? Fearful of the desire, and how vulnerable it made her, her heart thundering against her ribs, and she attempted to rise.

Matthew's arm tightened around her waist, and he gripped her arm. "I mean to talk to you, Katherine. It's more difficult for someone to avoid telling the truth while looking you in the eye."

Breathing hard, she ceased to struggle. The teasing seducer was gone. His gaze focused on her intently, his jaw stern and set.

Her heart sank. He knew! Someone had told him and he had just been testing her.

Matthew studied Katherine's wary expression and felt the tension in the way she held herself. Her attempts at using formality to hold him at bay both amused and irritated him. He asked a question that had been running through his mind since they first met. "Why did you choose to marry me?"

"You needed your freedom as badly as I did mine. You did not want to wed me anymore than I did you. And you were not interested in any reward you might gain from the marriage because you had resources of your own."

"You learned all that from one short conversation?"

"I did not hear all of it." Her violet gaze moved back to focus upon him. "But I did hear what you said about not wanting another wife. I felt certain, since you were so adamant, you would avoid doing anything to make the marriage a permanent one."

He plucked a reddish curl from her shoulder and twisted it about his finger, admiring the burnished highlights. Her assumption they would be able to annul the marriage was wrong. Even the fact that he had been coerced before witnesses was not grounds for annulment. What would she do when she learned they were truly bound?

His hand found a place to rest against her hip as he shifted her closer. Following her visit to his cell, the light floral scent that clung to her hair and skin had haunted his dreams for days. He breathed it in now and fought the urge to bury his face in the heavy mass of coppery hair close to his face.

It had been some time since he had held a woman in his arms. The soft womanly feel of her beneath his touch had him growing hard, his need stirring to insistent life.

Her eyes, the color of pansies, rose to his face then skittered away. She turned her graceful profile to him, the line of forehead, nose, and chin etched by the fire's light.

"I've asked Talbot to look over the will and help Edward settle the estate."

She stiffened and she searched his face. "Why would you do that?"

His jaw grew tight. "Have you thought that perhaps one of the reasons Edward was so eager to marry you to someone leaving the country was to cheat you of your inheritance?"

"He is the only male left in line for the title."

"But not necessarily everything else. Most fathers provide for their children."

Bitterness gave her voice an edge. "Not necessarily. Most fathers marry their daughters off, so they do not have to provide for them, someone else does."

His look of surprise must have been apparent for she hastened to add, "Edward said it was my mother's brother who left me a small inheritance."

"Talbot will see that you're inheritance is secured. And if he is an annoyance to Edward in the process—it won't concern me."

She laughed, her look of concern relaxing.

"What have you in store for Lord Rudman?" she asked.

43

"Nothing thus far, but should an opportunity present itself..."

"I hope that, before you leave England, such an opportunity arises."

The rapport between them restored, Matthew felt a vague regret in disturbing it, but he had to know if she had known all along they could not annul the marriage. He'd had time to resign himself to the situation. Two frustrating weeks to try to look at the change in his marital status as a positive one—for his daughter at least. "I've brought you a book from Talbot's library."

An expression first of surprise then confusion crossed her face.

He offered her the leather bound volume at his elbow. "I've marked the pages I thought you would find most interesting."

He rested a subtly protective hand against her hip as she bent her head to read the page, her lips slightly parted, her hair tucked behind her ear, her eyes intent upon the volume she cupped with one hand. Suddenly, the color began to leach from her skin.

"We can take everything slowly, Katherine."

She twisted away from him and rose to her feet. "Not bloody likely." Her voice sounded choked and the book slid unheeded from her hand to land on the rug at their feet.

For a moment, Katherine couldn't breathe. Panic had her heart drumming in her ears, and she crossed the room intent on escape. Her hand felt clumsy as she fumbled with the latch and wrenched at the door only to have it slam shut as he braced a hand against it from above hers.

Trapped. She was trapped. She thrust her elbow back into the hollow of his belly, and he grunted in pain as she swooped out from under his arm.

"You must calm yourself, Katherine," he said, his tone soothing as he followed her to the bed.

Slipping a hand beneath the pillow, she grasped the butt of the pistol and withdrew it from its hiding place. Cocking it, she thrust it squarely into his groin.

He froze.

"We are not doing this." Her voice sounded husky around the knot of smothering rage lodged in her throat. "How long have you known we could not annul the marriage?"

His gaze slid downward to the gun then moved back up to her face. With studied care, he eased back from her. "I suspected it from the beginning."

Resolve hardened within her. She would not be his wife. She would not be anyone's wife. She kept the gun steady in its position. "Move back."

"My father always told me never to point a loaded pistol at anyone lest you were prepared to fire it." He stepped back, his movements slow and measured, his hands palm out.

"My brother once told me so as well." She struggled not to allow her gaze to waver. "Back up." When he hesitated she added, "I should hate to give you a lead ball for a wedding gift."

A formidable scowl drew his black brows together. "If that's a jest, I don't find it amusing."

"I do not find it so either," she snapped, loosing some of the emotion that ricocheted through her. The flintlock wobbled and she steadied it with her other hand.

"Since when is it insulting for a husband to offer to take things slowly when initiating his wife."

"You are not my husband. You will never be my husband."

His look of speculation brought another surge of panic racing through her. Her legs felt numb with shock. Why had she ever believed Edward? He had known what she wanted to hear and had fed her the lies a piece at a time. Why had she been fool enough to believe anything he said?

She tripped over the edge of the rug shoving the metal barrel against him with more intimate familiarity than she intended.

"Have a care where you place your feet, Madame. I'm rather attached to that part of my anatomy and don't wish to be maimed by a careless shot."

She stifled an embarrassed moan and fought the urge to look down at the area where the gun pressed. "That would indeed insure a reason for annulment, would it not?"

"You don't need to do this, Katherine."

They reached the doorway of the dressing room.

"Yes, I do, Captain. I do not feel I can trust you to keep your distance since you have already resolved yourself to the situation instead of seeking out a solution to it." She drew a deep breath to steady herself for her heart raced so she could hardly breathe, and she was close to tears. "Please step inside the dressing room."

"And if I refuse?"

She swallowed and squared her shoulders. "I will have to shoot you then say it was an accident."

He studied her for a moment. "I've yet to force myself on a woman, Katherine."

"I am certain you truly believe that."

His frown deepened as his gaze once again probed hers. "I'll give you my word that I won't touch you."

"You already did, and you did not keep it." She motioned him back with the pistol. "Please step inside the dressing room."

With open reluctance, he stepped back over the threshold.

She closed the door and secured the lock. She leaned back against the portal, her legs shaking beneath her. Instant tears burned her eyes and she swallowed back the sob that raced up her throat and begged to be released.

His deep voice sounded muffled by the door. "It has been nearly five months since I've slept in a real bed and the floor is not an inviting prospect."

She smothered the quick feeling of guilt. "I am truly sorry, but I won't be trapped in a marriage I should grow to hate. And I refuse to be used at your whim like—like a piece of furniture. Tomorrow, we will find a solution."

****

After an hour's wait, the walls of the dressing room began to close in on Matthew. He rolled off the daybed to his feet and strode to the door to listen for any sound from without. Listening for an hour to Katherine's muffled sobs had not been a pleasant experience. Knowing she abhorred, to such an extent, even the idea of being married to him had been equally so.

He knelt before the door and inserted the buttonhook into the lock. Jiggling the metal stem and twisting it, he heard the satisfying click of the mechanism releasing. Rising to his feet, he rested his hand on the knob and turned it gingerly. Katherine only had one shot. There might be a good chance she'd miss, if she fired.

He stood back against the wall to one side as he gave the door a gentle push. It swung open wide. Silence followed. Tensed to dive for the floor, he stepped through the portal. His gaze swept the room for any threat.

Katherine, dressed in a simple cotton shift, lay curled on her side on the bed, her woolen robe draped over her feet. The flintlock pistol, with which she had threatened him, rested on the bedside table within easy reach.

His stocking clad feet made little sound as he crept to the table and picked up the firearm. He didn't relish being shot should she awaken.

His gaze fell on her features. The auburn crescents of her lashes appeared dark with moisture against the paleness of her skin and tear tracks marred her smooth cheeks. Her eyelids appeared red and puffy from crying, her pale pink lips pouting as a soft breath escaped from between them. The creamy perfection of her skin tempted him. He knew from experience it felt like warm silk.

His gaze trailed downward. The light muslin shift she wore followed the contours of her body like a lover's hand. The fabric caressed the full, unfettered thrust of her breasts and tapered to a dainty waist and slender hips. The folds of the garment, caught between her thighs, outlined the graceful shape of her legs. Matthew knew, in that moment, he had never seen anything quite as lovely as the woman who lay asleep before him. The liquid heat of desire raced down his body. He grew hard and aching with need. He found his hand outstretched, reaching for her before he caught back the betraying digits. His fingers curled into a fist, his mouth growing dry.

His eyes traced the classic perfection of her profile. She had brought hope and beauty into his small dank prison cell. That alone would have made it difficult for him to keep his distance. Now he had seen her like this, knowing she was legally bound to him, it would be nearly impossible. He didn't want a wife any more than she wanted to be one, but he'd had a fortnight to adjust to the situation. Having no choice had been a great qualifier in the process.

Marriage was after all like any other partnership.

There would be compromises and sacrifices, rewards and disappointments. It would be up to them to decide what they would make of it. She would eventually come around to realizing and accepting that. She had no more choice than he did.

For the first time all day, his thoughts turned to Caroline. A pain only partially dulled by time lanced through him. God how he had loved her! Never again would he leave himself open to such pain. Having married for convenience sake was a blessing. Neither of them had to grow emotionally attached to each other in such an arrangement.

His attention turned to the wide expanse of empty space beside Katherine. It had been more than four months since he had known the comfort of a real bed. He wondered if he could share the space beside her without reaching for her. He wouldn't force her to accept him as a husband. And in her current frame of mind that would be the only way she would. Matthew flinched. The realization steadied him and damped the flames of his desire to a controllable blaze.

Careful to keep his attention directed away from her, he tucked the flintlock beneath the mattress for safekeeping, then hurriedly stripped off his clothes, and turned down the lamps. Slipping between the covers, he bit back a sigh of pure pleasure and closed his eyes.

When she awoke to find herself in bed with him there'd be hell to pay. He didn't care. It would be worth it.

CHAPTER 6

Katherine opened her eyes to a wide, bare, masculine chest covered in swirls of dark hair. Shock held her immobile as her sleep-dulled mind leaped to complete wakefulness. A tremor of reaction raced down her body, and her heart drummed a frantic rhythm against her ribs making it difficult for her to breathe.

The light pressure of an arm rested against her back holding her, while her thigh looped over his with shameful familiarity. A tingling, wild heat traced the length of her body wherever his touched. She drew a slow, calming breath as she waited for the sensation to abate.

How had Matthew gotten out of the dressing room and how long he had been in bed with her? When he awoke, he was certain to be angry. Dread brought a hollow feeling to her stomach. The confrontation that was sure to come would surely be difficult. She lay motionless, fearful of waking him.

The slow steady rise and fall of his breathing beneath her head eased her anxiety and she began to relax. With her head cupped within the hollow of his shoulder, her cheek rested against the soft hair on his chest. The short curling matt did little to hide the well-defined muscle beneath. Curious, her gaze followed the narrow line of hair arrowing down the middle of his stomach. She realized her hand lay against the lower portion of his abdomen beneath the covers, her fingertips brushing hair there. Mortified, her cheeks burning, she eased her hand away, but knew not where to put it. She straightened her arm and laid it along her hip.

The bare skin of his thigh seemed meshed by warmth and moisture with hers. Tendrils of sensation raced upward to settle in the nether regions of her body. Katherine bit back a moan of frustration. Raising her head so as not to put any more pressure on his shoulder, she tilted her bent thigh upward then swiveled her hips.

The blankets layering the bed pulled away, baring more of his naked torso. Embarrassed, yet fascinated, her attention focused on the spot where the covers hung low over his hips. Realizing how unseemly her interest was, she forced her gaze upward.

The lower half of his jaw appeared shadowed by the stubble of beard, the heavy growth outlining the sensual curve of his lips and emphasizing the strong structure of his jaw. Her gaze followed the straight arrogant shape of his nose upward to the bridge. Well-arched brows traced the ridge of bone over his eyes. Dusky lashes fanned against the smooth skin of his high cheekbones. She stilled the surprising urge to trace the rugged masculinity of his features with her fingertips and test the texture of his skin.

Confused by the sudden desire, she eased into a sitting position only to find her shift caught firmly beneath his hip. She tugged on the tail of the garment and the fabric slid free so suddenly she almost fell over the edge of the bed.

He sighed in his sleep then turned toward her on his side. She swung off the bed just as his hand slid over the empty place where she had lain. The lean line of his hip, thigh, and buttocks lay bare to her perusal.

She stared at his long limbed, powerfully built body stretched out before her. Dark as a raven's wings, his hair hung in heavy waves along the side of his face and pooled like spilled ink on the pillow beneath his head.

He could have attacked her at any time during the night, yet he hadn't. The protective way he had held her in his sleep brought a quivering, uneasy feeling to the pit of her stomach. Now he lay completely vulnerable to her gaze and to the chill permeating the room. She moved around the foot of the bed to retrieve the heavy coverlet lying in the floor. Slowly she slid it upward over the sleeping man, securing his modesty and his warmth.

With a conscious effort, she dragged her attention away from Matthew. There was much to be done if she meant to leave for Summerhaven within the next few days. She had to get started. She slipped silently into the dressing room to gather her clothes.

****

"Where did she say she was going, Bradley?" Matthew shrugged into the waistcoat and began to do up the buttons.

The valet turned to answer the impatient inquiry, his narrow face as indomitably composed as always. "She said she had an appointment, sir, and told me to allow you to sleep as late as you would. I must say I've never known you to sleep so soundly, but you do look rested."

All those months of sleeping with one eye open to protect himself from Hicks had finally taken its toll. His gaze lingered on the discarded shift draped on the daybed. A vision of how she had looked while wearing it taunted him.

"Did she say when she would be back?"

"No, she didn't."

Niggling unease slithered into the pit of his stomach. Why had she left before the rest of the house had risen? Had she not wanted anyone to know where she was going? Or had she hoped to avoid him? Would she be back?

"Who did she take as escort?"

"Her maid, sir and Lord Willingham's driver." Bradley held his long coat for him.

He slid his arms into the sleeves and adjusted the cuffs of his shirt. At least she had taken a chaperone and her clothes still resided in the dressing room. An instant awareness of his duty to Katherine, as well as hers to him came to mind. Some rules would have to be set about their behavior if they were to appear a normal married couple. Her absence had already caused him embarrassment with Bradley and a certain amount of uneasiness.

Bradley bent to gather the discarded clothing that lay upon the floor next to the bed. A stocking lay just out of the man's sight between the bedside table and the frame. Matthew retrieved it and turning offered it to the valet. Spying dark brown spots upon the sheet, he tossed back the coverlet and stared at them. What the hell? There were flecks of blood upon the bed. Confusion and anger warred within him. He hadn't touched her. There had been no consummation. After being so adamant about it, why would Katherine create proof of an event that hadn't taken place?

"I'll have the maids change the linens, Mr. Matthew," Bradley said from beside him.

He nodded then turned away uncertain of his expression. What game was she playing? All the things he might do and say to her once she returned raced through his mind. Flipping her over his knee and paddling her precious behind ranked high on his list.

"Lord and Lady Willingham have held the midday meal for you, sir." Bradley's voice behind him drew him out of his contemplation.

"I'll join them now, Bradley."

As he entered the dining room, Clarisse rose from her place at Talbot's right to embrace him. "Is Katherine sleeping late?"

"No, she had an errand to run early this morn and has already risen and gone. She'll return shortly." Should she make a fool of him by extending her absence, she'd regret it.

Talbot shot to his feet with such suddenness his chair tipped over, striking the floor with a sharp crack. "Where has she gone?" His square-jawed features took on a concerned look, his stocky frame posed for action.

The sharp report of a door slamming came from the front of the house. The indistinct murmur of voices approached the dining room.

"Release me at once." Katherine's voice came from just outside the room.

"We shall see what your husband has to say about your behavior."

Still dressed in their cloaks, the two people entered the room followed by the Willingham's butler, Elton.

She jerked away from her uncle's grip, her cheeks flushed with temper. With the whispering swish of silk skirts, she crossed the dining room to stand at Matthew's side, a fact he considered quite brave after her behavior of the night before and this morning.

"She was parading up and down the street with only her maid for escort." Edward's ire filled voice rose in pitch. He cleared his throat.

Her gasp expressed her outrage. "I was not parading anywhere, Edward. Hannah was with me, and Lord and

Lady Willingham's driver followed us as well. I had errands I wished to complete early this morn lest my need of a conveyance was inconvenient." She rubbed her forearm as though it pained her. "You had no right to drag me into your coach and force me back here as though I were some kind of escaped criminal."

His eyes widened. "You have not told them."

She stiffened, her violet eyes growing dark, an open look of loathing tightening her features. "I will leave that to you, Uncle. It gives you such pleasure to spread the word far and near. In fact, it would not surprise me if it were your words alone that caused the latest round of gossip."

He drew himself up like a scrawny rooster, an image reinforced by the large flounce of white lace and silk protruding from the lapel of his waistcoat like the breast feathers of a cock. With his bony legs braced apart and his beaky nose high in the air, he looked as though he might crow as well. "You ungrateful little baggage."

"There is nothing wrong with a lady accompanied by her maid, running errands, Lord Leighton," Clarisse said.

Edward waved an impatient hand in the air. "There is when she has been witness to a murder and the men responsible have not been captured."

Matthew's gaze darted to Katherine's face as a stunned silence settled over the room. Though her features remained carefully devoid of expression, her hands clenched at her sides. He curbed the surprising desire to slide a protective arm about her waist.

"Elton, have two more places set for the meal," Talbot's calm tones cut across the quiet. He ran a hand through his thick crop of white hair making it stand on end.

"Yes, sir." The tall thin butler bent to return Talbot's overturned chair to its rightful position, then melted away.

"You knew about this?" Matthew turned his attention to his uncle.

"Yes." His uncle nodded.

What other information had been withheld? "Just when were you going to tell me?"

"This morning of course. I had no idea Katherine had

gone out."

Every eye turned on the woman beside him.

Her chin rose. "They will not show their faces in daylight, nor attack me on a busy London street."

"You cannot be certain, Katherine," Edward protested.

"Yes, I can. They are cowards. They would have too many witnesses should they do anything in daylight." She stepped away from Matthew to remove her cloak and handed it to the maid who appeared at her side. "I will not be treated as though I am to blame for what they did, nor shall I be locked away while they remain free."

"Both of you take a seat." Talbot motioned to the empty chairs on either side of the table. "We can discuss what can be done after we eat."

Elton once again appeared at the door. "Barlow has arrived with your maid and several packages, Madame Hamilton. He wishes to know where you would like them put."

Her lips parted, a frown creasing her brow. "Please ask him to put the bundles in our room, Elton."

Hannah appeared behind the butler, her cheeks flushed. The distress in her expression cleared when she saw her mistress. Katherine joined the maid in the hallway, her arm going around her in a soothing gesture. The woman nodded as she spoke to her then followed a man laden with paper wrapped parcels down the hall.

Katherine's attention settled on Matthew as she returned to the table. Her cheeks grew flushed and her lashes fell, but not before Matthew read the uncertainty in her expression as she approached him.

If what her uncle said was true, she could have been attacked and killed this morning while he slept. He had been remiss in his duty toward her, a duty of which he hadn't even been aware. Resentment flashed through him like heat lightning. He neither wanted nor needed any of this.

He held her chair for her and with a deliberate, exaggerated courtesy saw her seated, then took a place beside her. "You could have told me, last night."

She turned to face him, her features tight with control. "No, I could not."

He laid an arm across the back of her chair, his thigh touching hers as he focused his attention on her. "I'm listening now."

Her confidence wavered beneath his regard for a moment, then her jaw firmed and her spine straightened. She adjusted the knot of his stock, her hand lingering against the front of his waistcoat. "I would prefer to speak to you in private after the meal."

Surprised by the proprietary gestures and her courage in the face of his attempted intimidation, his fingers curled around hers, holding her hand against his chest. A sudden vision of how she had looked the night before intruded, bringing him to an instant state of painful arousal. A spike of irritation hammered through the hard-won control he held over his temper. "We shall speak in private about a great many things, Madame." Matthew bent his head to press a kiss within her palm and purposely nipped her skin with his teeth. He watched with satisfaction as soft color blossomed then receded in her cheeks.

"If what your uncle says is true, Katherine, you must be more careful in future."

Anger flared in her eyes as she met his gaze head on. "Perhaps I should begin to carry a flintlock for my protection. You would not happen to have an extra at hand?"

He thought of the weapon he had tucked beneath the mattress and smiled without humor. "I would have to be certain of your proficiency with firearms first, sweetheart. You wouldn't wish to shoot anyone by accident because you were unfamiliar with the rules governing weapons."

"Actually she is an excellent marksman," Edward said. "Her brother collected firearms and taught her to shoot." He frowned and looked down his nose at his niece from across the table. "Not that I agree with women participating in such activities."

One perfectly arched brow rose as Katherine's attention swung to her uncle. "You would prefer we be helpless and deferential at all times would you not, Uncle? Even when it is a danger to us."

"There is nothing wrong with a woman knowing her place, Katherine. I am sure your husband will instruct you in what that is." His expression of smug satisfaction bordered on being a smirk.

Matthew disliked the man's pettiness and the pleasure he derived from it. "I happen to approve of Katherine's ability to defend herself. There may come a time, I may need her to guard my back, as I'll guard hers."

Edward's expression darkened to one of displeasure. "Meaning?"

"You may leave the caring for my wife to me."

The man bared his teeth in an enthusiastic smile. "Gladly."

He viewed Edward's acquiescence with suspicion and wariness. It had come too easily. Had he charged blindly into the fray without first knowing all he should? Damn. What the devil had happened to the calm, deliberate man who captained a vessel two times a year? Had being imprisoned somehow addled his brain? Why was he even tempted to champion a woman who had completely deceived him? He looked down at Katherine's upturned face. She offered him a hesitant smile. He controlled the urge to shake her. Was he allowing his baser needs to rule the rest of him? Matthew shied away from answering the question.

CHAPTER 7

Katherine straightened her spine and turned away from the four pairs of probing eyes fastened on her. She concentrated instead on the view of the garden visible from the French doors of the study. Despite the woven intricacies of the hedges along the path, the fountain remained discernable, the nymph at its center, surrounded by frolicking water. Katherine gripped the doorknob, fighting the urge to escape the room and the expectancy of the people behind her.

"Will you not come join us by the fire, Katherine?" Clarisse asked.

Katherine rested her forehead against the coolness of the windowpane for a moment. "Of course, Lady Willingham." She forced herself to turn and face the group.

The empty place on the Chippendale sofa next to Matthew lay open and waiting. Katherine took the seat but left a wide section of a cushion between them.

Sliding forward to the edge of his seat, Edward's brows lowered into a sympathetic frown as he faced her. "I want to see justice done, Katherine, but not at the price of seeing your reputation damaged. Every time you are associated with what happened, there are suggestions made about what you may have been subjected to that night, as well."

Katherine shrugged and settled back into the corner of the sofa. Her gaze briefly touched Matthew's face then flitted away. "I am traveling to America. I do not care what anyone thinks I was subjected to."

"Your husband may feel differently. And through their association with you as their nephew's wife, Lord and Lady Willingham may feel you should show some restraint in whatever actions you are thinking about taking."

Lady Willingham spoke for the first time. "What your

uncle says is true, Katherine. Once your reputation has been sullied, it will follow you wherever you go. Should you come forward openly about what you saw that night, it will not matter whether or not they touched you. It will be what everyone will think."

"I think, in time, there may be a way for you to achieve justice without sacrificing anything, Katherine." Talbot ran his hands over the wooden arms of the Chippendale chair he sat in. "But it will take patience."

How could they put speculation above seeking justice for her family? She rose to return to the French doors, separating herself from the group once again. She was not only disappointed by their attitude but hurt by it.

"If I wait long enough, eventually they will die in their beds and God will serve them justice." Bitterness put an edge to her words.

"No one expects you to wait indefinitely, Katherine." Talbot laced his fingers together. "Eventually these men will be caught and punished."

Though they all meant well, they spouted the same cautious platitudes Edward had been offering her for months. She turned to face Lord Willingham, as her rage thrust through her control and over-rode her sense of propriety. "I wonder how differently you would feel if it had been your wife or daughter, who had been left lying in the street, beaten and bloody, her dignity torn from her, and her neck, bruised and raw, from a noose twisted until the life was strangled from her. I wonder how patiently you would wait, if every person you loved were suddenly ripped away from you, as my family has been from me."

She had been alone for months, but an overwhelming sense of abandonment swept over her. She turned away from them, her composure deserting her. With a twist of the knob, she opened the French doors and fled the room.

Driven from his seat, Matthew strode forward to follow her. Edward grasped his arm as he passed, his grip surprisingly strong. "We must speak about what can be done to protect my niece, Captain Hamilton. In the state she is in, she may well attempt something foolish."

If she were tempted to do something foolish, it would be because she had received little or no support from her only living relative. "You forced her to marry me to get her out of the country."

"I did not force her. She agreed to the marriage once she met with you. It was the only thing I could think to do under the circumstances. I am sure you have noticed how headstrong Katherine can be. Frankly, I found it exhausting trying to reason with her about the situation. She is too driven by her need for justice to listen to anything."

He could understand that. Had it been his own family he would have spent every waking moment personally hunting down the men responsible. He wondered why, with all the resources available to him, Edward Leighton wasn't doing that. He studied the man more closely. "Just what is being done to see these men are caught?"

"The local magistrate has hired some men to look for them, as have I. There has yet to be any news from them. It seems the brigands have grown more cautious since the attack upon my brother and his family."

His gaze shifted to Talbot. His uncle's frowning visage met his in silent communication.

"Of course she has been tormented by dreams of the man who attacked her." Edward's expression grew mournful. "It wasn't enough that she was nearly strangled to death, but for them to abuse her as they did her dear mother." He shook his head.

A dropping sensation struck Matthew's stomach. With the force of a blow, the reason behind her behavior of the night before and the purpose of the dark droplets on the sheet became clear. The adage that a horrible injury is numbed by the sheer magnitude of the trauma was true. When the numbness wore off, he would know how to feel. His face felt wooden as he turned his attention to Edward. "You must be mistaken."

The man started and looked up at him. "What do you mean?"

"It must be clear. Last night was our wedding night."

Edward's brow creased and he narrowed his gaze. "It's understandable, Captain Hamilton, that you wish to protect Katherine's reputation."

Was that not what her uncle should want as well?

The numbness began to recede as anger rushed in to replace it. He controlled the impulse to jerk the man out of the chair and shake him like the sniveling rat he was. Aware of Clarisse and Talbot's presence, he glanced briefly at his aunt. "Forgive me for speaking so bluntly in your presence, Clarisse." Focusing on Edward, he took a measured step toward the man. "Do you think me such a fool I wouldn't know the difference between bedding a virgin and a woman who is not?"

Edward's mouth opened and closed as he sought an answer.

"Shall I have the proof dragged from our marriage bed for your perusal? Should I call my valet down to testify to the blood upon the sheets?"

Edward shook his head. "I meant no insult."

"Yes, you did." He took several deep breaths at a bid for control that seemed just out of reach. He thrust his face close to Edward's. "Should I hear you have even hinted that my wife was anything but pure, as you just did to me, kin or not, I will call you out and take great pleasure and satisfaction in extracting your apology before I drop your cold, dead carcass overboard for the fish to pick over."

The man grew pale and he seemed to have trouble swallowing. "You can not threaten me like this. I am a Lord."

"Lord or not, makes no difference to me. This is not a threat, Edward. It is a promise."

He studied the man's sallow complexion with some satisfaction. "I hope I shan't discover there are rumors already circulating. I would hate to have to enquire just who might have started them. Though it might take some time to track it down, eventually, the truth always surfaces."

Edward remained silent.

Matthew straightened. "Talbot, Clarisse, please excuse me. I feel Katherine and I need a few moments away from the house. I thought it might be the perfect time for us to visit the Caroline." He returned his attention to Edward. "I will be certain to tell Katherine you wished her well, Edward."

****

Katherine watched the tiny brown wren pluck dismally through the fallen leaves for something to eat. The creature hopped close and cocked its head from side to side studying her. A breeze ruffled the heavy dark blue fabric of her skirt startling the bird and it skittered across the path and under a bush, it's tiny feet a blur.

She shivered beneath the chill of the wind. She preferred the cold to the oppressive atmosphere of the study. No doubt, they were planning to keep her under lock and key, as Edward had done. Resentment raced through her at the injustice of it. She had become a prisoner instead of the men responsible for her family's death. It did not matter that the cage was gilded, only that she couldn't go about with any freedom.

A movement from the path set the wren to panicked flight and it soared upward and away. Turning her head to see what had disturbed the creature, her attention settled on Matthew's tall form as he strolled toward her.

She studied the masculine appeal of his features. The strong angular shape of his jaw, the cleft in his chin, more than hinted at a strong will. She found an unusual beauty in the lithe grace of his powerful body. Thoughts of how he had looked that morning in bed brought heat rising to her cheeks and settling in other more intimate places. He was proving to be a distraction to her peace of mind, just as Edward had hoped.

He unfolded the cloak draped over his arm and, with a practiced movement, wrapped it about her shoulders.

She wondered how many women he had performed such a service for in the past. "You are very adept at that, Captain." The words were out before she could think to retract them.

"It comes from dressing a four year old who is seldom still." He took a seat beside her on the bench.

Shocked at the comment, her gaze leaped to his face. "You have a child?"

"Yes, a daughter." His black brows snapped together in a sharp V. "You didn't know?"

She shook her head. "Edward did not tell me." *He had a daughter*. The thought tumbled through her mind end over end. A sudden realization brought a sinking feeling of despair to the pit of her stomach. "Your wife, was it a recent loss?"

"Caroline died in childbirth four years ago."

Though his features remained composed, a tightening of the muscles about his mouth belied the ease with which he said it. She rested a sympathetic hand on his arm for a brief moment. "I am sorry." After a silence she added, "You must be eager to return home to your daughter."

"Yes, I am. I had promised her I'd be home for Christmas. Unfortunately, that isn't possible. I've sent a letter explaining that I've been delayed and will be there as soon as I can."

How he must resent her for her part in his delay. "How long will it take you to prepare your ship for the journey?"

"A month, if I'm able to hire a crew and get enough supplies aboard for the crossing."

"As I will be locked away here, perhaps you should be the one to inquire about the annulment. There must be someone who can offer you advice about it."

Instead of commenting on the matter he said, "Is that what Edward did, locked you away?"

Her quick perusal of his features reassured her of the genuine interest he showed to the question. "As good as. I was not allowed out of the house without him. While he was away, the servants kept watch over me to insure I did not leave."

"Where would you have gone?"

"Home." She breathed the word like a talisman against all the pain. Summerhaven represented the one place that harbored memories of her family untainted by grief. She longed to be there away from the smothering strictures of London society and her uncle's control.

"To the country estate in Birmingham you mentioned. You don't care for London then?"

She gave the question some thought. "No. I feel smothered here."

"Perhaps that's because you haven't had the opportunity to enjoy the city as you should."

She did not feel comfortable in a society where appearances meant more than truth. Nor did she have a place within the group. The women talked behind their hands and avoided her. The men made lewd remarks beneath their breath and more. "I will never be accepted here, nor do I wish to be."

His features settled into an aggressive frown. "Then why stay here, Katherine?"

She thought he would have understood. "Because this is my home, and if I allow them to drive me from it, they win. If I leave before they have been punished for what they did, they win as well. I am the only one who cares that my family is dead."

"And why is that?"

She shook her head. "My parents had many acquaintances, but few close friends. My father and Edward did not care for one another's company and were not close." After having lived with her uncle for a time, Katherine understood why her father had avoided his brother. His absorption in the frivolous concerns of dress and entertainment had worn on her patience. She had resented how easily he had stepped into her father's shoes and claimed all that had been his. He had resented the responsibility of caring for her. The combination had been an unhappy one for them both.

Guilt lay like a weight on her shoulders. Without compromising her own plans, there was no way for her to warn him of what she had done. Matthew would come to resent her as Edward had; she felt certain of it. "It is not my intent for you or your family to be harmed by your association with me."

His brows rose. "How might we be harmed?"

She brushed at the loose curls that dangled against her cheek. "Lady Willingham said there had already been talk about me among her acquaintances." She looked away from the steady regard of his pale blue eyes. "I suppose once a woman has been ruined, no matter the circumstances, she is expected to either end her life or hide herself away for the rest of it." She bobbed to her feet unable to remain seated.

His fingers curled around her elbow at the same time he rose to stand close beside her. "Was that the purpose of the blood upon the sheets this morning, to prove your innocence?"

Shocked surprise held her still. There had been no

consummation. Her thoughts raced from one possibility to another. They had been the only two in the room and neither had any injuries. She had not started her monthly flux. How? Her mind raced over the routine of the morning as she had dressed to leave. The only other person who had entered the room had been Hannah. She had tied her stays and buttoning her gown. She snatched back a groan. Hannah.

Her breathing grew shallow and quick as she fought the desire to scream and screech and pound the stone bench they sat upon. The effort it took to fight off her rising ire left her trembling.

"Now, I at least understand your locking me in the dressing room last night."

She swallowed and looked away from the compassion she read in his eyes. "I will not hold you to the marriage contract, Matthew. No matter what else should come to pass, when you sail to America it will be as a free man." She had given him her word and she meant to stand by it. She understood Hannah's reasoning behind what she had done. By passing the night untouched, proof of her innocence was lacking. Servants gossiped and consequently she would be damned for certain. Hannah had done what she thought she needed to protect her.

Her eyes rose to Matthew's face. His lips compressed, his features set in forbidding lines, he looked intimidating to say the least. She drew a deep breath and said what she thought she must to protect the woman. "As long as rumor is given more credence than the fact that my family is dead, I must do whatever I can to insure my credibility stands firm, Captain. I am their only witness, the only one left to speak for them."

"And you believe because you were attacked, that somehow weakens your credibility?"

Bitterness darkened her laughter. "In the eyes of English society it weakens my moral fiber, it lessens my value, and strips me of the respect that at one time was my due. Because I refuse to hide behind closed doors or bow my head in shame, I give insult to all with whom I have congress. Yes, one could say, it weakens my credibility."

It took all the courage she could muster to raise her

gaze to his face. The compassion she read in his expression brought a knot of tears to her throat. She swallowed against it, and grasping at her composure, raised her chin. "You need not feel responsible for me, Captain. I do not expect you to be."

The muscles in his jaw flexed. "Your expectations have little to do with it, Katherine. Lord Rudman and Edward might find it interesting should I neglect my new bride. I don't plan on ending my days in an English prison."

"I do not plan on ending mine locked away in a gilded one either."

"I suggest you take my arm then, Madame. I need to make a visit to my ship, and I don't trust you not to try an unescorted escape while I'm gone. You're going to accompany me."

Too surprised to take exception to his autocratic tone Katherine stared at him. When he offered his arm, she hesitated. "Are you not afraid you might be tainted by being seen with me?"

One black brow rose lazily, but his gaze remained steady. "I thought you were eager to escape the gilded cage, or do you prefer to be under the watchful eye of one of the maids?"

The reason she wished to avoid marriage at all cost came back to her with a vengeance. Knowing he had that kind of control over her infuriated her. Heat flowed beneath her skin. "You have no right."

His expression hardened. "Yes, I do. You are, before the eyes of God and man, my wife. After your unannounced departure this morning, and until I have time to make other arrangements, I intend to keep you close to me."

A vision of how the skin of their thighs had pressed together this morning came to mind. Shocked at the thought, her protest died on her lips as he grasped her arm and marched her down the garden path toward the front of the house.

CHAPTER 8

Matthew took in the hectic activity of the docks, and a smile spread his lips. The tension wound tightly inside him, eased just watching the scene. He had been dry-docked too long.

Seamen, dressed in faded homespun shirts and the loose fitting long breeches, scurried about like bees swarming a hive. The dank smell of the water, raw fish, unwashed bodies and the pitch used in repairing the vessels blended with the strong odor of the oils and spices being unload from an East Indiaman close by.

He grinned as he caught the delicate way Katherine wrinkled her nose as they exited the carriage. "The Caroline is anchored out into the channel. She'll be brought back into dock when we load her with cargo for the journey home."

He tucked her fingers over his arm and led her forward. Wooden docking platforms ran parallel to the Thames, offering access to the many vessels being unloaded. He avoided them, but walked along the wide, cobble-stoned street that ran before the warehouses and businesses built along the river. Midway down the wharf, he halted to point out into the channel. "That's the Caroline." His gaze ran over the lines of his ship from the bowsprit to the stern. He gave a satisfied nod, his spirits buoyant with relief. The anxiety over the ship's treatment had plagued many a day during his imprisonment. All looked to be in order. His gaze returned to Katherine to see her attention focused on the vessel.

"What do you think?"

"I think it is beautiful, Matthew."

"She. Yes, she is." He grinned. "We're going out to inspect her. Can you swim?"

"Yes, but I was hoping we would be using a boat to get out to her."

He chuckled. "Of course, but my concern was about

taking you out on the water."

He guided her across the busy thoroughfare. Hiring a small rowboat, he seated Katherine in the bow of the vessel and removing his long coat, draped it over the skirt of her dark blue wool gown. He settled in the stern and took up the oars.

After weeks of sedentary living inside a cell, he relished the physical activity of rowing. Katherine looked about with interest and asked a number of questions about the other ships being loaded. His attention was caught again and again by the curve of her lips as she spoke and the graceful beauty of the profile she offered him as she turned her head.

"What kind of ship is the Caroline?"

"She's an American built brigantine. She's not as large as some, but she's fast and sturdy."

"How often do you sail to England in her?"

"Twice a year. This is to be my final voyage as the captain of a sea vessel. I've responsibilities at home that I need to take up."

"Your daughter?"

"Yes, Emily misses me a great deal, and a ship is no place for a child to be reared. My father died last spring. I now have a plantation to run as well."

Her brows arched. "So you shall become a gentleman farmer there in America."

He pondered her description decided it met with his approval, though it didn't truly fit the responsibilities that went along with being a plantation owner. "In Charleston, South Carolina. My three brothers and I own quite a bit of property there. James owns a hotel and some warehouses, Stephen, a plantation of his own, and Thomas has a nobler calling, he's a doctor."

"It sounds as though your family has thrived there."

He read pain in the careful composure of her features before she turned her head to look away. Reminded of her grief and hoping to distract her, he pointed out the progress of a brigantine as it moved up the channel away from them under full sail.

The bow of the rowboat skimmed the side of the Caroline. He rose, braced his feet apart to retain his balance, and cupping his hands around his mouth, called upward, "Ahoy, Caroline. Is there anyone aboard?"

A freckled face appeared from above and a smile split the young boy's features crinkling his eyes to slits. "Cap'ain Hamilton. Henry's been worrying holes in the deck fretting about you."

"Well, you may tell him his worrying has been wasted, Georgie. Here I am, and I want to come aboard."

"Aye, sir." He hastened to remove a section of railing and lower a rope ladder.

Matthew secured the boat to a brass ring mounted on the bulkhead closest to them, then offered Katherine a hand.

She eyed the ladder with a frown, but rose to her feet.

"I'll be behind you to steady you," he said as she grasped the rung above her head for balance against the rocking of the boat.

"Perhaps you should put my shoes in your pockets." She slipped her feet free of the dainty slippers and handed them to him one at a time.

His weight kept the ladder from swaying. He aligned his body with hers as they climbed lest she lose her grip and start to fall. Even through her cloak, he felt her shoulder blades against his chest, the rounded curve of her buttocks against his loins as they ascended spoon-like topside. Her soft womanly body brushed back against him setting alight needs he had yet to assuage. He breathed in the scent of violets that lingered in her hair and wondered if her skin would taste as sweet. His heart hammered against his ribs as his blood heated and pooled leaving him hard and aching with an arousal that made it difficult for him to draw a full breath.

As they reached the deck, Georgie offered Katherine a hand and helped her aboard. After a quick look at her flushed checks and averted gaze, Matthew cursed his lack of control. He should have been better prepared to curb his response to her. The hollow feeling that had plagued him since learning of her attack returned with a vengeance. It wouldn't help her recovery from such an experience if he conducted himself like a randy fool.

Henry appeared from below the quarterdeck, and his gap-toothed smile of welcome eased the moment. Seeing

Katherine, he whipped his cap off and extended a smile to her. The few wisps of hair remaining atop his balding pate waved in the breeze.

Matthew produced her slippers from his pockets. He placed them upon the deck. She slid her feet into them. He turned to introduce his wife to the two and suddenly realized the awkwardness of the situation. "Katherine, this is Henry one of my crew and Georgie, my cabin boy. Henry, Georgie, my wife, Katherine."

Henry recovered first and wiped the dumbfounded expression from his weathered face with another smile. He bobbed his head and worked the cap between his hands as though he might strangle it. "Pleased to meet ye, mum."

The man actually blushed when she offered her hand and shook his.

Georgie flashed her a boyish grin and repeated the words.

Matthew's gaze swept the planking of the deck, bleached white in spots from many scrubbings. Ropes coiled at the ready lay beneath the spars from which they ran. Hatches were battened against the inclement English weather. Everything was in its place. Well satisfied with his crew's work, he offered Henry a smile.

He tipped his head back, closed his eyes, and soaked in the melodic creak of the deck beneath his feet. He opened his eyes. "She appears to have suffered no lasting effects from being boarded."

"Nay, Cap'in; the crew saw to that. We wondered, when last seein' ye, if ye were faring as well."

"There were times, I was uncertain as to my fate, Henry, but I am well, and ready to prepare for the trip home."

He followed Katherine's progress as she strolled to the port railing, her attention focused on the ships in the distance. The late afternoon sun set alight the burnished tresses coiled at the back of her head. A cold breeze whipped over the deck, dusting a rosy hue across the fragile curve of her cheek.

There had been men he with whom he had served who had possessed less resolve and courage than she did. She would be facing all of society's strictures as well as risking her life to see justice done. As she had spoken of standing for her dead family, the resentment and anger he had harbored had seemed petty and unimportant.

"When did ye wed, sir?" Henry asked, his expression curious.

"Yesterday."

His brows rose in surprise. He was quick to say, "I'm glad for ye, sir. Ye've grieved long enough. Yer still a young man and ye don't want to end up an old salt without a wife and children to go home to, like me."

Matthew had given little thought to more children. It didn't bothered him that his only child was female. His brothers were perfectly capable of keeping the Hamilton name alive if he should never have a son.

Katherine tipped her head back and looked up at one of the tall masts. The breeze coming off the water blew back her cloak, laying bare the slender line of her throat and the swell of her breasts. The shape of her upper body was held in tempting relief against the pale blue sky.

What a waste it would be if she denied herself the opportunity to be a wife and mother because of the events of that one night. The thought made him uneasy. He turned his attention back to Henry.

"We have less than a month to provision the ship and set sail, Henry. I'll need your and Georgie's help in gathering the crew we have left and hiring others. We'll start tomorrow. Have you any idea where Mr. Blevins and Mr. Ray may be residing?"

"Aye, sir. Mr. Blevins and Mr. Ray are at the Strutting Cock. They've been waitin' to hear from ye."

He smiled. "Good."

Katherine looked upward through the maze of guidelines connected to the sails. They looked like the work of a demented spider. What would it be like to board such a ship and sail away to places unknown? Being a woman, she would never know such freedom. Or would she? Once she had seen the criminals captured and punished, she would have only herself to worry about. If she was careful with her income, she might be able to do some traveling.

If everyone already thought her reputation ruined, she wouldn't have to safe guard herself against gossip.

They would think the worst anyway after the marriage ended. What more would they be able to say about her if she did as she pleased? Perhaps she would settle in another country all together.

Leaning her elbows upon the railing, she watched the activity on the dock. She longed for paper, ink, and quill to set down the images before her.

"What is it you're studying so intently, Katherine?" Matthew asked as he joined her.

"Everything." She leaned a hip upon the railing as she faced him. "Where besides England have you traveled?"

"France and Spain."

"That sounds like quite an adventure."

Bracing his feet upon the deck, he folded his hands behind him. "Actually, it was a very enlightening one. We were once boarded by pirates and lost some of our cargo. Two men were killed."

"You were not injured?"

"No. I was only a boy and of little consequence."

"When did you get your own ship?"

"Four years ago. I've made two voyages a year to England carrying cotton, indigo, rice, and tobacco."

Had he returned to the sea after his wife's death because of his grief? He had named a ship after her. That seemed testament enough of his devotion to her.

Who would grieve her loss should something happen? Hannah, her maid, would be the only one. The thought made Katherine more conscious of her solitude. Though Matthew stood beside her, she felt alone.

She shook off the feeling of self-pity and straightened her shoulders. "Are you not going to tour the ship?" she asked.

"I thought perhaps you would like to tour it with me."

"Certainly."

He guided her down a dimly lit passageway beneath the quarterdeck. He pointed out the galley and stopped at the first small cabin. Dim light filtered into the room from a small porthole. "This cabin is shared by my purser and first mate." The area was barely big enough for the bunks, one atop the other, and a small aisle for the men to get into bed.

The gentle pressure of his hand against her back guided her further down the hall to another cabin. "This is my home when I'm not on dry land," Matthew said as he opened the door. The room was no more than ten feet long and twelve feet wide. The dark paneling of the walls gleamed with care. Halfway between the door and the back bulkhead, a small brick fireplace hugged the wall, a kindling box beside it. A table and four chairs stood close by. Built directly into the opposite bulkhead, were a water closet, a washstand, and his bunk.

His desk, with a unit of cubbyholes constructed above it, faced his bunk. Maps were neatly rolled and stored within the compartments. A shelf atop it held three leather-bound editions on navigation and some metal instruments. A decorative molding around the edge secured them. A bay of windows took up the back bulkhead with a window seat beneath. Every area was designed with efficiency and took up as little space as possible.

"Being captain affords me the luxury of this much space. The men have to endure much more cramped housing."

She crossed the threshold of the cabin and wandered to the bank of windows at one end. Afternoon sunlight streamed across the floor and touched upon the bunk against the wall, a bed barely wide enough to accommodate two people. Her cheeks grew hot at the thought. Sitting on the window seat, she turned to look out upon the water.

Behind her, Matthew lit a lantern, drawing her attention. He crossed to the desk, and looked through the maps and charts there, then turned his attention to the metal devices on the shelf above.

She studied the play of light on his features, the wide expanse of his back and shoulders, so strong and manly. What would it be like to have such a man stand beside her against adversity?

Once he knew what she had done, it would be doubtful that he would continue to treat her with such understanding. Would he voice his displeasure in that biting tone he had used at the midday meal or vent his anger in a more physical manner? One seldom knew what men would do.

She quickly turned her interest elsewhere as he set aside the instruments.

"Do you wish to remain here, Katherine, while I inspect the rest of the ship?"

"No, I would like to accompany you."

Carrying a lantern in one hand, he guided her from the cabin and along the passageway. A dark square appeared in the deck and a narrow flight of steps disappeared into the depths below.

The pressure of his hand against her waist urged her down the rough wooden stairs. The lantern swayed as he held it aloft. Bunks hugged the walls supported vertically by wooden beams that ran from ceiling to deck with a narrow passageway between just wide enough for a man to slide in sideways.

Instantly, the room seemed to shrink to the dimensions of the small square of space upon which they stood. The dark sucked the air from the room making it difficult for her to draw breath enough to speak. A cold sweat broke out across her brow and coated her skin beneath her gown.

The deck swayed beneath her feet as the pressure of his hand steered her forward across the cabin to another passageway beyond. He made some comment about the crew's quarters, his deep voice sounding muffled beneath the drumming heartbeat that filled her ears. The air grew thinner as the bunks on either side closed their ranks about her. Gasping, Katherine turned and crashed into Matthew, upsetting the lantern. The lamp swung, the light rocking back and forth to a sickening tempo. She shoved past him and stumbled across the compartment to the stairs. Dizzy, the buzzing in her ears loud, she gained the top of the steps, then bracing a hand against the wooden paneling of the passageway, followed it to the entrance.

Out on the deck with the mid November sun overhead and a breeze like a tonic chilling her damp skin, her breathing eased and the hollow ringing in her ears receded. With her limbs weak, her body shaking with reaction, she found a seat on the steps to the quarterdeck above and half reclined upon them.

A subtle change in the movement of the breeze against her face had her opening her eyes. Matthew had braced a foot upon the bottom step and leaned down to gaze into her face. The masculine shape and size of him loomed over her. His eyes a pale, stormy blue, his lips a taut grim line, the controlled violence in his expression caused her heart to give an anxious jitter.

"If you have never spoken a true word before, Madame, you'd better do so now. Are you with child?"

CHAPTER 9

Matthew extended a long leg and braced a leather-shod foot against the seat across from him. The coach bounced and swayed in a soothing rhythm as it traversed the cobbled streets. The motion did nothing to ease Katherine's ramrod stiff posture as she sat beside him. Though he could only see her profile, her features maintained a careful lack of expression, her gaze fastened upon the passing scenery. She had said nothing since the scene on the quarterdeck, her silence carrying a weight that more than filled the space between them. The quick flash of pain in her expression, then her icy denial had left him with more questions than answers. The barrier of silence she had erected only made him want to goad her into a fight.

"I had every right to know, Katherine."

"And now you know, Captain." She continued to look out the window.

"Sulking isn't a becoming trait."

Her jaw went taut. "You have more chance of being shot for dallying with some other man's wife, than you have of my soiling your honorable name. Believe me, I shan't borrow it any longer than I must."

A satisfied smile tugged at the corners of his lips. He'd rather have her spitting insults than ignoring him. He folded his arms across his chest. "It was my resistance to such dallying that caused my troubles. And now that I've a new bride, I shan't have an opportunity to do any dallying, unless I do it with her."

Finally, her almond shaped violet eyes focused upon him, a warning glitter in their depths.

Another smile attempted to break free. He controlled it with an effort. "I don't intend to play the hermit the last weeks I spend with Clarisse and Talbot. Since you're my wife, I don't intend for you to do so either. Your presence will be required at the functions I attend, and if I know

Clarisse, they'll be many."

He frowned as the color in her cheeks subsided.

"You must know that will only cause more trouble for us both."

He didn't pretend he missed her meaning. "No one will dare offer you insult in my or Talbot's presence. And of course with the gossip spread about your deflowering from the household through the servants, some of the rumors will be laid to rest. That was what you intended."

Her expression remained controlled, but the tip of her tongue appeared to moisten her lips. "Yes."

"Well, you might as well take advantage of the situation."

The coach came to a halt, and he preceded her out of the conveyance. A length of fabric secured to the second floor balcony above fluttered in the breeze drawing his attention as he offered her a hand. The realization that it was the sheet from their marriage bed occurred to him in the same moment Katherine looked up and missed the second step. He staggered as he caught her unbalanced weight with one arm, breaking her plunge toward the ground. He had little time to register the soft feminine feel of her against him before she twisted away, her feet barely finding purchase before she focused her attention on the billowing proof of purity flapping against the façade of the house.

A sound somewhere between a groan and a gasp escaped her as her fingers clutched his stock. She turned shock-widened eyes up to him. "Oh Matthew—"

The distress in her tone had his hands curling around her waist to draw her against him. He brushed a soothing hand over her burnished curls. "It would seem someone else has taken a more direct route to ending the gossip."

Her voice sounded choked with emotion. "Please—make them take it down."

****

"Do you intend to question her about what happened, Matthew?" Talbot set aside the chess piece. He shook free of his coat and hung it on the back of his tall backed chair then poured them both a drink from a bottle set upon a small Pembroke drop leaf table against the wall.

76

Matthew stretched before the fire, and bracing his feet apart, folded his hands behind him. "I thought she might speak more freely once I had earned her trust. It seems that may be more difficult than I anticipated."

Talbot offered him the snifter, a teasing smile lightening his features. "You have never had trouble in the past that I can recall."

Katherine's embarrassment over the sheet had kept her withdrawn and tense all evening. Her complaint of a headache and subsequent withdrawal came as no surprise.

"You wouldn't happen to know who was responsible for the sheet upon the balcony." Matthew took a drink of the amber liquid and held it in his mouth, its smoky flavor like warm silk on his tongue.

"No, I do not. Clarisse thought it a crass gesture, but it may prove a beneficial one, once Katherine has recovered from her embarrassment."

"I've made arrangements for some of my own men to accompany us about the city. They'll be armed. I've asked Clarisse to speak with the servants. They should be careful to keep the doors and windows secured and their eyes open to any strangers lurking about."

His uncle's usual affability was instantly replaced with a serious expression. "You believe that there truly may be a threat to her then."

"I can't say for sure, but I'm not going to leave it to chance."

The older man laced his hands over the slight bulge of his belly. "I have been making inquiries into the recent attacks along the outskirts of the city. There is a particularly vicious band at work here, but no other deaths have occurred because of the robberies. Lord Leighton and his son were not armed, though the driver had a side arm, and Lady Leighton has been the only woman harmed in such a way. The driver was killed as well. Why would they shed blood if their only purpose behind the attack was monetary?"

"Perhaps there was a different purpose behind this attack than the others."

"I know you want to believe Edward had a hand in all this, but nothing points in that direction as yet, Matthew.

Perhaps once we have gotten a look at the will, we may know more. He does seem suspiciously eager to avoid me. Since Katherine is the only surviving child, I would think she would inherit at least enough to keep her comfortably, though she will not need it now."

Matthew tugged at the stock about his throat releasing the elaborate knot. "Had she not survived, Edward would inherit everything free and clear. He's led her to believe she'll only receive a small monetary settlement from her mother's brother's estate and nothing from her father. I find that a little suspicious, don't you?"

Talbot's white brows drew together in a frown. "Since he is executor of the estate, he would know."

"But he wasn't expecting to have assistance in settling everything, Uncle. As executor it would be easy for him to mislead his niece about her inheritance and her money could be allotted at his discretion."

Talbot's jaw thrust forward, his expression one of determination. "He will be disappointed if he thinks dodging me will keep him from giving Katherine her rightful inheritance. The courts and I will see the will, if I have to confront him in public about the issue. I am going to his apartment tomorrow morning before he can avoid me."

Matthew smiled. Talbot would settle the matter. "I imagine he'll be overjoyed to see you."

His uncle helped himself to another drink and leaned back against the desk behind him. "There is something that is not exactly suspicious but does reflect upon his character. After Edward approached me about a marriage between you and Katherine, I began to make inquiries about him. Until his brother's death, he was living on the fringe. Now, he has acquired some wealth he has wasted no time ingratiating himself to certain key elements of the ton, Lord Rudman in particular." With a grim expression Talbot's gaze rose to Matthew's face. "His eagerness to hand Katherine over to you without even inquiring into your character, does not reflect well on him either."

"No, it doesn't," Mathew agreed. He clenched his hands angry on her behalf.

"Rudman held all the so called proof of your crime and the courts were of course more eager to believe a peer than a Colonial gentleman. Had there been any other way I could have helped you, I would have, Matthew."

He nodded. "I know, Talbot."

"It is not a bad trade. Katherine is beautiful and refined."

Secretive, stubborn, distrustful.

"Obviously you found some common ground between you."

He referred to the sheet of course. Her words that morning about respect, honor, and credibility came back to him. He held his peace. "You knew Katherine's father?"

Talbot's gaze dropped to his drink. "Only as an acquaintance. There were rumors he abused his wife, but I could not say for certain they were true. I do know Ellen Leighton was as soft spoken as her daughter and just as beautiful."

"Before Rayford Leighton's death, he invited several very wealthy men to his country estate to meet Katherine. In my opinion, his eye was on the size of their purse instead of their reputation or their suitability. Two were gamblers, and the other old enough to be her father."

Anger tightened Matthew's jaw. "So he wanted rid of her, for a price."

"So it would seem. That attitude would be reflected in the will if he left her nothing," Talbot said. He shook his head as though the thought troubled him. He downed his brandy, set the glass on the tray, and collected his coat. "I am off to bed, as you should be, Nephew."

Talbot hesitated at the door. "I have been meaning to give these to you all day and it continued to slip my mind." He withdrew a stack of letters secured with a wide ribbon from the inner pocket of his coat. "Edward gave these to me the afternoon of the wedding, so I might deliver them to you." He extended the papers. "If he wanted her dead, Matthew, why would he drag her back to Willingham's today, so determined to see her safe?"

He shook his head. "I don't know Talbot." He hesitated to admit that part of his suspicion of Edward stemmed only from his own treatment at the man's hands when so many other things played into it.

Setting aside his empty glass, he accepted the small bundle and murmured a good night. His name, written in a feminine hand, graced the front of each letter. So, she had written to him. Why had she not told him? He pulled the ribbon free and opened the first letter. The anxious tone of the note brought a frown to his face. She had not known he was still imprisoned. She had spoken the truth about that at least. Matthew quit the room to go upstairs.

****

Katherine rose from the bed with a sigh. Half an hour of quiet had gone a long way to ease the dull throbbing at her temples. While getting her night shift, she checked the paper-wrapped parcels stacked next to the chest in the dressing room. Concerned that Matthew would be curious about them, she looked about for some place else to put them.

Hannah's sudden appearance at the door gave her a start.

"Lady Willingham sent me to help you undress."

She nodded and turned giving the abigail access to the row of tiny buttons down her back. She eyed the daybed with its bent wood ends and rolled pillows. The thought of another night in bed with Matthew, reeked havoc with her emotions and brought a feverish heat to her skin. Spending her nights on the daybed would be a wiser option, if a less comfortable one. The idea offered her no feeling of relief and made her doubly determined to keep her distance from her temporary husband.

Dressed only in her shift, she moved back into the bedroom and sat down before the dressing table. Hannah removed the pins from her hair. The auburn mass unrolled down her back and stray curls sprang free.

Considering confronting the maid about the blood on the sheets, she studied the other woman's reflection in the mirror. She had aged in the last few months; the death of Katherine's family had left its mark upon Hannah's heart as much as it had her own. Her hand covered the maid's. Looking into those faded brown eyes, Katherine couldn't bring herself to say anything. "I can do this, Hannah. It has been a long day for us both. You should rest."

A smile laced with sadness touched her lips. "I shan't be about to do things for you when you leave for America, Katherine." She began running the brush through the thick locks.

She wished she could tell her she wasn't going. She turned to face her. "Why ever not, Hannah?"

"I went to the south of France with Lady Ellen before the trouble there broke out. I nearly died from seasickness on the trip there and back. I couldn't tolerate a longer voyage. I would surely be sickened unto death."

A painful feeling of abandonment struck her bringing a knot to her throat. "But you are the only family I have left."

Hannah's eyes grew unnaturally bright. "That isn't so. You'll have a whole new family now. Three new brothers, and Lord and Lady Willingham seem to have taken to you. You'll have a child to keep you busy."

"That does not make up for what I have lost already, what I would lose if you were not with me." Upset by the thought of separation, she had to swallow several times against the tears that threatened. Since birth, Hannah had cared for her. She was as much a part of her family as her Uncle Edward. More so. Love forged a stronger bond between them than blood ever could.

"You're a married woman now, missy. You have a responsibility to your husband. It's your place to be at his side wherever that may take you."

"Where ever I go, so shall you."

"Not if I don't wish it." The woman's chin firmed, her expression determined.

Hannah had served her family, had served her, for nineteen years. Perhaps she truly wanted to be free. "And, if I do not leave England?"

The maid stared at her in surprise. "What nonsense are you spouting now, Katherine?" She set aside the brush. "Of course you'll be leavin' with Cap'in Hamilton as soon as his ship is ready. And, you'll do well to be thankful for havin' a kind and generous husband to care for you. It's what Miss Ellen wanted for you, a young and handsome husband who could keep you safe and give you healthy children. She spoke of it often."

"I know what she spoke of." Better to sow the seeds of doubt now so she wouldn't be so disappointed in her later. "You know the Captain married me to get his freedom back and his ship, nothing more. He still grieves for his wife."

"'Twill take some time, but he'll learn to care for you too. He behaves warmly to you already."

The pretense he had adopted so readily was a regrettable success. "The weight of all the gossip will kill any affection he may harbor for me, Hannah. The difficulty of having a wife with a soiled reputation may prove too burdensome for him."

Hannah's doubt stretched plainly across her features. "He looks to have strong enough shoulders to bear the burden, missy. Now that the neighborhood has seen with their own eyes proof that the rumors are untrue there'll be no need for him to worry."

There was no shaking the woman's faith in the man. She did not even know him, yet she had accepted him in a way Katherine couldn't—or had she just refused to?

Uncomfortable with the thought, she fired a blunt question at the woman. "You would not know how that proof came to be or how it ended up hanging from the second floor balcony, would you?"

The maid gave her a mutinous look.

"You have placed me in an awkward situation with the Captain, Hannah. He was very upset about it this morning. After all, he was in a position to know nothing happened."

"Had you done your duty something would have," she fired right back.

Katherine's anger fled. "It makes no difference if he is handsome, or kind, or generous, or wealthy, if he does not love me."

Hannah focused on her with what Katherine knew to be the woman's most intimidating frown. "Are you afraid to care for him? Afraid he'll treat you as your father did your mum?"

She flinched. "I will not allow any man to raise his hand to me. Never again." Bitterness lay like a stone inside her chest. "I would sooner live alone and unloved the rest of my days than have to tolerate such behavior." Old rage blended with the new to make her voice husky. "My mother knew little kindness from my father and knew no mercy from the men that attacked us that night. I could do little about my father, but I will see the others punished, if it takes a lifetime to do it."

Hannah placed a hand upon her shoulder. "You can't do it alone. You have to seek help where you may."

"Do you think one woman's life, her dignity, means anything to them?" Katherine shook her head. "Only my father's and brother's life will count if justice is ever sought on their behalf. Had she survived they would have blamed her for what they did to her, just as they blamed me. Because we are women, we mean nothing."

"Unless we're loved," Hannah added. "You have to give love to receive it, Katherine. If you're too afraid to give of yourself, you never will. You'll be cheatin' yourself, and you'll be cheatin' your husband."

She bit back the words, "I do not have a husband." A niggling guilty feeling had her biting her bottom lip. She was deceiving everyone, including Hannah. But what else was she to do when she couldn't depend on their help or support?

Struggling with her frustration and anxiety, she remained at the dressing table for several moments after Hannah left. If Matthew grew curious about the packages in the dressing room, he might discover their contents. She had to make certain they were hidden or at least placed where he would not notice them. Returning to the room with the dressing table chair, she eased the door closed, lest Matthew return while she hid the packages. Climbing atop the chair, she hefted the heavy paper wrapped parcels atop the armoire then jumped down.

As her feet touched the floor, the lamp went out leaving an inky blackness that fell like a cowl around her. The air thickened to the consistency of syrup. Katherine gasped. Her mother's voice, muffled and pleading, rose out of the darkness, her sounds of pain, animal moans that went on and on. "Momma." The word escaped on a sob. Katherine shuddered. A blurred image of men standing in a circle watching something upon the ground accompanied by the loud rhythmic sounds of heavy breathing flashed through her memory. Katherine clapped her hands over her ears, blocking the sound, panic making her fight against the emotional anguish it represented. The memory receded leaving her nauseous and dizzy. She reached out and shuffled forward. Disoriented, her hand brushed the face of a chest of drawers. She turned to the right, cracking her knee on a drawer left partially open. The opaque fabric of the room closed in around her. Her chest ached with the effort it took for her to breathe. Shivering, a clammy sweat coating her skin, She stumbled forward with her arms straight out before her. Her hand pressed flat against the door. For the first time, she noticed a sliver of light penetrating across the bottom. Her fingers fumbled at the knob trying to turn it. The slick glass slipped from her grasp, then caught, but didn't turn. Thinking she was locked in she slapped her palm against the door, her breathing too labored for her to cry out. *Dear God, get me out!*

The door opened so unexpectedly she pitched forward and would have fallen had Matthew not caught her. Trembling, her ears filled with the sound of her own panting sobs, she clung to him, her face pressed against his waistcoat.

Several moments passed before her panic eased. She grew aware of the gentle pressure of his hand cradling her head and the strength of his arm supporting her. The softer contours of her body melded with the taller more muscular angularity of his bringing, a fluid weightiness to her lower limbs. A languid heat suffused her skin as the desire to press closer imbued her.

She jerked back, distrustful of her own feelings, more than of him. "Did you lock me in?"

His eyes went from blue to gray. His sensual mouth took on a taut angry line that emphasized the hard masculinity of his features. He looked like a dark angel, with his beard-shadowed jaw, dusky brows, and the inky black hair. Katherine told herself it was fear that brought an added weakness to her legs.

His arm tightened around her his expression grim. "I don't go in for petty reprisals. If ever I wish to seek retribution from you for any wrong you've done me, Katherine, I can promise you, I'll not play the sneak about it. The door wasn't locked."

His biting tone and the unflinching directness of his gaze had her sighing. Once again she found herself in the position of having to apologize to him. "I am sorry."

"You're afraid of close spaces."

"Dark, close spaces," she admitted, her gaze focused upon the stock that hung loose about his neck.

"But you came into the prison."

"I had no choice. Edward was willing to give me to whoever would have me. I had to find some way to protect myself."

His jaw went taut.

"At first I thought I might smother." A shudder shook her. "Mr. Hicks provided a distraction. He made me angry when he began to beat a prisoner. And—you had a window."

"Such as it was. What were you doing in the dressing room?"

Guilt settled once again upon her shoulders. "Looking for something. Then, the lamp went out."

"I left it lit last night. The oil must have burnt low." He kept an arm about her as he guided her to a chair.

Matthew sat down then drew her down on his thigh. She stiffened and tugged at the hem of the shift she wore. She attempted to rise, but he restrained her, tightening his hold upon her waist.

"It's time we spoke."

"About?" She tugged at the hem of her shift again only succeeding in stretching the fabric across her breasts.

"You."

He tried to focus on her face and ignore the display as he studied the growing tension of her features and the reflective wariness in her gaze.

"What is it?" she asked.

"Are there anymore problems that you've neglected to share with me?"

"No."

Her quick denial made him suspicious. "Perhaps you'd better tell me."

She flashed him a furious frown and tried to rise.

His grasp tightened against her hip bringing her against him. He breathed in the clean floral scent of her hair and skin, the musky scent of woman. His attention focused upon the reddened bottom lip that pouted at him so prettily and he fought back the urge to taste it. "As long as we are wed, I've a duty to protect and provide for you."

"Your duty must first be to protect your family."

Her eagerness to thrust aside any connection to them made Matthew uneasy. "My aunt and uncle have embraced you as my wife, Katherine. You made certain of that this morning."

She moved restlessly upon his thigh and braced a hand against his chest keeping some space between them. "That was not what I planned."

She had duped him, no matter what her reasons. Surely, she understood she couldn't continue to take advantage of his good graces indefinitely. "You knew what you were doing when you placed the blood upon the sheets. I don't remember being awakened and taken into your confidence before you did it. Now that we are caught in the trap, we've no choice but to make the best of it."

She stiffened visibly and her violet gaze darkened then shifted away.

"I didn't appreciate waking this morning to your absence and not knowing where you were or when you would return either. I expect to be apprised of your whereabouts from now on."

"And may I expect the same, Captain?"

Her attempt at formality made him angry. "Certainly." He inclined his head. "There is little hope of an annulment, Katherine."

"If you were to seek out some other woman, I could seek a divorce decree." Katherine said.

Her eagerness for him to be unfaithful struck him as insulting. His jaw grew tight as he fought back the tide of anger. "You might not find the idea of being wed to an adulterer distasteful, but I find the idea of being one so."

Katherine grew still, watchful.

He drew a deep breath. "Talbot can arrange a meeting for you with the court appointed administrator."

"I would appreciate that." Her voice took on a husky note. "You do not think Edward has been honest about my inheritance, do you?"

"No, I don't."

He ran a hand in a circular movement over her back then immediately regretted the gesture. She felt so fragile and feminine beneath the pressure of his hand. He didn't want to stop.

"I am not surprised. I guess it is obvious that I do not particularly trust him either." She tucked a long strand of chestnut hair behind her ear and folded her arms against her waist pressing together the rounded weight of her breasts, exaggerating the cleavage between. Such a display of warm creamy flesh had his palm tingling with a desire to touch. He searched her face, but found no evidence that she knew what she was doing. He tamped down the burgeoning need that brought a hitch to his breathing and made his breeches feel uncomfortably tight.

Her throat worked as she swallowed. "What Edward will never understand is how unimportant the money is. I almost pity him because of that. He cares nothing about losing his brother."

The statement struck him as more telling than any other she had made. He had known the pain of grief, but had not known it in reference to one of his brothers. They were related through blood, their bond forged more through a wealth of shared experience and years of caring. The knowledge that he was loved and accepted by them somehow made him more than what he would have been without them. Katherine had been stripped of that. She was left with an uncle, whose care had been questionable at best, and whose attitude had solidified her suspicious beliefs against men. He wanted to throttle Edward Leighton and hang his scrawny carcass from the front balcony of Willingham's.

He ran a hand down her arm and discovered the warm satin of her skin. His arousal tripled bringing sweat to his brow and a heavy beat to his heart. He reminded himself that she was recuperating from a brutal attack and the loss of her family. She didn't need, nor would she welcome, the advances of a randy husband. Those thoughts steadied him. He dragged his attention back to the problem at hand.

"You said my duty was to protect my family. It would be better if you would share your concerns with me now so I might do that."

"They will come, eventually."

He tensed at the certainty of her tone and probed her expression. No fear appeared evident only an unwavering acceptance that brought a hollow feeling to the pit of his stomach. If she felt she had nothing else to lose, what would she do? He didn't care for the answer he derived.

"I've already made arrangements to insure your safety, Katherine."

Her brows rose.

"When you go out, several of my men will accompany you. Until others are hired, the grooms here at Willingham's will patrol the grounds in shifts at night."

"You do not intend to lock me away?"

"Not yet." He purposely adopted a stern expression. He cupped her chin to insure he had her attention. "The first hint that you're deliberately placing yourself in harms way, I'll do so."

Her fingers folded around his wrist. "It is not my intent to immolate myself in the name of justice, Matthew. My family made too dear a sacrifice, so I might live." The bottomless well of pain and grief he glimpsed in her eyes stirred his sympathy. For a brief moment, she actually allowed him to draw her close and offer her comfort. But all too quickly, she pulled away.

She went to the bed to don her robe then strode to the French doors leading out onto the balcony. He rose to stop her. She stood gripping the doorknobs, her forehead resting against the wood, her slender body taut with emotion.

He laid a hand upon her shoulder. "You can't run away from your pain, Katherine."

"If I could just get clear enough to breathe, maybe it would ease."

"Your brother, was he very much like you?" he asked trying to distract her.

Her throat worked as she swallowed. "In looks, yes. Johnny had an insatiable appetite for knowledge. He would have enjoyed your ship and would have made a nuisance of himself asking questions about it."

She straightened, and though no tears were in evidence, she appeared pale. "If you will summon a maid to refill the lamp, I can sleep in the dressing room upon the day bed."

He wouldn't allow himself to dwell on why that idea displeased him so much. "You survived last night unscathed, didn't you?"

"Yes, but—"

"When the servants make the bed in the morning, they'll believe we are at odds with one another or worse yet, that I've mistreated you in some way."

"I had not thought of that." After a pause, she said, "Then...I must insist you wear something more to bed than what God blessed you with, Captain."

The stiff formality in her tone made him grin. "I wasn't aware a little bare skin had caused you such distress, Mrs. Hamilton."

"Surely you see the need to be sensible about this, Matthew. Though I had a brother, he was not in the habit of parading about unclad."

His grin broke out into a smile. "I suppose not. There was a custom in America that you might find interesting, Katherine. It was a courting ritual between sweethearts that became popular just before the war."

"We are not sweethearts."

He smiled at the tenacity of her reminder. "But this may solve our problem."

She eyed him quizzically as he strode to the bed. He threw back the heavy quilts and folded the sheet in half to one side then spread the covers back into place. "I don't intend to be stitched into the sheet but this may ease your mind to some degree." He straightened from the task. "It was called bundling. The man would be stitched into the sheet to insure he wouldn't touch his beloved during the night. The purpose was to allow them time to know one another in privacy without the proprieties being dismissed."

Her violet eyes glinted with disbelief.

"'Tis true."

"You are expecting a great deal of trust on my part, Captain."

"No more than I'm willing to give you, Katherine. I didn't take advantage of you while you slept."

She looked away, two bright red spots of color staining her cheeks. "Are we to travel the same path over and over?"

He studied her profile. "You said I didn't give you an opportunity to confide in me last night. I won't make that mistake again. As we are man and wife, you may seek my council, if you will." He paused to give her an opportunity to speak and frowned when she remained silent. "Should you attempt to make a fool of me a second time, I won't be so understanding."

"One wing-like auburn brow arched to a haughty angle. "Why is it men always offer aid in such a way it insures them control of the situation? Should I want to jump into the Thames, why is it you could not say 'let me hold your cloak,' instead of, 'jump in at this spot and be sure to remove your shoes and bonnet?'"

He threw his head back and laughed. He tugged at a long waving curl that fell over her shoulder. "I suppose, as men, we are expected to take control, provide protection, and care for our ladies."

"I am not one of your ladies."

The resentful gleam in her deep violet eyes and the challenge it represented he found very tempting. "You are for now, Katherine. You are for now."

CHAPTER 10

Katherine slid deeper behind the boughs of the yew bush, the garden wall at her back. A sigh of relief escaped as she listened to the groom's receding footsteps. The man took his duty seriously for he had passed that way thrice since she had been there waiting. Another ten minutes, and she would have to return to the house. At any moment, she expected to see several servants advance upon the garden in search of her. Anxiety raced through her and she fought the urge to rub her arms.

At the sound of horse's hooves upon the cobbled street outside the gate, she leaned out of her hiding spot to look through the wrought-iron bars. The dark mahogany gleam of the coach looked familiar. Hoping the darkness of her morning garb would catch the driver's attention, she stepped forward and raised a hand.

The man perched atop the conveyance pulled back on the reins to stop the vehicle. As he climbed down, his sand-toned hair and dark blue long coat brought a smile to Katherine's lips, her anxiety receding.

His feet had barely touched ground when the coach door flew open and a group of roughly garbed boys climbed out. She was puzzled how so many could have fit in so small a space. And what was their purpose in riding about in her family's coach?

"Clear the way lads," the driver spoke from the street behind them.

She focused upon the man. "William—"

The head groom of Summerhaven offered her a smile as he jerked his tricorn from his head. "I know they're a ragged bunch, Miss Katherine, but they'll work hard and quick and not cost you as much as men will. They'll have the likenesses up before anyone knows what they're about." He lowered his voice, "They can use the money for food as well."

Her attention returned to the children. Their

clothing, little more than rags, was filthy. Some had no shoes, others did not have coats. Some had neither. Hungry eyes stared out of faces gray with grime.

Pity clenched inside her. She nodded. "A good meal before they start should give them strength to do the job well. And another afterward as a reward."

The man grinned his agreement. "Yes, my lady."

She raised the mechanism to unlatch the gate and held her breath as the portal swung open with the soft rasp of metal on metal. "The bills are here in three bundles. You purchased the tacks and hammers?"

"Yes, just as you instructed."

She withdrew a small pouch of coins from her pocket. "This should cover the cost of their food and leave enough for their pay as well."

William tucked the pouch inside his coat. "I went by the Bow Street Agency as you wished. They've agreed to handle any reports that may arise from your posting the prints."

"Good." She laid a hand upon his arm. "God willing and with a little luck, justice might yet be served for your brother and my family."

He covered her hand with his, his callused fingers rough upon her skin. "It's a dangerous thing you're doing. Are you certain this is what you want to do?" His hazel eyes studied her face, his expression grave.

Had Edward been more interested in pursuing the men instead of enjoying her father's title and money, had anyone else helped her, perhaps she would have a different choice to make. As it was, she had no other. "Yes, I refuse to wait any longer."

He gave a brief nod. "You've only to send Hannah, and I'll come for you. If there's trouble, send for me."

"I will."

"Come lads, we've work to do."

Two of the larger boys came forward, hefted the bundled bills, and carried them back to the coach.

He lifted the last batch then paused. "Thank you, Miss Katherine."

Reading the suppressed emotion in his face, she fought the tears that rose close to the surface. "You do not owe me any thanks, William. Your brother died trying to protect my family and myself that night. I will do whatever I can to see his killers caught."

"They'll do whatever they can to see that doesn't happen, Lady Katherine. Have a care for yourself."

****

"You did well, Mr. Ray." Matthew closed the ledger and extended a hand to his purser, Carson Ray.

"The English didn't interfere with the sale of the cargo, Captain. In fact, Whitcomb, Lord Rudman's clerk, was fussy about the books being kept just so."

"It was no reflection upon your ability to keep the books, Mr. Ray."

The younger man's features settled into grave lines, his heavy brows drawing together into a frown giving his broad face the pugnacious look of a bulldog. "If the charges against you were any measure to judge him by, its no wonder Rudman must guard his back." A smile just shy of a smirk curved his lips. "Every crewman aboard knew they were false, Captain. The English knew it as well and tried to intimidate us into testifying against you. The crew stood their ground together."

"For their loyalty and yours I'm grateful, Carson." He retrieved a bottle from the bottom desk drawer. Pouring two fingers of bourbon into short glasses, he extended one to the purser. The two drank in silence for a moment. "The return home shall be my last voyage as Captain of the Caroline. If you and Mr. Blevins are still interested, at the end of the passage you may purchase her."

Ray's smile, though laced with restraint, fairly beamed. "Aye, Sir."

"Finish your drink, and go tell Blevins."

"Aye, Sir." Ray tossed back the rest of his drink and hastily excused himself.

Matthew propped a booted foot upon the chair beside his. It had to be done and at least he would be assured the steady hands of command would pass to those he trusted. Through the hardships they survived at sea together, Ray and Blevins had earned his trust as he had earned their loyalty. The Caroline deserved to be passed on to those who would treat her with care and respect.Frowning at the uncharacteristic sentimentality, Matthew set aside the empty tumbler and rose to don his long coat.

He paused on deck to enjoy the last of the late afternoon sunlight as it fell into the haze of gray-brown smoke hovering low over the London sky. The smells of dank water, pitch, and the stew Webster was cooking in the galley blended with cacophonous familiarity. Life at sea was a combination of beauty and ugliness, excitement and boredom, action and tedium, but it was always a challenge. He wondered if he would find life as a "county farmer" held such a diverse appeal.

Upon reaching the dock, he found Barlow, the Willingham's driver, waiting atop the coach in the deepening shadows of the warehouses, two men perched beside him riding shotgun on either side, a footman standing ready by the open door.

Had there been a disturbance at the house? "Is all well at Willingham's, Barlow?"

"Yes. All is well, Captain Hamilton. Lady Willingham thought to save you the trouble of hiring a hackney, sir."

Relief brought a smile to his lips. "Good, I have one more stop to make before going home, Barlow." Matthew gave the driver directions. He swung himself aboard the coach and settled back against the leather seat.

Periodically throughout the day, he found his thoughts wandering to Katherine. Each time, a niggling unease accompanied the lapse in concentration. He hadn't trusted her promise that morning to stay close to the house unless accompanied by Clarisse and his men. She had seemed too sincere. He had instructed Clarisse, Elton, the butler, and several maids to keep an eye on her movements throughout the day. He wondered how they had fared.

The coach came to a stop. He shook free of his cloak, took out the flintlock pistol he had tucked in the waist of his breeches then laid it on the seat. To enter an establishment armed so late in the day might be misconstrued.

By the time he had concluded his business, the afternoon light had waned, leaving the street purple with shadows. He tucked his purchase carefully inside his long coat and approached the coach only a short distance away.

A man stepped out from behind a rain barrel at the

mouth of an alley. Matthew stopped every nerve in his body instantly alert. All he could see in the dim light were the rough condition of the man's clothes and the long stringy hair that hung over his face.

"Me master sent me to warn ye, gov'na. The girl ain't worth the trouble she'll be to ye."

Stunned at the blatancy of the warning, he strained to see the man more clearly and judge what kind of threat he might be. "Obviously your master thinks otherwise or you wouldn't be here."

The man's voice sounded hoarse and raspy. "She'd be worth more to ye dead than alive. Ye could have all that comes to 'er and a tidy sum besides. All ye 'ave ta do is turn 'er over to us."

He shook his head. "That isn't likely to happen, my friend. My wife is worth much more to me alive."

Willow thin, his chest rose dramatically as he heaved a great sigh. "I was afeared ye'd say that. It'ain't worth dyin' over a woman." He lunged at Matthew, his approach swift and silent.

Matthew pivoted to one side avoiding the blade that passed within inches of his side. He settled into a defensive crouch as the two faced off circling one another. "You need to take your own advice and walk away," he warned.

Barlow shouted a warning.

Matthew turned at the streak of movement he caught out of the corner of his eye, another attacker approached from his left. He swiped at Matthew with a knife. Matthew dodged to avoid the blade then grabbed the man's arm just above the wrist and jerked him forward throwing him off balance and slamming him against the brick building face first. Turning, Matthew drove an elbow into the heavier man's back hard enough to mash the air from the attacker's lungs. The man dropped his knife and fell to the ground gasping for breath.

Matthew scooped up the knife as the wiry one closed in with a downward thrust that ripped through the fabric of his sleeve and grazed the skin beneath. Skill guided the upward thrust of his own blade catching the man between the ribs.

The assailant caught his breath and staggered back

in pain. Blood, black in the dim light, gushed from the wound, and he pressed a hand to it. He turned and staggered away, down the alley.

The two men riding shotgun atop the coach with Barlow dropped from the driver's seat of the coach. Flintlocks in hand, they ran past Matthew in pursuit of the heavier attacker who had gained his feet and fled down the street.

Barlow reached Matthew, and paused outside the alley to offer him a pistol. "I couldn't get a clear shot, Captain Hamilton," he said his tone apologetic.

"It's all right Barlow. I was a little busy myself."

"I could see that—bloody bastards."

Barlow held the lantern aloft and took one side of the alley and Matthew took the other. They followed the blood trail down the garbage and sewer strewn passage.

"He'll need help once we find him, Barlow."

The trail came to an abrupt end one block over. The two guards came toward them from down the street, breathing heavily.

"He caught the back of a coach that was pullin' away as we rounded the corner, Cap'in Hamilton. We couldn't see nothin' about it, only that it was black," one of the men said when he had caught his breath.

"You did your best, men. We'd best report the incident to the magistrate, then go home. Barlow, would you happen to know who that may be?"

"Aye, Captain Hamilton. 'Tis Mr. St. John, sir."

Until that moment, Matthew had refused to think about the repercussion he might face for defending himself if the man died and his body was found. St. John, being Rudman's flunky, could once again twist the truth in order to imprison him. As badly as he wished to avoid it, he had to report the incident.

"We'd best get back to the coach then and get it done."

"Yes, Sir.

****

Katherine felt constricted by the walls of the house, the servants, even the clothes on her body seemed to be squeezing the breath from her. Grabbing a shawl from the back of a chair, she stepped out onto the balcony to breath in the chilly night air.

She had done it. There was no turning back. By tomorrow every man woman and child, or at least as many of them as she could reach, would know the face of one of the men responsible for her family's death. She was certain that, by now, every print was tacked up for the world to see. Tomorrow, when the first papers she had had printed were sold upon the street, everyone, high and low, would be able to recognize him and know what he had done. And then? Someone would report to the watch patrols or perhaps one of the magistrates, and he would be brought to justice. He would lead them to the others. He had to. Tears flowed freely down her cheeks. He had to. She wiped them away with the hem of her shawl.

She had not allowed herself to think about how Matthew and the Willinghams would view what she had done. She had done what she felt was right, what she had felt had to be done. And for the first time all day she had time to reflect how it would affect Matthew and the Willingham's. Gossip would abound. She would become an embarrassment to them and to Matthew. She wouldn't be able to bear facing Matthew's censor for having lied to him. Talbot and Clarisse's disappointment in her would be just as bad. After they had embraced her as one of their family, she had stabbed them in the back with a letter not a knife. They would resent her for that, and she could not blame them.

She would have to send a note to William. They would have to leave for Summerhaven tomorrow, after Matthew left for his ship. If she distanced herself from them, it might spare them the worst of it.

Her breath escaped on a sigh, forming a plume of white. The cold moist air around it swallowed up the vapor. Katherine bent to rest her forehead against the concrete balcony railing and fought against the tears that threatened once again. For one week and three days, she had known what it was to be a part of a family again. That would all be gone tomorrow.

****

Lord Rudman lived behind high walls. Matthew wondered as they followed the cobbled drive through the gate why the man bothered, since he could not keep his wife in, and he couldn't keep her suitors out. Since returning to Willingham's from prison, he had become privy to several rumors about Jacqueline Rudman and her penchant for straying from her marriage bed. At the time he had known her, she had not been so focused on self-destruction. He wondered what had happened to change her.

He had little time to ponder the thought as the flat façade of the house came into view. Lanterns on poles lit the drive and steps. The large evenly spaced windows spread across two stories in symmetrical rows. The door, in the center of the ground floor, framed by half columns holding a pediment above, looked too small for the rest of such a grand house.

A tall, thin man in black answered the door at his knock, his hollow cheeks and eyes appearing ghoulish in the lantern light.

I'm here to speak with Mr. St. John. I was told he was here to see Lord Rudman. My name is Matthew Hamilton."

Looking down his long thin nose the man asked, "Have you an appointment with his Lordship, sir?"

"No, I haven't, but I'm here to report a crime to St. John. He is one of the magistrates here in London?"

"Yes, sir, he is. Why don't you come in, and I'll send one of the maids to the library with a note."

He took a seat in the wide entrance hall to wait and watched as the butler wrote the note and sent it on its way.

To block out the dull throb of his injured arm, Matthew studied the ceiling design and counted the railings of the dark mahogany banister that ran down each side of the staircase. He had begun to grow restless when the hurried tap of a woman's shoes on the gray marble floor drew his attention.

Jacqueline Rudman paused to speak to the butler. Her pale curls looked glossy beneath the light of the chandelier overhead. The bodice of the pale green gown she wore was gathered beneath her breasts in such a way that it came together between them. The neckline plunged dramatically displaying a wealth of pale creamy skin. As she turned, Matthew glimpsed one pale rose nipple as it peeked above the fabric.

Sitting beside a table within the shadows, she didn't see him until she was almost upon him. The genuine surprise and delight he read in her face had his stomach sinking.

"Matthew, what are you doing here?" She approached with both hands extended as though to grasp his, and he swiftly took just one.

"Lady Rudman. Good evening." He bent over her hand briefly.

"There's no need to be formal, Matthew. We are, after all, old friends."

"I'm not here on a social matter, Jacqueline. I'm here on a matter of business with St. John."

Her pale brows rose. "What kind of business?"

"I'm sure you'd find it uninteresting. I'm waiting for his meeting with your husband to end."

"Yes, of course." She laid a hand on his sleeve, then with a frown turned it palm up. Her soft gasp had the butler stepping close to observe them. "You are bleeding, Matthew."

He looked down at his arm. He parted the fabric of his coat where the man's knife had torn through it. He was surprised at the depth of the cut. He removed a handkerchief from one of his inner pockets and offered it to Jacqueline. "It's just a scratch, but perhaps you should keep your distance. I should hate to ruin that lovely gown."

"Nonsense." She wiped her hand clean with the handkerchief. "Richard, have someone bring a basin of water and some bandages for Captain Hamilton."

"Yes, Madame." The butler bent his head and went down the long wide hallway toward the back of the house.

"You must take off your jacket, Matthew, so we can clean the injury. Come in here." Jacqueline pulled at his uninjured arm.

"Here will be fine, Jacqueline."

"No, here does not suit at all. I have guests coming any moment. I do not want them upset."

Reluctantly, he allowed her to pull him into the room. He looked about the drawing room taking in the white paneled walls with their gold tipped relief designs. Two

Chippendale sofas were arranged before the fireplace with numerous smaller chairs curved inward on each side. A secretary sat against one wall, the books enclosed on either side of it protected by glass doors. The rug beneath his feet was thick, the colors rich. Jacqueline had married a man who could easily provide well for her, and from the look of everything from their home to the gown she wore, did.

He shed his torn jacket and draped it across the wooden back of a Sheraton armchair. His shirtsleeve looked worse for wear, but had staunched the bleeding to some degree. He pulled the cuff back to view the injury. The four-inch cut bled sluggishly. The edges needed to be drawn together with a few stitches.

"What happened Matthew?" Jacqueline asked standing close as though fascinated by the cut.

"That's what I'm here to speak to St. John about."

Jacqueline frowned, a speculative light flooding her green gaze. "Surely Avery had nothing to do with your arm being injured."

"Of course not."

"I doubt St. John will listen to anything you have to say. I fear Avery has colored his perception of you. My husband has not completely forgiven you for taking liberties when you first arrived from Charleston."

His jaw tightened with anger, especially virulent because he had to swallow it back. "You know damn well, I didn't take liberties, Jacqueline. I tried to convince you to leave the Caroline that evening without offering you insult."

"I was angry, Matthew. After the relationship we had enjoyed the year before, you dismissed me out of hand."

"I greeted you amiably, offered you refreshment, and then sent you on your way, as I would have any other married woman. I don't have affairs with married women, Jacqueline. I won't come between a man and wife, it only stirs the pot."

Jacqueline sauntered up against him. Careful not to come in contact with his bleeding arm, her fingers smoothing the tails of his stock as she leaned slightly forward to show her décolleté at its best advantage. Her breasts were all but exposed in the gown. Matthew wondered why Rudman would permit his wife to display herself in such a manner for anyone but himself. Matthew was surprised how unaffected he was by the sight.

"After all we shared that fall, you cannot blame me for wanting to recapture some of that excitement. You are the most accomplished lover I have ever had. And you remember how good things were between us."

He stepped away from her and turned to present the injured side of his body to her hoping the threat of bloodying her gown would hold her at bay.

"We are both married now, Jacqueline."

"What is it you want, Hamilton?" Avery Rudman entered the room, a harsh scowl drawing his already bulldog-like features into even more folds. St. John followed on his heals. The magistrate's eyes narrowed, his long thin face, badly pitted by scars, taking on a tight closed look as he recognized Matthew. His thin, loose-limbed frame looked almost fragile next to Rudman's bulk.

Matthew turned to Jacqueline. "Please excuse us, Lady Rudman."

"Richard has not brought the water and bandages yet. I will see what is keeping him."

He murmured his thanks. Jacqueline walked through the door, the fabric of her gown making a swishing sound. She flashed him a coy smile as she drew the portal closed.

Avery Rudman scowled at the exchange and turned a hostile gaze upon Matthew. "Why have you come?" He sounded no more welcoming now that his wife was gone than he had before.

Matthew nodded toward the magistrate. "I was told Mr. St. John was here."

"So he is."

"Then I'm here to see him. If you will excuse us, Lord Rudman."

St. John's dark eyes narrowed. "His Lordship can stay. You have nothing to say to me he can't hear."

He raised one brow. The man's eagerness to sloth off even the outward signs of his station did not bode well. "I was attacked outside a jeweler's shop. Two men tried their best to stab me to death. I unarmed one and wounded the other. My driver and I looked for the one I had injured, but they both escaped in a black coach."

"Well, you look as though you survived the ordeal well enough." Lord Rudman nodded toward his bloody shirt. "Richard will be here with bandages in a moment. By all means bathe your wound and bandage it. I have guests arriving."

"I'm not finished," Matthew said when Rudman started to turn away. He focused his attention on the magistrate who had yet to speak. "You know that my wife's parents were killed by a band of highwaymen."

"Yes." The man nodded.

"I believe the men who attacked me were members of that gang."

"And why would you think that?" St. John raised a thick, speculative brow.

"They wanted me to turn Katherine over to them for money. She's the only witness to what happened that night."

"They said all this before they attacked you?"

"Yes."

Rudman snorted his disbelief. "And assuming all this is true, you expect him to do what?"

Rudman's tone and attitude infuriated Matthew. He bit back the angry words that begged to be spoken.

He focused on St. John once again. "Katherine has never done anything to you. For her sake, I'm asking you to look for the man I injured. He'll have to seek help from someone. He was bleeding badly. These men attacked me on a city street. Next, it could be Talbot and Clarisse, or Lord Leighton. They'll go through them to get to Katherine because she's a threat."

"Then, I suggest you do your duty by the girl and protect her, Hamilton. She's your wife," Rudman interrupted again.

Matthew shook his head and reached for his coat. He slipped his injured arm into the sleeve gingerly. "These men are ruthless. They raped and killed an innocent woman and shot the men. They're a threat to anyone they come into contact with. That means the populace of London. If you won't search for them for Katherine's sake, then at least do it for duty's sake."

St. John's pock-marked features flushed red with

temper, and his mouth became a grim line. "I do not need you to tell me what my duty is."

"Katherine's family hasn't been the only ones robbed, though they are the only ones killed thus far. The next might be Lord Rudman or yourself."

Rudman's gaze turned suspicious. "Is that a threat?"

"I won't even honor that with an answer. You would do well to get your flunky to take action before someone else is hurt."

Rudman remained silent. Disgusted by both the men's attitudes and St John's refusal to do his duty, Matthew didn't try to hide the contempt he felt for the two men. He strode to the door and swung it open impatiently.

The Butler stood just outside with a maid who held a basin of water and some cloths.

"Matthew, you cannot leave without seeing to your arm," Jacqueline said as she rose from the chair he had vacated in the hallway.

He grasped at his temper in an effort to be civil. "Thank you, Lady Rudman, but I'll see to it when I reach home. My wife is waiting for me and I'm late. Have a good evening."

He brushed past them all and vacated the house. He paused on the steps just outside the front door to take a deep breath of the cold night air to clear his head and cool his temper. He didn't know why he had wasted his time.

Seeing two other coaches approaching up the drive he hastened to board his own to avoid being caught up in the throng of the Rudman's guests. The footman slammed the door closed then almost immediately the coach rolled forward. As he settled back against the leather seats, Matthew realized he had just been treated to the same frustration and futility that Katherine had experienced for the past four months. There had to be something they could do.

CHAPTER 11

Elton opened the door at Willingham's.

"Were there any problems today, Elton?" Matthew inquired as the butler took his tricorn and cloak.

"No, sir. Madame Hamilton spent some time in the kitchen going over recipes with cook. Then, she and Lady Willingham left for a time to have tea with Lady Abington and her daughter."

Matthew nodded, though his thoughts were more on the first statement the butler had made. "You said she spent time in the kitchen going over recipes."

"Madame likes to cook."

"That's...interesting." He had never known any English lady to do more than plan the menus. "Has she a talent for it?"

Elton's solemn composure cracked enough for a slight smile to hook one corner of his mouth upward beneath his mustache. "I am sure you shall discover that at dinner, sir."

He smiled. "For certain. "I'd like water sent up for a bath, Elton."

"I'll see to it, sir. Lord Willingham has asked that you join him for a drink in the library, before you go upstairs, sir."

"Very well. Thank you, Elton."

Talbot stood at the fireplace, a drink in his hand. He offered Matthew a smile and a crystal glass of amber liquid. "You are a bit late are you not, Matthew?"

He accepted the glass of brandy, relieved to be within the folds of his own family again. "There was some trouble earlier this evening. It delayed me."

Talbot frowned. "What sort of trouble?"

"I was attacked outside a jeweler's shop, after going in to retrieve a gift."

Talbot's mouth flew open in surprise. "Attacked by whom?" he asked

"By two of the men who attacked Katherine and her family. They were actually there to bargain with me. They wanted me to turn her over to them for a fee."

Talbot shook his head, his features registering disbelief.

"They decided to repay my refusal with knife play. One of them was injured, and the other escaped down an alley."

"Where the hell was Barlow and the two men I sent with him?" The man's shock grew into outrage.

"The whole thing happened so quickly they didn't have time to react. Besides, it was nearly dark, and none of them could get a clear shot without hitting me."

"Blast and damnation!" Talbot's exclamation was explosive.

He placed a hand on the older man's shoulder as his face became florid with color. "It's over and done with, and I'm still in one piece."

"You are sure you are all right?"

He ignored the twinges of pain the long narrow cut across his forearm gave him. "I'm fine. Now, is there some reason why you wanted to see me? "

His uncle frowned at the question. "We were going to make ourselves scarce and attend a dinner at the Arkwrights, but under the circumstances I believe we should stay here."

"I think it would be better for you and Clarisse to go on with your plans, with the appropriate precautions of course. I think you should double the number of men you take with you. As for telling Katherine and Clarisse what happened tonight, I'd like to hold off on that." He had thought about it in the coach on the way home while he bandaged his arm with a handkerchief. It would alert the women to the danger certainly, but Katherine was already traumatized enough by what had happened. As long as he could keep her close and ensure her safety, there was no need to tell her. "Why do you suppose they thought I would hand Katherine over to them for money?"

"Since money is so important to them, perhaps they thought you might be open to that as well."

"They knew about her inheritance. One of them said she'd be worth more to me dead than alive. Meaning, I assume, that I would inherit whatever she claims from her parent's estate. How would they know any of that?"

Talbot shook his head. "I do not know unless they were sent by someone intimately involved with Edward Leighton or Lord Rudman."

He drew a deep breath. "I also had the pleasure of reporting the incident to St John in Avery Rudman's presence."

Talbot's features settled into a scowl. "I am sure that was pleasant."

He raised a brow at his uncle's sarcasm. "Is there a problem with Katherine?" he asked changing the subject.

"If you put it like that there may be."

"You said only you and Clarisse were going out to dinner. I thought perhaps she was ill."

"Your aunt is concerned that you have not had enough time together of late."

He was being told he had been neglecting his bride in a not so subtle manner. A smile borne of half amusement and half wry deprecation, curved his lips. If he had neglected Katherine, it was out of self-preservation. He awoke every morning breathing in her scent and cradling her against him as though she belonged there. It felt too right. Having her beneath his hand without being able to caress her was slowly driving him mad.

"I thought it best that Katherine be introduced to certain elements of marriage slowly. I'm unsure of how much she witnessed, and was subjected to the night her mother died. I didn't want to press the matter too quickly or too often."

The explanation, not entirely untrue, cleared Talbot's frown and had him nodding. "I see. Has she spoken of that night at all?"

He shook his head. He hadn't tried to urge her to speak of it for fear of stirring memories that might once again spark her fear of him.

"Your aunt has been upset all evening, Matthew. She believes that Katherine has given up hope of ever being accepted by her peers, and that she has resigned herself to it."

He tried to ignore the hollow feeling that struck him just beneath his ribs. If he left her behind, as she wanted him to, her fate would be sealed. She would be alone and defenseless against the judgment of a society that was all too quick to point a gleeful finger at any whisper of impropriety. The thought of abandoning her went against every honorable instinct he had. But short of throwing her over his shoulder and forcing her onto his ship, how was he to persuade her to accept their marriage?

"There's little we can do to force them to accept her, Talbot. It may cause Katherine more distress if Clarisse presses the issue."

"I believe that is what has upset her. Katherine yielded to her wishes just to please her and has been silently miserable."

Matthew wondered what other things his wife had held back just to keep the peace.

****

A few moments later, Matthew tapped upon their bedroom door and frowned as his bid for entry met with silence. Opening the portal, he scanned the chamber only to find it empty but for the lingering feminine smell of scented soap. He paused to enjoy it, for it had been some time since he had shared such things.

He enjoyed women. The way they smelled, the softness of their skin, the sound of their voices, their laughter, the way they moved. He found more pleasure in his wife than he should. That thought brought to mind his own restraint when interacting with her. Was he keeping her at arm's length because it was what she wanted, or because he wished to avoid growing attached to her?

Despite both their attempts to remain in control, he was beginning to know his wife. Katherine didn't fuss over her appearance, yet appeared neat and feminine even in the dark mourning garb she was required to wear. When angry, her cultured tone grew clipped. When moved, her voice sounded husky and soft. Her smiles were rare as pearls. He had never heard her laugh with any humor, and that piqued his concern.

Though she tried hard to cover it, her wariness when in the company of men truly bothered him. Her normal outspokenness and confidence seemed to dwindle away, and she withdrew into herself. He was at a loss as to what to do about it.

A flicker of color in the dressing room caught his attention, and he crossed to the door to look in. As he watched, Katherine folded a cream-colored shift and placed it in the drawer of the chest. He couldn't discern her expression, but sensed an air of melancholy in the slump of her shoulders and the bend of her neck. Her damnable English reserve, combined with the wariness she exhibited toward him, kept a distance between them he believed he had no right to cross; yet, he found he wanted to more and more.

As his desire grew stronger, so did his guilt. He had certainly not been celibate since Caroline's death, but the relationships he had pursued had been based on lust, not on any lasting affection on his part. He had certainly liked the women he had bedded, but he had never been tempted to make any of them a permanent part of his life.

Until Katherine.

He woke up in the night, hot and hard, aching to make love to her. He wanted to taste the soft white skin just behind her ear and work his way down to her toes. He wanted to cup the full firmness of her breasts in his hand then lathe them with his tongue until the nipples were taut and she begged him for more. But most of all he wanted to break the careful composure she donned like a cloak and see her features flushed with passion and hear her moan with pleasure. Just thinking about it stirred his blood and made him sweat. He knew his reactions were probably heightened by his earlier experience. How much better a way to reaffirm life than by making it. He could only hope she didn't notice the obvious signs of his arousal.

"Good evening, Katherine."

Katherine looked up at the sound of his deep lazy drawl. It slid over her like a warm caress. Swallowing against the emotions swamping her, she struggled to gain control, when really all she wanted to do was to run to him and throw herself at him to be held. "Good evening," she managed after a moment.

"Elton said you've been in the kitchen cooking today. Is that right?"

"Mrs. Parkins was kind enough to allow me to share her kitchen and bake some bread. I find it relaxes me."

"It seems Clarisse and Talbot have been invited to a dinner party tonight and will be out for the evening."

"Oh." The tight knot to her stomach relaxed somewhat. At least for one night she wouldn't be subjected to a barrage of dinner guests. Nor would she have to endure the women's whispered comments made purposely within her hearing and the men's bold, speculative glances that teetered on being leers. After tomorrow, such behavior would be mild compared to what would follow. She had to be strong, for herself and for her family. She had done what she had to do.

She looked up at Matthew and wondered if he would understand that. Light from the oil lantern etched one side of his face with a pale glow and cast bluish highlights in his hair as he stepped into the room. He wouldn't be prepared for the situation in which he would find himself embroiled. He deserved better from her.

"Matthew—" his name came out in a breathy, soft tone, and she turned to rest her hand upon his arm. If she warned him now, he might find a way to stop her. She couldn't allow that. The knot of dread that had settled in the pit of her stomach tightened painfully. She had become a sneak. She had lied through omission. How much farther she would have to go in order to see justice done?

Guilt had her going on the offensive. "You have instructed the servants to spy on me."

He didn't try to deny it. "To watch over you, for your own protection."

Katherine nearly snorted at that. "I helped you escape your prison only to find one of my own."

"Where do you wish to go that you can't with my knowledge, Katherine?"

She shook her head. "Knowing that my every movement is being observed is what I find objectionable. Elton has hung over my shoulder all day and, I am certain, reported to you as soon as you walked into the house."

"I've a duty to keep you safe, Katherine."

Between her father's actions and her uncle's, she'd had enough of duty to last her a lifetime. Men did all manner of things against you in the name of duty. "Save your duty for something or someone you truly care about, Captain."

He blocked her attempt to go around him by stepping in front of her. "You're so busy trying to keep a distance between yourself and everyone else you don't realize it's already too late. Talbot and Clarisse already care about you, as do I."

She noticed how reluctantly he said it and anger spiked by hurt, lent her voice an edge. "I do not need your grudging declarations of care and concern. And you would be wise to keep your distance. Neither of us would like to endure the embarrassment of an emotional entanglement before you leave. In fact, it might be wise for us to seek an end to this as quickly as possible."

He grasped her chin forcing her features upward for his perusal. His features were a study in light tinged angles and shadows. His jaw was taut with control. "You know as well as I do that will not be possible. And even if we could, we'd have to produce proof that we haven't been lovers. How difficult will that be, Katherine?"

She gasped as pain lanced through her and couldn't control her reactive flinch. "You may always accuse me of coming to our marriage bed soiled. I am certain the court will have no qualms in accepting your petition for divorce then."

The pressure of his fingers about her jaw relaxed. He ran his fingertips along the curve on her cheekbone and jaw in a caress that brought a flutter to her stomach. "Do you believe you must be punished in some way because you survived that night?"

"No." *She* didn't, but others did.

His touch branded her with heat, the steady regard of his pale blue gaze inspired an airless feeling beneath her ribs and brought to life an empty ache low in her belly. Her mouth grew dry with longings to be closer. She laid a hand against his chest whether to hold him at bay or bring him closer she didn't know.

Matthew swore, his tone laced with frustration. In a snap, he crushed her to him. His hand thrust through the soft curls at the back of her head as his mouth covered hers. His lips and tongue tempted, tasted, and then plundered the depths of her need, drawing from

Katherine a response just as wild and impatient as his. With a groan, she looped her arms about his neck urging him closer.

He obliged by running a hand down her spine to mold her body to his. His kisses grew languid and hot. She felt boneless. She didn't think she'd be able to stand had he not held her so close.

She drew a shuddering breath when his mouth left hers to nibble her earlobe, his breath warm against her skin. Sliding one hand upward beneath his bound hair, she pulled free the black cord that held it and buried her fingers into the lush rich strands. Matthew's mouth came back to hers and their tongues thrust, and parried. When Matthew sucked upon her tongue, an insistent ache raced through her and she groaned aloud.

After tonight, no other man would treat her with respect as he did. She would never know this pleasure with any other man. She would not want to. That knowledge seeped into her passion-clouded mind and brought an ache of loss deep inside her that was almost unbearable. She cupped his face between her hands and felt the texture of his skin beneath her palms. She fed from his kisses as though each were the last she would ever experience.

"Katherine—" Matthew spoke her name on a ragged breath. He buried his face in her hair and held her as he struggled to get his breathing under control.

She sensed his withdrawal. Embarrassment had her drawing a deep breath. She lowered her hands and took a step back. It was self-preservation alone that had her dragging her pride around her like a shield.

"Katherine—" he said again.

"Please, don't." If he voiced one word of apology or regret, she wouldn't be able to bear it.

Matthew raked his hands through his hair and swearing beneath his breath he strode back into the bedroom. It took all the courage she could muster to follow him.

Matthew shook free of his long coat and she gasped. The lower half of one sleeve was dark with blood. "What happened?"

"Just an accident." He untied his stock and began to

remove the ruined shirt.

Going to the dressing room, she filled the washstand basin with water. He followed her, his arm banded by a handkerchief. "Come, let me see how bad it is," she urged. He seemed reluctant to let her, but finally stepped close to the basin.

"You should have said you were hurt when first you arrived." She pulled him forward and untied the handkerchief. "Webster or Georgie could have done a better job bandaging it."

"They weren't about when it happened, so I had to tie it myself in the coach."

The cut ran across the middle of his forearm and was deeper in the center than at the edges. She thought it was too straight to be anything but a knife wound. She swallowed against the sudden rush of fear that cut off her breath for a moment. She positioned his arm over the basin and began to gently bathe away the dried blood. The coppery smell made her queasy, and she breathed through her mouth until the feeling passed.

She paused to look up at him, her throat feeling tight. "Tell me I have not brought trouble to you."

He smoothed a dark auburn curl back from her cheek. "You haven't. Sometimes the docks can be a dangerous place, Katherine. Knives are a sailor's first choice of weapon when in a fight. I was just at the wrong place at the wrong time."

She continued to study his features for a moment before going back to the task at hand. She wanted to believe him, but knew she shouldn't. "You will need a few stitches. I will ask Elton to send for a doctor." If this incident was somehow caused by the men who had attacked her family...Fear clenched like a fist in the pit of her stomach. She had to draw them away somehow. She had to leave tomorrow.

****

Katherine gripped the corner of the pillow and fought the urge to weep. The finality of what she had planned had come crashing down upon her at dinner. Every time Matthew had spoken, she had caught herself studying his expression in a desperate bid to remember it. Every touch of his hand had become precious. His protectiveness when

112

they were in social situations—his penchant for sharing his cloak and his body heat in the coach—and his hand covering hers in the bend of his arm when they walked together—had all become gestures to hold dear in her memories.

How many times had he unfastened her gown, just like any other husband? Or touched her cheek, or smoothed back a wayward curl? How many times had he shared some passing thought or observation and made her feel privy to his inner thoughts? And why had she not done the same in return? What could it have hurt? Regret tasted like bitter ashes in her mouth.

It did no good to torment herself with questions, or dreams of something different. The very needs and desires that had brought them together would keep them apart. An ache of loss squeezed her heart and she turned her face into the pillow to fight against a fresh wave of tears.

"What is it, you are mulling over?" Matthew asked his tone hushed.

The fire's pale glow threw flickering light across the bottom of the bed just enough to see his profile. Katherine swallowed twice to clear her throat, but her voice still came out weak and husky. "I was just wondering...if we had met in a different manner...but then we would have probably never met at all."

"Despite my close relationship with my aunt and uncle, I doubt a lowly sea captain would have been invited to court."

"Neither was I."

"You didn't have a coming out?"

"No."

Matthew turned on his side facing her. "Why not?"

Katherine drew in a breath laced with his scent. Even that she would remember. "My father wished to choose my husband."

"It seems you would have had a better chance at a good match during the season."

"A title, wealth, all the things that we are told our husband's must have, did not mean to me what my father thought they should."

"What was it you were looking for?"

You. The word poised on the tip of her tongue and she swallowed it back. "I did not know. I just resented being put up for auction like a prize mare with a good bloodline."

He remained silent for a moment, and she wondered if she had shocked him with her bluntness. When he threw back the covers and rose, she thought she had angered him.

Lighting a small twig of wood at the fireplace he lit the oil lamp beside their bed. "Come here, Katherine." He motioned to her.

Studying his face she wiggled free of the covers and slid to the edge of the bed.

Dressed in the disreputable cut off trousers he had taken to wearing to bed, he bowed to her and somehow made the gesture as courtly as it would have been had he been fully dressed. "Captain Matthew Hamilton, Lady Katherine, how do you do?"

"I do very well, Captain Hamilton." As she took in the muscular definition of his thighs, stomach, and chest, she bent her head to hide her smile.

"It would thrill me if you would share that smile with me, Lady Katherine, and the thought that brought it to your lips." "I was thinking that, should all suitors dress as you are right now, there would be less time spent on pretentious flirtation."

Matthew chuckled. But when his warm gaze swept down her body, clad in her night shift, her limbs grew weak and weighty and her cheeks hot. She pressed her hand to the front of the gown as her heart fluttered.

"Is your dance card filled, Lady Katherine?"

Her throat tightened with emotion at the question. "No."

"Will you share a dance with me?" He offered his hand.

"We have no music," she said as she placed her hand in his and allowed him to draw her to her feet.

"I will count the beat." He guided her to an open space, unobstructed by furniture. When he lifted his hands palm up she placed hers in them. He named a simple country dance. "Do you know it?"

"I believe so."

"Though it is written for six, we should do very well. I will count and you come toward me then back, then toward me and back—" He went through each step, his hand brushing her shoulder, pressing her hip as he guided her in practice. Then they were dancing in earnest as he counted the beat and they stepped forward almost touching, then backed away. He was turning her, casting off and stepping down the section of carpet and meeting her again.

To Katherine, their steps mirrored their relationship to date, for it had been fraught with tantalizing closeness and loneliness. They were poised between commitment and parting, trapped there by circumstances they couldn't control.

They stopped, a little out of breath. Katherine, her hands tucked behind her, tipped her head back to look up at him.

Matthew cupped her cheek, his pale blue eyes intent. "Better?

He had sensed her upset and done all this to make her feel better. With this last sweet action he captured her heart.

CHAPTER 12

"Where is she?" Matthew demanded. Concern lanced through him, kicking his heart into a gallop. He cautioned himself to remain calm.

"I don't know, Cap'in. Georgie and I 'ave been over ever' inch of the Caroline. We 'aven't been able to find 'er." Henry's gaze shifted to the water, his salt-worn features creased with worry. "Ye don't suppose she fell overboard?"

"You didn't hear anything, and Georgie was on deck with her fishing off the bow. She couldn't have fallen overboard." Matthew's gaze swept the deck looking for any nook or cranny they might have missed. After his experience the night before, he had brought Katherine on board with him to keep her safe. What could have happened? "Go below and search again. Maybe she's in the galley with Webster. She likes to cook."

"Aye, Cap'in."

"Georgie."

The boy stepped forward. "Aye, Cap'in."

"What was Katherine doing when you last saw her?"

Georgie's freckles stood out on a face pale with fear. "She was sittin' on the quarterdeck on a crate drawin' the deck bellow, Cap'in."

He should never have insisted she accompany him today. But there had been something in her manner this morning. She had been withdrawn, more so than usual, upset, or...something. Could she have somehow rowed ashore?

He climbed the steps to the quarterdeck and turned to search the lower deck from the higher perspective. If someone had sneaked aboard and taken her, Georgie would have heard something. If she had fallen overboard, there would be some sign of it. The sketches she had been working on would have been scattered upon the deck or in the water. He narrowed his gaze against the glare of the winter sun. A chill wind whipped across the deck and rippled the lashed sails above his head and he glanced up.

He tracked something white as it fluttered and looped through the air then sailed outward to disappear over the aft rail of the ship. He tilted his head back to follow the line of mast and spars to the crow's nest overhead. His breath caught and held, his jaw tightening against the stream of oaths that leaped to his tongue.

"Georgie."

"Aye, Cap'in."

"Go below and tell Henry I've found her."

Georgie tipped his head back following Matthew's train of sight then his mouth dropped open in astonishment. "How ye goin' ta get her down, Cap'in?"

"The same way she got up there. Go tell him."

"Aye, Cap'in." The boy ran across the deck and disappeared below like a jackrabbit into its hole.

Matthew approached the ladder and took several deep breaths to calm his temper. He mounted the ladder to the crow's nest.

Katherine moved the charcoal across the paper with quick sure strokes. At this distance, the people were tiny forms moving about the ships docked along the quay. The buildings, constructed one next to the other parallel to the docking area, created a monotone hued backdrop. The late afternoon sun reflected off the windows, setting to light the drab facades of the warehouses.

In the crow's nest, a stinging, cold breeze blew away the scent of tar and the pungent odor of the river. Her cheeks and nose burnt from the chill. Her fingers were numb. The heavy sweater she had found in a chest in Matthew's cabin kept her torso and arms relatively warm despite its warn spots. It covered the upper part of her thighs nearly to her knees. She thought that a good thing since she had exchanged her gown for a pair of breeches she'd brought along in her bag. A knitted cap held her hair back and kept it from whipping about her face.

She would have to go back down soon. Her toes were aching from the cold and would soon be numb as well.

"Why are you up here, Katherine?"

She jerked, caught unaware by Matthew's sudden appearance from below. The crow's nest had little room to spare once he stood beside her. His pale blue gaze flashed like heat lightning, the set of his jaw grim and angry. A nervous shiver of apprehension raced up her spine.

"I thought it would offer me a more interesting view of the dock."

His gaze raked her from head to toe. "What the hell do you have on?"

"A pair of my brother's old breeches and a sweater I found in your cabin. I hope you do not mind me wearing it." She pulled at the edge of the garment as his gaze settled upon her legs.

His jaw worked for a moment. "I can see you're dressed as a boy. But why?"

"It seemed more practical since I was climbing around the decks of the ship. The wind kept blowing about my skirts, and it was neither comfortable nor modest."

His gaze narrowed. "Practical they may be, but if you were aiming for modesty you've failed. The breeches show the shape of your legs and the stockings show even more. Were I not the only one here to see them, I'd be stripping them from you and putting your gown back on."

Taken aback by the possessiveness of the threat, she stared at him. "I suppose you would rather I had climbed up here in a gown."

"I'd rather you not climb up here at all. During a storm the wind alone can toss you out of the basket."

"It is not storming, Matthew, and I was careful."

"Careful would have been content to roam the deck below." He pointed downward.

"But look what I would have missed." She waved an arm in the direction of the docks.

He gave the view only a cursory look. "You'd have missed having your cheeks burnt by the wind and your nose red as a raspberry. You look half frozen. Bundle your things together. We're going down."

Had she not been so cold, Katherine may have argued further just on principle. She rolled the charcoal sticks she held into a piece of paper and slipped them into her breeches pocket. Withdrawing a handkerchief, she wiped her stained hands as best she could. Tucking the cloth back into her pocket she kneeled to secure the small drawing board and the sketch she had rendered within the leather portfolio Johnny had fashioned for her. She buckled the strap along the flap, slipped her arms through the leather straps at the side, and settled it on her back.

She paused to look one last time at the dock, the warehouses, and the city that stretched out behind them in the distance.

"You do not know how fortunate you are to have been able to experience such freedom, Matthew."

"What do you mean?"

She studied his features. Cold had slapped a ruddy tint into his cheeks. With his black brows drawn together in a frown and a shadow of beard darkening his jaw, he looked dangerously handsome.

"No matter where you go, or what you do, no one will try to force you to adhere to rules that clip your wings before you are even able to spread them. Whether it is you, or my uncle, or some nosy someone who takes it into their head that I need protection from my own impulsiveness, I will always have someone hanging over my shoulder watching my every move. There will always be someone trying to force me to adhere to what they think is respectable behavior when all I really want to do is be free to be what and who I am."

His blue gaze raked her again. "Do you wish yourself a boy, Katherine?"

Disappointment nipped her heart and made her feel suddenly tired. "No. I have never wanted to be anything but what I am."

"Even men have to adhere to rules, Katherine. Even we have to acknowledge our limitations. Had I been free to do as I pleased I wouldn't have spent nearly three months in a jail cell."

"It was because of that, I thought you would understand."

"Understand what? That you delight in doing outrageous things to cause trouble?"

She flinched as pain lanced through her. His resentment of her had finally bubbled to the surface and though she had warned herself repeatedly to expect it, it still caught her unaware. Uncertain of her composure, she stepped to the opening at the center of the crow's nest and grasping the rope sides of the ladder, she mounted the wooden rungs. Holding tight to each bar, she began descending to the deck below.

Matthew breathed an oath and followed her. He had hurt her. He had seen the quick flair of pain in her eyes and the way her features stiffened into that damnable emotionless mask.

But, by God, he had his limits too! When first he'd seen her in the crow's nest he'd felt fear, gut clenching, breath stealing fear. Once he had climbed up to her, she'd seemed so unaffected, so at ease surveying the world below in the thigh hugging breeches and his sweater, he'd wanted to shake her and kiss her at the same time. Even the cold hadn't affected his rampant desire to rip the breeches from her. He had had but two choices: rage at her or ravish her. He'd chosen the only option open to him.

He looked down to check her progress and saw her reach the bottom of the ladder.

Henry and Georgie stood at the railing looking over the side of the ship. Matthew swore again as Edward gained the deck.

The man's bearing stiffened the moment he spied Katherine and he stomped toward her. His movements angry, Edward grabbed Katherine by the shoulder and shook a paper in her face. "Did you do this?"

The words carried to Matthew, though he couldn't hear Katherine's reply, and he hastened his efforts to reach the deck. The sharp sound of a slap landing against flesh and a soft cry had Matthew twisting to look over his shoulder. Katherine staggered and fell to one knee. Edward clenched the neck of the sweater in his fist and drew his hand back for another strike. Katherine threw up an arm to ward off the blow.

A feral growl of rage tore from Matthew. Unmindful of the distance beneath him, he leaped to the deck landing in a half crouched position on the balls of his feet. A red haze clouded his vision as he sprinted toward Katherine and her uncle. Edward, his features still twisted with anger, looked up at Matthew's approach. The momentum of his stride carrying him forward, he punched Edward in the face and felt the satisfying crunch of bone beneath his fist. Blood spurted, the powerful stroke driving the man backward, his arms flailing as he sought to regain his balance. He struck the bulkhead of the quarterdeck with a meaty thud, staggered, then fell to the deck. He lay writhing upon the bleached planks, holding his nose and squealing in pain.

His bloodlust still burning hot, Matthew dragged the man to his feet by the collar of his coat and the back of his pants. Edward's feet scrambled for purchase as Matthew half dragged, half marched him back to the railing then threw him forward toward the open balustrade. Edward caught a post, barely saving himself from pitching head first into the water. His movements clumsy, unbalanced, he swung around to face Matthew. The man's nose appeared squashed to one side and was already swelling in the midst of a face smeared red with blood. He cowered back as Matthew crowded close, his fists clenched.

"If you ever lay a hand on my wife again, I'll kill you. Get off my ship."

"You do not know what she has done," Edward managed, his voice a mewling whine that resonated strangely through his shattered nose.

"I don't give a damn what she's done. You'll never raise your hand to her again." Tempted to heave him over the side, Matthew stepped back. "If he's not off my ship in five seconds, throw him overboard, Henry."

The man stepped forward his expression gleeful. "Aye, Cap'in."

Matthew spun on his heel. His gaze swept the deck in search of Katherine.

"You will be sorry you ever married her," Edward said.

Amazed at the man's persistent desire to dance with danger, he turned to look over his shoulder. "If I do, it won't be her I'll hold responsible, Leighton. It will be you."

CHAPTER 13

Katherine watched Matthew's long purposeful strides eat up the distance between them. His coat was ripped at the shoulder, and the dark blue waistcoat and lace trimmed white shirt he wore beneath were spotted with blood.

"Are you all right, Katherine?"

"Yes."

He caught her elbow and guided her down into the ship to his cabin. He moved immediately to the washbasin to cleanse his blood-streaked hands.

The sickening coppery scent wafted upward. A memory of Johnny lying in a pool of dark rust, his skin white, cut across her thoughts like shards of glass. Struck by a wave of nausea and a hollow ringing in her ears, she sought the support of the window seat. She bent double to rest her head on her knees.

Several moments passed before the awful woozy feeling subsided and the cramping queasiness diminished. Still shaky, she sat up and dragged the knit cap from her head freeing the heavy braid she'd secured within it. Her skin clammy with sweat, she brushed the rough sleeve of the sweater over her forehead.

His expression grim, Matthew handed her a damp cloth. He peeled the straps of the pack she still wore from her arms and set it aside.

The coolness of the cloth eased her burning cheek very little. The genuine concern she read in his expression as he watched her had her throat tightening with emotion.

"I am sorry, Matthew."

"For what?"

"For involving you in this. Had there been any other way I would not have."

"Perhaps you should explain to me what you've done," he said, his tone quiet.

She fished inside the pocket of her breeches and brought forth a piece of paper. She smoothed the wrinkles from it then handed it to him "It is only part of it. The rest tore away and blew out into the water."

He bent his head and silently perused the small section of paper. His features grew still as he began to read.

Her hands fisted then she twisted the cloth she held as she watched him. Of all her regrets, losing his respect would be the hardest for her to bear.

"When was this hawked upon the streets?"

"Today. Fleet Street refused to print it. They said it would inflame the populace. Do you not find that amusing? Everyone I have met, save your family, seems to thrive on gossip, the worse the better. I paid to have it printed and sold."

"The day you slipped away, this was what you were doing."

"Yes. I could not tell you what I was about. You would not have allowed me to do it." She paused to draw a deep breath. "I had to do this, Matthew. The longer the killers go without being caught, the less chance they will ever be punished." She cleared her throat then continued. "Edward would not help me, nor would he allow me to speak about that night to anyone who would."

"My mother was a gentle, unassuming, beautiful woman. She never harmed another living thing in her life. My brother and father did not deserve to die trying to defend her. Nor did our driver."

"Why would Edward be so upset with you over this, Katherine?"

"He believes that appearance is everything. He will not forgive you for breaking his nose." Bitterness laced her tone. "It shall curtail his schedule of engagements, until he deems himself presentable again."

One black brow rose. "He shouldn't have hit you." The flat dangerous gleam that lit his eyes brought a hitch to her breathing. One broad shoulder lifted in a shrug. "'Twill take about the same amount of time for the bruising to subside from his injuries as it took him to release me from the cell. There's a sort of justice in that."

She bit her lip. "You are not angry at me for what I

have done?"

Matthew tossed the paper into her lap. "Not because of this."

But he was angry—no, furious. The cool control she witnessed was more frightening than all her father's violent rages. She felt as though a great storm built before her and there was no shelter available to protect her from it. She looked away. "There is more. I did drawings of the man I remember from that night and hired a man to do prints of him. I have had them posted in every pub and alehouse around the city and offered a reward for information about him that will lead to his arrest. Once he is captured, he will lead them to the rest."

When he remained silent, the knot of anxiety in the pit of her stomach grew to painful proportions and she looked up.

"Anything else?" he asked, his expression benign as he took the rag from her and turned her face to examine the damage Edward had done.

"No," the word came out almost a whisper.

"I'll ask Webster to prepare some tea and see if we have some liniment to put on your check. You'll have a bruise by morning."

Her mouth dry as dust, she swallowed painfully. "What about Talbot and Clarisse? I do not want to cause them any trouble."

His pale blue eyes focused on her so intently her stomach did a slow roll.

Matthew got to his feet and crossed the room to his desk. "We'll be staying the night aboard ship. I'll have Henry deliver a message to Talbot and Clarisse." He withdrew paper, quill, and ink.

"Please tell them how sorry I am."

"That, my dear, will be something you'll have to convey when face to face with them. You owe them that much."

She flinched from the biting tone of the comment. She had never been more aware of his size and strength in comparison to her own as he came to stand over her. He braced a hand upon the bulkhead that framed the window seat and studied her for a long silent moment.

"I understand why you've printed the story and have

had the likeness printed and posted. I can even admire your courage and determination in seeking justice for your family. But—you've lied to me repeatedly since we exchanged the vows that made us man and wife. You've lied to me by omission and through trickery and deceit. Because of that you've make it difficult for me to know what is truth and what isn't. You've made it impossible for me to trust you."

He drew a deep breath. She could see the effort it took for him to rein in his temper.

"If it's your hope to provoke the killers—you may get your wish. If someone is hurt, they won't be the only ones responsible."

He straightened. Katherine had never thought to see him direct such a flat, cold look at her. "I'll return shortly. While I'm gone make yourself presentable."

She had not the spirit left to take exception to his dictatorial tone. When the door clicked shut behind him, she released the breath she was holding. Her entire face aching, her limbs shaking uncontrollably, she slid back upon the window seat and folded her arms around her up drawn knees.

She had expected his anger, but she had not expected his disgust. She had been prepared to face the disapproval and contempt of strangers, but not Matthew's. She had only herself to blame.

****

Matthew swore aloud as he pulled against the ores. His temper banked a fire beneath his ribs that made him want to beat his fists into something more than Edward Leighton's face.

"Do ye want me 'elp, Cap'in?" Henry asked as he held the lantern aloft.

"No."

"Yer missus aint 'urt, is she?"

"No—Yes. She'll have a bruised cheek by tomorrow."

"That bastard 'it 'er, but she didn't cry. Most women would 'ave been a wailin' like a pack of 'ounds at a 'unt. But she just got up and dusted 'erself off."

Matthew swore again with less heat, his temper cooling. He focused on the dimly lit dock in the distance.

"Makes ye wonder if 'e ain't done it before."

Someone had. She had talked about her mother and brother, but had little to say about her father.

"Is she in trouble, Cap'in?"

Matthew gave a gusty sigh and stopped rowing. The boat bobbed gently upon the water, drifting toward the dock. "Yes, Henry. There are men who may try and harm her, the men responsible for her family's death. There will be people who may sit in judgment of her, though she had no control over what happened."

"The men stood with ye when charges were brought agin ye, Cap'in.. They'll stand with 'er as well because she be yer missus, if you ask it of 'em."

Matthew shook his head. It could be dangerous for his men.

"Webster, me, and Georgie will stand with 'er Cap'in."

Katherine had worked her magic upon the men in only an afternoon. A niggling jealousy took root. She had never tried to work it on him. He had slept with her for nearly a fortnight, held her against him in sleep and in waking, and still she denied the burgeoning intimacy between them. The trust he had thought he had earned was just within his mind.

The thought was still tormenting him when they reached the dock, and he sent Henry to find a handsome cab to have a few moments alone. The seaman returned with the conveyance, and Matthew swung himself aboard the coach.

It had grown completely dark by the time they pulled to a stop before Willingham's front steps. Matthew exited the coach, but when Henry moved to climbed down from atop the conveyance, he waved him back. "Stay where you are, I'll not be long."

As he reached the steps, a woman's laughter, high and pure, carried to him on the still air, like the tinkling of bells. Matthew paused to look overtop the shrubbery toward the west entrance. Beneath the soft glow of light escaping from the window above them, he glimpsed a man with a slender blonde woman wearing a black cloak. As he watched, the fellow cupped her small, pointed chin in his large hand and pushed her back against the brick wall and kissed her. The plum of moisture their breathing released obscured both they faces, but Matthew recognized the woman as one of the maids.

With a shrug, he continued up the steps to knock on the door. Elton let him in and offered to take his cloak.

"There's no need, I'll only be a moment upstairs. Are my aunt and uncle home?"

"No, sir. They have gone to Lord and Lady Abingdon's house to play cards."

Perhaps the news had not reached them yet. "When they return, please tell them Katherine and I have decided to spend the night aboard the Caroline. And please see that my uncle receives this." He reached inside the inner pocket of his coat and withdrew a copy of the paper that had been hawked that afternoon, as well as a note. Talbot would understand their absence.

It took only moments for him to pack a satchel with their belongings. The thick hall runner muffled his steps as he walked down the passageway toward the stairs. A strange rhythmic squeaking caught his attention. Curious, he stopped to listen and decipher from which direction it came. As he continued down the hall, he discovered a chamber door standing ajar. Resting a hand against the portal, he pushed it open further. Light from the hall sconce behind him shone inside the room, casting dark shadows in the corners. From the doorway, the coverlet on the bed was wrinkled but nothing else appeared disturbed. Shaking his head, he continued on downstairs.

Elton waited in the entrance foyer.

"We'll return late tomorrow evening, Elton."

"I shall be sure to tell his lordship, sir."

One of the maids was just outside the west entrance when I came in. You may want to check the door is secure.

"Of course, sir.

Matthew exited the house and glanced toward the west entrance as he walked down the front steps. The man and woman were gone. It was too cold to linger outside for long. He drew his cloak close and called to Henry to join him inside the coach.

The man settled back against the leather seat as though he feared the pressure of his body might mar it.

"'Tis too cold to be atop the coach if you don't

have to be, Henry. Besides, I have something to discuss with you." "Aye, Cap'in."

"The trouble we discussed earlier—"
"Aye, Cap'in.
"I may have to take you up on your offer."

CHAPTER 14

Katherine rose from her perch upon the window seat and smoothed the wrinkles at the front of her dark gray gown. She joined Georgie at the table and started helping him clear the tea things away.

"You don't have ta help me, Miss Katherine. I can do it."

"I know, Georgie. I do not mind."

His attention focused on her cheek and he grimaced in sympathy. "Is there anythin' I can get for you, Ma'am?"

She shook her head and touched the swollen side of her face gingerly. The initial burn had passed and had settled down to a persistent dull ache. "No, I do not believe so."

With a nod, he went back to gathering the heavy china tea service upon the tray.

"My pa used to pound on me some. He'd get drunk and come home. Used to pound on my ma some too, 'til she died."

She focused on his young features and found his freckled face both funny and endearing. His attempt to ease her embarrassment and pain reflected a chivalry he had obviously learned at Matthew's hand.

"The Cap'in took me off the docks in Charleston and made me his cabin boy."

"How old were you?"

"Ten."

A knot rose in her throat. She had married a good man, a strong man; she didn't need anyone to point it out to her. His penchant to protect those weaker than himself would one day get him killed.

"You were very fortunate to have found him."

Aye, I was." He nodded.

They both were. Had he been any other man she would probably be sporting a black eye or worse for her recent behavior. He had shown greater restraint than her father ever had.

She realized that she'd been waiting for him to behave like her father, and he was just not going to. He would never raise his hand to those smaller or weaker than himself. She supposed she presented a very frustrating problem to him always doing things that tested his temper and leaving him no recourse.

In less than a fortnight, he had managed to show her how different men could be from her perception of them. She had painted them all with the same callous, unfeeling brush her father and uncle had placed in her hand. Now, she knew there were those who weren't out to manipulate and dominate those weaker than themselves.

The door behind her opened without a warning knock, and she turned to look over her shoulder. Beads of moisture glistened in Matthew's dark hair and wet the shoulders of his cloak. He tossed the leather valise he carried onto the bunk and removed his cloak then hung it on a peg at the door.

She collected a towel from the washstand and went to offer it to him. Matthew studied her features, his gaze sharp. "A white flag, Katherine? I'd have thought you'd sooner fight to the death than surrender."

"A flag of truce, so that we may negotiate," she suggested.

"I have negotiated with you before and come out the loser."

"Will ye be needin' anythin' else, Cap'in?" Georgie asked from the door.

"No, Georgie." He crossed the cabin in two long strides to open the door for him.

The silence that stretched between them with Georgie's departure grew taut as sail canvas. He removed his long coat and hung it beside his cloak. He unwrapped the stock from about his neck and hung it there as well.

Katherine turned away and went to the window seat to look out upon the water. The reflective light of the cabin limited her vision to a small patch directly beneath the window. The warm yellow lights of the lanterns behind her turned the dingy gray water a milky green.

He tossed a cream-colored piece of paper on her lap as he sat down beside her. "I've read it. Is there anything that you neglected to include in the story?"

She had hoped to avoid telling him the more personal parts of the story, but if she held anything back now he would view it as another betrayal. As she strove to avoid looking at him, all she felt was a bone deep pain and tiredness.

The wooden bulkhead behind her felt cool through the thinness of her gown as she rested back against it. It grounded her in the present so that the past could not wound her so bitterly.

"I do not remember everything about that night. Had the guns been in the coach, we might have had a fighting chance."

"The guns?"

"My brother's guns. There was a compartment beneath the seat where they were kept, but when we opened it to arm ourselves they were gone. Even the powder and shot were missing. Edward said one of the servants must have discovered them while cleaning the coach and taken them to sell."

"That sounds a reasonable assumption." He shifted and braced a hand on the back of the desk chair.

"My mother made me get inside the compartment and hide. I heard gunshots and her screaming. I don't remember what happened next. It is as though time just ceased to be.

"The only face I remember is the one I drew. I remember being cold, and everything looked as though I viewed it through the bottom of a glass. My legs were slick with blood, and my gown clung to them as though it were alive."

His movement as he released the chair back brought her gaze to his face to find his expression wooden. She wondered what he hid behind that control. Revulsion? Pity? "It was from the shot in my side, not what you are thinking. He told me that came later."

"You said nothing of being shot." His tone was subdued, careful.

"Here." She touched her waist. "The ball tore through my stays and into my side. It took the surgeon some time to pick out the whalebone fragments. In the end he told me it was probably the undergarment that saved my life."

She fell silent as she struggled to retain her composure. "All I remember after being shot is a weight pressing down on top of me and a rope tight about my neck squeezing my throat so that my head pounded. I couldn't breathe. There was a light in the distance. I thought at the time, if only I could reach it, I would be safe."

"Who is he?" he asked.

She stared at him confused.

"You said 'he' told you."

"Edward." She drew her legs up and looped her arms about her knees, hugging them hard.

Silence settled between them weighted with emotion. She turned to look out upon the water, away, unable to bear whatever she would see in his expression.

"When was it Edward began searching for a husband for you?"

"Barely a month later. He said we would have to be quick about it before rumor made it impossible for him to find me a match. He insisted my immigrating to another country would be for the best." She finally looked at him, but his attention was directed at the bare wooden floor beneath his feet. "I wanted to tell you everything before the wedding, but— you were never released from prison and my notes were never delivered."

"It wouldn't have changed the outcome of things, Katherine." He rose to his feet and looked for a long moment out into the darkness. "I'll have Webster prepare a meal," he said as he crossed to don his long coat and cloak. "I'll be up on the quarter deck should you need me."

She rested her forehead against her up-drawn knees as tears ran unheeded down her cheeks. He hadn't looked at her a single time. Her chest ached with the pain of his rejection. She had never dreamed anything could hurt so much.

****

Matthew pounded his fist against the railing of the quarterdeck. Knowing she had been abused when injured made him sick, but it also thrust to life a rage he had tried to ignore for days. He could ignore it no longer. It twisted like a thing alive in the pit of his stomach. He wanted the men responsible for this, dead. They were out there somewhere free to do as they pleased while she stayed huddled beneath decks, afraid and outcast. He wanted to rail at the injustice of it.

When had he begun to care so much about this stranger he had married? From the moment she had walked into that dirty, dim cell and offered him her hand and his freedom. She had invaded his thoughts, his dreams. Even when he was concentrating on other things, she was like a tune that threaded its way though his mind.

Now that she had posted the bills and had the story hawked upon the streets, he couldn't leave her behind when he left England---but he had known that all along. She was his responsibility. *His wife.*

She was determined that their marriage would be a temporary one though there was no way for them to end it. By making the story public, she had backed them both into a corner, in more ways than one. He was furious with her for that, but in a way, he was also relieved. Relieved because the choice had been taken out of his hands.

Acknowledging that made him uncomfortable. He had faced situations on board ship and made decisions under circumstances that any hesitation might have meant life or death. Never had he vacillated over anything as he had about Katherine. He had tried to avoid facing why. Now he had no choice, but to confront it. He was afraid of loving her. Afraid of loving her and losing her, as he had Caroline.

He had wanted Caroline, gotten her with child, and caused her death. He wanted Katherine, possibly more than he had ever wanted any other woman. Wanted her so much, he dreamed of making love to her. He knew if he started touching her, there would be no way he could keep himself from taking her. He just wasn't that self-sacrificing.

And what if they made love and she conceived? Just the idea twisted his stomach into painful knots. He raked his fingers through his hair and groaned in frustration. The black cord that bound it at the nape of his neck came loose, and he stuck it in his pocket.

After speaking of the rape, making love would be the last thing she would be ready to do. But the desire to lay claim to her, to wipe out her memories of that night and fill her mind with only his touch, his kisses, his body, was so strong every muscle felt knotted with the effort to resist.

He slumped down on the top step of the quarterdeck and studied the rigging above as he allowed the familiar feel of the ship beneath him to soothe his rampaging emotions. He could not face her until he had himself under control. If he went below now he'd likely carry her to his bunk, and take her, and damn the consequences.

Katherine deserved better than that.

****

The numerous humiliations her father had heaped upon her had taught her well. Facing Matthew after their earlier exchange was one of the most difficult things she had ever done. Katherine kept her composure intact for pride's sake alone and forced herself to respond to his attempts at conversation as though nothing were wrong. By the end of the meal, her hold upon her emotions was tenuous. Anger and pain warred inside her, threatening an eruption of either tears or violence.

Georgie returned for the dishes. Where he had lingered to talk to her before, a frown flitted across his face as though he sensed the tension between her and Matthew, and the boy hurried through the chore and left.

The door had barely closed behind him when Matthew moved to the desk and said, "Please come here, Katherine."

She hesitated then, girding her composure, strode across the cabin to join him.

He opened a drawer and removed a small bottle. "I have some liniment for your cheek." He pulled the cork from the vessel and moistened a small scrap of linen.

She flinched, as much from the strong smell of the medicine as the unexpected emotional pain his touch caused.

Matthew murmured an apology and hurried to finish the task then set aside the medicine. His fingers grasped her jaw raising her face for his perusal. "I shouldn't have shown such restraint with your uncle," he commented. "Is it very painful?"

Surprised by his concern, she studied his expression then shook her head.

"Not all men hit."

"I know."

"Do you? You don't look as though you truly believe it." His black brows knitted together in a frown, his mouth set in a ridged line that bespoke of temper held in check. "The only thing I have for pain is a bottle of brandy. Would you like a dram?"

"No."

He stepped behind her to unfasten the buttons of her gown. She had, had a difficult time getting in and out of the garment earlier in the day and, though she resented his help, it did make the task easier. She held the gown close against her as the buttons gave way. When he unlaced her stays as well, she turned to look over her shoulder at him.

Matthew rested his hand upon her shoulders beneath the fabric and though the frown still lingered, his lips no longer looked compressed.

"Thank you." Though she sought to dismiss him, her voice came out just above a whisper. His calloused fingers ran lightly over her collarbones. Her breasts grew tight, the nipples puckering beneath the bodice. She wondered how he could inspire such feelings when only a few hours before she had thought he found her repulsive.

He wasn't behaving that way now. She wished she understood more about men. She couldn't read anything that was going on behind his face.

He removed his hands as though he just realized what he was doing. "I'll leave you to prepare for bed."

She nodded. His long strides took him to the door. She bit her lip against the urge to speak his name. He had behaved the attentive husband before in public and some of that had bled over into their private moments together, but there had been something different in the way he had touched her, addressed her. If it was pity he was feeling, she wanted no part of it.

She undressed, washed, and pulled the nightshift Matthew had packed for her out of the valise. Her stomach plummeted when she saw it. A wedding gift from his aunt, the garment was made of some fine soft material so diaphanous it was nearly non-existent, held together at the shoulders and sides by thin strips of ribbon. The most substantial part of the gown was the lace that bordered the hem and neckline. For a moment, she allowed herself to think about what it would be like to wear such an item for Matthew, had their marriage been a normal one. The way he made her feel when he looked at her, nearly stole her breath. For the first time, Katherine was glad she couldn't remember everything that had happened that night. It would have spoiled the way she felt about Matthew.

When he sailed for America, she would at least have the memories of every touch, every kiss, every time he held her to ease the loneliness.

CHAPTER 15

Matthew returned to find Katherine before the fireplace, a quilt from the bunk forming a pool of color around her hips. The neckline of the shift scooped low as she leaned forward to draw her hair over one shoulder and run her brush through the heavy mass. When he thought of this small cabin in years to come, he would see her there before the fire just as she was now. Even the dark purple bruise that discolored one cheek couldn't detract from the perfect contours of brow, cheek, chin, and jaw. The glossy sheen of her dark auburn hair looked rich against the pale smoothness of her shoulders.

He unbuttoned his shirt as he moved to stand beside her. "Will you help me with my boots?"

Slipping from beneath the quilt as though reluctant to give up its cover, she rose to do as he asked. The soft cotton shift, wrinkled and misshapen from being compressed beneath her stays, clung to her waist and hips. She bent to grasp the heel of his boot and for a moment, her unbound breasts were almost totally visible to him. Desire like a hot ferocious wind raced through him, stealing his breath. He grew hard with arousal. He wanted to drag her onto his lap, spread her legs and thrust up inside her. With those visions playing in his head, he gripped the edge of his chair and wrestled to maintain control. He had to avert his gaze before offering her his other boot, and nearly sighed in relief once the shoe was off and set aside.

He peeled the stockings from his legs then rose from the chair. "Was there something wrong with the nightshift?" he asked as he shed his shirt and draped it over the back of a chair.

When Katherine didn't answer, he turned to look at her and found her huddled upon the seat. He caught a glimpse of her tear-wet face before she buried it in the quilt. He approached her with a sense of relief, for the

137

tears he had awaited all day had finally erupted. He bent and scooped her up, quilt and all, and carried her to the bunk to stretch out beside her and hold her. It took some wrestling to extract her from the blanket, but finally he had her pulled close, the cover over them both. He brushed the hair back from her face and welcomed the slender feel of her pressed tightly against him. As Matthew kissed her brow and murmured soft words of comfort, he acknowledged to himself how good it felt to actually behave like a husband. She was so alone, so self-contained. It was difficult to break through the barriers she erected between them. The more she needed, the higher the walls grew. He felt the tension in her body as she struggled to suppress the tears even as she shed them. The only time she showed no restraint was when they kissed. He found some hope in that.

"I need my handkerchief," Katherine said, her voice thick with tears. Embarrassed by her lose of control, she turned her face away when he rose to retrieve a large square of linen from his coat pocket and returned to the bunk.

She knew her face looked flushed from crying, her eyes and nose red, and she hated him seeing her in such a condition. Katherine mopped her face. He barely gave her time enough to do that before molding her against him once again.

"I think I've decided on a punishment for your refusal to tell me things," he said as he continued to stroke her hair.

She went still, shocked by the idea. "I am not a child. It is not your place to punish me for anything."

He smiled. "I think every time you decide to hold back from me, I'm going to kiss you, Katherine."

A sound, part sigh, part laugh, escaped her, and she relaxed. "That is not a threat."

Matthew propped himself up on an elbow and looked down at her. He smoothed the damp curls that lay against her forehead. He bent his head and lowered his mouth to hers. The pressure of his lips felt more comforting than anything else. She curled a hand around the back of his neck holding him close. The ache of despair slowly eased away and a bone melting heat replaced it. He turned her against him and stroked her back with a gentle, warm pressure that made her want to wiggle closer.

She placed a hand against his chest as though to hold him at bay, but her fingertips curled against his skin as she fought against the urge to caress his broad chest and discover the texture of the hair covering it.

His tongue brushed the seam between her lips and her mouth parted. He tasted of the wine he had drunk at dinner. He smelled of soap and his own musky scent that hinted of vanilla and spice. Her tongue mirrored the undulating movement of his as her hand moved restlessly over the thick pelt of hair on his chest.

He cupped her buttocks molding her against him. She had slept with him for nearly a fortnight. She hadn't seen him completely nude since that first morning, but she had felt, more than once, the change his body went through when early in the morning she would awaken to find him molded against her from behind. She had felt the empty ache between her thighs and had fought the urge to wiggle back against him. The desire to rub against the heated hardness beneath his breeches was nearly impossible to resist. She groaned beneath the pressure of his kiss as his tongue writhed and twisted around hers.

Tentatively she stroked his back with restless caresses and bent her knee along his hip opening her thighs in an instinctive invitation.

He groaned and ran his hand the length of her thigh and back up again. His callused palm felt rough against her skin as he worked his way beneath the hem of her shift to her hip. His mouth left hers to touch the thundering pulse in her neck. His tongue traced the shell-like contour of her ear, his breath warm, moist upon her skin. She shivered as a thousand delightful sensations raced through her.

He eased the shift upward, but Katherine clung to it anxious about losing its cover. She wanted more. She wanted to feel his hands all over her body. She wanted to touch him all over as well. She wanted to spread her legs and bring him inside where the aching emptiness tormented her, but taking that last trusting step was difficult.

His pale blue eyes looked luminous with heat as he

drew back to look down at her. His fingers traced the scar on her side and suddenly conscious of its ugliness, she covered his hand with her own.

"Don't, Katherine. Don't hide from me any more." He ran his hand beneath the shift, his fingertips grazing her skin from her collarbone down the center of her body to her navel. "You're beautiful, as beautiful as I knew you would be."

She felt beautiful beneath the weight of tenderness and desire she read in his face. He bent his head to kiss her once again. Beneath the shift, his hand cupped her breast, kneaded the taut flesh, and gently pinched the tightly budded nipple. When he pulled the garment upward again she wiggled free of it.

She drew a shaky breath as he slid downward, and latched onto one distended peak, the suction he applied causing rivulets of sensation to travel from her breast downward. As he caressed the inside of her thighs, she wanted to roll her hips, to urge him on. The tentative brush of his fingertips against the sensitive wet heat between her legs had her whispering his name. Instinctively, she closed her legs around his hand even as her body moved beneath his touch. One long finger eased inside her. She groaned at the foreign rush of pleasure that spiraled deep within her. She grasped his hand unsure if she wanted to stop him or urge him on.

He moved his finger in a flickering movement that sent a tremor through her entire body, and she bowed her back opening her thighs to push against his touch. His mouth transferred to the other nipple, and he drew upon it hard, his tongue lathing the underside. A hungry heat pulsed within her, and she tilted her hips upward, seeking more, trying to draw his finger deeper. In between strokes, once again, he flicked the digit. A breathless moan was wrenched from her as pleasure spiraled tighter and tighter against the ebb and flow of his touch building toward something wondrous. With one last flickering movement it came upon her in a rush that rolled over her so sweetly she gasped Matthew's name and nearly wept from the joy of it.

Slowly, gently Matthew removed his hand from between her thighs. He unbuttoned his breeches and shook free of them then slid upward between Katherine's parted thighs, his bare skin brushing hers. His arousal rested boldly against her.

He smoothed back the tousled locks from her cheek and looked down into deep violet eyes still slumberous with release. Her hands ran up his back then back down.

"I have wanted very much to touch you, Matthew."

He gritted his teeth against the urge to thrust inside her right then. "I don't need any encouragement right now, sweet." He bent his head to kiss her. "I want you, Katherine. I've dreamed about being with you like this for weeks."

"I know." Her open mouth moved to his shoulder and he shuddered. She was so naturally sensuous. All that quiet reserve on the outside hid the passion just simmering beneath the surface waiting to be tapped. God, how he wanted her.

"Do you want me, Katherine?" He wasn't even sure she understood what he was asking but he could go no farther without hearing her consent. He drew back to look down at her.

"Yes." Her violet eyes looked almost black, the pupil nearly swallowing the iris.

He guided himself to the entrance to her body and eased inside her slowly. She was so hot and wet and tight, he thought he might go mad from the pleasure of it. His muscles shook with the effort it took not to plunge deep inside her. He felt the tension of her body, the resistance of his invasion, but finally he could bear it no longer and with one quick thrust seated himself to the hilt.

Her momentary gasp of pain had him going completely still. His body ached for release so badly he couldn't bring himself to withdraw.He looked down at her, shock ripping through him in a rush.

She drew a deep breath as though girding herself. "Does it hurt every time?" she asked her fingers combing through the hair at his nape.

No woman could act that ingeniously. She didn't know! Matthew had a moment to think of what she might have seen and experienced that night. He had soothed her fears after more than one nightmare since they had been wed.

He wanted to laugh at himself and at her. He wanted to shout with relief and joy. Whatever else had happened, they hadn't molested her. They had to talk about this, but sheathed inside her body, he couldn't bring himself to start such a conversation. Knowing she was untouched, that she was truly his alone, only intensified his need.

"It doesn't hurt at all if done right, Katherine. It's been some time for me." He rubbed his beard-roughened cheek against her soft one and turned his lips to hers. He kissed her lips, her nose, her brow, moved by tenderness and a desire to give her pleasure once again, if he could.

With long, slow, kisses he soothed the tension from her body. When she looped her arms around his neck and clung to him, he began to move inside her. Her hips began to rise to meet him as she caught his rhythm.

He lost himself in her, filled with a craving he could no longer contain. Their skin melded with the sweat the friction of their bodies created. He felt the frantic heat that suffused her skin and brought a ragged intensity to her breathing. Her hands cupped his buttocks urging him deeper. Her body clenched around him, squeezing, massaging. He lost all will, and buried himself as deep as he could inside her and groaned aloud as his seed spilled forth in a pulsing release that went on and on.

CHAPTER 16

Katherine woke to the sound of rain against the window and the feel of a naked man spooned against her from behind. A blush flared in her checks at the unfamiliar sensation. The moist heat of their skin melding together in spots, and the intimacy of their position sparked a melting weakness in her lower extremities. Matthew's hand lay curved around her breast and though he remained asleep, she felt the tempting tingle his touch ignited.

They had shared an intimacy that went deeper than she had ever expected. She still felt connected to him though their bodies were separate. She would never forget his gentleness, the tenderness she had read in his face as he had come inside her. He had given her such wonderful memories to cling to after he left England.

The almost physical pain she felt when she thought about that had her closing her eyes to keep the tears at bay. When he left, he would take part of her with him. She wondered if he would feel the same about her.

She was grateful for all he had given her. He had taught her how to trust again. He had taught her that to love didn't have to be painful and that the sharing of her body didn't have to be degrading as she had expected it to be.

Her checks felt hot as she thought about her uncontrolled response to his touch, his kisses. Since living with her uncle and staying at Willingham's she had met any number of men. She had never experienced the instant pull of longing she felt with Matthew. Somehow, she thought it might be a very rare occurrence. She felt that was as it should be. She couldn't imagine feeling for anyone else as she did for him.

She eased from beneath the covers to use the water closet. The call of nature answered, she slipped Matthew's shirt on and buttoned it around her to ward off the early morning chill that permeated the room. The flounced cuffs hung over her hands and the hem struck her just above the knee. As she folded back the sleeves, she studied Matthew's reclining form.

He slept with one hand stretched over the pillow she had just vacated. She traced with her gaze the light dusting of hair on his arm, the strong graceful shape of his hand and looked around for her pack.

She wanted to draw him. When her memory grew clouded by time, her drawings would aid her in remembering him more clearly. Her throat ached as she collected her pack and opened it. Withdrawing several sheets of paper, she sat down at Matthew's desk. Using a piece of charcoal, she quickly sketched his reclining form. Asleep, he looked younger even with the heavy shadow of beard darkening his jaw. The intensity of his gaze, his personality, was relaxed for the moment.

She worked for nearly an hour while Matthew slept. Her attention remained focused on him so intently she was only vaguely aware of the chill in the room.

He stirred, and she froze. For the first time, she wondered how he would feel about being drawn while in so vulnerable a position. Her stiff muscles protested as she rose from the chair to put away the drawings. Black dust from the charcoal coated the desk, and she quickly wiped the wooden surface clean with a rag. She walked to the washstand and scrubbed her stained hands and washed her face.

Matthew threw back the bedclothes and rose to his feet. Her mouth went dry just watching him. His skin looked dark against the white bandage around his forearm. Broad of shoulder and wide of chest, his muscular torso tapered to a lean waist and hips. Dark hair grew in swirls across his chest then arrowed down the center of his flat stomach to blossom into a dark thatch that framed his sex. Long and hard, it jutted out from his body as it had the night before. His long legs looked as powerful and well shaped as the rest of him. He brushed her mouth with a quick kiss then disappeared into the water closet.

Her cheeks burning, she poured water into the bowl and soaped a rag. Leaving the shirt on, she ran the cloth between her legs to ease the soreness there. She jerked it away as Matthew left the water closet, and offered him a tentative smile as his reflection appeared in the mirror next to hers. His arms went around her waist, and he nuzzled the sensitive area between her neck and shoulder. Katherine shivered in response as delightful tremors raced down her spine.

"You're cold. Come back to bed." He gave her no time to respond, but scooped her up and carried her to the bunk.

"Woman, those have to be the coldest feet I have ever felt," he complained as he cradled her close to share his warmth.

She laughed as she tossed the wet rag toward the washbasin and missed.

"What have you been doing while I slept?" he asked.

She saw no reason not to tell him. "I have been drawing."

He grasped her hand still slightly stained with charcoal and studied it before he bent his head to kiss her palm. "It's more than just a casual entertainment to you, isn't it?"

"Yes. I think I may be able to make a living with it, if I can find an agent willing to sell my paintings for me."

"Why would you have to have someone act on your behalf?"

"When a man paints, it is his profession. When a woman does it, it is a hobby. When a man sells his wares, it is business. When a woman does it, it is unseemly. People will pay a great deal more for paintings done by a man than a woman as well."

"It sounds as though you've experienced those problems first hand already."

She nodded. "A month before his death, my brother sold two of my paintings for a hundred pounds apiece. I had been offered ten pounds for both a month before."

"How did your father feel about your success?" he asked.

"He never knew. He thought my drawings a waste of time."

"Was he like Edward and insisted you be dependant upon his good graces?"

She studied his features for a moment. The probing intensity of his gaze had her biting her lip. Did the sharing of her body entitle him to other intimacies as well, or had it only opened his desire for them?

A knot of tears rose in her throat. She turned her back to him.

Matthew sighed softly from behind her, but when she wiggled back against him, he slipped an arm around her waist to hold her.

"He burnt my drawings and paintings until I learned to hide them successfully. He destroyed my paints more than once. My mother smuggled more back during her trips with him to London. He thought me too strong willed and had launched a campaign to cure me of it, because a husband would expect me to be meek and subservient to him at all times."

His arm tightened around her. "Not all men expect that, Katherine. In fact, most, I'd wager, would want their wives to be able to take charge of their household in their absence."

"Did you?" she asked.

He remained silent for moment. "Caroline and I were only married a year. We were apart only once during that time, and my father was there to see to things. Without him there to take my place, I'd have depended on her to make decisions in my absence."

Some of the tension eased from her body. Matthew's hand slid beneath the fabric of the shirt and captured one of her breasts. Her mouth went dry as he began to fondle it. His hot aroused flesh moved against her intimately. She tilted her hips back against him in response, as desire leaped through her.

His hand ran in a slow provocative caress down the center of her body. She parted her thighs as his fingers honed in on the moist pressure that built between her legs. He nibbled her ear lobe as he parted her with his fingertips and found the tiny sensitive bud hidden there. Katherine bit her lip to keep from groaning aloud at the tempting pleasure he inspired.

He pushed inside her. She felt sore and his possession was a pleasurable pain as he sank deep inside her. As he began his slow careful movements, she pressed back against him finding his rhythm.

His lips grazed her shoulder, her neck, and he nibbled her ear. "Is it too much, Katherine? I don't want to hurt you."

It was not enough. She reached back to touch him, her hand sliding down his hip to his tautly muscled thigh. She knew they could not continue with this. For every time she shared her body with him she moved closer to becoming the very thing of which everyone accused her.

She could not be his wife, only a temporary mistress. She had promised to let him go, to find a way of releasing him from the marriage. She had to stand by that promise.

She pulled away and turned to face him. The warmth she read in his pale blue eyes was nearly her undoing. His large hands ran in restless circles up and down her back. "It's all right, Katherine. We don't have to make love."

Make love. Those two words brought to mind a realm of possibilities they could share if only he truly loved her. Knowing this would be their last intimate moments together, she was torn by her need to be as close to him as she could get, and a desire to end it now. As she looked into his face, her heart ached with a bittersweet need too deep to deny.

She traced the curve of his cheekbone and the flat plain of his jaw with her fingertips. His beard felt prickly and rough against her skin. She sat up on her knees and straddled him. He rested his hands on her hips beneath the fabric of the shirt his pale gaze intent with interest.

She bent and kissed him, her lips parted to drink in the warmth of him. The heavy mass of auburn curls fell over her shoulder to drape across his chest. She tasted his skin as she kissed the hollow of his throat. She explored the round flat nipples that peeked through the hair on his chest and felt his response as they beaded beneath her touch.

Matthew ran restless hands under the shirt and over her bare back. She unbuttoned the shirt. She dipped low to rub her breasts against his chest, loving the roughness of the hair there against her skin. Matthew murmured her name, his voice husky. The lance-like hardness of his aroused male flesh brushed against her thigh.

She slid downward to rest her cheek against his chest

then turned her lips against the steady beat of his heart. She wanted to hold him close, to feel his body against hers, to draw him inside her and be a part of him, for the last time.

She curled her fingers around him and was surprised by the velvety soft heat of him. The skin there felt tender, yet his flesh was swollen and throbbed beneath her touch. She looked down into his face and wiggled forward to lean down and kiss him as she guided him inside her. As her body enveloped him, tears of loss welled up making her throat ache. She closed her eyes against the pain, and focused on the intimate connection between them.

Never again would she know this closeness with any other man. Never again would she feel free to offer her body or her heart to anyone.

He caught her lips with his, his kisses slow and languorous as he cupped the tender weight of her breasts and gently kneaded them.

She began to move against him in response. Her body adjusted to his possession and the initial soreness eased. A heart wrenching pleasure began to build inside her.

He grasped her hips, guiding her in a slow deep tempo of motion. Every kiss left her hungry for another, every touch inspired an answering caress. She could not get close enough, could not touch him enough, could not draw him deep enough, to last forever.

Their bodies strained toward each other, their short deep thrusts growing faster and more frantic. He groaned her name and his thick, husky tone triggered an answering part of her. She tried to hold it off wanting more time, more of the closeness she had found. A wave of pleasure pulsed through her working outward from the very core of her body to her fingers and toes. She cried out as the end rushed toward her. As she felt Matthew's release echo deep inside her, a feeling of such sorrow coursed through her, she turned her face into the bend of his neck and clung to him.

An abrupt pounding on the door, interrupted before their hearts had even begun to slow. "What is it?" he called from beneath her.

"It's a message from Lord Willingham, Cap'in. There's been some sort of trouble at the house," Georgie called through the door.

Katherine eased from her position on top of him. With a murmured apology, he rose and quickly slipped on his discarded breeches from the night before. He strode to the door and opened it, blocking Georgie's view into the room with his body.

"Lord Willingham needs you to come at once, Cap'in. His man is on deck waiting to drive you back to the house."

"Did he say what kind of trouble, Georgie?"

"Something to do with one of the maids being attacked, Cap'in."

"Tell him I'll be with him immediately, Georgie."

"Aye, aye, sir."

Hearing his comment about one of the maids, Katherine rose and began to gather her clothes.

"There's no need for you to accompany me, Katherine."

"Of course there is. He did not say who it was that was attacked or where. What if it should be Hannah?"

"Whoever Talbot has sent can tell us the details. As soon as we're both dressed we'll go up on deck and ask him for more information."

"It must be serious if Talbot wants you there. I will not be left behind," she argued as she looked through the valise from the night before for a fresh shift. A frantic sense of fear tied her stomach into knots. Talbot wouldn't have sent for Matthew if the incident weren't serious.

She emptied the water out of the bowl on the washstand and refilled it. Even though they had shared their bodies, she found herself too shy to abandon the shirt she still wore. She washed quickly, aware of Matthew watching from behind her as he set out clothing for them both.

She held the garment against her as she moved to the bunk for the fresh shift he had laid on the bed.

He peeled aside the collar of the shirt and kissed her shoulder. "Do you remember on our wedding night when you met me at the door covered from neck to ankle in that ugly wool robe?"

She nodded. She focused on the dark beard that covered his jaw for fear she might cry if she met his gaze.

"Covering yourself from head to toe was more provocative than if you strutted around naked, though the latter would certainly garner a response. I'd want you if you wore sack cloth and ashes."

He wanted her. But what of affection and love?

"There are things we must talk about later when there is more time, Katherine."

She nodded again, not trusting her composure enough to speak. She rose on tiptoe to press her cheek against his. "I must dress." She moved to the bed and turning her back to him, shrugged free of the shirt and quickly donned her shift. Matthew appeared behind her as she tugged her stays in place and pulled the strings snug and tied them for her. He was there again to button the numerous tiny buttons down the back of the gown he had packed for her. Katherine busied herself with trying to brush the tangles from her hair and braid the heavy mass as she waited for him to finish dressing.

As she smoothed the wrinkles from her gown, she thought, just once she would like to wear something festive and colorful for him instead of the drab gray or black of mourning. There would be no time for that now.

CHAPTER 17

"The authorities have been notified, Captain Hamilton," Elton, the Willingham's butler, said as they settled into the small rowboat he had arrived in. The sailor he had hired took up the paddles and began to row them ashore.

"It was one of the downstairs maids who found Margaret this morning. Her cries for help awoke some of the other staff, and Lord Willingham was notified. He seems to think that Margaret slipped downstairs to meet the man and he turned on her for some reason. Nothing was disturbed inside the house."

"That at least is a relief," Matthew said.

"Margaret is the young blond maid with the lovely skin, is she not?" Katherine asked from beside him.

"Yes, Madame." Elton nodded, his expression solemn.

"She was not much older than I am," she commented, her voice weak and thready.

Matthew placed an arm around her waist for though her composure seemed intact, she looked pale.

"With the guards patrolling the grounds, I'd be interested to know how he got by them and into the house," Matthew said.

"She would have had to let him in herself, sir. The side entrance was locked. I checked it myself before retiring."

The man's words shocked him. It couldn't be. Surely it hadn't been the woman he had seen outside last night? Had he walked past the man moments before he killed her?

The trip from the docks to Willingham's progressed in silence. Matthew kept his arm around Katherine throughout the short journey. He was troubled by her abrupt withdrawal into silence and attributed it to shock and concern for the maid. His own concerns lay like rocks in the pit of his stomach. Why hadn't he called out to them as he'd gone into the house?

"How did you know her, Katherine?" Matthew asked as he braced them both against the sway of the coach.

"She brings in the morning paper at breakfast," she answered. "I know the names of all the servants."

Surprised, he fell silent again. He wondered how many of the servants he could name. Very few, he'd guess.

Elton hung back as the footman opened the door and lowered the steps. Matthew exited the coach and reached up to offer Katherine a hand. A crowd hung outside the entrance to the grounds, their silence giving an air of foreboding to their arrival. Two burly men dressed in camel colored knee breeches and dark coats stepped forward as Matthew and Katherine mounted the stairs with Elton behind them.

A small cart with two horses harnessed to it blocked the drive. Two men bearing a blanket-covered stretcher rounded the corner as they stood on the steps.

"This is Lord Willingham's nephew and his wife," Elton informed one of the men as the other brushed past them and went to lower the tailgate of the cart. The man flipped back the cloth covering the woman's face revealing blond hair surrounding a pale grayish face. A blue ribbon dangled from around her throat.

Matthew's pushed aside his own reaction as Katherine staggered and grasped at the concrete banister of the steps. Matthew caught her arm partially breaking her fall. She raised shock-glazed eyes to his face, her hands clenched at her throat as she huddled upon the narrow step. Matthew bit back an oath. Had the man been able to curb his curiosity for one moment more she would have been spared seeing the girl entirely.

He knelt upon the step prepared to lift her, but she held him off, her hands grasping his upper arms so tightly he felt the pressure of each finger. Her eyes appeared so large and dark, her face looked as though it had shrunk around them. The bruise upon her cheek stood out in stark contrast to the pallid color of her skin. "He's been here."

For a moment he stared at her in confusion, then realization dawned. "How do you know, Katherine?"

"The ribbon. It is the same as the one he used to strangle my mother. A blue ribbon." She clenched both fists against her lips, as though to hold back some sound that rose inside her. "Oh, God! It is my fault." She began to rock as though in pain. "You warned me that someone would be hurt."

He scooped her up, intent on getting her inside the house and away from the prying eyes of the men standing around them. Elton opened the door for him, and he carried her into the entrance hall.

Hannah sat upon a bench along the wall waiting for their arrival. She sprang to her feet upon seeing them and rushed to Matthew's side.

"She knows." It was a statement not a question. He set Katherine on her feet and the two women reached for each other immediately.

"He used a blue ribbon," Hannah said.

Katherine's posture was stiff. He realized she was struggling to hold onto her composure. "I saw it."

Listening to the women talk in short terse sentences sent concern rushing through him. He watched as Hannah hugged her offering her comfort.

"It is my fault she is dead, Hannah. I should have warned the staff more clearly. I should have given each one of them one of the prints. She may have recognized him and we could have caught him. She'd still be alive." Her voice, choked and husky, held a broken note of sorrow. Her skin retained the paleness of shock. The fact that she turned to Hannah for comfort, instead of him, made Matthew uneasy.

"You'll need to talk to Talbot about this, Katherine. Everything you tell him and the magistrate may help them capture the man or men responsible."

She turned to look over her shoulder at him, her eyes wet with tears, her expression so raw with emotion and vulnerability he fought the urge to reach for her. Her posture, her pointed avoidance of seeking him out for comfort, made it clear she had distanced herself from him again. He didn't know if it were triggered by their return to Willingham's, the murder, or something else, but he didn't like it a damn bit and didn't intend to endure it.

He wasn't going to stand by and allow the open, giving woman he had made love to last night and this morning, to slip away without a fight. As soon as she had calmed, he intended for them to talk about the situation.

"Will you join us, Hannah? You may have something useful to add to what Katherine has to say."

"Aye, I will, Captain Hamilton." The woman nodded.

"I want to do it now," Katherine said as she straightened away from Hannah and wiped her eyes with the small handkerchief the maid offered her.

He grasped her arm and guided her down the entrance hall to Talbot's study. As concerned about the situation as he was, he had to admire Katherine's strength and determination. Caroline had been more malleable and less independent. He wondered what his brothers would think of his choice. Regardless of how they had wed, he had made a choice to have her and to keep her. With her headstrong, iron will, things would certainly never be boring between the two of them.

Matthew gave the door a short, sharp rap. The portal opened almost before his hand had lowered to his side.

Talbot's white hair looked mussed, as though he had threaded his fingers through it repeatedly, and his stock hung askew.

His expression changed from irritation to open relief. "Matthew, I am glad you have returned." He stood back for the three of them to enter the study.

"Katherine and Hannah have some things to tell you they think may be useful."

Talbot turned toward the women. "Please come in and sit down." He motioned toward the chairs before the fire.

He turned to look over his shoulder at a man behind him standing before a large Queen Ann desk. "Lord Harcourt, please join us."

The man who stepped forward had a slight, wiry build and moved with bold, confident strides. His light brown hair, brushed straight back from his forehead and tied with a black lace, bared his wide flat cheekbones and pointed chin. His brows, bushy and thick, arched above brown eyes that held a sharp intensity. His other features appeared so exaggerated; his small narrow nose seemed almost an afterthought.

Talbot quickly made the introductions then said, "Lord Harcourt read Katherine's story and had asked to speak with me this morning, but since it is Katherine's story to tell, I believe he should speak directly to her."

"With your permission of course, Mrs. Hamilton," Lord Harcourt added.

She settled on the edge of a high-backed chair. "I will do whatever I can to help."

Lord Harcourt studied her for a moment. "There has been a rash of similar attacks upon women across the city, Mrs. Hamilton. The general populace is not aware of it because it was feared that it would cause a panic. Your mother was not the first and this young woman here today will not be the last, if he is not captured. You are the only one to survive such an attack. You can identify the killer and that makes you very dangerous to him."

"Anyone who has seen the prints is a danger to him now, Lord Harcourt. That is why I have offered a reward for his capture."

"But they cannot testify to his actions as you can, Mrs. Hamilton. You must be very careful."

"Of course." She nodded.

"Lord Willingham has hired some men to protect you and his family. I believe you will be secure here at Willingham's."

She made a dismissive gesture with her hand. "He strangles women with a blue ribbon. He has brown hair with blond mingled through it, and I believe green eyes. He is a big man with large hands. He is handsome, but he has a cruel set to his mouth. He reminds me of someone I have met of late, but I cannot quite identify whom. Something about his jaw—" She rubbed her temples. "I only remember parts of the night I was attacked, Lord Harcourt. I remember being on a horse and being shot. I remember my brother's and father's faces gleaming white in the lantern light. I remember seeing a light in the distance and I remember the man's face who tried to strangle me with a thin rope." She rose to her feet. "I can offer you one of the prints I had made with his likeness."

"That will not be necessary, Mrs. Hamilton. I already have one." Lord Harcourt rose to his feet as well.

"Then if you will excuse me, I would like to go to my room."

"Certainly."

Hannah rose to follow her and Katherine stopped to turn to the woman. "If there is more that you can tell Lord Harcourt, you must stay, Hannah. I am going up to lie down."

Hannah hesitated then lowered herself back into her chair.

The door closed behind Katherine, but Hannah remained silent for a few moments.

"What is it you wish to tell us, Hannah?" Matthew prompted the woman when she remained silent.

"The man is a monster. He tortured Lady Ellen before he killed her. I cleaned and prepared the body m'self. She was cut some across her thighs and belly and the ribbon had dug into her throat so deep I had to have help cutting it free." She hugged herself and began to rock as tears streamed down her face unheeded. "They'd done other things as well, more than one of 'em." Overwhelmed, she wept and Matthew laid a comforting hand upon the woman's shaking shoulders. She gathered herself and wiped her face and blew her nose. "Miss Ellen was so sweet and soft spoken, a real lady, they had no right to shame her so."

"We almost lost Miss Kate as well. She'd been shot in the side. She near died from losin' so much blood. Another coach came up the road and scared him and his men away. That 'twas what saved her from the worst of it."

"Who was it that told Katherine she had been molested like her mother, Hannah?" Matthew asked.

"It had to be Edward—Lord Leighton. Had I known he had claimed such a thing, I'd have spoken with her about it," Her expression took on a momentary narrow eyed look. "'Twas untrue. Lady Kate wasn't harmed like that. You know that don't you, Capt'in Hamilton?"

"Yes," Matthew said briefly.

The woman blinked to clear her vision, and focused on his face. Heat crept upward in his cheeks. It was one thing to make love to one's wife, quite another to admit as much to your wife's maid, and to do so with two other men looking on.

"Why don't you go upstairs and lie down for a while too, Hannah. I'll see to anything Katherine might need."

She nodded and stood up. The wrinkles around her

eyes and mouth appeared to have deepened in just the few moments she had spoken to them. "Thank you, Cap'in Hamilton." She placed a hand upon his sleeve. "I know Miss Kate will be safe with you."

"I'll do my best to see she is, Hannah."

She nodded and left the room.

"Tell me about Lord Leighton," Lord Harcourt said immediately.

Matthew nodded. "After I have told you about something I saw last night."

****

Katherine shoved the feather-laden sack into the drawer of a chest inside the dressing room. It had taken her some time to clear away the feathers spilled from the mutilated pillow. She saw no reason for Matthew to experience the same sense of violation and fear she had on discovering it. She shivered as goose bumps crawled across her skin. Knowing the killer had been inside their room made her almost ill with revulsion.

She checked the bed for the third time for any further proof he had been here.

Had they been asleep in the room, there was no doubt in her mind that Matthew and she would be as dead as the downstairs maid.

Katherine wanted to wail with grief and guilt at the woman's death. It was her fault. Had she not persisted with her plans, the woman would still be alive. She would have to learn to live with that. At the moment, she wavered between tears and nausea and a feeling just shy of panic.

Her continued presence placed Matthew and his family in danger. She couldn't live with that. She wasn't willing to lose anyone else she loved to these killers.

She placed the note she had composed on the bedside table, picked up the small bag she had packed, and left the room. There were no servants about when she went down the back stairs to a hallway just outside the kitchen. The side entrance where they had removed the body was just down the hall.

A man stood outside the door, a musket cradled in the bend of his elbow and a pistol stuck in his belt. She didn't recognize him though she understood his purpose for being there.

"Where would you be going, girl?" he asked, his green eyes sweeping the plain gray dress beneath her cloak.

She hesitated only a moment with the valise in her hand. She adopted an accent just shy of the more cultured tones she had learned at her parents heals. "I'll be leaving here for home. I didn't sign on to risk my life for a bunch of rich gadders, only to clean for them." She stepped across the threshold and closed the door behind her.

"I wouldn't desert the ship jest yet, love. Ye'd probably be safer here with me outside the door than on the streets."

"I won't be on the streets. I even have me a coach waitin' at the back gates. You wouldn't want to walk with me there would you?"

He looked from right to left then grimaced. "I can't leave me post, but I'll watch ye as far as I can."

She flashed him a smile then with a sigh of relief walked down the path she had taken her wedding day. With each step she took, she felt the strain of the ties she had made with Matthew and his family pulling at her. They would care for Hannah and keep her safe, safer than the woman would ever be with her. She made it to the back gate without meeting another guard and gingerly lifted the latch. Cracking the gate only as wide as she needed, she slipped through.

She stifled a squeak of fear as a hand came to rest on her shoulder.

"Sorry, Miss Katherine. I didn't mean to frighten you." William took the valise from her.

"Are the men you have hired at Summerhaven, William?"

"Yes, I've got four waiting for us at the corner. They'll ride guard."

She nodded. "The guns are beneath the seat?"

"Yes, everything is just as you asked for it to be. Are you sure you want to do this?"

She swallowed against the knot of tears that lodged in her throat. "There was another murder last night, William. A maid inside the house was killed. I cannot put Matthew and his family in any more danger. I feel as though I no longer have a choice. I have one stop at Fleet

Street to make and then we can be on our way."

William's ruddy complexion paled with the news. He took her elbow and escorted her down the street to the coach.

She eyed the four men who stood guard before the conveyance. They looked tough and hard. Each had a flintlock pistol tucked in the waistband of their breeches and carried a musket.

She settled into one of the coach seats, and William slammed the door. She felt the sway of the conveyance as the men positioned themselves on the vehicle.

With a jerk, the coach pulled away. Regret rode her hard with every step the horses took. She had known all along that she would have to say good-bye and that it would be painful to leave him no matter when or how it happened. At least she knew now what it was to be, if not loved, at least wanted. But the knowledge brought her no comfort. She had given herself to a man because she loved him, and he had taken what she had to offer for desire's sake and nothing more. Matthew might care for her, but caring wasn't enough. She deserved at least as much as she was willing to give. Didn't she? Tears blurred her vision.

If only they had met before she had been ruined, he might have been able to care for her more. Perhaps if they had, had more time, he could have learned to love her. Pain settled like a hard lump just beneath her breastbone. Love was like breathing, it just was. It could not be forced, and it could not be denied.

She supposed she had loved him from that first night when she had backed him into the closet. It had not been him she was afraid of, but herself. And now she was frightened for him. She hoped leading the men away from Willingham's would be enough. As long as those she loved were safe, she could face whatever she had to.

****

"Continue to purchase the goods we will need for the trip, Carson. I'll return as quickly as possible from Birmingham." Matthew fought to keep his voice even, when in truth he wanted to growl the orders at his purser like an angry lion.

"Aye, Captain. All will be ready when you return,

sir."

He nodded. Keep Georgie busy with his studies while I'm gone. We've been reading Shakespeare's sonnets. The book is in his sea chest."

"Aye, Captain."

He drew deep breaths to try to stem the anger that pulsed through him white hot as a star. Once he got his hands on Katherine, she would regret this. Her disappearance had set the entire household at Willingham's into a panic and given him a host of anxious moments. The desire to be off, to race to her side was so strong he could barely contain himself. The end of the month long deadline he had been given was drawing near. His need to delegate authority among his men so that all would be ready on the Caroline for their voyage was the only thing holding him back.

He swung the leather valise off the bunk and flipped leather saddlebags over his shoulder. "We can share a boat back to shore if you like."

"Thank you, sir."

An icy wind whipped across the deck of the ship as they arrived topside. He ignored the discomfort, eager to get aboard the row boat and be on his way. The sudden appearance of a blond head and billowing cloak at the ship's railing brought an oath to his lips.

"Is there a problem, sir," Carson asked at his side.

"No," he said his tone short. "Take these to the boat. I'll be there in a moment."

"Yes, sir." Carson accepted the articles then strode down the deck to the railing. Matthew watched as he tipped his tricorn to Jacqueline then moved on.

"Hello Matthew," Jacqueline breathed as she joined him.

"Lady Rudman," He tipped his head to her in greeting.

Jacqueline's smile faltered then widened. "How formal you sound," she said in a cajoling tone as she brushed the tangled blond curls from her forehead where the wind wreaked havoc with them.

Impatience thrust through his control. "What is it I may do for you Jacqueline?"

Her green gaze ran down him and she smiled. "I

learned from an acquaintance that your wife has returned to her home in Birmingham to pack for her journey and thought perhaps you were lonely."

He stared at her for a moment. "What acquaintance? When did you learn of it?"

"I do not mind your knowing who told me. 'Twas Matilda Herrington. Her husband has investments with the paper, and he mentioned it to her."

He shook his head. "And, how would she have known about Katherine's trip?"

"Well, it is to be announced in tomorrow's paper."

He swore as disbelief and anger ripped through him liked the crest of a wave. Damn the woman, did she not know the danger she was placing herself in?

"Really, Matthew you were never so rude before."

Jacqueline's tone drew his attention back to her. Tamping down his emotions he said, "I apologize for my language, Jacqueline. I haven't got time right now to be sociable. I'm on my way to meet my wife at Summerhaven."

"Sociable." She repeated the word, a frown drawing her pale brows together, her eyes narrowing. "Is that how you describe our past relationship, as *sociable?*"

He mentally girded himself for the battle to come. "No, Jacqueline. But from now on, all I'm interested in is a social connection between us, nothing more."

Her lips tightened, her green eyes acquiring the wide-eyed look of a cat getting ready to spit, snarl, and attack. "You are dismissing me, as though I were nothing."

"No, Jacqueline. I'm accepting my responsibilities and committing myself to my marriage. That means staying faithful to my wife. It isn't that difficult to understand. You might want to think about how much you risk every time you act on impulse."

Jacqueline's cheeks grew a hot, angry red and her mouth went tight. "How dare you call me to task for my behavior. I was not the only one in the bed we shared, Matthew."

"No, you weren't, but that was another time and place when we were both free to pursue other pleasures and entertainments. You are not the only one in your marriage bed, Jacqueline. If I were your husband, I wouldn't wish to share it with another man. Should he find out you are here pursuing me, how do you think he will react?"

"You would not dare tell him," she said with a toss of her head.

He stepped closer to her, his gaze fastening on her face intently. He couldn't risk being imprisoned again and he wouldn't. He had too much to lose. "Your visiting me here won't just affect your marriage. It can affect mine as well. If you persist, I will tell him. Go home. Pursue your husband with as much persistence as you are showing me."

"But...he is old, Matthew," she almost wailed.

"You had no problem using your imagination when we were together." He shrugged.

Jacqueline's features settled into sulky lines. She turned on her heel and stomped across the deck to the railing. She flashed him one more look laced with resentment and longing before she backed down the rope ladder.

"Trouble, Cap'in?" Henry asked as he joined him at the railing.

He looked out on the water at the rowboat's progress that bore Jacqueline back to shore. "Should Mrs. Rudman return, deny her access to the Caroline, Henry. She's no longer welcome on board."

Henry started to smile then caught himself and bobbed his head instead. "Aye, Cap'in."

He backed down the ladder, his thoughts already focused on the journey ahead. He had perhaps a day to reach Katherine before the murderers took the bait.

CHAPTER 18

Darkness pressed in on Katherine, weighted by the heavy sound of her breathing and the frantic beat of her heart. She scratched at the surface of the door searching for the latch to open it. The wood peeled away in splinters, piercing her palms and making them slick with blood. Low mewing came from the other side of the panel and she called out to her mother and brother.

A dull metallic gleam caught her eye. Her fingers traced the shape of the object. Nails poked along the edge of the door digging into her fingers, and she jerked her hand back.

The groans grew weaker. She was suddenly overwhelmed by a feverish desperation to reach what lay behind the door. Katherine shoved against the portal unmindful of the spikes that poked her flesh and tore wounds into her arms and sides.

The door popped open so suddenly she staggered and nearly fell down the long flight of stairs that stretched before her. Fear of what lay below held her suspended on the edge. A tormented moan called to her. Compelled to follow the sound, she ran down the steep flight.

She burst from the stairwell into a pale golden circle of light, barren and cold. Johnny, his chest bloody, lay crumpled at her feet, his eyes staring sightlessly up at her. A primal sound of grief tore from her throat, but was lost in the sound of howling behind her. Fear lanced through her lightning quick, stealing her breath. She jerked around. A pack of Wolves, ten in all stood behind her. Their eyes glowed, lit from within by an unholy fire. Their movements stealthy, their fangs bared, they began to spread out to encircle her. Katherine shuffled backwards, her limbs nearly frozen with fear. A large beast, twice the size of the rest, inched forward, his gaze intent upon her, his body tensed to spring.

She turned and ran into the darkness. Brush tore at

her clothing and hair as she pushed through the waist-high brambles that blocked her way. The animals' baying grew louder, their hot breath nipping at her heels. Wild with fear, Katherine broke free of the underbrush into a clearing.

The hard crushing weight of something large hit her from the side knocking her to the ground. She screamed as white fangs, dripping with saliva gleamed above her, snapping at her face. She gripped the fur on either side of the animal's head to hold him at bay. He shook his head, twisting from her grasp. His teeth sank into her arm, tearing at her flesh. Pain arched through her as blood, coppery and hot, splattered her cheek and jaw, the salty taste of it permeating her mouth. She threw up an arm to shield her face as he lunged forward and ripped into her throat, cutting off her guttural cries in midstream.

Suddenly the wolf was not a wolf at all, but a man, his face young, his features hard and cruel. The blood that soaked the ground glowed silver, then blue and became a scarf. He pulled it tighter and tighter about her throat, blocking her air, crushing her windpipe.

Katherine woke to the harsh gasping sound of her own breathing. Her hands clawed at her throat tearing at empty air as she surged to a seated position. Her sleep-clogged mind began to clear and a sob of relief bubbled up from her fear-parched throat. Her limbs felt weak and rubbery. The linen sheets, twisted about her, were clammy with sweat. She reached for Matthew, needing his presence to reassure her. The bed beside her was empty. For a moment, overwhelming loneliness compounded her response to the dream.

She pressed her face against her up-drawn knees. Seeing her brother's blood soaked body and empty eyes each time the dream came to her, was almost more than she could bear. She experienced the crushing loss as though it had just happened. For months, she had been plagued by the images. Not just of Johnny, but of her mother, her father, and James, their driver. It always ended in her running from the killers and being caught and brutalized.

Anger so deep it made her chest feel tight, brought a heated flush to her skin. It overpowered the soul shaking terror of only moments before and replaced it with a strong resolve. She was through running. She'd had enough of being afraid.

Untangling herself from the bedclothes, she rolled to her feet and reached for the butt of the flintlock pistol on the bedside commode. She crossed to the window and looked out.

"Come get me, damn you," she challenged.

Frost coated the rolling contours of the grounds. The reflective light of a new dawn etched the surface of the paddock railings with silver. Though the stables stood in shadow, she could see the doors stood wide, an open maw waiting to conceal anyone who stepped through. It could harbor any number of attackers.

She frowned, annoyed. She had asked for the doors to be closed and secured just for that reason. It was too late to do anything about it now. Setting aside the flintlock, she reached for the discarded gown at the foot of her bed.

The fragile light of a single candle lit her way as she traversed the long hall to the gallery just above the front stairs. She left the taper upon a table in the entryway hall and let herself out. Sunrise was only moments away. The air felt icy and looked achingly clear. Folding her cloak closer about her, Katherine paused to listen to the crisp silence, her breath shooting white plumes of steam into the air. The grass beneath her feet made a brittle crunch as she walked across the slopping front lawn to the stables.

Outside the building, she hesitated and listened for any unfamiliar sound. A bay colored horse with a white blaze poked an inquisitive head over a stall door and nickered to her. She entered the structure and paused beside the animal to rub its velvety nose and pat its neck.

Sultan neighed from the other end of the building, the shape of his head midnight dark in the shadows. Katherine hesitated just out of reach of the darkness. A feeling of breathlessness seized her, the low ceiling and wooden walls of the stalls closing in around her. She tried to step forward, but her legs felt too heavy to move.

Sultan stomped his hooves and called out, the sound loud and shrill in the enclosed space. Katherine drew a deep breath and closed her eyes. She rested a hand upon the stall door, grounding herself. The walls were not creeping closer. The ceiling was not going to fall. The dark was not going to reach out to smother her.

It was time to return to some sense of normalcy, to reclaim her life. In the past, it had been her habit to come to the stables and see Sultan every morning. She could do it again. It would actually be no worse than going into the prison.

The thought brought Matthew to mind. She had tried to avoid thinking about him but again and again, he crept back into her thoughts. She wondered how he had felt about the letter she had left for him, explaining her reasons for leaving, and apologizing for having to do so. He would understand. She hoped her absence did not cause him trouble with Edward or Lord Rudman.

With something else to focus on, her anxiety began to ease, and she moved slowly down the stable's wide central aisle, pausing to stroke or pat each occupant who thrust a head out. Katherine hurried past the gaping blackness of a couple of empty stalls.

She sensed movement behind her and swung to face it bringing up the flintlock she clutched in her right hand. Strong fingers grasped her wrist in a hold too strong to break aiming the pistol downward. Katherine jerked back in panicked surprise and lost her footing. A strangled yelp was torn from her as she stumbled backwards, the momentum of her fall encouraged by the pressure of a large masculine form forcing her back into the darkness of an open stall. The flintlock flipped end over end off into a corner. She landed in the thick hay, the hard masculine planes of the man's body tangled with her own. She raised her knee, her intent vicious, and made glancing contact with the man's thigh.

"I'm finding your penchant for trying to shoot me or unman me annoying, Mrs. Hamilton."

"Matthew—" His deep voice, so devastatingly familiar, caught at her thundering heart, and her limbs went weak with relief. Just as quickly, her temper flared. "What the blazes do you think you are doing? You scared me half witless."

He smelled of outdoors, horses, and sweat. The masculine contours of his body adhered to her feminine form in a way she found too disturbing to ponder. The stall was so dark that she could not see his features, but could make out the silhouette of his head and shoulders looming over her.

She attempted to free the hand tangled in her cloak and realized how helpless she was with his fingers still looped around her wrist holding the other down as well. "Let me rise, Matthew."

"When I'm ready."

His implacable tone sent a jolt of anxiety through her. She realized the quiet even timber of his tone was deceptive. Without being able to see his expression, she couldn't judge his emotional state, but obviously he was upset.

"Coming out here without escort, under the circumstances, was dangerous and foolish. Had I been the man you depicted in the bills you had posted, you would now be dead."

Unable to argue against the truth, she turned aside the comment by saying, "I am sure you did not ride all this way to lecture me on caution."

"No, I didn't. I rode all this way because I don't intend to bury another wife, regardless of the fact that you're a lying, sneaky, manipulative bit of fluff who needs her backside blistered with the flat of my hand."

She caught her breath and fought against the instinctive desire to struggle against his greater strength. She knew from experience how easy it was to provoke a man already angered. "I expected that you would be annoyed because I left, but I thought it would be better for you, your aunt, and uncle if I distanced myself from you. I explained all that in the letter."

As Matthew shifted above her, Katherine grew more aware of the intimacy lent to their positions by the darkness of the stall. The bold masculine lines of his body fit with hers like two links in a chain, his thigh resting between hers, the heat and shape of his male member pressing against her hip. Her heart began to thunder anew as a familiar tempting heat pooled between her thighs. Her lower limbs began to tremble.

Inexplicably, Matthew pushed up and off her drawing her to her feet as he stood up. Shackling her wrist with his fingers, he pulled her out of the stall to the open door. His jaw was covered by a heavy growth of beard, his clothing wrinkled and coated with dust. Travel weary and dirty, he was heart-stoppingly handsome despite the angry scowl that marred his features. He turned to face her, the movement aggressive enough that she took a step back.

"I warned you once that should you ever put yourself in harm's way on purpose that I would lock you up. Do you remember my saying that, Katherine? Do you really think I don't know what you're doing here?" His fingers tightened about her wrist and he gave her a shake.

"You have no right."

"Oh yes I have, *Mrs. Hamilton.* We have consummated our marriage and as of two nights ago you are physically, officially, and morally *my wife.* You may even now be carrying my child, or has that possibility just slipped your mind?" His blue gaze bore into hers, his brows clapped together in a frown that grew more harshly intimidating by the moment.

She forced her chin up though her lips trembled with a combination of guilt and anger. "Yes, it occurred to me, but I mean to stand by the original agreement, regardless. You do not want a wife anymore than I want to be one." She jerked her arm free of his grasp. "Go back to London; I do not want you here." She turned and stormed away from him, so frustrated and angry, she was afraid she might resort to scratching, kicking, and biting at any moment.

The weight of his angry footsteps behind her made her want to break into a run, but she fought the impulse. Never again would she be intimidated by a man's anger.

She reached the front of the house before he snagged her arm just above the elbow and jerked her to a stop. They both froze at the loud clinking sound of a firearm being cocked.

"Are you all right, Lady Katherine?" a man asked from just beyond the corner of the house.

Katherine focused on Matthew's face, dark with anger. "Yes, I am fine, William."

In an attempt to smother her own frustration and bring a more amiable clime between them, she turned to introduce the two men. "Matthew, this is William our coachman. William, Captain Matthew Hamilton—my husband."

William tipped the barrel of the weapon skyward and approached them with the blunderbuss resting against his hip, his finger still on the trigger. He eyed Matthew with more than a little distrust. "There was a disturbance down the hill a ways. Rory and I left for just a moment to see what or who was about."

"You were gone long enough for me to stable my horse and for Katherine to come down to greet me. Is it just the two of you guarding the house?" Matthew asked.

William's gaze shifted to her, and she gave a brief nod. He turned his attention back to Matthew. "There are ten of us. We're taking it in shifts."

She saw Matthew's jaw tense as he absorbed the information. He turned a looked of amazed disbelief upon her and shook his head. He drew a deep breath in an obvious bid to control his temper. "My men will be arriving later in the day. There are an even dozen of them, all armed."

A sharp crack sounded from down the hill and chunks of masonry from the corner of the house splattered outward just above Katherine's head. Matthew shoved her to the ground and covered her body with his own. "Crawl," he ordered. "Get in the house."

She struggled with her skirts but managed to make it to the front door. William waited for them there. Stretching his arm upward, William turned the knob and opened the portal. He motioned Katherine in ahead of him and she rushed to comply.

Matthew pulled the door shut behind them and leaned back against the wall to avoid the windows on each side. "They were hoping for a lucky shot and almost found it." His pale blue eyes fairly blazed as they settled on Katherine's face.

"Anyone hit?" called a voice from the stairs. A man appeared from the second floor landing pulling on a shirt, his carrot red hair disheveled, his suspenders hanging around his hips.

"No, Franklin. We're still in one piece," William yelled back. "There'll be two coaches coming. 'Twill be help coming to join us. Pass the word."

"Aye,sir."

William passed Matthew a pistol. Matthew nodded his thanks. "I left mine in the stables."

Katherine felt naked and helpless without a weapon of her own to make her feel in control. Time stretched as they waited for a barrage of fire. After ten minutes passed, Matthew got to his feet careful to stay clear of the windows.

She took the hand he offered to help her up then bent to brush the dirt from her skirts to hide the fact that she was shaking. She straightened her shoulders in an attempt to project more confidence than she truly felt and pushed impatiently at a curl on her forehead. "I will make some tea and start breakfast. The men will be hungry. I imagine you are too, after riding all this way." She felt Matthew's gaze boring a hole between her shoulder blades as she walked away from them.

Matthew stared after her for a moment then shook his head, part in amazement and part in admiration.

"Lady Katherine has more steel in her backbone than any man I know." William spoke from beside him.

Matthew glanced at the man. "She'd better have. She'll need it before this is over."

CHAPTER 19

Matthew wiped the streaks of dirt from his face with a linen handkerchief. The time he and five of the men had taken to circle the grounds and look for the shooter had been well spent. "They've pulled back for now, but it won't last long. We don't have much time to secure the house and grounds. Is there any place we may hide the horses and coaches when they arrive?" Matthew asked. "The first thing they'll do is cut us off from them."

"We can hide them on one of the tenant farms, but we'll have to keep at least a few horses in order to reach them quickly. The Cooper's and Sunderland's farms would be the closest." William pointed at two areas on the rough map he had drawn.

The man had been agreeable to everything Matthew had suggested thus far, but it didn't escape his notice that the deference William had shown Katherine was conspicuously missing.

"Keep the tack in the house and turn the horses out in one of the pastures. Better to have to run them down than to have them burnt alive if they set fire to the stables."

"Yes, sir."

The "sir" was offered more from habit than respect. Matthew pushed back a feeling of irritation and concentrated on the task at hand. It didn't matter as long as they could pull together when needed.

"Your men are more experienced with the animals than mine. I'll trust you'll see to this."

"Yes, sir."

"As much as the kitchen needs the light, I don't like that open bank of windows at the back of the house. We'll have to find something to cover them that won't appear too conspicuous. Have you any ideas?"

William shook his head.

"I 'ave a idea," one of the men said.

Matthew turned. With the exception of himself, the man standing close to the fireplace towered at least a head above everyone in the room. His shoulders and chest looked thick with muscle beneath the rough fabric of his coat.

"Andy, isn't it?"

The man removed his cap as he stepped forward. "Aye, sir."

"How do you propose they might be secured?"

"Interior shutters can be built, to secure them from the inside. 'Twon't look pretty, and they won't protect the glass from bein' broke, but they can be removed when the trouble's past."

He nodded. "Can you do it?"

"Aye, sir, but I'll need materials and tools."

"We've tools and lumber enough to see to it. I'll show you where they are," William said.

"See to it Andy."

"Aye, sir."

"Then that should do it for now." At his nod all the men, but William and two others, began filtering out to assume their duties.

Matthew stood at ease against the desk behind him. "Please close the door behind you, Andy," he said as the last of the men exited the room. The man flipped his cap back on his head and swung the portal shut.

William stepped forward, his gaze serious. "James the driver killed that night, was my brother. I mean to see justice is done for him." William rested his hands on his hips, defiance in his stance. "I'm here for Lady Katherine's sake as well. She put herself between me and her father from time to time in the past as did her mother and brother. I'll do whatever I can to protect her."

Matthew folded his arms across his chest. "I appreciate that. Katherine's health and safety are of the utmost importance to me." He purposely aligned his features into lines of control as the cold wave of anger he had held in check since learning William was responsible for bringing Katherine here came crashing to the fore. "Should you ever transport my wife from beneath my protection again, without my knowledge or my orders, there won't be a force on earth that will keep you safe from me."

William's fair skin flushed bright red. He opened his mouth to speak only to close it. The movement of his two companions behind him had him raising his hand to stay them. "You have a valid point, sir. Had it been my wife or daughter, I'd be angry as well. It won't happen again."

Matthew continued to study the man's features for a moment. William's gaze remained steadily on his. Certain as he could be of the man's sincerity, Matthew nodded. "My uncle, Lord Willingham, is doing all he can to call attention to this matter in London. Hopefully it will do some good."

"Hopefully, sir."

"I'm committed to seeing this through, William, for my wife's sake. But I can only spare three days here. I have to return to London, and Katherine is returning with me." Even if he had to tie her up and bodily carry her and put her in the coach.

William nodded, his lips twitching as though he read his thoughts.

"Lady Katherine is used to finding ways to accomplish things she feels are important," he said.

Matthew's brows rose at the diplomatic way the man expressed Katherine's actions to date. "Since you are aware of my wife's habits, I'll depend on you to help me see she doesn't put herself in any more danger than she has already."

William grinned. "Yes, sir."

****

Matthew surreptitiously watched Katherine as she loaded and checked the priming of the weapons lined up on the dining room table. He hadn't thought to find her working at such a task or that she would be so proficient at it. Every time he thought he had begun to know her, she surprised him. Edward said she was a marksman, or rather, a markswoman. He wondered how good her aim might be.

"I thought there might be a call for extra weapons." Her violet gaze fastened on him at the door. "These were my brother's. I suppose they belong to Edward now, but since we will be defending his house I am sure he won't begrudge us their use."

"Does Edward even know how to shoot?"

"I do not know. As foppish as he may be, sometimes I think there may be more going on inside his head than just the cut of his jacket and the knot in his stock."

"How to count his money?"

She nodded. "That too."

The quickness of her answer had him smiling.

"I need help preparing the rooms upstairs for your men, Matthew."

"Lead on, I'm free at the moment."

The hollow echo of their shoes against the marble floors sounded loud in the silence. The hall opened to the left into a wide staircase that climbed upward to a gallery that swung both right and left. The polished wood of banisters and floor shined in the meager light cast by the oil lamp that sat upon a table in the hall. He paused to admire the style and grace of the architecture.

"I have been cleaning a little on my own since I arrived, but most of the rooms still have covers on the furniture." Katherine paused by the table to light another lamp.

"Do you have any idea what you're inviting by coming here like this, Katherine?"

"Yes, I know. I left Willingham's to spare you and your family any involvement in this. Why did you feel you had to follow me?"Because duty and honor and something else he wasn't quite ready to admit to her or himself had demanded it. "You're my wife."

"No, I am not." She stopped and turned to face him. The golden glow of the lamp she held added warmth to her pale skin and set to light the coppery curls that had escaped her braid. "Just because we shared a moment of passion does not mean we are man and wife. You married me to escape prison and to get your ship back. I married you to escape Edward. I do not expect you to defend my honor or my life. Go back to London, get on your ship, and sail back to your family. Go with my blessing. I do not want you here." She swung away from him and continued down the hallway.

He followed unwilling to believe she didn't want his help, didn't want him. The latter thought stung deeper than the first. He was used to getting any woman he wanted. He found it insulting to be dismissed with such resolve by his wife.

"To leave now would be as dangerous as it is to stay, Katherine. I won't leave here without you."

She stopped, her hand resting upon the mahogany banister. He watched her throat work as she swallowed. Her eyes looked suspiciously bright as she looked over her shoulder at him. "I did not want you involved in this, Matthew."

"I already am. Lord Harcourt was offering you his help, Katherine. Talbot and I were both committed to protecting you and helping in any way we could. "Why couldn't you be patient?"

"I have been patient for nearly four months. I needed an end to it." Her voice cracked with emotion, and she turned away and climbed the stairs.

They turned right at the top. Their footsteps sounded muffled as they followed the thick maroon runner down the hall.

"I will try to find you another shirt, and I will brush your coat to remove the dust. I am afraid there is nothing here quite big enough to fit you."

He found the way she mixed caring for his comforts while encouraging him to leave confusing, but hopeful.

She pushed open the first door on the right. "This is my father's room." The heavy canopied bed set against one wall dominated the room. Dark brocade fabric draped across the top and down each post. The curtains, made of the same fabric, were drawn against the afternoon sun. No fire had been laid and the room was chilly.

Noticing his interest she said, "He liked to have the light blocked out when first he awoke."

Had her father been a mean drunk and meaner when suffering from a hangover?

She squatted to open the bottom drawer of a tall chest. "His shirts will probably be tight across the shoulders and chest, but will do until yours can be washed."

He shook free of the dark blue wool long coat and handed it over to her. "So once again I'm coated in dirt." He grimaced as he unwound the stock from around his throat. He shook out the fabric sending a cloud of fine particles into the air.

"I promise not to begrudge you a sliver of soap or a bucket of water." She brushed the fabric of his coat vigorously. She went still and her deep violet gaze rose to his face wide with apology.

He smiled to put her at ease. "Your expression at the wedding was—memorable."

"I worried that morning that I wouldn't know you at the church without your beard. You looked such a bear with it."

"A tamed bear," He said bitterness rising in him.

"Not tamed." She shook her head. "Your willingness to engage Mr. Hicks in battle negated that."

He raised a brow, surprised at her astuteness in reading the situation.

"When men gain a little power, they immediately abuse those beneath their control," she said.

"Not always, Katherine."

Her quick return to the task at hand expressed her uncertainty more profoundly than words. She flipped the heavy braid of auburn hair over her shoulder drawing his attention to it. Her hair's natural curl feathered soft rings about her face and against her neck while the rest struggled against the weave of the braid. The lamplight shot copper through the rich wine color. He controlled the urge to release the ribbon that held it prisoner and rake his fingers through it. He knew its texture would be slightly course, each strand warm with light and life.

Her cheeks, flushed deep rose by the chilled moist air trapped inside the room, looked creamy smooth. He remembered the warm satin of her skin beneath his touch. He wanted to lift her into his arms, carry her to the bed, and settle things between them in a more physical manner.

He turned aside to hide the discomfort of his arousal from Katherine and moved to the wash stand in the corner. The pitcher was dry.

"You will have to wash in my room. The fire is lit, and I brought water up last night."

After her adamancy only minutes before, he was surprised by her willingness to share her room with him. Perhaps she was as confused by her feelings about him as he was about his for her. He hoped so.

"You know there's no way ten men can defend this house successfully."

"I know."

Her soft agreement had him turning to face her. "Then why?"

Her gaze dropped from his face and settled upon the floor. "I will not run and hide from them any more. If they must come, it will be here, on my terms."

He felt a hollow feeling beneath his ribs. What she spoke of was a last stand.

He studied the resolve in her expression, in the set of her shoulders, and her stance. He had to admire her courage and determination, but he also had no intention of seeing her dead or brutalized like her mother. "In that case, the sooner my men join us, the sooner we can take care of this—inconvenience," he said. "They should arrive before dark."

"Then, we have little time to prepare their rooms."

A sudden idea struck him as they left the room and continued down the hall. "It wasn't you who put the blood upon the sheets that morning."

She hesitated so long he knew she was picking her words carefully.

Before she could formulate an answer he said, "It was Hannah."

She lifted one shoulder in a dismissive shrug. "She was trying to protect me."

"And you took the blame on yourself. Are you always so protective of the people you care about?"

Her eyes wide and dark touched his face briefly then skittered away. Her features settled into the taut lines of composure he had learned hid her strongest emotions.

As he followed her into her room, he struggled to suppress the smile of relief that threatened to break out. She had left London to protect him because she cared for him, not because she didn't. He was certain of it. Now all he had to do was get her to admit it.

CHAPTER 20

Katherine shifted upon the high backed chair. The musket she held lay heavy in her hands. A faint smell of oil and gunpowder emanated from the weapon. The firearm offered her some sense of protection, but didn't ease the anxiety that tightened her muscles and made her feel slightly nauseous.

The one brief, hard kiss Matthew had given her before slipping out the back door of the house now seemed paltry and did nothing to ease her fears. One kiss, one touch, would never be enough should something happen to him.

"Please let him be all right," she whispered for the hundredth time since he had left before dark with two other men to flag down the coaches and prevent them from driving up to the house. A hundred different disastrous possibilities had gone through her mind since—one being that his own men could shoot him by accident.

"There's movement."

She recognized William's voice from the back of the house and had to force herself to remain where she was. She could not leave her post in case they chose that moment to attack. It took all her self-control not to leap to her feet and run to the back of the house.

"There's the signal. Hold your fire," William yelled. The words passed through the house in a haphazard echo.

A sudden barrage of gunfire sounded from the back of the house. She ran to her position at one side of the window to peek out. Pitch-blackness reflected back at her. The clouds had covered what little moonlight there was. She could see nothing but black on black shapes.

She couldn't just sit and not know what was happening. "Andy?"

"Aye, Lady Katherine." His voice came from across the hall.

"Can you take my place here? I want to go upstairs to the second floor."

"Aye, Lady Katherine."

She waited until he was in place. Taking her musket and pistol, she ran up the stairs.

Two men came out into the hallway at her shout. "They're pinned down, Lady Katherine. We can't see anythin'," one complained. "Should we fire, we might hit one of our own."

Having her fears realized paralyzed Katherine. Light—light—they needed some kind of light. "One of you, come with me." She rushed down the hall to the third floor stairs. She was breathing hard, her heart galloping wildly as she turned at the landing and moved on to the end of the hall to another flight.

Reaching the top of the narrow steps leading to the attic, she jerked the door open. Cold moist air crept out like fingers clawing at her shoulders and arms. The darkness appeared so thick it seemed to have texture. Her breath caught as a wave of claustrophobic anxiety glued her feet to floor just outside the doorway. Her limbs felt leaden. Each breath felt weighted and hard to draw.

The sound of a moan carried to her from the darkness. "Momma?" she breathed. The sound of her mother crying and pleading came back to her and she shuddered. She fought against the feeling that should she take a step forward, the blackness would swallow her.

"I'll get a lamp from the hall table." Franklin's voice sounded far away, the rapid tattoo of his footsteps as he leaped down the short flight of stairs and ran down the hall, a distant pattering.

She leaned against the door facing and closed her eyes against the opaque curtain before her. Johnny's skin glowed white in the lantern light, his blood spread in a rusty pool beneath him. She forced her gaze away from her brother's body lying at the bottom of the coach steps. Horses and men were clumped together, their faces blurred ovals without features. She had to remember. She tried to focus on the face closest to her.

"Here, Lady Katherine." Franklin took the flintlock pistol she held and pressed a small oil lamp into her hand.

His action broke her concentration. There was no time for this. Shaking, she raised the lamp high and stepped into the attic. The light, as feeble as it was, held back the darkness. She forced her feet forward, her thoughts on Matthew and the men with him. Trunks lined the walls of the room. Setting aside her weapons, she opened first one, then another, slamming the lids down when she didn't find what she sought.

Swinging up the lid of the third trunk, she spied the cylindrical tubes. She stuffed two into Franklin's arms and hefted two herself.

"What are these things?" he yelled as they ran down the stairs.

"Fireworks."

****

Matthew ducked as another shot cut through the brush and plowed into the dirt in front of him. He swore beneath his breath. They couldn't go forward, and they couldn't turn back. The highwaymen had them caught in a crossfire. If someone didn't do something soon, they would be cut to ribbons.

A muffled moan sounded from the man at his right. He reached out a hand to touch his arm. "Where are you hit Jackson?"

"My leg. I'll never be able to run, sir."

"Then, I guess I'll have to carry you."

"If you see a chance to make it to the house, take it, sir."

A high-pitched whistle sounded from above. An explosion overhead had Matthew ducking closer to the ground. Light spilled down over him. He looked up as bright orange sparks lit the sky and bathed the group in a yellowish glow. A loud concentrated barrage of gunfire came from every window of the house in front of them. The smell of burnt powder hung thick in the air as clouds of smoke drifted on the breeze.

With a shout, he jumped to his feet. "Run for the house, men. They're covering us." Thrusting his musket into the injured man's hand, he levered Jackson to his feet, and bent to heft him over his shoulder as another round of fire came from the house.

Lead shot pinged through the brush at his right. He

ran for all he was worth, the weight of the man he carried throwing off his balance and making each step a struggle. The overhead light faded quickly. Matthew waited to feel the bite of a lead ball ripping through his back.

A bright yellow glow of an oil lamp outlined an open doorway as he reached the back of the house. Brick particles exploded outward as a shot hit the wall just inches from his head. He felt the slight sting as tiny bits of masonry splattered his neck. He leaped through the door and dodged to the right out of the way of the men who followed him. Breathing hard, he lowered Jackson to the floor and turned to check the rest of his men. A quick head count reassured him they had left behind no one. One man's arm was bleeding and another was already ripping open the sleeve to check the injury.

"Webster, there are loaded weapons and shot on the dining room table one door down to the right. Distribute them to the men and spread out through the house."

"Aye, Cap'in."

He bent to see to Jackson. The man had been hit in the thigh. The ball had traveled through the muscle and out the other side. Meaty flesh showed from the hole in his breeches. As long as fabric hadn't been carried into the wound, he'd have a chance to heal. Despite the blood, Matthew inspected the breeches for missing pieces. A semicircle of fabric held by a thread dangled from the edge of the opening. He fit it together.

"It's all there, Jackson. There's no cloth in the wound."

"Praise be, sir," the man said through gritted teeth.

Taking a knife from his boot, Matthew cut open the leg of the garment to expose the wound. He caught a glimpse of Franklin's bright red hair as he appeared at his side with a bowl of water.

"Where the blazes did you get fireworks?" he asked as he glanced up. He shook free of his coat and ripped free the sleeve of his shirt to make a temporary bandage for Jackson's leg. He rinsed away the blood from the wound and inspected the injury more closely.

"Lady Katherine got them from the attic. Her brother, John, saw fireworks on one of their outings to London and purchased a few. Master John had a liking for anythin' to do with powder or shot."

"The more I hear about my wife's brother, the more I'm certain I would have liked him a great deal."

"I'm sure he would have liked you as well." Katherine's voice, slightly breathless, came from behind him.

He glanced up in time to catch the movement of her eyes as she ran them downward in a quick inspection, searching for wounds.

"Your neck is bleeding," she said, her features carefully composed as she set aside her weapon and kneeled beside him. Her hands shook, belying her outward calm as she gave the wound a quick inspection.

"It's just a nick from a bit of brick. Jackson's in worse shape than I."

Her dark violet eyes looked almost black against the paleness of her skin. She smelled of spent powder and smoke. Bits of hair had escaped her braid to hang in spirals on either side of her face. She had never seemed as beautiful to him as she did in that moment.

She nodded, her attention swinging to the man on the floor. "Franklin, clean and bandage the Captain's neck while I see to this man."

"Yes, Lady Katherine."

Matthew caught Jackson's attention focused on Katherine's face as he got to his feet and a quick wry smile twisted his lips. Even though he was injured and in pain, she had managed to capture the man's attention enough to distract him.

****

Katherine pressed the sleeve Matthew had torn from his shirt to the man's wound to staunch the worst of the bleeding. She shoved aside the spent weapons the man still held and guided his hand over the bandage. "Hold tight to that while I wash my hands."

She rushed to pump more water and quickly scrubbed her hands clean of powder and grime. The action gave her time to gather her scattered wits and shaky emotions. Thank God, thank God, Matthew was all right.

When she returned to the bleeding man on the floor, she was able to offer him a calm façade and a reassuring smile. "What's your name?" she asked as she began to clean away the blood and gore from the wound.

"Jackson, ma'am. Jerome Jackson."

"Your accent sounds close to my husband's, Mr. Jackson."

"My husband" the words reverberated through her mind. She couldn't allow herself to think how close Matthew had come to being killed. She focused on the young man before her. His dark brows scrunched together in a frown of pain and his teeth clenched against it, his bush of black, curly hair fanned out about his face.

"You're in good hands, Jackson," Matthew said from her right.

"Aye, sir."

Matthew laid a hand on her shoulder for a brief moment. She fought against the quick tears of relief that stung her eyes.

Sporadic fire from upstairs served to remind her of the threat outside. There were twenty-three men standing between her and that threat, but nothing standing between them and the men determined to kill them all.

Matthew left with William. She forced her attention back to Jackson. "Are you from Charleston, too?"

"Yes, ma'am."

She kept him talking as she cleaned the wound and staunched most of the bleeding. "I'll have to bind this, Mr. Jackson."

"Yes, ma'am." He nodded.

She called to one of the men to stay with Jackson. Instructing him to keep pressure on the wound, she ran up the servant's stairs to retrieve some fabric from her sewing basket. Once again, the darkness held her back. She waited for the sound of her mother's voice, but all was quiet. Forcing herself to step over the threshold, she left the door open behind her. She had just enough light from the hallway to see what she was looking for. Basket in hand, she paused sensing something was wrong.

Quiet had settled over the house. The firing had stopped. Relief flowed through her. Perhaps they had gone. If they had, what then? She didn't want to think about it. She could not protect the men who were here. She could not even protect herself. She had been an idealistic fool spouting on about justice when what she had really wanted was revenge. And it wasn't she who was paying for it, but Matthew and the men. It wasn't worth anyone else dying. Why hadn't she realized that before it was too late?

CHAPTER 21

Matthew watched as Katherine circulated from man to man pouring them tea from a pot that looked too big for her to lift. From a basket, she produced bread with thick slices of ham wedged between. He remembered a time when his mother had done the same for men on the front line. No doubt, she would have found a kinship with the woman he had married. She had done him proud tonight in front of his men, had done herself proud.

He rose from his position at one of the windows to join her. The soft candlelight etched the side of her face with light and touched her hair with copper highlights. Grabbing the cloth she had used to handle the kettle, he lifted it from the floor.

She turned to look up at him. "I can get it."

"I'm sure you can, but everything is quiet for the moment. I don't mind helping."

"I only have the men upstairs to see to."

"Lead on, Mrs. Hamilton."

Her gaze rested on him for a moment before she turned to do as he suggested.

"Jackson said he was feeling much better."

"Good." Her throat worked as she swallowed, her eyes glowed suspiciously bright. "He'll have to be still otherwise, he'll start bleeding again."

"He seems to be doing well. As long as the wound doesn't fester, he'll heal."

"I hope so. 'Twas lucky the shot didn't hit the bone, or 'twould be a different story."

They paused outside one of the bedrooms not as well lit as the rooms downstairs. He watched her as she braced herself to enter the room.

"The space is not close, Katherine."

"I know. 'Tis the darkness that makes it seem so."

"You weren't afraid at Willingham's."

"You were there in the dark with me."

"I still am."

Her eyes looked so deep a violet they appeared almost black as she looked up at him. "I wish you weren't," she said, her voice nearly a whisper.

For countless moments, the hallway receded as their gazes met. Each breath she drew, he seemed to draw in sync. The touch of her hand against his cheek, the look on her face of emotions, unhampered by control, brought him a sense of hope. Then, she turned away to lead the way down the hall but he felt more encouraged than rebuffed.

They worked as a team serving the men tea and the food she had prepared. On the third floor, he retrieved the weapons she had left in the attic while she extinguished the oil lamps.

On the second floor, he tugged her into her bedroom where a fire and a lit candle had been left burning. "I thought we could share what was left of the tea and the food." Setting aside the guns and pot he still carried, he went to the basin to wash his hands. By the time he had dried them, she had poured him a cup of tea and set out thick slices of bread and ham on a cloth before the hearth. He placed another log on the fire to chase away the chill and settled there with her.

They ate in silence for a moment. "Will you tell me about your little girl?" she asked, surprising him.

He broke off a crust of bread and chewed it as he compiled his answer. "When Emily was born and Caroline died, for a time it was difficult for me to look at her. Even as a baby, she looked just like her mother." He chewed slowly for a moment. "Of late, I've realized she has a great deal of me in her as well. She has a stubborn streak that runs bone deep. She's been allowed to do as she pleases. She can twist her uncles around her little finger."

"And her father as well?" "Not as much, but yes, she has a way about her. It's difficult for me to be harsh with her, since I feel her behavior is partially my own fault. Because I've been gone a great deal, she and I haven't exactly reached an understanding of who's in charge yet."

She smiled.

"In fact, she reminds me of you."

One well-arched auburn brow rose in reaction to his observation. "You're not in charge of me."

"You couldn't have made that clearer than when you left a note behind and expected me to let you go."

She looked away.

"I'd have been here sooner, but I had to go to the Caroline, find my purser, and turn everything over to him."

"I'm sorry for inconveniencing you." She bundled up the bread left over and put it back in the basket.

"I have less than a fortnight, Katherine. I have to leave England."

"You should have stayed in London. You could already have been on your way back to your family."

When she started to rise, he grasped her wrists, stilling her movements. "You don't know about Rudman's edict, do you?"

She looked up, her brows furrowed with a frown. She shook her head. "What edict?"

"I have to be away before the fortnight. If not, he has threatened to have me thrown back in that hell hole again."

Her lips parted in surprise. "He can't do that. You haven't done anything."

"That didn't stop him the first time."

She jerked her hands away and scrambled to her feet. "Damn him, and damn Edward for not telling me." She snatched up the basket and swung it as though she wanted to throw it.

He got to his feet. "Would it have made any difference?" he asked, searching her face.

For a moment she remained silent, her mouth softly parted. The struggle she felt was, for once, plain on her face.

He decided he didn't want to hear her answer. His mouth swooped down to cover hers. She tasted of tea and ham, sweet and salty, and smelled like a blend of flowers and gunpowder. He wanted to revel in that fragrance, in her taste. Though her lips parted beneath the pressure of his, she held herself apart from him, the basket clutched in her hand. Matthew broke the contact long enough to wrestle the thing from her and set it aside.

His hand trailed down her back molding her more tightly against him. The full thrust of her breasts pressed

187

into his ribs. The tightening pull of arousal shifted into a full-fledged need. He wrapped her braid around his hand to pull her head back and find, with his lips, the throbbing heartbeat at its base. Her skin pulsed with warmth and life. He wanted to taste it, all of it.

He cupped the weight of her breast, and through the fabric, rubbed the nipple already beaded there. Her hand covered his. "We cannot, Matthew." Her voice sounded breathy and weak. He could feel her trembling.

She shivered as he traced her ear with his tongue. "There are a hundred different things we can do, all of them pleasurable, Katherine."

His mouth caught hers in a blatant seduction, his tongue tempting hers to respond and when she finally did, he groaned in relief. She belonged to him. It was up to him to prove it to her.

The laces at the front of her plain, gray gown gave way with a quick tug. The sleeves of her gown fell down her shoulders, opening the modest neckline of the garment to him. The soft weight of her breast in his hand, and the responsive curl of her fingers around the back of his neck, felt more a victory than any battle he had ever fought.

She pulled the black ribbon loose to free his hair and ran her fingers through to caress the nape of his neck. He ran a hand into the bodice of her gown to caress the pale soft skin open to him. The touch of her tongue against his fired his blood. He cupped her buttocks to lift her against him and felt her hips tilt against the hard ridge of his erection as her arms went around his neck.

The bed seemed too far away as the thrust and parry of their tongues became torpid and hot. She pulled and tugged at the ill-fitting shirt until she parted it to run eager hands over his chest and back. Matthew managed to bare her breasts, though her stays prevented him from uncovering more. Responsive to his every touch she rubbed the rigid peeks against his chest, her skin like warm silk against his. Blood pooled in his groin making him throb with need. He groaned as he bunched the material of her gown upward and lifted her off her feet.

She put her legs around his waist. Her mouth moist, and hot, fastened onto his shoulder, and she sucked. He nearly lost his footing as thoughts of her doing that to his distended member turned his legs to water. He staggered to the bed and fell across it with her beneath him.

He buried his face against her breasts, breathing in her scent. His mouth latched onto one pebble hard nipple as his fingers found the wet open heat between her legs. He shoved the bundled fabric of her gown up around her waist baring the lower half of her body. As he slid downward, his feet found purchase upon the floor. Cupping her hips, holding her captive, he pressed moist heated kisses across her belly.

As he laved her skin with his tongue and tempted her with his fingertips, her hips moved in a parody of lovemaking. The soft gasping sound of her breathing came to him as he sucked the inside of her thigh while he rubbed the tiny nub of flesh above her passage, then thrust one finger deep inside her. The tight, wet feel of her as she closed around the digit had him grinding his teeth in a bid for control. The desire to bare himself and take her was almost more than he could stand.

When he lifted her to his mouth and thrust his tongue into the very heart of her, she made a strangled squeak of surprised pleasure. He tasted the sweet, salty heat of her upon his tongue, felt the slow roll of her hips as she reached for completion, and his hips moved in time with hers.

Finally, he could bear it no longer. His hands trembled as he unfastened his breeches, his breath coming in short choppy gasps. He braced both knees upon the bed, and balancing himself upon one hand, drove deep inside her.

She bowed her back and cried out. His name became a litany moaned to the pounding beat of his heart as she grimaced in the throws of her own climax. He thrust once, twice, three times. His seed spilled forth in a wave of intense pleasure that left him floating like flotsam upon the soft rise and fall of her breasts.

Katherine smoothed the soft strands of raven dark hair and cupped the back of Matthew's head. His breathing had finally slowed to a normal rhythm. He wiggled down where he could rest his cheek upon her breast. His long legs hung off the side of the bed, a position she knew couldn't be comfortable, yet, he seemed content to rest just where he lay. She had no desire to dislodge him and continued to stroke his hair away from the side of his face enjoying the moments of replete silence they had been cheated of the last time they'd made love.

How had she thought for even a moment she would ever be able to deny him, and herself, the pleasure they gave each other? How foolish she had been. This connection she felt to him was too strong.

She laid an arm over her eyes. She didn't want to think too much this time. She didn't want to find regret creeping up to drain this feeling from her again.

"Are you all right, Matthew?" she asked after nearly ten minutes had passed and he still had not moved.

"No, I may never be the same. You have drained my strength as surely as Delilah drained Sampson's."

"Your hair is still there, my Lord." She ran her fingers through the thick layer at the nape of his neck.

"Sampson had not traveled three days on horseback before she sheared him."

"If you wish to sleep, you can do so. I will wake you if anything happens."

"As much as I would like that, the men might begin to wonder where you and I have gotten to while they're guarding our backs."

"I suppose you are right," Katherine heard the regret heavy in her own voice.

He rolled over with a groan and sat up on the edge of the bed. Denied the cover of his weight and warmth, she crossed her arms over her bare breasts.

"Don't move."

She looked up at him to see his gaze intent upon her. A slow smile curved his lips as he ran a hand up the inside of her thigh to the bare band of pale white flesh just above her garter. His touch instantly set to light a tingling heat in her most intimate spots. She bit her lip as she struggled to control her expression.

"You look beautiful, decadent, and very well serviced, Mrs. Hamilton. I would like to do it all over again, even though it would probably kill me."

She laughed aloud then clapped a hand over her

mouth to stifle the sound.

His devilish grin brought a weakness to her limbs and made her wish he had the strength to do as he wanted. "Come, sweetheart." He offered her a hand as he rose to his feet. "I'll play ladies' maid as I promised when first we married and help you make yourself presentable again."

"It may take the both of us to repair the damage." She allowed him to pull her to her feet. Her legs were weak, her shoes gone, her décolleté stretched wide leaving her breasts exposed, not to mention the stickiness between her thighs. Her hair curled in wild wisps about her face where her braid had come undone.

How he could think her beautiful after all that, she could not fathom.

Aware of him watching her every move, she adjusted the neckline of the shift and pulled the laces of her gown to close the gap and cover her breasts. She heard Matthew sigh and looked up to see him watching her with a pained look of regret; a blush heated her cheeks. She turned away to go to the washstand and bathe her face and hands. She wet a cloth and turning her back to him, raised the hem of her gown and wiped away the evidence of their lovemaking.

He had kissed her there, and it had felt so good she had wanted to writhe with the pleasure of it. Her face felt hot with the memory, and her heart beat like a caged bird against the bars of her ribs, even as her body thrummed to life with the feelings he could so easily inspire. These minutes they spent together were exciting, fulfilling and the most precious she would ever know. He was so very, very precious to her.

She turned as he set her shoes on the floor in front of her. He offered her a hand as she slipped her feet into them.

His shirt hung open to the waist. The thick mat of dark hair on his chest, beckoned her to touch. His hair hung down his back and across his shoulders. She watched as he retrieved a partially filled teacup from the rug before the hearth and drank from it. The dark shadow of his beard colored the underside of his jaw. Just to look at him made her want him.

She stepped close and began to button his shirt. Matthew cupped her elbow as he watched her.

"You must check the men, they will be missing you. And I must clean up here and return everything to the kitchen. 'Twill be dawn soon."

When he remained silent, she looked up to find his pale blue eyes fixed on her, and the look in their depths stole her breath. He bent his head, and she rose on tiptoe to meet his lips with her own. The kiss was soft and sweet and so tender, tears pricked her eyes. When it ended, she leaned against him and felt the weight of his arm holding her securely.

"Do you want anything more to eat?"

"No, I am satisfied, for the moment."

She drew a deep breath and stepped away from him. She was well aware he wasn't talking about food. There would be a reckoning between them once they returned to London. A painful reckoning. She saw no way for the outcome to be a happy one for either of them.

She could not change the fact that she had been raped. She could not change the fact that her reputation was in tatters. That would follow her even to Charleston, should she go with him. She would become a social burden to him, an albatross hanging about his neck. She wouldn't be able to bear that. She would slowly die inside seeing his resentment build as he had to defend her honor again and again. Even if he should learn to love her, the strain of that burden would eventually sour his feelings for her. It was just too much to expect of any man.

She had to hold tight to the moments they had right now. They would have to be enough. But even as she thought it, she couldn't ignore the aching hunger for his love that gnawed at her, nor her fervent wish that things could be different.

CHAPTER 22

Katherine fastened a dark blue ribbon around her long braided tail of auburn hair and brushed it back over her shoulder. She bent to retrieve the food basket, relieved Matthew had insisted on taking the heavy kettle back to the kitchen on his way downstairs. Reluctant to blow out the candle dimly lighting the room, Katherine left it on the nightstand.

She had just entered the kitchen when Franklin appeared in the doorway.

"Might I have another cup of tea, m'lady?"

"Certainly, Franklin, but 'twill take me a moment to brew it."

A shout from the front of the house had her tensing, and him swiveling to face the door.

A shout came from upstairs. "The stables are on fire."

A glass panel in the door shattered spraying Katherine with shards of glass. Oily liquid splashed across the floor onto her feet followed by a trail of fire that ignited the kitchen curtains then raced toward her. Katherine squeaked in fear as she leaped back away from the flames.

Shielding his face from the heat with his forearm, Franklin jerked the curtains from the window. Grabbing a shovel from the hearth, he beat at the flames.

The smell of burning lamp oil rose strong in the room. Katherine grabbed a heavy tin of flour and threw it on the liquid to try to soak it up.

"Get out a 'ere," Franklin shouted as he beat at the fire like a man possessed.

A cloth covering the worktable in the center of the room caught fire with a quick swoosh, and the basket she had just placed there, began to smolder.

As the flames crept closer, she backed up the servant's stairs. Hot air blew up the stairwell like an open oven door. The yellow-orange glow of the fire reflected on the walls down below. She turned and ran down the hallway toward the other end of the house. She had to warn the men on the second floor of the danger and urge them to go down the front stairs to safety.

****

The sound of glass shattering came from other parts of the house. Matthew jerked the blazing curtains from the library window and stomped on them to muffle the flames. The fire finally out, he went to the door to see who was shouting. The mirror in the hallway reflected the angry amber haze of a fire on the curved staircase that led to the second floor. The men had stripped their jackets off and were using them to beat at the flames.

"Webster," he shouted to one of the men. "Why are you not going for water?"

The man turned, his face half covered by a beard. "The kitchen's aflame as well. They're burning the 'ouse from around us."

Matthew turned to look down the hall to find flames curled around the kitchen door leading out into the hall. "Webster, gather the men on this floor. We need to get out and take cover."

"Aye, sir."

He ran down the hall to the kitchen. Heat blasted him in the face. Franklin was still battling the blaze with a wet towel. Flames undulated up the back wall of the room to the ceiling in a fluid dance that was almost beautiful.

"Get out, man," he shouted above the roar of the conflagration.

"Did Lady Katherine make it down the front stairs?" Franklin shouted back.

Shock punched the air from Matthew's lungs. His wife was trapped on the second floor.

****

Katherine heard the unmistakable sound of a shot and she stopped at the corner of the U-shaped corridor to peek around the turn. Cold air blew directly at her from an open window at the end of the hall. A man stepped from one of the bedrooms into the pale light of an oil lamp, his face in shadow. She opened her mouth to call out to him just as he turned and looked down the hall at

194

her. The dull light etched his jaw line, cheekbones and brow ridge leaving the rest in shadow. His features appeared grotesque, mask-like, his mouth a gaping hungry maul, his eye sockets empty of light and life. Looking past the trick of light, recognition struck her. The hard line of his jaw softened as he smiled gleefully. He raised a flintlock pistol, and she ducked for cover.

Panic raced through her. She ran back the way she had come, stopping by a lamp just long enough to extinguish it, her legs shaking with reaction, her breathing ragged. Darkness swallowed her and for a moment, she couldn't breathe. She pressed back against a doorway hoping the it would cover her should he come around the corner firing. Her fingers fumbled against the wood, and she found the doorknob. She slipped inside the room and closed the door softly. She searched the area beneath the knob for the key to lock the door. It was gone.

Had he killed the men who were guarding the upper story windows? She wondered where the others might be. Where was Matthew?

The darkness, cloying and cold, embraced her. She closed her eyes against it.

"'Twill do no good to 'ide," a voice said from outside in the hall.

She jerked and caught her breath.

"The fire is spreadin' at both ends of the 'ouse, Katherine. 'Twould be better to allow me a clear shot than to burn to death with the men down the 'all."

Her stomach clenched with dread. Had he injured them? Tied them up? Or could he have already killed them and was using them to draw her out? She had to find a weapon.

She shivered, clammy and cold with shock. Katherine shuffled to the right, and slid her hand along the wall. Her knee came in painful contact with something, and she ran her hand over the surface of the piece of furniture.

It was a cabinet. She was in her brother's room. That knowledge alone eased her fear. She drew a deep breath and rested her cheek against the cool wood. She opened the doors and ran her hands over the surface within. It was empty, just as she had known it would be. She had taken all the firearms in the house to the dining room below and loaded them herself. Biting her lip to still its trembling, Katherine stepped away from the cupboard. The desk was close beside it. She held her hands straight out before her. Her fingertips brushed more wood, and she felt the rounded back of the chair that stood before the desk. The tools Johnny had used to repair the weapons might offer her something with which to defend herself.

She froze as a sound came from outside in the hall. A slender sliver of light appeared along the bottom of the door then moved away. He had lit the lamp. A heavy crash startled her, and she jerked. The sound of breaking glass came from the room next door. A strange glow pulsated from just outside the heavily draped windows across the room to offer her a small amount of light.

She ran careful hands over the desk top. Assorted tools lay scattered across the surface, but none she could use as a weapon. A rod used to load a pistol rolled away from her. The sound of it striking the floor reverberated through the room. She scooped it up from the floor and prayed he had not heard it.

The muffled sound of shouting came from downstairs accompanied by the faint smell of smoke. The fire downstairs was spreading upward. She had to get out of this room.

The thread of light appeared from beneath the door once again. "I've set the second story alight, Katherine. 'Twill reach ye soon."

He was mad. He was setting the whole house ablaze in order to kill her. Her eyes darted to the window where light flickered and glowed. Dear God, he had set the room next door on fire. Did he know where she was? Had he heard the rod fall?

The door opened. She froze. There was nowhere to hide.

****

Matthew eased the window open just wide enough to slide through then dropped in a crouch behind the cultivated bushes lining the side of the house. Smoke rolled out the next window, covering his progress, and urging him to cough. He paused long enough to cover the lower half of his face with a handkerchief. Bending at the waist, he ran a hand along the exterior wall and made his way around the back of the house. Heat from the flames engulfing the kitchen drove him from the cover of the brush. He threw up a hand to protect his face from the hot shower of sparks that exploded with the loud pop of shattering glass. He looked up at the second floor. Several rooms on the second story were ablaze, but others were, as yet, untouched by the inferno.

He had to get up there and find Katherine.

****

Katherine squeezed herself in between the desk and the gun cabinet and pulled the open door back in front of her. She gripped the pistol rod tightly and raised it in a stabbing position. She'd go for his eyes should he move the door. She couldn't see the man, but marked his progress by the light of the lamp he carried.

"The fire is spreadin' closer, Katherine. Let me end it for ye. 'Twill be easier than burnin' to death." For a moment, she thought he might have seen her, and she tensed, preparing for him to jerk the door out of the way and grab her.

She felt the pressure of his steps through the bottom of her feet as he crossed the rug. He paused to stand on the other side of the cabinet door. She pressed back against the side of the armoire. The rustle of her clothing sounded loud.

He shouted and heaved the lamp down on the hardwood floor at the base of the bed. Fire leaped to the cloth draperies that hung to the floor and swept up one heavy ornate post. She clamped a hand over her mouth as a scream of rage and fear ripped up her throat. He was destroying her home, the last thing she had of her family. Tears trailed down her cheeks.

Despite the building heat, she forced herself to wait as his heavy tread crossed to the door and moved away down the hall. She shoved the cabinet door out of the way, and immediately had to throw a hand up to shield her face. Flames raced along the canopy and leaped to the curtains at the window.

Fearful of being heard, she ran to the door and peeked out. From the glow of the burning rooms, the hall looked empty. Smoke hung in the hallway like fog. The heat was building. Her gown felt uncomfortably tight

197

against her skin already growing damp with sweat. Crouching low, she hugged the wall and hurried down the passageway, pausing at each doorway, until she reached the corner. Easing forward, she poked her head around the turn. A hand shot out grabbing her hair. Jerked forward so quickly, she lost her footing. She landed on her hip and cried out in pain.

Eye level to the man's crotch she punched upward with the steel rod she held tight in her fist and felt the give of tender flesh beneath the point. The man gave a bellow part pain, part rage and slapped her across the face. Tiny points of light exploded in her vision.

"You bloody bitch!" He jerked her hair so hard she thought he might tear it from her head.

On her back between his spread thighs, she kicked up with her foot landing a solid blow to his groin. Clutching himself, he fell across her, driving the air from her lungs. Wild with panic, she shoved and clawed her way free. He grabbed her skirt and she jerked the fabric, tearing it away.

Her vision blurred. Ears ringing, she limped against the pain of her bruised hip and staggered down the hall away from him. The smoke soon forced her to her knees, and she crawled through an open door. The room was hot, the floor warm beneath her hands. She curled behind the bed and paused to try to clear her head. Nausea rolled over her, and she fought against the urge to heave.

The staggering thump of his steps sounded from the hall. He bellowed her name. Katherine groped in the dim light for somewhere to hide. The open door of a dressing room beckoned her and she scurried inside. It was empty and smelled musty from disuse. Afraid she wouldn't be able to breathe, she hesitated to close the door.

She jerked with a squeak of surprise as the door slammed shut with such force her ears popped. Panicked, she climbed to her feet and shoved against the portal with all her strength, hurting her shoulder and hip. Darkness, ink black and stuffy pressed against her. When she heard the jiggling sound of a key turning in the lock, she beat against the wood with her fists and screamed in frustration and fear.

She heard his voice muffled and hoarse, close against

the door. "Ye'll die, bitch. Not the way I wanted, but ye'll be dead just the same. No one will find ye now. I'd have preferred to have a taste of ye first, like I did yer mum. But this will do."

Waiting for the fire to reach her in the locked dressing room frightened Katherine more than facing anything he might do to her. At least outside of the room, she'd have a chance to escape, to possibly survive. "You sniveling coward. You haven't even the courage to face me."

"Courage 'asn't anythin' to do with it," he said through the door, his tone a snarl. When he continued, he sounded almost amiable. "'Tis time we're both short of, m' lady. The fire's nearly 'ere. It shouldn't be long now. 'Tis the sound of you chokin' on the smoke 'twould please me. 'Twould sound like your mother when I choked the life from 'er."

Rage and fear collide inside her, and Katherine swallowed against the emotions. "If I am to die, I would like to know who my killer is."

"Me name is Jaime Stone."

"No, not you. Who is the man in charge of you? Who sent you to kill my family?"

"'Twas yer Uncle who ordered the deed. Ye were there, ye saw him. And ye don't remember a thing."

Her legs gave way, and the darkness beat against her face. Her heart throbbed in her throat and against her temples. She slid down the door until the hard surface of the floor rushed up to meet her. One scene after another flashed through her mind, a kaleidoscope of color and emotion, sickening and painful as her mind ripped aside the protective curtain it had drawn over the memories.

She remembered Edward kneeling between her mother's thighs, her nude body like alabaster in the flickering flames of the coach lanterns. He had been fastening his breeches as she stood at the coach door. He had raped her mother along with the other men, and she had seen it—heard her mother begging him to stop and asking why over and over.

The sound of something being dragged across the floor on the other side of the door brought her back to the present.

"'e should 'ave let me take care of ye and saved us all the trouble and worry ye've caused. Ye'll not be causing anymore."

CHAPTER 23

Matthew took cover behind a clump of brush and watched the two men who stood at the base of the ladder braced against the side of the house. Had there been one, he'd have taken the chance in overpowering him. As it was, the two were well armed with both pistols and knives.

The smaller man paced restlessly around the base of the ladder going beneath it in a circle. Every few moments he looked up at the window above, his body tense.

Smoke drifted out of the open portal in wisps and puffs, growing thicker with each passing moment. Anxious frustration niggled its way up his spine to tighten the muscles in his neck and shoulders.

"If 'e fries, the old man will 'ave our 'ead."

"Jaime knows what 'e's about. This ain't the first 'ouse 'e's burnt."

A man's head appeared out the window and he swung a leg over the sill and searched for the first rung with his foot. The two men below braced the ladder, as with stiff movements, the third man descended on the rickety structure.

"'Tis 'bout time. I didn't relish comin' in after ye, boy," the slighter built man greeted him as he reached solid footing.

The new arrival's face appeared gray in the dim fire light, his blond hair hanging about his face, lank and damp with sweat. He wiped his forehead with his sleeve and turned. Matthew recognized the man from Katherine's drawings immediately.

"I wouldn't 'ave expected it of ye. I can take care of meself."

"The girl—ye've taken care of 'er."

"Aye, she'll not be troublin' us again." He slapped the smaller man on the back. "'Tis time for us to leave before the fire is seen and 'elp arrives."

201

For a moment, shock held Matthew frozen as the men's footsteps receded. "No." The word reverberated through his skull. She couldn't be dead. He wouldn't believe it until he saw her body. Held it in his arms. He ran to the ladder. He barely noticed how the thin structure shook beneath his weight, his attention focused on the window above.

Smoke billowed out of the opening making his eyes sting and his throat to seize up, despite the kerchief tied about the lower half of his face. He gulped what little air he could and dove head first through the window. The air was a little clearer close to the floor, and he was able to get a few shallow breaths, without coughing. The floor felt warm to the touch, the air dry and hot. Sweat beaded his forehead and had his shirt sticking to his back. Matthew stayed low to the floor and looked into the first room on the left. Thick hazy smoke filled the chamber. Two men were bound to the bed posts at the bottom bed. Matthew crawled quickly to the one closest to him. The man's shirt was blood stained, his complexion grayish-white. Matthew briefly touched his throat to check for a pulse. Finding the man dead he moved on to the other.

His hands a reddish purple, the man had twisted around trying to free himself from the ropes until they had dug into his arms and cut off his circulation. His eyes were open but the gag that bit into either side of his mouth was sopping wet with saliva keeping him from shouting. Matthew recognized him as Jess Thornton, one of his crewmen.

Jess's breathing was labored as though he had been fighting the ropes for some time and had exhausted himself. Reaching into his boot, Matthew brought forth a knife. He cut loose the kerchief and ropes.

"My wife—did you see her?"

Jess shook his arms as though they pained him and clenched his fingers into fists as he worked the blood back into his extremities. "No, sir, but I 'eard 'im callin' to 'er and talking to 'er further down the 'all. The bastard shot Willy."

"There's a ladder just outside the window at the end of the hall. Can you make it without me?"

"Aye, sir. 'e didn't shoot 'er. I'd of 'eard the shot. She

may still be alive, Cap'in. I think I 'eard her calling out down the 'all, so she 'as to be close."

"If she is, I'll find her. Get out as quickly as you can and stay close to the ladder. I may need you to hold it for us."

"I can stay and 'elp you find 'er, Cap'in."

"If I have to carry her out, I'll need you manning the ladder. I don't know how much time we have."

"Aye, sir."

They both paused at the thickening smoke in the hallway.

He slapped the man's shoulder to urge him on. "Go. I'll be right behind you with Katherine."

The air, like hot tar against his face, tasted oily. He crawled down the hall into hell.

****

Sweat rolled in rivulets down Katherine's spine and she tugged at the lacings of her gown loosening the bodice. Curls clung uncomfortably to her forehead and neck. Exhaustion dragged at her. Her hip and shoulder ached from throwing her weight against the door.

The smell of smoke, acrid and bitter, tickled her throat with every breath she drew, making her cough. Her throat, nose, and eyes burnt. She felt light headed. Settling on the floor where the air seemed clearer, she rested for a moment. Her movements clumsy, she used the hem of her petticoat to wipe her face and stem the irritating running of her eyes and nose.

A need to close her eyes and rest tempted her. She could do so if she could quiet the cough that plagued her.

Had Matthew and his men escaped? She prayed so. Tears of emotion joined those that ran down her face. She was grateful for those moments they had shared earlier. There had been no discord between them to mar the experience. She wished Matthew was here in the dark with her holding her and at the same time, she was glad he wasn't. He had so much more life to live, a life without her, just as she had been telling him. But she hadn't really believed it.

She had been waiting, hoping, for some miracle to prevent their separation. And now, just as her memory had returned giving her a reason to hope, it was all going to end. It was so unfair. And she was waiting again, waiting to die. Her family had died trying to protect her and she was lying down and letting life slip away. She should be grasping at every moment left to her.

She forced herself to her feet though her limbs felt weak and uncooperative. Her lungs burnt with every breath. She threw herself against the door again and again. Her ears rang and she bent at the waist and almost wretched as forceful coughing seized her. She braced a hand upon the door. The wood gave way unexpectedly, and she fell sideways. Her elbow connected with the door facing and pain lanced up her arm. She writhed on the floor in pain, coughing and gasping for air.

Matthew's pale blue eyes above a blue kerchief stained with smoke came within her view. Her arms went around him and for a precious moment, she held on. "I knew you'd come," she croaked.

"We have to go, now, Katherine." He pulled away from her. "Can you crawl?"

"Yes," the word came out a whisper and she nodded. She rolled over onto her knees like a sow bug finding its feet. The world spun then righted itself leaving her feeling nauseous and woozy. Matthew half guided, half dragged her to the bedroom door.

The flocked wallpaper burnt in spots. The flames danced gleefully against the ceiling. They had surely been dropped into hell. They inched their way down the passageway. Her skin felt hot and dry stretched taut by the heat. The window beckoned only a few feet away, the curtains burning to ash whipped and flew through the air above their heads.

She watched in amazement as Matthew plunged a hand into the flames and jerked the fabric from the window then slung it away. He looped a leg over the window facing, reached back to grasp her arm, and dragged her to her feet.

"Just a few more feet, sweetheart, and we'll be clear. Come to me, Katherine."

Her limbs felt sluggish, and his image appeared blurred around the edges. She pushed up the wall to her feet and would have crawled head first out the window had he not reached in to drag her leg over the edge of the window frame. Her feet couldn't find purchase on the narrow rungs for though her mind told them what to do, she lacked the coordination.

She looked up as a rumbling like thunder sounded from behind her. A wall of fire rolled like a ball straight toward her. Startled, she jerked, losing her balance, and pitched sideways off the ladder. She came up short with a jerk, Matthew's hand clamped around her wrist. Glass splintered and fell around them like shards of frozen rain. It nipped and sliced at them as the ladder slid sideways along the wall of the house. Flames leaped up from the hem of her dress and she screamed. Her feet were boiling.

She looked up into her husband's face just as he released her hand and she fell into oblivion.

****

Jess caught Katherine, her weight knocking him to the ground. Matthew saw the man roll to his knees and beat at the burning fabric that encircled her ankles.

The ladder swayed like a willow branch, the fire beneath him burning the wood. One of the rungs broke with a loud crack and the flimsy structure gave way. He fell. Swinging his arms in an instinctive attempt to stay upright, he landed flat on his back in one of the evergreens. He couldn't breathe and a thousand rough wooden points thrust into his ribs. Stunned, it took him a moment to roll out of the bush and attempt to stand. He tumbled face down on the ground gasping for air, coughing up some of the smoke he had breathed, and aching with a multitude of cuts and burns. He forced himself to his feet, concern for Katherine driving him. Once upright, he staggered toward Jess.

"'Twas her shoes that were burning, Cap'in. I don't think she's burnt bad. Just a blister or two on her ankles."

Matthew tugged loose the kerchief from his face. His hand throbbed as though he'd been using it to pitch hot tar.

Falling to his knees beside Katherine he used the cloth to wipe away some of the oily soot staining her face. She lay so still fear raced through his veins, and his heart surged in his chest. He pressed an ear to her breast and found the steady beat of her heart.

"She's swallowed a lot of smoke, Cap'in. Might take

her a time to come around."

He knew he had done all he could and slumped to the ground beside his wife.

"Go see where the rest of the men might be. I'd like to know if they all got out of the house, Jess."

"Aye, Cap'in."

Matthew lay back into the cold damp grass, too exhausted to move.

****

Matthew watched as two men stirred the ashes and smothered the last sparks left burning with buckets of water. Over half the stately house Katherine called home was a burned out shell, and the rest was smoke damaged and uninhabitable.

He turned to look over his shoulder at his wife. Awakening after a day-long sleep, she had insisted on seeing what was left of her home. He had argued against it, but she had been adamant. Concerned about the stress, arguing put upon her smoke strained throat, he had given into her, against his better judgment.

Bundled in blankets, Katherine looked like a child perched in the doorway of the coach. Her forehead and cheeks appeared a feverish pink, as though she had been out in the sun too long. The added color would have been becoming had her features not looked so drawn, her eyes and cheekbones so prominent. He moved to stand beside her and extended a bandage-wrapped hand .

"It can be built back, Katherine."

She shook her head. "There would be no purpose." Her voice was a wispy croak.

He frowned at the sound and wondered how long it would take her voice to return to its normal timber. "Are you warm enough?"

She offered him a faint smile and nodded.

"Are you ready to return to the inn now?"

Grief etched lines around her mouth, but no tears fell. She looked one last time at the house and gave a brief nod.

He motioned to the two men who stood nearby and they climbed atop the coach. Four others, heavily armed, moved to make room for them. After everything that had happened, he was taking no chances.

Ignoring twinges of pain, he grasped her arm to steady her as she rose to take her seat inside the conveyance. She spread the blankets over them both to share the warmth. Leaning lightly against him she fell silent, her gaze directed on the passing scenery.

"'Twas Edward who had my parents and brother killed."

She spoke with such certainty he studied her expression for some clue as from where such an idea might have come.

"How do you know?"

"I remember what happened that night. I remember seeing Edward there among the men—taking his turn."

He stared at her; the image her words evoked brought a hollow feeling to the pit of his stomach.

Her features remained composed.

"No one will believe me, and I have no proof, just my word. And we both know how much credence they will give that."

"We'll think of something. There has to be a way." He slipped an arm around her and drew her against his side. "Lord Harcourt may have some suggestions. We'll contact him as soon as we arrive in London."

"His name is Jaime Stone."

"The man from last night?"

She nodded. "He was the man who tried to strangle me that night."

His arm tightened around her. "His was the face you drew. I recognized him last night from your drawings, but there was nothing I could do."

"I believe you did enough." She placed a hand against his chest, her head finding a place in the hollow of his shoulder. "Your hands—"

"Are much better this morning." He attempted to distract her. "If you feel up to it, when we reach the inn, I'll let you take the out the stitches the doctor put in my arm. They're itching like the devil."

She nodded.

Matthew pressed a bandaged hand to her cheek. He was finding the injury more and more inconvenient. Thus far, the only benefit had been Katherine helping him dress before their sojourn to the house, something he had found most pleasurable even though neither of them had been in any condition to act upon it. Caring for one another, offering each other comfort, came easily between them. Sharing a life or death experience, he believed, had cut through all barriers between them.

"He expected me to die so he told me his name. He told me about Edward. It was the shock of it and the smoke filled dark, like being trapped beneath the coach seat once again, that brought the memories back to me."

"You'll be doubly dangerous to him now--and to Edward. If Jaime Stone can be caught, he could be a witness against Edward."

"But would he speak against him when he would condemn himself as well?"

"He'll be condemned anyway for his part in the women's deaths in London. He'll have nothing to gain or to lose—if he can be caught."

"How do you think that might be accomplished?"

He shook his head, though an idea had formed, an idea too dangerous to be entertained. He wouldn't see her placed in any more danger than she was right at this moment.

"We'll speak with Lord Harcourt when we reach London and decide what can be done."

She nodded and nestled against his side once more. The coach's sway rocked them against one another and reminded Matthew of their trip from the church on their wedding day. The pressure of her breast against his ribs had affected him then, just as it was doing now, despite the ache and soreness of bruised and abused muscles.

"I was not raped."

He had wondered when or if she would broach the subject.

"I know."

She drew back to look up at him.

"Since the first time we made love."

"Why did you not say something?" There was an accusation in her tone.

"Do you not remember my saying that there were things we needed to discuss as soon as the trouble at Willingham's was dealt with?"

She nodded.

"When I came upstairs, you were gone."

For the first time, her expression held a hint of guilt.

"We had consummated our marriage, Katherine. Did you really believe I would allow you just to walk away?"

"It was never my intention to trap you in a marriage you did not want, Matthew."

Anger thrust through the barrier of his control. Was she once again trying to wiggle off the hook? He'd be damned if he'd let her. "Have you heard any complaints pass my lips?" He grasped her chin and turned her face to him, his gaze delving into her hers. "I wanted you and you wanted me."

Color flooded her cheeks making them appear berry red. "I cannot prove my innocence any more than I can prove Edward's guilt."

"Innocent or not, my intention was to take you, Katherine. I knew in the moment that I joined my body with yours what I was doing. Did you really expect me to leave you behind when I sailed for Charleston after what had happened between us?"

"Any other man would have ignored it and gone."

When would she concede that he might be different from the father she kept expecting him to behave like. "I'm not any other man."

"I know."

Those two softly spoken words took the angry wind right out of his sails.

He kissed her, hungry for the taste of her, the touch of her tongue against his, the feel of her naked and responsive in his arms. A wave of possessive heat rose up inside him. He wanted to rip the gown from her, lay her back against the leather seat and bury himself between her thighs to claim her, to be held within her. To renew the bond he felt between them.

When he broke the kiss, he was breathing as hard as she. He rested his forehead against hers and closed his eyes, seeking to control the passion that had slipped its bonds and left him aching. "That day in the crow's nest—I wanted to tear those ridiculous breeches from you and take you then and there."

"You were so out of sorts I would never have guessed." Her prim English tones had him chuckling. She rubbed her cheek against his, her breath moist upon his ear. "I have had similar thoughts about you, Matthew."

His breath left him as the blood pooled in his groin. The touch of her fingers upon the buttons of his pants had him biting back a groan of excitement. For the first time, he gave the men riding atop the coach a thought and fumbled clumsily at the leather shade on the window managing to close it just as her hand closed around him. He swallowed against the rising tide of pleasure her touch evoked, his heart beating harshly in his chest.

Her eyes looked dark, a sleepy look of desire relaxing the pain sharpened contours of her face. She moistened her lips with the tip of her tongue. "I am always amazed at how hard you are, yet so soft." She stretched upward to touch her lips to his and he turned his mouth full on against hers, his lips and tongue as hungry for her as the rest of him.

He spread his legs wider as she fondled him and caught back another groan. Her untutored, gentle exploration left him gasping. "Let me come inside you, Katherine," he urged his voice a husky murmur.

Shy, uncertain, she struggled to lift her skirts, retain her grip on the blanket, and straddle his lap all at the same time. He smothered the sound of his mirth against her shoulder. He felt like a clumsy lad again, fumbling his way beneath the skirts of his first love as he tried to help her. He caught the answering gleam of her smile as she pulled back to kiss him.

Passion overpowered his laughter and he cupped her buttocks with his bandaged hands and slid lower against the seat to better align their bodies. The moment she sank down upon him, merged with him, their breathing seemed to catch, hold, and then find a corresponding rhythm. She tilted her hips forward then back, catching the sway of the coach, pushing him deep then sliding away. The pleasure of it was maddening. The joyous, generous, sharing of the act gave him a feeling of acceptance, of mutual possession.

He became impatient with the slow, gentle pace, and he was soon thrusting upward urging her on. The soft breathy sounds she made as she neared release pushed him toward his own. He caressed the soft skin of her parted thighs with his fingertips. He explored the tender wet heat between and found where their flesh met and blended. When he finally touched the desire swollen nub he sought, Katherine's hips bucked. He stifled the repetitive murmur of his name with a kiss, as she came apart in his arms. Her unfettered reaction raced through his body, whipping through his control with a force that thrummed in his ears like the wild beat of a wind blown sail. His release followed hers.

He held her, his face pressed into her shoulder as their breathing slowed and their heartbeats steadied. He longed to feel her skin against his own, not just that part of her that remained connected to him but all of her. He wanted to stroke her back and kiss the pale creamy flesh of her thigh just above her garter. He wanted to explore every inch of her and learn where every touch would bring her the most pleasure. He wanted to ride with her and discover how she sat a horse. He wanted to dance with her again to see how easily she could follow his lead. He wanted to see if she would as easily learn the names of his servants as she had the ones at Willingham's. He wanted to keep her safe so they could accomplish all of those things and more. It would be so.

They swayed to one side, the steep movement of the coach throwing them off kilter. Matthew placed a hand on the seat to keep them erect and raised the corner of the shade to see where they were.

"We will arrive at the inn shortly."

She drew back to look into his face.

It was impossible for Matthew to stifle the satisfied smile that jumped to his lips. It widened further, when her color deepened.

"The bunk, the bed, the coach. I wonder how many other places we may do this, Mrs. Hamilton, before we grow old and cock up our toes. My property is most extensive in Charleston. We'll have plenty of time to think about it on the voyage there."

"You are incorrigible, Matthew." She eased away from him and turned her back to rearrange the layers of petticoats and gown that had twisted around her waist. He passed her a folded handkerchief.

"We could christen the crow's nest if it weren't so

cold."

Slowly she turned to look over her shoulder at him. "It is a tempting thought, Matthew." She slid back against the seat to draw the blanket high under chin as though she were cold.

He could no longer ignore her change of mood or her withdrawal from him. "But—" he said for her.

"I cherish the moments we have together. When you touch me, I—I shall never feel anything close to it again in my life." Her dark violet eyes rose to his face, pain in their depths. "No matter how many times we make love, it will never change things. There is no way for me to repair the damage the rumors have done to my reputation. I have been insulted more than once by my uncle's acquaintances. Imagine how much worse it will be when your friends do it beneath your own roof. And it will happen. There is half a world between our countries, but it seems a short distance for gossip to travel."

"I've been gossiped about myself, Katherine. It means nothing to me. As long as we stand strong together we can face a few rumors."

"You know it is more than that." She shook her head. "Your wife will be whispered about, be called a whore, and be propositioned. And being the honorable man that you are, you will be obliged to defend me. I will not see you hurt any more than you already have been. I do not want to see the respect and care you show me change to resentment and frustration when it happens again and again, and there is nothing you can do."

He grasped her arms and thrust his face close to hers. He wanted to shake the stubborn pride right out of her. Didn't she know that he didn't give a damn about the gossip? He knew the truth. "I'm not leaving you here in England, Katherine. You're my wife. You could be carrying my child. You belong to me."

"And what are you going to do when a man calls me a whore within your hearing? Kill him and be hung? Will you leave your daughter fatherless because of me?" Tears ran down her cheeks. Her hands clenched his shirt. "If I could change things I would. If I could make love with you in that crow's nest with the summer sun warming our skin, I would do it. But I will not make you a social outcast because you feel honor bound to recognize a marriage that was thrust upon you against your will."

He wouldn't allow her to use that as an excuse. "That was a lifetime ago, Katherine. Things have changed now."

"You said you made love to me the first time because you wanted me. I made love with you because I trusted you would treat me with respect and gentleness. I wanted to know what that was like because I had already accepted that I would never know those things with any other man. Every time we have been together since has given me another memory to cherish."

He swore viciously. "I never expected you to behave like such a coward, Katherine." He released her and settled back in the corner of the seat and crossed his arms. "I never expected you would give up without a fight."

For a moment, she looked as though he had slapped her. "There is no way to fight this, Matthew."

"How do you know? You haven't even tried. You're just lying down and letting Edward walk all over your pride and your honor without trying to take it back. You're doing exactly as he wants you to do."

It was difficult for him to watch her try to recover her composure without offering her comfort.

"What do you want me to do?"

"Do you want to stay with me, Katherine? Do you want to be my wife?"

Her eyes looked like rain-washed violets. "Yes, I do."

Relief raced through him easing the tension from his neck and shoulders. "Then allow me to stand by you, Katherine. Allow me to be a husband to you, not just a lover."

She bit her lip and looked away. "I never realized—" Her voice dwindled away, her cheeks growing flushed beneath the burns. "It was never my intent to just—"

He raised one brow and let his silence fight the battle for him though he had an uncomfortable moment thinking about all the women in the past that he had treated in a like fashion. "A husband wants to feel he is in his wife's confidences and privy to her thoughts and feelings. I'm willing to wait for those things, as long as I can be assured they will eventually be offered."

"Very well."

She didn't sound happy or certain, but he'd take it. He knew she had feelings for him, otherwise, she would have never allowed him to touch her the first time. Every time she touched him, kissed him, he felt it. If it took her some time to say the words, he could wait.

"What can we do?" she asked.

"We can stand firm together. That's what married people do."

CHAPTER 24

Katherine stirred more honey in her tea and sipped the hot, sweet brew to ease the raw feeling in her throat. Every time she coughed, it felt as though the inside of her chest had been scalded. When she spoke, she had to push the sound out through a barrier. Tea and time seemed to be the only medicine for it.

They had avoided the common room downstairs and had their meal served in their room. The aroma of roasted lamb, vegetables, and meat pie lingered in the air with the smell of wood smoke from the fireplace. She had tried to ignore the constraint between them. She felt somehow more exposed than she did when they were making love. Sharing her body with him felt natural. Sharing her feelings was more difficult.

"'Twas fortunate that you insisted we load the coach and leave it in one of the tenant's sheds, otherwise we would both be wearing borrowed finery," she commented as she caught Matthew toying with the pale cream lace that edged the ruched back of her gown. Her dark mourning garb had gone up in smoke, and now the brighter colors she had desired to wear to attract his attention were indeed doing that.

"Do you wish me to remove your stitches now? I asked the inn keeper's wife for a pair of scissors in order to do so."

"Aye, if you want to." He rose and she helped him removed his long coat and draped it over a chair. She unbuttoned his sleeve and rolled it back, exposing the stitched cut on his forearm, along with several bruises. She scrubbed the scissors at the washstand then returned to the table to sit next to him.

"Have you spoken to Mr. Jackson to see how his injury is faring?"

"Yes. There is no sign of infection."

"That is indeed something to be thankful for." She

215

bent over his arm. "It is truly a wonder that you did not tear these loose." She quickly snipped one side of each knot on the sutures and plucked the ends from his skin. She tossed them into the fire. She lightly touched the red scar that marked his forearm, then each bruise. Every time she saw another bruise appear, she felt regret for all the pain she had caused him.

"I am deeply sorry for all the trouble I have brought you, Matthew. Had I left the situation as it was, none of this would have come about. Two people have lost their lives because of what I set in motion. I shall have to learn to live with that."

"Two people lost their lives because there are bad people who will prey on those weaker than themselves, Katherine. They would have come after you, whether you had made the matter public or not. You're a witness to their crimes and too much of a threat to ignore. Lord Harcourt recognized that and cautioned you before you left London."

Frustration flickered across his face. "Jaime Stone is a killer, Katherine. Should he discover you are still alive, he'll continue to pursue you. You're his only failure, his only mistake." He fell silent a moment. "What if we were to pretend you perished in the fire? Few people, other than our own men, have seen you since the blaze. If we can limit the number of people who know you are alive it will alleviate the danger for you until the men can be captured."

She was silent as she considered the idea. "I will do whatever you think best, if it will lessen the danger to you and the other men."

He nodded.

"It may be a good idea to check with the innkeeper and inquire about Mr. Drake."

"Drake?" Matthew frowned.

"Garrett Drake. You met him at our wedding dinner. He was one of Edward's guests."

His brows rose. "You saw him here?"

"Yes. When we arrived back from Summerhaven, he was standing at one of the windows watching us."

"I'll inquire about him and speak with him about the situation before I meet William." He reached for his coat, and she rose to help him into it. "We're going to talk with some of the tenants this afternoon about clearing away the debris from the fire. It wouldn't do for someone to be hurt or injured because they got too close and part of the structure fell. We also have to arrange for some of the horses to be boarded until the stables can be rebuilt. That will be up to Edward to decide, I suppose, but we can't transport them all to London with us when we leave on the morrow." He bent his head to brush her lips with his own.

"I've arranged for one of the men to stand guard just outside the room, while I'm gone. Keep the door barred."

"I will. I am still a bit tired. I plan to rest while you are gone."

He smoothed back a stray curl from her cheek. "Keep the flintlock on the bedside table close at hand."

"I will. I'll be fine."

"I'll be back as soon as I can." He kissed her again.

Warmed by his concern, she smiled at his reluctance to leave her. "No one knows I am here, Matthew."

"Every man in the common room knows you're here, Katherine. Did you not notice their interest?"

"No." She had been too flustered by all that had transpired between them in the coach to notice anything else.

He shook his head. "We'll have to be a great deal more careful from now on."

She caught his arm and tried to keep her anxiety for him out of her expression. "Have a care for yourself as well."

His pale blue gaze fastened on her features for a moment, and a smile curved his lips. "I will." He opened the door.

She barred the door behind him then stood for a moment listening to his footsteps recede down the hall. Silence settled over the room so profound she hugged herself. The chamber was empty without him.

She was a weak pathetic fool so in love with her husband she was only putting off the inevitable. She could not help herself.Though she saw no way the damage could be rectified, she wanted to believe that it could. Hope gave her more time to spend with Matthew. Hope gave her time to lock away more memories of their time together.

Damn Edward Leighton and his scrawny, selfish, foppish ways. Every time she thought of him, the blood rushed to her ears and her head felt as though it might fly apart. Unless he could be forced to publicly admit he had started the rumors and recant them, she knew there was no hope of mending the damage. He had to be the one who had spread them. He was, after all, the one who had assured her that she had been molested in the first place. Why had she ever lent credence to what he said? Why had she not remembered sooner what happened that night?

She wanted to rush back to London and confront him, but he was much too devious to openly admit what he had done. He would have to be encouraged to do so in some secretive way. If one of the men with him that night could be captured, they would have proof. But how could that be arranged? And even if it could, would the word of a criminal be believed above the word of a ton?

The thoughts raced through her mind until her head ached with them. She moved to the door and cautiously raised the heavy wooden bar that secured the door then peeked out into the hall. Jess Thornton sat just outside, a musket held across his knees. He rushed to his feet. His face and hair cleaned of soot, he appeared much younger than she had thought him the night before, not much older than herself.

She offered him a smile. "Jess, would you be kind enough to go downstairs and ask for one of the maids to come up?"

The man frowned and moved from foot to foot in indecision. "The Cap'in gave me orders not to leave here for any reason, ma'am."

She nodded. "I understand. Should a maid come by within the hour on another errand, could you stop her please?"

He nodded, his smile laced with relief. "For certain, ma'am."

"Have you eaten? The Captain and I have some meat pie left from our meal. Would you care for it?"

He grinned. "Aye, ma'am, I'd like that."

She closed the door. She left the pie in the pan in which it had been prepared and cleaned a fork for him at the wash basin. She poured a cup of tea from the pot, though it had gone tepid, and returned to hand it out the door to him.

Jess set aside his musket to accept the pan and cup. "Thank you, ma'am. I'll secure a maid, if I can."

She smiled at his eagerness to please. "It is not a pressing matter. One will be up shortly to remove the dishes, I am sure."

She barred the door and busied herself stacking the dishes on the tray and straightening the room. The task took little time, and she settled in a chair near the window and gazed out a narrow opening between the curtains. The gently rolling terrain reminded her of the view from her bedroom window at Summerhaven, and her throat ached with tears.

The consuming anger she had felt from the time her family had been killed had mellowed with each loss that had followed. A woman and man were dead, and the home that had harbored such sweet memories of her mother and brother was destroyed. It was painful, certainly, but it was also freeing. The events had narrowed the focus of what was truly important. She could bear any material loss, as long as Matthew was safe. She would do whatever it took to see that he was. Just as he had done for her.

He had walked through fire for her. Would a man do that for honor's sake alone? Would he not have to harbor some deep affection for her to brave such danger? He had spoken of desire and the possibility of her carrying his child, of his possessiveness, but not of any deep abiding affection. But when he looked at her with concern, did she not see caring as well?

It was enough. Every moment they had together, every word spoken between them, every touch they shared, fed the emptiness in her heart. He brought her pleasure and happiness. She would hold on to that for as long as it lasted.

She closed her eyes, exhausted by her thoughts. Her body ached in a dozen different spots, and she felt bone-tired. She rose from her chair and stretched out on the bed. The noise that filtered up from the common room downstairs had grown less boisterous as the noon hour had passed. She kicked off her slippers. Matthew would be back soon. She drifted off.

She woke to a brief knock on the door. Feeling groggy and disoriented, she looked about the room. The shadows had lengthened and the light from the windows had the dullness of late afternoon.

"'Tis the maid, m'lady." The timber of a female voice came through the door.

Katherine's head felt heavy, her limbs stiff as she slid off the bed to her feet. She brushed at the curls that clung to her forehead. The wood bar felt weighted as she lifted it and opened the door. Gray eyes, wide with fear, met hers. Katherine caught the sight of a man's boot just beyond the opening. The girl's throat was clamped so tight between Jaime Stone's thumb and fingers the skin was already bruising. Her mouth hung open as she wiggled and squirmed and clawed at his hand struggling to breathe. Katherine tried to shove the door closed again, but Jaime heaved his shoulder against it, thrusting into the room and dragging the girl with him. He flung her aside. Her head hit one of the chairs, the crack of bone against wood, sharp and sickening. She fell to the rug and lay still.

Katherine turned and scrambled toward the bedside table for the flintlock. She came up short as he grabbed the back of her gown and spun her around slamming her against a bed post. Her breath exploded from her with a whoosh, her side and shoulder numbed by the blow.

She lashed out, her nails biting deep into Jaime's face, drawing blood. He bellowed in pain and shoved her back. He punched her with a closed fist along the side of her head knocking her to the ground. Lights exploded across her vision. Weak, addled, her vision a blur, she rolled to her side and struggled to get her feet beneath her.

"Ye're goin' ta die, bitch." Jaime withdrew a blue ribbon from his pocket. He grasped the front of her gown and dragged her away from the bed. Flipping her face down, he straddled her back, pinning her to the floor. She blocked the ribbon with her hand as he looped it around her neck. The strand cut into her palm as he tightened it, pushing her knuckles into her throat, and making her gag. She rocked from side to side, fighting against the pressure of his weight. Her heartbeat drummed in her head. Black dots swam in her vision as the ribbon pressed into the sides of her neck.

****

"The randy beast is more trouble than he's worth," William complained as they shut the stall door on Sultan. The big bay snorted and pawed at the straw beneath his feet.

After all the trouble they had experienced getting him from the paddock to the inn, Matthew agreed. "He belongs to Katherine, and after everything else she's lost, I'm determined that she won't lose anything else she values."

The horse thrust his nose between them in an aggressive bid for attention and both men jerked back. Sultan neighed as though amused at their reaction. Matthew shook his head and patted the glossy neck. He spoke softly to the animal and the horse cocked his ears forward and focused his attention on Matthew. His eyes shined bright, intelligent.

"If my hands were in better condition, I'd give him the ride he needs. Perhaps you might want to take on that detail, William."

"Yes, sir. After I've cleared the dust I've eaten all the way back from the Ansley's meadow from my throat."

Matthew grinned. The man had been more than helpful in finding facilities for the horses and buying feed and straw for them. They had had a productive afternoon. "I'll buy you a pint for your trouble and treat the men as well. They've more than earned it this afternoon."

William nodded in agreement. "They'll let you, I'm sure, and be grateful for it."

The two men left the stables and walked around to the front of the inn. The common room had cleared considerably since the noon hour. The desultory sound of the two bar maids' voices as they took the men's orders, carried into the entrance hall.

Matthew tossed a small pouch of coins to William. "See everyone gets a pint and order me one as well and I'll join you. I want to check on Katherine."

He climbed the stairs, his steps eager. He had been dogged by worry all afternoon though he had left her locked in the room with Jess posted at the door. The longer they were away, the more anxious he became lest Katherine grow restless and want to leave the room. He began to relax when all remained quiet as he reached the landing that ran along the second floor. He turned the corner toward the back of the house.

Jess's lean figure came into view. He sat slumped in his seat, his head resting on his chest. A discarded metal pan and teacup were stacked next to his chair. Anger had Matthew's pace quickening. He had trusted the man to remain alert while guarding his wife and he had fallen asleep at his post. He grasped the man's shoulder to shake him awake. The body slumped sideways out of the chair and fell to the floor. Blood ran in a thin line down his temple and cheek.

"Katherine," Matthew breathed her name for he hadn't the air to shout as he leaped over the prostrate figure and shoved against the door. The portal swung back hitting the wall with a bang. His momentum carrying him into the room, he tripped over a woman's body on the floor and braced a hand on the floor to catch his balance.

Jaime Stone straddled Katherine's hips as he pulled on a blue ribbon laced around her throat like the reins of a horse. The muscles stood out in his forearms as he stretched her neck back. Her face was a deep reddish color from the strain, and Matthew thought her neck might snap in two.

He launched himself at the man knocking him over and forcing his face into the floor. He pounded his bandaged fist into Jaime's back. The man twisted beneath him nearly succeeding in throwing him off. They rolled together into the table. Plates and cutlery scattered across the floor as a leg gave way beneath their combined weight and the tabletop crashed to the floor narrowly missing both of their heads.

Jaime punched upward, landing a glancing blow to Matthew's chin. His head snapped back, but he punched back, connecting a solid blow to the other man's mouth.

His lip split and blood ballooned down his chin. The ribbon still clenched in Jaime's fist trailed around his arm as he locked his fingers around Matthew's throat and squeezed. Matthew pounded him in the face repeatedly then twisted away, breaking the man's hold.

Matthew braced his foot on the floor and attempted to rise. Jaime swung around, one of the knives from their noon meal clenched in his fist. He thrust forward and Matthew staggered backward over one of the table legs and went down flat on his back. Jaime was on him in a second, thrusting downward. Matthew caught his wrist, holding off the blow. His grimace feral, the man spat blood in Matthew's face and growled like a snarling wolf.

He put all his weight behind the knife trying to force the blade downward. Matthew's arm shook with the strain of resistance, his muscles aching.

The loud report of a firearm's discharge reverberated through the room accompanied by the thick smell of spent gunpowder. Jaime's head jerked back. His surprised expression became obscured by the blood that blossomed out the hole in his forehead. His body went limp and he slumped forward. Matthew pushed him sideways and the man fell to the floor and rolled onto his back, his hand still gripping the knife. His brassy, green eyes gleamed in the dull light as they stared sightlessly at the ceiling.

The pounding of running feet in the hallway seemed far away as Matthew shoved himself away from the body and half staggered to his feet. He wiped the blood from his face with the sleeve of his coat and turned to look for Katherine. She stared past him at the body on the floor as she lowered the flintlock to her side, the barrel still smoking. Her eyes appeared black with shock as they rose to his face, and she took an unsteady step toward him. In three long strides, Matthew caught her against him, holding her tight as relief rushed through him, so intense he felt light-headed.

William, his gun drawn, pushed inside the room followed by three others brandishing arms. They froze at the door taking in the scene. William stepped to the door to answer the shouted inquiries from the hallway. The three men who accompanied him circled Jaime Stone's body, their expressions a mixture of satisfaction and morbid curiosity.

Katherine coughed and pressed a protective hand to her throat as she drew in a deep breath. "The maid." It was painful to watch her speak, but welcome to hear.

He guided her to the bed and pressed her down on it. He kneeled by the woman and gently eased her onto her back. A huge purple bruise discolored her forehead and a good size knot protruded from it. She moaned and her features creased in pain as she started to regain consciousness.

Jess staggered into the room, supported by a man on either side. His face looked pale and a thin stream of blood dripped from his chin. "Mrs. Hamilton, ma'am. I'm sorry."

She made a movement with her hand negating his apology. Matthew offered her a hand as she rose to her feet. A purplish bruise was forming on either side of her throat. It stood out in stark relief against the pale skin as she tipped her face upward to look at Matthew. "It is over."

To protect him, she had killed the only witness against Edward they might ever have.

"William." Matthew turned to the man as he stood at the door.

"Yes, sir."

"Get someone in here to see to this woman and start asking everyone you can if Jaime Stone was staying here and if he had any traveling companions. Don't allow anyone to leave the inn until they've been questioned. And post someone at the stables so no one will be tempted to slip away."

"Yes, sir."

"He had to be staying here to know you were still alive, Katherine. He's been watching for an opportunity."

She nodded and bent to sooth the maid at her feet as she opened her eyes. The woman began to cry and touch her forehead.

"Andy." Matthew spoke to one of the men standing guard over Jaime Stone's body.

"Aye, sir."

"Go down and get some brandy and be quick about it."

Matthew bent to take the flintlock from Katherine's grasp. She stared at the weapon as though surprised she held it. He squatted on the balls of his feet and grasped her jaw to capture her gaze with his. "It isn't over, Katherine. We're going to find out who's behind all this, once and for all. We're not leaving England until we do."

CHAPTER 25

Katherine eased the blood-smeared wrappings from around Matthew's hand. The blisters had broken and the cloth had adhered to them making it difficult. She dipped a sponge in a basin of water and moistened the fabric to loosen it. Matthew shifted in his seat, his impatience palpable.

"You could just jerk it loose and be done with it," he said.

She glanced up at him. "I suppose that would be a solution if it would not tear your skin away as well." The words came easier, which was amazing considering the added trauma to her throat. The muscles felt sore each time she turned her head and she fought the urge to cough.

"I need to be downstairs with the men, Katherine."

"I know. But, I need to see to your hands first."

He focused his attention on her. "Are you feeling better?"

"Yes." She wasn't interested in how she felt, she just needed to touch him and know he was well. She peeled back the saturated fabric and lifted it away from his palm. The blisters had indeed broken and the skin had torn loose, leaving raw flesh exposed beneath. Areas had cracked and bled. She grimaced at the damage and, as gently as possible, bathed his hand and patted it dry.

She stuck her finger in the concocted salve the innkeeper's wife had given her, and spread a generous amount over the injuries. She placed a protective pad of fabric over his palm then started winding strips of fabric around his hand and between his fingers.

She clipped the end of the strip and tied it securely in place. "Better?" she asked, looking up.

"Yes." His grudging admission made her smile.

"Why is it men will suffer in silence rather than take the time to see to their injuries?" She motioned for him to

226

extend the other hand.

He shrugged. "I haven't heard complaints from you either." He placed his hand palm up on the table.

She remained silent for a moment as she unwound the bandages. "I have had worse, just not quite so many at one time."

He ran his fingertips along her arm garnering her attention. She looked up and read the question in his face.

"Your father?"

She nodded. "He drank sometimes and became mean with it."

He frowned. "There is no excuse for it, Katherine."

"No there is not."

She finished cleaning and bandaging his hand, then rose to toss the dirty bandages into the fire.

They both turned at a knock on the door. Matthew armed himself with a flintlock though it was awkward for him to fit his finger against the trigger. "Who is it?"

"'Tis Garrett Drake, Captain Hamilton." Drake's cultured tones sounded muffled, but recognizable through the door.

Matthew pointed the pistol toward the ceiling as he raised the wooden bar and opened the portal. She moved to stand beside him.

Drake carried his cloak over his arm. Moisture glistened in the dark, wavy strands of his hair. "I was informed you had inquired about me earlier, but I was already out. I heard you had some trouble earlier this evening and have come to offer my assistance, should you or your wife need it."

"The trouble has been dealt with, Mr. Drake." Matthew motioned for the man to enter. "A man knocked out one of my men and attacked one of the maids and Katherine. He was killed."

The man's features went stiff. "Who was this man? Do you know?"

"His name was Jaime Stone. He was wanted for the earlier attack and murder of Katherine's family."

Drake frowned and nodded his head. "I see." He coughed then cleared his throat. "I hope you weren't badly hurt, Mrs. Hamilton."

"Not badly," she answered.

His brows rose at the hoarse sound of her voice, and his gaze focused on her throat. "It was close, I take it."

Katherine's hand moved to her neck, and she touched the bruises there. "Yes, it was. Had Matthew not returned when he did, I would surely be dead."

"How fortunate you were in time, Captain. Is there anything I might do to assist either of you?"

"No." Matthew shook his head. "But thank you for the offer."

"Then I'll leave you to recover." Drake turned toward the door then looked over his shoulder. "Your hands. I heard they were injured in a fire."

"Yes, Summerhaven was burnt to the ground last night. The house was set ablaze by the man killed this evening."

"It would seem you are either very lucky or a very adept fighter to have survived both attacks." He paused, waiting for a reply.

"A bit of both," Katherine said. Her gaze met Matthew's. It was miraculous that he had found her in the dressing room during the fire. The timing of his return during the second attack was equally so.

"I imagine Edward will not be pleased by the property loss. I believe he had hopes of selling the house and property."

"The land is still there." Matthew shrugged, but his hand rested against her waist in silent support. "The house will have to be rebuilt."

"I suppose that can be left up to whoever buys the property."

Matthew nodded.

"I will be leaving for London early tomorrow morning. If you should need me to transport Mrs. Hamilton there, while you finish your business here, I am at your service."

She placed a hand on Matthew's arm, not liking the idea, and his attention swung to her for a moment, then back to Drake. He inclined his head. "I appreciate the offer, but I prefer to keep Katherine with me. After nearly losing her twice, I'd feel more comfortable keeping her close at hand."

Drake nodded. "I understand." He tipped his head to

Katherine. "Should you need anything at all, don't hesitate to call on me."

"Thank you, Mr. Drake," Katherine murmured.

Matthew closed the door behind him and slipped an arm around Katherine's waist. She rested lightly against him and pressed her cheek against his chest. "Mr. Drake's eyes are a most unusual green, don't you think?"

"I'm not in the habit of noticing other men's eyes, Katherine."

She laughed at his tone. "They're like cat's eyes, green with gold flecks. They make me feel uncomfortable when he looks at me." She shivered feeling a chill and pressed closer.

He tipped her face up to him, a thoughtful frown drawing his brows together. He brushed her mouth with his own. When he smoothed the hair back from her face she winced. She remained still as Matthew explored the area and found the knot there.

"We are a pair, Mrs. Hamilton. 'Twould do us both good to lock ourselves away for about a week and allow all the bumps, bruises, burns, and other marks a chance to heal."

She smiled. "Yes, it would."

"My mother used to kiss our injuries better. When we both feel up to it, we'll have to see if that truly works." His devilish smile eased her anxiety and brought another smile to her lips.

"I must go down and speak to William, but I'll not be long."

She was learning, once he had something on his mind, little could distract him. In that, they were very much alike.

****

Katherine woke with a start, her heart racing. She reached out to the space beside her to find Matthew gone, the sheets beside her still warm. She sat up in a rush, alarmed, and looked around the room. Firelight touched on the surface of the two chairs that sat before it, the table against one wall and the washstand. A movement at the window caught her attention. She drew a relieved breath as Matthew stepped out of the shadows. His long easy stride brought him back to the bed.

229

A tremor of reaction shook her. "What is it?"

"Nothing, sweetheart." The lean line of his hip and the muscular shape of his thigh were etched by the firelight as he shucked the breeches he had donned and slipped beneath the covers.

"Are your hands troubling you?"

"A bit." He drew her against his side.

She found a familiar place to rest her head in the curve of his shoulder and pressed close. "I can change the dressings."

"Shhh. In the morning before we leave." His lips brushed her forehead.

The tension slowly drained from her body, and she closed her eyes. The steady even beat of his heart lulled her. "You could tell me what you are waiting for."

She sensed his smile though she couldn't see it.

"Nothing. My thoughts are a bit restless after such a day."

She ran a soothing hand over his chest, the texture of the hair there rough against her palm. She knew he was disappointed, as was she, they had not found anyone in the inn associated with Jaime Stone.

"What will we do, Matthew?" she asked on a sigh.

His arm tightened around her. "They will be found."

"There's so little time. Lord Rudman—"

"Talbot and some of his associates will help me deal with Rudman."

"They couldn't influence him before."

"I don't think you understand how much sympathy and support your situation has garnered, Katherine. Talbot was already receiving offers of help from many of his associates the day after you left. By the time we reach London, perhaps he will have some good news for us."

"I hope so."

An instant surge of anxiety raced through her body as a brief tap came on the door. Matthew moved to rise, and she grasped his arm to hold on to him.

"'Tis just Webster reporting in. He is on watch."

She forced her fingers open to release him. The combination of events in the past days had her so on edge that she suspected an attacker around every corner and imagined a threat at every sound. She supposed it would take her some time to recover her balance.

He slipped into the breeches again and armed himself with the flintlock on the bedside table.

Visions of Jaime Stone bursting through the door ran through her mind. She rose to follow him.

Webster's voice outside the door eased her anxiety a little.

"All's well, Cap'in. 'Twas just as you believed."

"The men?" Matthew asked.

"They're on their way."

"You impressed on them how much care must be taken, Webster?"

"Aye, Cap'in. There was no need. After everything that's happened, they have an interest in seeing it through."

Matthew nodded. "Good."

Katherine crept closer, curious about their conversation. As she peeked around Matthew's shoulder, Webster bobbed his gray head in a nod of acknowledgement His toothy grin, nestled in a thick, grizzled beard, further eased her anxiety.

"All's well, Miss Kate."

"I am glad to hear it. What else are the two of you planning?"

"Two of the men are going ahead as scouts and to apprise my uncle of everything that has happened," Matthew explained.

"Oh."

"Change the watch, Webster and get some sleep. We'll be leaving at first light."

"Aye, Cap'in." The man tipped his head to Katherine then he moved down the hall.

"There is something more." It was a statement not a question, and she hoped he would settle her concerns by explaining.

Matthew closed and barred the door. "The air is chilled, get into bed."

The pressure of his hand against her waist urged her forward.

"Tell me." She slipped beneath the covers and turned back to him.

"There's nothing to tell, Katherine." He tossed the

breeches at the foot of the bed and got in beside her. "'Tis only a few hours until we'll be leaving. We both need to sleep."

"You are getting back at me for not being open with you earlier."

"No. I've told you before, I don't go in for petty reprisals."

She gave a sigh and flopped on her back. She winced as her neck muscles protested the movement.

He turned her on her side and moved to cradle her back against him. His thighs tucked beneath hers, and his manly parts nestled against her buttocks. She became distracted as a familiar lassitude invaded her lower limbs and she suppressed the urge to push back against him. Every muscle in her body felt sore, her ankles were blistered and bandaged, and she was covered in bruises. And still she wanted him. The change in Matthew's condition in response to her had her smiling.

"If you are very still, it will go away," he whispered.

She laughed, the sound reduced to a snicker because of her throat.

His hand crept beneath her shift and followed the rounded curve of her hip. When he pressed his cloth covered hand against the flat plain of her belly, Katherine's mouth went dry with desire and it took all her control not to wiggle against him.

"It is a constant source of aggravation to me that I can't touch you, Katherine." He bent his lips to her shoulder.

She swallowed against the knot of emotion that rose in her throat. "You do touch me, Matthew." She reached back to run an encouraging hand up the length of his upper thigh and heard him catch his breath.

"If we move very slowly, very carefully, perhaps, we can make love without causing any further harm to one another," he suggested, his breath warm against her ear.

She shivered and guided his hand upward to her breast. With a movement of her hips, she felt the heated length of him slide between her legs. "Take your time, my lord; I am not in any rush."

His mouth, open and parted, found the sensitive area between her neck and shoulder. She twisted around, her lips seeking his. The hot, torpid kiss went on and on. She wondered if she would ever get enough of him. She hoped not. She hoped they'd never get enough of each other.

The velvety hardness of him brushed her thigh and she turned to push back against him, her fingers guiding him to the opening of her body. With a gentle push, Matthew entered her. His hand cupped her lower abdomen holding her back against him as he thrust up inside her, seating himself to the hilt. The slow thrust and counter-thrust of their joined bodies ebbed and flowed, binding her closer and closer, pressing him deeper and more tightly inside her. He was around her, inside her, possessing her, loving her. She felt as though she never wanted this touching, giving, sharing to end. She cried out in joy, in regret as, with a hot pulsing rush, it did.

CHAPTER 26

Matthew braced his feet against the sway and bumps of the coach and adjusted the shade on the window, so the light would not beam directly into Katherine's face.

The same thoughts had played through his mind since they had turned over Jaime Stone's body to the local constable and answered his questions. The man Matthew's men were trailing had to be involved. If they lost him, they would not get another chance. *They had to succeed.*

"You have been quiet for nearly and hour. Is there something disturbing you?"

He looked down into Katherine's deep violet eyes and smiled. He was besotted with his wife. The prim cut of the gown she wore did nothing to dampen the immediate response that quickened his heartbeat every time he looked at her. He felt amazed by the courage and resilience she had shown throughout the last few days.

"I was just wondering how Clarisse and Talbot will respond to everything we have to tell them."

"They will find it all difficult to believe, I am sure." She drew a deep breath. "I am more concerned about how I will react when I see Edward."

He frowned. "You have to find a way to hide your feelings, Katherine. Until we find a way to prove he was there, it will just be your word against his. If you confront him with what you remember that night, he may find a way of covering his tracks more completely."

"I know. I keep seeing him as he was that night." She covered her eyes with her hands as though that would block out her memories. She shuttered then dropped them in her lap.

He tucked her fingers in the bend of his arm in a show of comfort. He wanted to share what he was doing with her, but if it didn't work, she would be disappointed once again. "Perhaps Talbot and the barrister have found something."

"Perhaps."

She fell silent, her gaze focused out the window. A frown flitted across her face. "There are British soldiers riding along side the coach, Matthew."

He raised the leather shades and looked out. Four men rode parallel to the coach on each side.

She clutched his arm, her eyes wide with fear. "You don't suppose something has happened to Talbot or Clarisse?"

Concern lanced through him. "I hope not."

Willingham's gate came into view, and they pulled through the entrance and came to a stop before the house. His stomach muscles knotted with concern as the troops surrounded the coach.

Webster hastened to climb down and lower the steps. Matthew swung down from the coach and offered Katherine a hand. The sound of several muskets being cocked gave him pause. He looked up to see the assembly of eight armed soldiers pointing their guns at him. "Stay where you are, Katherine."

One man dismounted, his uniform designating him an officer. His livery appeared snowy white against the deep red of his coat. His blond hair hung straight down each side of his face. He strolled rather than marched to stand before Matthew. He doffed his hat and tucked it beneath his arm.

"Captain Matthew Hamilton?"

"Yes."

"Lieutenant Marshall Endicott. You are under arrest for the murder of Lady Jacqueline Rudman."

For a moment his mind could not grasp what the man had said."Jacqueline is dead?"

Lieutenant Endicott frowned but pressed on. "Will you surrender your arms, sir?"

Katherine stepped down from the coach between him and the men, and Matthew's heart clenched as eight muskets came to bear on her.

"My husband has been in Birmingham with me for several days, sir. There has been some sort of mistake. He cannot be responsible for this."

"Step aside, Madame." The man reached out to grasp

Katherine's arm, and Matthew caught his wrist preventing him from touching her.

Time stood still as several guns were cocked atop the coach. Matthew glanced up. All six men above had armed themselves.

Talbot stepped out the front door with Clarisse at his side. Elton's tall figure stood at attention behind them. "What the hell is going on here?"

Beads of moisture shown on the young officer's forehead. His gaze strayed upward where the barrel of a musket pointed at him. "Captain Hamilton is under arrest, sir."

Talbot's bushy, white brows rose. "For what?"

"The murder of Jacqueline Rudman, sir."

Talbot's face grew red, his features creased in a frown. "That is ridiculous. Jacqueline's death occurred after Matthew had already left for Birmingham. Avery Rudman has gone too far this time."

"I have orders to transport Captain Hamilton to Newgate, sir."

Matthew watched the change come over his men's faces. They had already seen him taken away once. They would not allow it again. He pulled at Katherine's arm. "Get behind me, Katherine."

"No. If Lord Rudman is involved, they could just as well have orders to shoot you and say you were resisting."

Endicott's face stiffened. Several of the soldiers on horseback shifted to a more purposeful posture. "I am an officer in His Majesty's Army, Madame. I do not shoot prisoners without reason."

Clarisse stepped down the stairs to the drive and right into the path of several firearms. Matthew's heart stuttered. Someone was going to get hurt.

"Lieutenant," Clarisse addressed the man, "I suggest you accompany my nephew and his wife into the house, and we will sort this out like civilized people."

"It is not my job to sort anything out, Lady Willingham, just to follow my orders."

Katherine advanced on Endicott, and he took a step back. "You are not taking my husband to that—place."

Matthew said the only thing that would put an end to the confrontation before it escalated any further. "Yes, he is."

She turned to look over her shoulder at him, her eyes wide with shock.

"It will be all right, Katherine. We both know I didn't harm Jacqueline Rudman. I have witnesses that will testify to that." He swallowed and struggled to retain a calm demeanor as he turned to the Lieutenant. "I am going to order my men to lower their fire arms. I suggest you do the same, before someone gets hurt. We have unarmed civilians in the line of fire. It wouldn't do your career any good if one of them is shot and killed."

The young soldier couldn't completely hide the relief that flickered across his face. "I agree, sir."

Matthew glanced upward and met each man's gaze. "Lower your weapons men. I'll need you to testify as to my whereabouts instead."

"Lower your weapons." Endicott called out to the men on horseback then turned to face Matthew. "I will need your weapon, Captain."

Matthew spread his coat wide, pulled out the flintlock pistol at his waist, and offered it to the man butt first. "I would ask you for a moment to speak to my wife and my aunt and uncle, Lieutenant. I will need them to see to my defense."

"Of course, sir." The man nodded.

"How was Lady Rudman killed?" he asked.

Endicott studied his face for a moment. "She was strangled, sir, with a blue ribbon."

Katherine caught her breath and bit her lip. As her gaze focused on his face, he read the fear in her expression.

Matthew motioned for Talbot and Clarisse to join Katherine and him at the base of the stairs.

"Talbot, you will need to contact Lord Harcourt immediately. I will need him to testify as to the investigation he is leading. Jacqueline came to the Caroline the day I left for Birmingham." He felt Katherine shift in response to the news. "My purser on the Caroline, Carson Ray and my first mate, Henry, can testify I sent her on her way in full view of everyone on deck. Carson rowed ashore with me from the Caroline afterward and he saw me mount my horse and ride away. What day was it that Jacqueline was killed?"

"That same afternoon, Matthew," Talbot said, his brows drawn together in a frown, his worry palpable. "They found her body in her coach in an alley just off the docks. Her driver had been knocked unconscious, and she had been molested and strangled."

He met his uncle's gaze. "They could argue I suppose, that I doubled back, knocked out the driver, and murdered her. There have to be witnesses to what happened, Talbot. If it was broad daylight, someone had to have seen something."

"We will find them, I swear it. You will not languish in jail again for something you did not do, Matthew."

Clarisse placed a hand on Matthew's sleeve, her pale eyes, so much like his, focused intently on his face. "We will do whatever it takes to set you free, Matthew. No matter what that may be."

"A coroner's inquest as soon as possible might be helpful. Isn't that how things are done here?" He forced a smile to his lips, though he had never felt less like smiling. He turned his attention to Katherine.

His throat felt thick with emotion as he looked down at her. Her eyes had never seemed so dark, nor her skin so pale. He could think of only one thing to say. "I haven't wanted any other woman, since the first time I saw you, Katherine."

"I know."

The open trust in her face was nearly his undoing.

"I'm coming with you."

"No. We both know Newgate is no place for a lady, sweetheart."

"My place is with you, no matter where you are, Matthew."

He cupped her face in his bandaged hands and closing his eyes, rested his forehead against hers. "I need you here, fighting for me, covering my back."

He felt her hands grip the fabric of his coat tight. I—"

He kissed her, drawing her in against him to feel the imprint of her body against his. When he raised his head, he read in her face the words she had started to say. "Tell me when I'm a free man again."

"I will." Her hand lingered against his cheek.

"In light of your injuries, we'll use your coach to transport you, Captain." Endicott motioned to his hands.

He released Katherine and stepped away. "Andy, Webster, and Franklin, you'll stay here with my wife. I'm counting on you to help keep her safe." He looked from man to man. "All of you."

Andy, the quietest of the bunch, said, "Won't nobody bother 'er whilst we're around, Cap'in 'amilton." The men climbed from the coach and moved to stand beside her.

"I am coming with you, Lieutenant. I will see Matthew settled, and know where he is housed," Talbot said. He hastened to collect his cloak from Hampton at the door. He swung himself aboard the conveyance.

Matthew climbed inside the vehicle. He took his seat. His gaze settled on Katherine's face through the window. With a jerk, the coach pulled forward. His last view of his wife was of her standing on the steps with Clarisse, her hand clenched tight against the frogs that held her cloak in place, her body held taut against the golden glow of the setting sun.

****

Katherine watched the coach turn outside the gate. She thought she might scream if she didn't find some outlet for the rage and fear building inside her.

"Clarisse, do you know where Lord Harcourt lives?"

"Yes, I do."

"Good, you may give Andy directions."

"Andy." She turned to the big man directly behind her. "Please go around back to the stables and see that a horse is saddled for each of you."

"Aye, Ma'am." The man started off at a jog.

"Webster." Emotion gripped her throat as she read the concern in the man's face. For a moment, her composure deserted her, and tears threatened. She cleared her throat. She had no time for tears, not while Matthew remained confined in that hell-hole. "I need you to go to Lord Rudman's house and fetch the driver of the coach who was attacked. Lord Harcourt will wish to speak with him, as do I."

"Yes, Mrs. Hamilton"

"Franklin."

The man's red, bushy hair stood on end as if he had

been caught in a windstorm. Katherine smiled, despite the fear and worry bringing a hollow feeling to her insides. "Go to the Caroline and find out where Mr. Ray might be. Have him come here immediately. Bring Henry as well."

"I'll be there and back before ye can blink."

She nodded. "I know I may count on you. Do not take no for an answer. If someone is out, inquire where they are, and hunt for them until you find them. As soon as Lord Harcourt and I have had time to speak with everyone, we will decide what can be done."

****

Matthew listened to the scrape and clamor of metal doors slamming closed deep within the prison. The nauseating smell of urine and filth made his throat burn. The sounds of fear and misery echoed through the halls, more wrenching than any he had ever heard.

He eyed the filthy cot with its straw mattress with distaste, and took a seat on the only chair in the room. The cell was much like the one he had occupied before, but this chamber also had a pocket of brackish water in one corner where rain had leaked from somewhere above.

He focused on the barred window high on the wall where a small piece of sky was visible. His thoughts turned to Katherine, and the first time he had seen her in a room like this one. Her gaze had strayed to the window as she staved off her fear of close spaces. He wondered at the courage it had taken for her to face her fears in such a manner.

A knot of emotion rose in his throat as despair crashed down on him. He had done what he needed to do to prevent anyone else from being hurt, but now, as he sat in this cell; he wished fervently he'd had an opportunity to fight. He wanted to smash something and yell at the injustice of it. Avery Rudman wanted someone to blame for his wife's death, and because of Matthew's earlier relationship with her it was he. He wondered how many times he was to pay for meeting her. Would he pay with his life for those few, brief, stolen moments that happened months before Rudman had ever married her?

Matthew raked his fingers through his hair.

"I knew ye'd be back," a familiar voice said from the

door.

Matthew looked up.

Hicks's broad, piggish face pressed close to the barred opening in the door. His small eyes narrowed as he smiled. "Murdered a Lord's wife, I 'ear. Ye'll not be leavin' 'ere this time, lest it be in a box."

A key twisted in the lock. Matthew got to his feet.

"'Tis a standin' order that all murderers be ironed." Hicks threw a pair of rusty shackles to the floor at Matthew's feet. "Put them on."

He looked at the chains then studied Hicks's face. A satisfied smile played around the man's mouth. Hicks wanted him to resist. Matthew's gaze moved to the open door, and he caught the furtive movement of a shadow to the right. He wondered how many there might be waiting for Hicks's signal.

Matthew bent to pick up the shackles and eyed the cuffs. With both his arms and ankles secured, he would be bent at the waist and unable to straighten up. He would be helpless to defend himself should Hicks and the other guards attack him. He wondered if Rudman had ordered the guards to kill him.

Probably so.

A sense of calm settled over him, as resolve took the place of his despair. He had been hungry for a fight, and Hicks was providing him with one. He might as well take advantage of the opportunity. A smile curved his lips as he focused his attention on Hicks. "Why don't you invite the others in, Mr. Hicks, and we'll get down to business?"

Hicks's smile listed and died, his features taking on a hard look. "'Tis my pleasure, Yank." He looked toward the door.

Matthew swung the chains, hitting him in the side of the head. The man staggered sideways and fell head first into the door blocking the portal, just as two men crowded through armed with clubs. One tripped and went down across Hicks's limp figure. Matthew swung again barely missing the two and the sound of the metal links hitting the door clanged, making his ears ring.

The two ducked and scrambled on all fours back out of the cell. Matthew adjusted his hold on the shackles. He spun one length of chain with a metal cusp around and around as he converged on Hicks's limp form.

"Ye'll be punished for attackin' 'im," one of the men warned.

"I'm in here for murder, and they can only hang me once. Now which one of you would like to be next?"

The two eyed each other. One lunged for the door and slammed it shut. "Get the key, 'urry," he urged.

"'icks is still in there, Charlie."

"Better 'im than us. 'is Lordship will be more upset should the bloke escape."

The key rattled in the lock and the tumblers turned.

Matthew's blistered hands protested as he grabbed Hicks by the back of the coat and dragged him to the bunk. He tossed the shackles next to the bed and hefted Hicks onto it. The side of the man's head and face had already begun to swell with a multitude of lumps. Matthew eyed the injury with some satisfaction. He clamped one of the metal cuffs around the guard's wrist, and then pulled the ring of keys from his belt. He tried several before finding the correct one with which to lock it. He had just finished securing the last one around Hicks's ankle when the man began to moan and come around.

He removed the short club from Hicks's belt then leaned against the wall and crossed his arms. Hicks's beady eyes fluttered open and settled on Matthew. He frowned and looked addled. When he started to sit up, he came up short and flopped back. His eyes widened in surprise, and then fear, as he eyed the chains that held him to the bed frame. "Charlie," he bellowed.

Matthew left him to his struggles and strode to the door. He tried several keys in the lock until he found the one that fit. Temptation niggled at him, urging him to open the door and take his leave. If he did, his actions would be discerned as an admission of guilt. If he didn't, he could be hanged for a murder he didn't commit. With an oath, Matthew slammed the club he held against the door and heard a yelp of surprise from the other side. He held the key in place as someone attempted to force another into the lock from outside.

He flinched and ducked as an explosion went off close to his head. A cloud of smoke and the smell of burnt powder leeched into the cell. Hicks bellowed again, the sound more frantic than before. A chunk was carved out of the wooden bed frame where the lead ball had ricocheted off the ceiling and nearly struck the man's hip. "Damn ye, Charlie. Ye're goin' to kill me afore 'e does. Put that pistol away."

His ears ringing, Matthew slid down the wall of the cell where he could hold the key in place and stay out of range. Hicks's outraged expression triggered a chuckle that built into a full-blown laugh. Hicks glared at him, which only served to amuse him more, and he laughed again.

"Ye're crazy, Yankee," he accused.

Growing sober once again, Matthew nodded. "'Twould do you well to remember it, Hicks. With a noose waiting for me, I've nothing further to loose if I decide to snap your neck."

"Ye won't do it."

He raised one brow and focused his attention on the man. "I haven't forgotten a moment of your treatment when last I visited this establishment. Think back on all you did and ask yourself if you really believe that."

Hicks considered his words for a moment. His bellows for help echoed off the walls of the chamber, and he began to struggle again.

Sighing, Matthew shook his head. It was going to be a long night.

CHAPTER 27

Katherine hugged herself to still her tremors. Her eyes burned and her fingers were stained black with ink, but several drawings of the men she had seen that night were completed, as well as another of Jaime Stone, and one of her uncle.

Her attention rested on the drawing room door just visible from her seat in the library. She looked at the clock on the mantle again and grimaced when she realized only five minutes had passed.

"Have a cup of tea, Katherine. It will help pass the time." Clarisse poured the brew in a cup and set it on the table before her. Talbot leaned over and added a splash of brandy from the glass decanter he held. He poured the tea Clarisse had set before him back into the pot, and filled his cup with the stronger libation.

She cradled the teacup in her hand as she wandered to the window to look out. Darkness pressed against the glass unrelieved by moon or stars. Rain ran in a steady stream down the panes catching the light of the lamp behind her. She wondered for the hundredth time if Matthew was all right. To picture him locked away at the mercy of Hicks again was almost more than she could bear.

"Mrs. Hamilton." Lord Harcourt's spoke from behind her.

She turned to face him, her heart beating in her throat so hard she couldn't speak.

"Could you bring the drawings you have finished to the drawing room?"

"Certainly." The word came out a whisper. She set aside the untouched tea and rushed to comply with his request. Her hands trembled with a combination of hope and fear as she gathered the sketches.

"I know how difficult this must be for you," Lord Harcourt said as he walked beside her.

244

She doubted that the events she and Matthew had survived in the last few days had ever fallen within the realm of his personal experiences. "I appreciate your help in this matter, sir. I would not want Lord Rudman to doubt the evidence because it came from a source he thought biased. I am certain he will find you an acceptably neutral representative for justice."

"I am honored by your trust, Mrs. Hamilton." He opened the door and stood back to allow her entrance.

The men, six in all, came to their feet as a group as she entered the room. Her gaze fell on Henry first. His gnarled hands clutched his hat as he turned it round and round. He bobbed his head in greeting and offered her a shy smile. She did not recognize the man beside him and paused while Lord Harcourt introduced him as Matthew's purser Carson Ray.

"Mr. Ray." She offered him her hand. "I appreciate your coming to testify on my husband's behalf."

"It's my pleasure, Mrs. Hamilton." His mouth thinned, making his square-jawed face appear stubborn. "I've sailed with the Captain for several years now. I have no doubt that he is innocent, ma'am."

"Thank you."

"I have sent two men to collect Lord Rudman's driver, Mrs. Hamilton. He should be here any moment," Lord Harcourt said.

She nodded and stepped to the table to spread the drawings out.

Hampton appeared in the doorway. "There is a gentleman at the front door who wishes to speak with Captain Hamilton, Mrs. Hamilton. He is quite insistent. He says he is one of the Captain's men."

"Show him in, Hampton."

Jess entered the room, his dark hair slick with rain, his clothes dripping with water. "I have to speak with the Cap'in, ma'am."

"The Captain isn't here, Jess."

His teeth chattered as he spoke. "We found them, ma'am. They're hiding out at an ale house on the east side, at a place called White-Cross Tavern. I left Hollis standing watch while I came back here to tell the Cap'in."

"How do you know you have found the men, Jess?"

William stepped forward. "One of the maids saw a man with Jaime Stone at the inn before we arrived. She gave a description of him to Captain Hamilton and me. When nothing came of our questioning everyone at the inn, he ordered a watch put on the stables. The man the maid described sneaked out near daybreak and rode out. Captain Hamilton sent Jess and Hollis to follow him and see where he went. 'Twas his belief that he would lead them back to the rest of the highwaymen."

Heedless of the water the man dripped upon the rug, she grasped Jess' arm to lead him to the table where she had just spread the drawings. "Do you see the man's likeness here?"

"That one," Jess pointed at the sketch of a thin, rat-faced man. "They called him Badger."

Katherine's throat grew thick with tears as her gaze traveled from one man to the other. "If he was traveling with Jaime Stone, perhaps he was a party to Lady Rudman's murder or a witness. He has to be captured."

William, Andy, Franklin, and Webster started checking the priming on their weapons.

"Wait." Lord Harcourt's voice carried over the noise. "It would be best if His Majesty's troops were involved. None of you have authority to arrest them."

"You do, don't you?" Webster asked.

Lord Harcourt turned to Katherine. "What of the Captain, Mrs. Hamilton?"

She felt as though something inside her grew tighter and tighter until she could barely breathe. "These men bore witness for my husband, Lord Harcourt. Will it be enough to prove his innocence?"

The man's gaze dropped from her face giving her his answer.

"Then go. But please capture them alive. It may be Matthew's only chance."

****

Matthew listened to the squeak of rusty metal as one of the men worked at the hinges of the door. Eventually they would work free the portal and there would be nothing he could do to keep them out of the cell. A wooden club would be little protection against a loaded flintlock.

The only advantage he had over them was the

darkness. Hicks's presence compromised that for he was constantly taunting him and calling out to the others. Matthew unwound the stock around his neck. Hugging the wall, he edged his way slowly around the cell to the cot.

"Don't ye touch me, Yankee."

Matthew stuffed the stock into the man's mouth and tied it around his head. Hicks's cries diminished to grunts and whimpers, and Matthew wondered why he hadn't gagged the man hours ago and saved himself the bother of his constant noise.

The man Hicks referred to as Charlie called out. "Hicks—Hicks, are ye all right?"

Matthew crept back around to the door and squatted down to wait.

The men began to beat at the metal. Matthew crossed over to the back side of the portal where the door would give way once the hinges were free.

He had just decided that he preferred Hicks's bellowing to the pounding when the door shifted sideways. The lock gave way. A man rattled off a string of colorful curses as the door toppled back. It seemed to take an inordinate amount of time for it to settle on the dirt floor.

Matthew hugged the wall as closely as he could. He blinked as the light of a lantern extended into the room. A man stepped onto the door and eased just inside the door facing, his flintlock pistol cocked and ready. Matthew grasped the top of the weapon wedging his bandaged hand between the cock and the steel preventing it from discharging. He jerked the firearm out of the guard's hand at the same time he swung the club. The wood connected to the man's skull with a sickening thud. The guard fell to the ground and lay still.

He then found himself face to face with the other guard. The man's eyes rounded with shock, and with a high-pitched yell, he swung the lantern he held at Matthew's head. Matthew ducked and glass chimney splintered against the stone wall, splattering oil across it. He thrust upward with the club and struck the man under the chin, driving him back out into the passageway. The man lost his footing on the metal surface of the door and fell against the rock wall. The busted lantern clanged as he lost his grip on it and it struck the floor. Tossing aside the club, Matthew gripped the butt of the pistol and pointed it in the man's face.

"I believe you are in a spot of bother, my friend," Matthew said, imitating the upper class English accents of the ton.

With a look of resignation, the man leaned back against the wall and spread his hands in surrender.

****

"Come sit and rest for a moment, Katherine." Clarisse patted the settee beside her. "I will tell you of Matthew and his brothers when they were younger; it will pass the time."

Recognizing the couple's attempts to distract her, she looked from one to the other and read the same strain and worry she felt on their faces. "Forgive me. Both of you. I know you are as concerned for Matthew as I am. I have not been very considerate of how you must be feeling about all of this."

"Damned helpless." Talbot's hands clenched and unclenched as he stood at the fireplace. He raked his fingers through his hair making the white strands stand on end atop his head.

She settled beside Clarisse and the older woman clasped both her hands. She swallowed several times as ready tears threatened.

"I knew in the coach after the wedding Matthew was smitten with you."

A smile tempted Katherine's lips for the first since Matthew's arrest. "I was with him as well." The heat of a blush crept upward into her face and for a moment, she wondered how much she might share with them.

"I tried not to become attached the first days of our marriage. To him, to the two of you." Katherine looked up at Talbot. "We struck a bargain during that first meeting at the jail. The marriage would be annulled as soon as I received whatever inheritance my mother left me, and he had his ship back and could sail for Charleston. Then Hannah hung that ridiculous sheet off the balcony and confused the issue."

"So that is who it was." Talbot sat in one of the chairs

248

before the fire. "Matthew never said a word."

"Of course not." Clarisse's blue eyes searched Katherine's face. "Matthew would have never said anything to disparage Katherine's reputation."

Katherine caught herself smiling again. "With the rumors, Hannah thought to protect my reputation. I truly meant to stick by the agreement. I planned to leave before the papers were hawked and the bills posted. I thought if I were absent it would give Matthew time and reason to annul the marriage."

Talbot leaned forward in his seat. "Matthew would have never left you behind. Honor alone would have prevented him from doing so.

"I know." She tucked a stray curl behind her ear. "I delayed leaving for Summerhaven a day too long. He refused to allow me to stay home that day and, in truth, I wanted one more day with him, before we had to part."

She brushed at the tears that trailed down her face. "Your nephew is difficult not to love."

"Then why would you even try?" Clarisse asked as she gathered Katherine against her.

She relaxed against the other woman, grateful for her understanding and comfort. "I thought, at the time, to protect him from all the trouble I have caused. It is because of me he is in prison again."

"No it is not." Talbot shook his head, a scowl darkening his features. "It is because Avery Rudman's jealousy has blinded him to the truth."

Hampton appeared at the library door, and Katherine sat up. "Lord Rudman and his driver are here, my lord."

Talbot rose and withdrawing a handkerchief from his coat pocket offered it to Katherine. "Show them in Hampton."

"Who are you to command my driver's presence, Talbot?" Avery Rudman demanded as soon as he cleared the doorway. His features, set in aggressive lines of displeasure, appeared drawn and haggard.

"It was not by my invitation, but by Lord Harcourt's, Avery. Though there is nothing untoward about my wanting to speak to the man, is there? My nephew has been accused of a heinous crime, a crime of which he is innocent. I intend to do everything I can to prove that."

"His innocence is a matter of opinion." Rudman scowled, his bulldog like jaws trembling as he ground his teeth.

"Not just my opinion. He is innocent."

Katherine stepped between the men when it appeared the conversation was only going to deteriorate into an argument. "My husband told me about your wife's visit to him on the Caroline that day, Lord Rudman. I am sure your driver told you that she left after only a few moments, as all the men on deck that day can attest to, as well. Matthew's purser, Carson Ray watched Matthew mount his horse and ride away in the opposite direction. He was coming to me at Summerhaven."

"So you say. He could have easily circled back."

"What reason would he have to do that?"

"Revenge against me for having imprisoned him. Revenge against her for having caused it."

"If you knew my husband, you would not believe that, Lord Rudman."

The man's jaw flexed. "You are his wife; of course you will defend him."

"I am his wife because you and my uncle both wanted rid of a problem. I will ask you at another time, what Edward promised you to gain your cooperation in that matter. Right now, I am more concerned that an innocent man may lose his life because you harbor an unreasonable hatred for him." She delved into the man's eyes seeking any softening and found none at all. "I would like to speak with your driver."

"I thought Lord Harcourt was here to do so."

"He has been called away for a short time. In the interim, I would like to speak with the man. Unless there is some reason you do not wish me to."

Rudman hesitated then said grudgingly, "John is waiting in the hall."

She strode to the door and paused just outside the room to still her resolve against the discouragement that threatened to overwhelm her. Arguing with Rudman was like throwing oneself against a stone wall. She had promised Matthew that she would fight for him, she would watch his back, and she would do it. She straightened her shoulders, though every inch of her ached with exhaustion.

The man leaned forward in a chair, his elbows braced on his knees, and his hat held in his hand. He straightened as she approached, and rose to his feet. For a moment, she studied his elderly features wondering if once again their hopes would be crushed.

"Good evening."

The man bobbed his head and tugged once at his coat to straighten it. "Good evening, miss."

"Might I ask your name, sir? Lord Rudman called you John."

"Yes, miss. John Abner."

"Mr. Abner, my name is Katherine Hamilton. It is my husband who has been arrested for Lady Rudman's murder."

The man's gaze wavered and fell. "'Tis sorry I am for your trouble, ma'am."

"Thank you, Mr. Abner. Will you please join us in the library?"

He hesitated then nodded. His steps slowed as they reached the door, and She placed a hand upon his coat sleeve. "We just wish to ask you some questions about the day Lady Rudman died. It is very important that you share with us everything that happened that day."

The man nodded again. She studied his face as they entered the room. His attention focused on Avery Rudman first as he sat in a chair by the fire then swung away to touch on Clarisse then Talbot. She directed him to a seat across from Clarisse, so as not to allow Lord Rudman an opportunity to intimidate him with a look or gesture.

"Talbot, would you retrieve the drawings I have done from the drawing room?"

"Of course."

She pulled a seat close to the man's and sat down. "How long have you been a driver for Lord Rudman, Mr. Abner?"

"More than a score of years, ma'am."

"Lord Rudman has been very fortunate in having you, I am certain. I am also certain he depends on you to be discreet about any private matters you might become aware of as well."

Rudman shifted in his seat and cleared his throat. Abner glanced in his direction.

"We depend on the people who have been in our employ for a lengthy time, to look out for our best interests."

"Yes, ma'am."

She leaned forward in her seat and tried to capture the man's gaze with her own, but he evaded looking at her. "My maid, Hannah, has been with me since I was a child. She is more than a maid. She is part of my family. After my parents' and brother's deaths, she was the only person I could depend on to care for me, to remain loyal to me."

"I heard about the trouble, ma'am. Everyone has spoken about it."

"I am sure they have." She paused as Talbot handed her the drawings. She smoothed the top one of Jaime Stone against her knee.

Abner's gaze fastened on the drawing and he swallowed.

"My family was attacked by highway men on the road to our home. The men killed my father and brother outright, then they tortured, raped, and strangled my mother." She swallowed against the pain. "My mother had concealed me in a compartment inside the coach. I tried to escape and mount one of the horses to go for help. I was shot, and when I fell from my horse, one of the men put a ribbon around my neck and tried to strangle me to death.

"He thought he had succeeded in killing me for a time. Since my marriage, he and the other highwaymen have tried to kill me numerous times to insure that I cannot testify against them. Had it not been for my husband's efforts, I would not be alive here before you now."

Lord Rudman swung to his feet. "I don't see what any of this has to do with my wife's death."

Her gaze swung from his face then back to his driver's. "Mr. Abner, will you look at the drawings I have done? You may have seen one of these men in the area that day."

The man's hands trembled as he took the papers from her. He stared at the portrait of Jaime Stone. The wrinkles around his eyes and mouth seemed to deepen, and his eyes filled with tears. He looked up at Avery Rudman then away. "I can't, your Lordship. I know what I promised, but I can't see an innocent man hung for something the likes of this one did." He shook the papers as though angry. "It was him and another man. Lady Jacqueline had just returned to the coach from the ship. I was helping her up the steps when the one came up behind me with a knife and threatened to stick it between my ribs. This man," he tilted the papers, "forced her into the coach. The skinny one forced me to drive into the alley. He promised they would not harm us, the other one just wanted to ask Lady Jacqueline where the Captain had gone. That's all he said he wanted." He swallowed and withdrew a handkerchief to dry his face as tears continued to stream down his face. "When the big one got out of the coach, I knew she was dead. He had a strange look in his eyes, lifeless, dead, like his eyes were made of green glass. The one atop the coach with me struck me three times and knocked me onto the street below. I hit my head. I awoke when one of the seamen from the docks stood over me and shook me awake. He stayed with me until the constable could be notified."

Katherine bent her head, her relief so staggering it took a moment for her to breathe. She raised the driver's hand to her cheek. "Thank you, Mr. Abner. You cannot know how grateful I am to you."

"It was his fault she was there to begin with," Rudman said as he sank back into his seat. He rested his chin on his chest as he gazed into the fire, his flabby features empty of emotion.

She forced herself to her feet. "Matthew sent her away, Lord Rudman. What else did you expect him to do?"

"I wanted him to die. I thought maybe she might—" he broke off what he had begun to say. "I wish him dead still."

She steadied herself against the back of her chair as her heart began to beat in her ears like a drum. She thought of Hicks's wide, thick-lipped face and the pleasure he derived in beating the prisoners. "What have you done? What more have you done?" The rising pitch of her own voice steadied her, and she grabbed his shoulder to give him a shake.

"It was his fault she was there on the docks."

"Matthew went to you weeks ago, and asked you to help him pursue these men. If you are going to point a finger in his direction, then point one in your own as well, Lord Rudman. Had you done your duty, they may have been in prison instead of preying on your wife. Or did you know about them even before that? Did you ignore their threat because Edward asked you to?"

Rudman's expression grew blank. When he looked up, she read the pain of the damned in his expression. "Talbot, we must go to the prison, now."

"It is probably already too late," Rudman murmured.

Those words staggered Katherine's hopes and sent shards of fear through her. "You had better pray that you are wrong, Lord Rudman. Otherwise, you will hang right along with Mr. Hicks."

****

Matthew settled the rickety chair on firmer ground then propped his feet on the door facing while he rested the flintlock on his stomach.

"Throw out the pistol." St. John's voice came from down the hall.

"No. I told you half an hour ago I would surrender it to Lieutenant Marshal Endicott whenever he arrives. Until then, I intend to keep it."

"You're only diggin' yourself a hole, Captain. Ye can't just take guards prisoner and expect us to go along with it."

"Well, you didn't just expect me to go along with their plan to abuse and kill me either, did you, St. John? What else has Avery Rudman ordered you to do?"

His words met with silence for a few minutes.

"If you have proof of his Lordship's involvement in this, I'm willing to listen."

Matthew snorted. St. John was in Rudman's pay. The man would kill him the first opportunity he got. "Lieutenant Endicott may question these men and get whatever proof needed. Until he arrives, ask the other inmates about Hicks's penchant for beating and tormenting them, for his own pleasure. That should give you proof enough."

A chorus of voices called out accusations down the passageway, and Matthew looked over his shoulder at the guard.

"Seems you are not beloved, Hicks."

The man glared his hatred. The gag prevented him from speaking.

"Who is this Endicott bloke?" Charlie asked from his position on the floor next to Hicks's cot. His wrist lay atop the reclining guard's rotund stomach, held there by one of the four manacles.

"He is one of His Majesty's Guard and known for his brutality. He talks like a gentleman, but has the heart of a pirate. How else do you think he was able to arrest me?"

Charlie exchanged a look with Arthur, the third guard and his manacle mate. Matthew could almost hear the men swallow, and turned aside to hide his smile.

A sound in the passageway had Matthew rushing to his feet. He took a position against the wall just inside the door and pointed the flintlock upward.

"Matthew—"

Katherine's voice had him tensing. Were they using her to draw him out? He leaned forward to see who might be with her as she stepped upon the metal door. Her wet slippers fought for purchase on the slick surface and he caught her hand and pulled her to him. She steadied herself against his chest as he shielded her body with his own. He braced himself to face whatever threat might follow and was surprised when none came.

She clung to him with her face pressed against his chest and after a moment, he realized she was crying. His hand tangled in her hair, wet with rain, as he cupped her head and held her close.

"What are you doing here?" he asked when she seemed to be regaining her composure.

"You are cleared. Lord Rudman's driver identified Jaime Stone as Jacqueline's killer."

Relief had him drawing a deep breath, and he kissed her.

"Lord Rudman as good as admitted hiring someone here to kill you. I was so frightened. I thought I might be too late."

"So you rushed here to save me."

"Of course." Her violet eyes rested on him. The worry and fear of the experience had etched dark circles beneath them.

"And you braved the dark."

She looked about her as though noticing her dank, close surroundings for the first time. "It would seem so."

"Why?" he prompted.

A frown flitted across her face then cleared. Her eyes moved over his face with a look that brought a feeling of fullness to his chest.

She cupped his face in her hands. "I love you."

"I told you I was going to kiss you every time you held something back from me," he said, his voice husky. His mouth covered hers, and he tasted the sweet truth of her words in her eager response.

"Captain Hamilton," Lieutenant Endicott's cultured tones came from just outside the door. "I hear you are once again in a spot of trouble."

Matthew broke the kiss unable to stifle his laughter. "Indeed, Lieutenant Endicott. Please join us, so we can sort it out."

CHAPTER 28

Matthew propped his feet atop a small stool and crossed his arms. It was a sorry day indeed when a man couldn't have a moment alone with his wife to give her a gift and share aloud his thoughts and feelings for her. It seemed the entire household had a purpose for being in their rooms and disrupting their every moment together. First, Clarisse had come up to bring Katherine a selection of ribbons with which to do her hair. Then one of the maids had delivered the velvet gown Katherine would wear to the dinner. He had been called away for a few moments by his purser to discuss a small problem with a shipment of some of the goods he had purchased, and now, Hannah had come up to help Katherine dress.

He watched Hannah brush and loop Katherine's hair into an intricate design at the back of her head. He listened as the two women discussed what color ribbon would best match the gown Katherine planned to wear. He decided that he had missed being privy to a wife's toilette. He derived pleasure from listening to her feminine tones as she spoke, the soft fragrance of her scent, the look of her perched on the small chair before the dressing table while Hannah attended her.

Katherine's skin glowed warm and smooth in the lamp light. The tightened stays stretched the fabric of her shift against her breasts, outlining their full shape. Matthew felt the blood race to his groin and shifted in his seat with a murmured oath. Katherine and Hannah both turned their attention on him, their enquiring expressions bringing a self-deprecating smile to his lips.

"I'll wander downstairs to see if Talbot has returned. He may have news. I'll return shortly to escort you to dinner." He paused behind Katherine to brush a kiss against her bare shoulder and watched as her cheeks blossomed with color. His gaze captured hers in the mirror. He read the anxious distraction in her expression.

257

"Hannah, I'd appreciate your staying with Katherine until I return."

"Certainly, Mr. Matthew."

He made his way downstairs to the entrance hall. He watched from the landing as one of the maids put the finishing touches on a centerpiece of greenery and holly berries on the hall table.

Christmas would pass before they would set sail. He would once again miss the holiday with Emily. He wondered if there would be any way he could make up to her for his long absence. His earlier letters to her would not reach her for at least another month. He drew a frustrated breath. Perhaps they could have another Christmas celebration when they reached Charleston. It wouldn't be the same. It wouldn't heal the disappointment she would undoubtedly feel now. There was no hope for it. He could not sprout wings and fly across the Atlantic to join her.

He descended the stairs and walked down the hall to the library. He gave the door a cursory knock then opened it.

Talbot turned to look over his shoulder, from his position at the French doors. "Come in, Matthew."

"How is Katherine faring?" He joined Matthew.

"She is anxious to get this behind her."

Talbot nodded as he poured brandy into two glasses then offered him one.

"Lord Harcourt has somehow managed to keep the arrest of the highwaymen quiet thus far. It will come as a surprise to Edward."

"And the will?"

"A forgery and not a very good one at that. He paid a fortune to have a copy registered only weeks before his brother's death. The man responsible has been captured and admitted to the fraud. The original will has probably been destroyed. We will not know until his apartments can be searched."

"It will make no difference to Katherine. The money and properties meant little to her without her family."

"I wonder if you know how rare it is to find a woman so unconcerned with wealth."

"I do. As my wife, she will never want for anything,

but she seems content as long as she has a stick of charcoal or a quill in her hand with which to draw."

"The paintings you brought back from Birmingham are extraordinary."

"Luckily they were packed before the stables burnt. They were hidden beneath the floor in the tack room." Matthew's jaw muscles tightened. "Her father thought her interest unfeminine and a deterrent to her finding a husband. He burnt the bulk of her drawings and paintings along with her paints just before he was killed."

"'Tis a shame her father could not celebrate her gifts and view them as such," Talbot said a frown drawing his pale brows together. "From what I have learned, Lord Leighton was consumed with controlling his properties. That included his wife and children. Of course, he would view Katherine's ability as something out of his realm and want to quash it."

"The bastard." His jaw muscles tightened with anger.

Talbot grinned. "Katherine told us of the marriage bargain the two of you made when you first met."

Matthew's brows rose in surprise. Her penchant for holding things back, or understating them, always threw Matthew. He found her willingness to open up to Talbot and Clarisse a pleasant surprise. Perhaps she was learning to trust a little.

"I take it the marriage is not going to be dissolved."

"No. Not even if it could." His tone sounded gruffer than he intended, and he grimaced.

Talbot chuckled. "We did not think so."

He smiled at his uncle's obvious look of pleasure.

"What of Avery Rudman?" he asked changing the subject.

"He has been stripped of his commission and is under house arrest until he can be taken before Judge Townsend. I believe they will plead dire emotional distress and he will be spared the noose, but it will be some time before he will be allowed his freedom. And as for Hicks and his cohorts, they are already residing in the very jail they guarded."

"Had Rudman chosen someone more intelligent and less intent on brutality he may have succeeded in seeing me dead."

"Let us be grateful that he didn't."

Talbot paused. "If everything works out as we hope, you know that it will probably take some time to settle the Leighton estate. You will have to bring Katherine back in order for her to claim whatever inheritance the court awards her."

"Yes, I know. When next we come to England, Emily will travel with us so you may see her."

"Indeed and your brothers as well, if you can manage to persuade them to join us."

"I will." His gaze settled on Talbot. "I can't begin to thank you for all you have done for me. After all that has happened—"

Talbot slapped him on the back. "We are family. We stand together."

"Yes, we do." He cleared his throat against the emotional obstruction that caused his voice to sound husky.

The two settled before the fireplace to sip their brandy.

"Harcourt knows what time to be here?" Matthew asked.

"Yes. He knows what to do. He said the men have decided to be cooperative in exchange for a few comforts until their trial."

They lapsed into silence for a time then Talbot commented," It has a chance to work. In any case Edward will get the scare of his life, even if his nerve holds."

He nodded. "And if we don't get him for murder, there's at least a possibility of charging him with fraud and forgery."

"Indeed."

Matthew set aside his glass and rose to his feet. "Katherine will be becoming more anxious by the moment, and acting as though she isn't. I'm going up to join her."

"Your aunt said something interesting last night just before you arrived home. She said she knew the two of you were going to be fine together on the coach ride to Willingham's from the church."

His brows rose. "We didn't know ourselves, Talbot."

Talbot shrugged. "She said it was the way the two of

you were already banding together to care for one another before we ever reached the house."

He paused in thought. "I suppose she was right."

Matthew dwelt on his aunt's observation all the way upstairs. Hannah was fastening the last few buttons along the back of Katherine's gown when he entered the room. Her deep auburn hair was swept up, leaving bare her neck and shoulders. He studied the contrast of the deep wine colored velvet against her flawless skin. The color seemed to darken her eyes and make the pale rose of her lips and cheeks appear redder.

Her beauty fired his desire and passion, but her inner beauty nurtured and sustained it. The way she looked at him with love and caring, filled the hungry emptiness Caroline's death had left behind. Clarisse was right. Love had come to him in the damp, dingy prison cell and taken root in his heart. And for the life of him he couldn't think why he had been so afraid of it.

Katherine turned to face Matthew. He stared so intently at her she thought perhaps something was amiss with his uncle. "Is Talbot well, Matthew?"

He smiled. "Yes. All is well." He stepped forward to stand before her and take her hands in his. "You look beautiful, Katherine. I shall be the envy of every man here tonight. Don't you agree, Hannah?"

"Yes, Cap'ain Hamilton." Hannah's smiled and pressed a stray auburn curl in place. "There are some things Lady Willingham wished me to do."

Katherine watched her maid as she slipped out of the room. Hannah was pulling away from her, putting distance between them in order to make the parting easier, but it only made Katherine more aware of how much she would miss her.

"She hasn't changed her mind about sailing with us?" he asked.

She shook her head and bit her lip. "Your aunt has offered to give her a position here."

"She'll be safe here."

"Yes, I know. It is just difficult to think of her being so far away."

Matthew squeezed her hands. His desire to comfort her was easy to read in his expression. "She may change her mind."

She shook her head. "She says it is time for me to stretch the ties of one family in order to have another."

"That is all you'll be doing, Katherine, stretching them, not severing them completely." His hand lingered against her cheek. "And you'll be back to see her, possibly within the year."

"Do you think so?"

"With Rudman in jail, there will be no reason why we can't return for a visit, whenever we wish."

She remembered Hannah saying that her mother had wished for her a kind and generous husband. She thought Matthew might even surpass her mother's expectations.

"I have something for you." He removed the small bag from his inner coat pocket. "I purchased these for you some time ago and missed the opportunity to give them to you. I thought to give them to you at Christmas, but the gown you are wearing would display them as perfectly, as it does you."

She caught her breath as he pulled the necklace from the pouch. The fragile collar of pearls supported a teardrop shaped pearl much larger than the rest. As he fastened the band about her neck, the large pearl came to rest in the hollow of her throat.

She looked in the dressing table mirror at the necklace, amazed at the gift. She had owned few pieces of jewelry and certainly nothing like this. "It is truly beautiful, Matthew." Her fingers touched the dangling pearl as she turned to look up at him. Her throat felt tight with emotion and it took an effort to suppress her tears. "Thank you." She slipped her arms around his neck and tiptoed to press herself close against him and brush her lips against his cheek.

He turned his lips to hers, and she gave herself up to the warmth and pleasure of his kiss. She drew a breath to steady herself as he grazed her cheek then her forehead with his lips.

"No matter what happens tonight, know that I will stand with you against whoever tries to hurt you."

"I know, Matthew." She drew back to look up at him. "It will ease the need for you to stand against so many, if

Edward confesses."

"If that doesn't happen, it won't change the way I feel, Katherine." He touched the necklace. "I purchased this the night the doctor stitched my arm. I knew then I would never be able to leave you."

Her gaze settled on his face. Something in his expression set her heart to flight. "I have always known you were a man of honor, Matthew, and that you would not do that willingly."

"Honor be damned, Katherine." He made an impatient gesture with his hand. His pale blue eyes focused on her face with an intensity that turned her limbs to jelly and brought a smile to her lips. Hope suffused her, a waiting tension keeping her from drawing a full breath. He was going to say the words.

A knock sounded at the door. Katherine wanted to groan aloud her disappointment. Matthew quick scowl and whispered oath reflected that as well. He released her and strode to the door.

Hampton stood on the threshold. "Lord Harcourt has arrived and requests you and Mrs. Hamilton join him and Lord Willingham in the library, sir. It seems very important."

"Thank you, Hampton. We'll come down right away."

Katherine joined him at the door. She smiled for he looked quite ferocious with his dark brows drawn together and his lips compressed. "I love the necklace, Matthew."

His expression softened. "After this evening is over, no matter the outcome, you and I are going to lock ourselves away from everyone so we might speak without interruption."

She laughed. "I shall make myself available to you whenever you wish, my lord."

He smiled. The look in his eyes held a rakish charm that brought heat to her cheeks. "I shall remember you said that, sweetheart."

CHAPTER 29

As she and Matthew entered the library, Katherine's attention went to Lord Harcourt and Talbot where they stood before the fireplace. As she viewed their expressions, a sinking feeling struck the pit of her stomach. "What has happened?"

"Two of the highwaymen, a man named Brock and another named Jones have been killed. Another inmate stabbed them to death with a broken spoon handle. Since none of the men admit to being the leader, we are concerned someone may have paid the man to commit the murders."

"Two men are dead in the two days that have passed since their arrest. It seems too coincidental to be a horrible run of bad luck," Talbot said.

"I don't believe in luck," Matthew said. "Too many things have happened in the last few weeks for me to have faith in random events."

"The other men who were captured, is there a way they could be moved to a section of the prison and guarded by your men until their trial?" Katherine asked. "Just in case."

Harcourt smiled and inclined his head. "That has already been done, Mrs. Hamilton."

"And Mr. Badger?" she asked.

"He has sworn to do his part. He recognized the drawing you did of your uncle and agrees with your account of that night."

She nodded, her throat growing tight with emotion. Matthew's hand rested against the small of her back in silent support.

"What of Mr. St. John?" she asked.

"We have as yet been unable to locate him. My investigation into how he was handling his office has uncovered several cases, much like your husband's, Mrs. Hamilton. It would seem St. John would arrest whoever

264

Rudman had a grudge against, and evidence would be presented against them by Lord Rudman. After studying the evidence presented, most of the men have been freed." Harcourt turned his attention to Matthew. "The evidence in your own case, Captain Hamilton, has been reviewed and deemed fraudulent."

Harcourt gathered the cloak that lay across one of the chairs before the desk. "There is much to be done before Mr. Badger is to make his appearance. I shall see you later in the evening."

She offered her hand. He was quick to take it.

"Thank you for all you have done and all you are doing."

"It is my duty and my pleasure, Mrs. Hamilton." A smile flitted across his thin lips. "Talbot, Captain, I'll be back shortly." Harcourt strode purposely out the door.

"I must go see how Clarisse is faring. The guests have already begun to arrive." Talbot gave Katherine's hand a brief pat and slapped Matthew on the shoulder in passing.

Silence settled between them, with his exit.

The fresh bandages she had applied to Matthew's hand looked snowy white against the black of his long coat. His blue satin waistcoat hugged his torso and emphasized the long lean line of his body. He turned to look at her. His hair shined with bluish highlights. Gazing into his pale blue eyes made her feel as though her heart might beat its way free of her chest.

"How are your hands feeling?" Her voice sounded husky, and she cleared her throat.

"A little stiff since the blisters are healing." He folded his hands behind him and braced a foot upon the hearth. "And your ankles?"

"They are nearly healed."

His attention focused on her face. "I know it will be difficult for you to face Edward."

"Yes, it will." She drew a deep breath to steady herself.

He guided her hand through his arm. "Remember what I said. We'll stand together as a family. It will be all right, no matter the outcome."

Conversation paused as they entered the drawing

room and Katherine became aware of every eye focused on them as she and Matthew stood at the door. Some of the couples Katherine recognized and some she did not. Clarisse and Talbot had chosen those attending carefully with thoughts of earning support for Katherine should Edward confess.

Clarisse and Talbot greeted them. "Edward is being fashionably late. He is not here yet," Clarisse said just above a whisper.

Katherine's stomach twisted with nerves. If he did not come, it would spoil the affect they were hoping a public admission would have. "What should we do if he does not come?"

Matthew gave her hand a squeeze. "We'll think of something. We may confront him at his apartments tomorrow. I think I'd prefer a few minutes alone with him anyway." His expression promised a more physical retribution than planned.

"Lord Leighton and Mr. Drake," Hampton announced at the door.

Katherine sighed in relief and turned to face her uncle.

Edward greeted the Willinghams then turned to her and Matthew. Bruises from his recently broken nose gave the area around his eyes a yellowish look. He pointedly ignored Matthew and bowed to Katherine. "Greetings, Niece. I am glad you have returned safely from Birmingham."

She wondered how he could face her so calmly after what he had done to her mother. She had to swallow back the nausea that rose in her throat before she could answer. "We are safe, but I am afraid Summerhaven is not as it was before. Or has Mr. Drake had an opportunity to tell you?"

"Tell me what?" Edward frowned.

"We were attacked by the highwaymen once again, Edward. Summerhaven was set ablaze. The house was nearly burnt to the ground."

Edward's jaw went slack with shock. "But—but—" He wheeled about to face Garrett Drake. "Drake did you know of this?" His voice rising in pitch drew the rest of the guests' attention.

"Yes, Edward. I was in Birmingham staying at the same inn as Captain and Mrs. Hamilton when it happened. I am sorry I did not think to prepare you for the news on the way here."

Edward's expression settled into a stilted composure as he tried to gain control of his emotions.

"The house can be rebuilt, Edward," Matthew said.

"We are hoping the men might yet be captured," she said.

"It might have profited you to be more aggressive in your search for them," Matthew said.

Edward looked as though he had swallowed something, and it had lodged in his skinny neck. "Perhaps so."

"In any case," Katherine added, "had it not been for Matthew, I would have been killed. One of the men locked me in a closet and left me to burn to death."

She became aware of how closely their conversation was being observed when there were several gasps. A twittering of voices followed. Fresh gossip was hard to come by, she thought bitterly. How often she had been the brunt of it because of Edward? Her resolve hardened.

"I am sorry you have had to go through another ordeal, Katherine." Edward said, his eyebrows drawing together in an expression of sincerity.

For a moment, she almost believed him. "It has proven beneficial in some ways, Uncle. I have begun to remember things from that night. I am certain I shall remember it all—eventually."

Edward's Adam's apple bobbed, and he looked a little pasty around the eyes and mouth. She allowed herself a little satisfaction from his discomfort. She felt hungry for revenge and wondered how it might feel to plunge a butter knife into his black, hateful heart. "I am glad you are able to join us tonight. We shall be sailing at the end of the week. This will be our last chance to visit with one another. You must sit with me at dinner."

"I am certain there are others who would wish the opportunity to enjoy your company, Katherine."

"Indeed," Garrett Drake said. "I had hoped to sit beside you, Mrs. Hamilton. I am fascinated by your artistic abilities. I had hoped to discuss with you the possibility of commissioning a painting for one of my drawing rooms. With your husband's permission of course." He gave a slight bow in Matthew's direction.

She felt both surprised and a little wary of his sudden interest. She found anyone so closely associated with Edward a little suspect. "Since we are due to leave so soon, Mr. Drake, there would not be time for me to complete such a work."

"There would be no rush. It could be shipped to me, at your discretion, from Charleston."

"My wife will be too busy settling in once we arrive in Charleston. When we return at a later time, if you still wish to discuss it, I would not mind Katherine taking on the commission, if she desires to."

Drake smiled. "When do you hope to return?"

"We haven't discussed any long term plans, other than enjoying being a family. It should be within the year, if possible."

Drake nodded. "I will keep that in mind. Come Edward, we have monopolized enough of Captain and Mrs. Hamilton's time. There are others who wish to speak with them." he drew Edward aside.

Katherine watched Drake push a drink into Edward's hand as the next guests stepped forward to greet them. Katherine felt more than a little frustrated by the man's intervention. She had hoped to keep Edward close.

"Clarisse has placed Edward beside you at the dinner table. You'll have time to keep him off balance until Lord Harcourt brings Badger in to identify him," Matthew said, his lips close to her ear.

Lord and Lady Abington approached with their daughter, Amelia, and her fiancé, Morris.

Katherine dragged her thoughts back to the moment at hand, and turned to smile at them. Lord and Lady Abington passed on after only a few words, but Amelia lingered with Morris, a tall thin young man with a rather prominent nose.

"I have brought you a small token of thanks for what you did the day you visited, Mrs. Hamilton. You truly saved our wedding from disaster," Amelia said, her voice soft.

"I did not do anything that your mother would not have done eventually. She wants your happiness above all other considerations."

"I know she does, but she did have her heart set on my wearing her wedding gown."

Morris motioned to one of the maids serving drinks. She set aside the tray and rushed to bring him a parcel. He handed it to Amelia.

"I hope you shall be able to use these to draw with while on your journey to Charleston," Amelia said as she presented Katherine with the paper wrapped gift.

Katherine pulled the ribbon tied around the parcel. Her gaze fastened on the pale blue strip. She blocked out the memories that threatened, and folded back the paper. A smile leaped to her lips. Two fresh quills, a bottle of ink, several sticks of charcoal, and two sticks of sepia colored chalk lay in a protective cushion of paper.

"Thank you, Lady Amelia. This is a very kind and generous gift."

"It is just a token of our thanks and our support."

Morris spoke for the first time. "We have both been most impressed with the courage you have shown in your pursuit of justice, Mrs. Hamilton." His eyes moved about the room. "There are quite a few here who feel the same. If it is support you need, all you need to do is ask for it."

Surprised and amazed, Katherine extended a hand to Morris. "Thank you."

"Who is that young man?" she asked Matthew when the couple drifted back to Amelia's parents.

"His father is Lord Hallowell, an advisor to the King," he said as he helped her bundle the gifts back inside their wrappings. "You could probably gain the King's ear if you wanted it. What was it Amelia meant about your saving their wedding from disaster?"

Katherine crumpled the ribbon in her hand as Matthew motioned to one of the maids. The woman took the gift away with instructions to put it in their room.

"Lady Abington desired to pass down her wedding gown to Amelia. It was an ugly creation and completely unsuited to her. I just stated the obvious to the lady and drew a gown more flattering to Amelia."

"Which I doubt made you very popular with her

mother."

"Actually, Lady Abington was very open to my suggestions once she saw how thrilled her daughter was with the drawing. She even thanked me later for having saved her from pressing the matter and causing Amelia unhappiness."

Matthew shook his head. "I didn't realize you had such a gift for diplomacy."

She laughed. "At the time, I was not intent on diplomacy, just honesty. I did not think I had anything to lose by being honest with Lady Abington, since I had already been rejected as unsuitable by the ton anyway."

"It seems that tide has turned now," he commented as other guests came forward to greet them.

For a time, Katherine found it difficult to track Edward's movements about the room. She worried that he might find a way to slip away and avoid the coming confrontation. She experienced a wave of relief when Hampton appeared at the door and announced dinner.

Edward's displeased frown looked fierce as he held her chair for her at the table and waited for her to sit down. He turned away from her immediately to speak to the woman at his right.

Her gaze wandered around the room taking in the subtle lighting of the candles overhead, the minute care that had been taken with the centerpiece on the table. For a moment, she wished that the occasion could be one of celebration, instead of one fraught with tension and subterfuge.

Hampton slipped into the room and bent over Talbot's left shoulder to murmur something in his ear. Katherine looking down the table at him, saw his brief nod of encouragement. She laid the crumpled ribbon beside her uncle's plate and smoothed it out.

She caught Garrett Drake's attention focused on the ribbon. His green gaze touched her, his square-jawed features taut, his mouth compressed. She shivered as Jaime Stone's features came to mind.

Edward reached for his wine glass, spied the ribbon, and jerked his hand back. "What is that?" He pointed to the ribbon with equal parts revulsion and anger in his expression.

She dragged her attention back to him. "It is the ribbon Jaime Stone tried to strangle me with," she lied without compunction. "I carry it in hopes that it will help me remember what happened that night."

Edward's expression smoothed. "That is not the ribbon. It was discarded."

"I am not speaking about the first time, Edward, but while we were in Birmingham. He broke into our room at the inn and tried to strangle me. Matthew fought with him and Jaime attempted to stab him, would have stabbed him, had I not shot him. I killed one of the men responsible for my mother's death." She focused on Edward's face searching for any hint of guilt or regret. His gaze held nothing but a glassy, startled look. Katherine purposely touched the ribbon with her finger.

"You-you must not dwell on what happened, Katherine."

"I could understand the enmity others felt toward my father. But my mother never hurt anyone. She was gentle and kind and loving. Johnny's one fault was his insatiable curiosity. What harm could he have done to anyone?" She pressed her finger up and down the ribbon.

Edward placed a hand over hers stopping the movement. "They were just in the wrong place at a most inopportune time, Katherine. Their deaths were not punishment for any action they took."

His touch made her skin crawl. It took all the control she could muster not to jerk her hand from beneath his.

"It was my mother who was punished, Edward. I heard her begging them not to hurt her." She pulled her hand loose from his to rub at her temples as though in pain. She looked from the ribbon to Edward's face. She saw the rising panic in his expression and rose to her feet. "I saw you there, Edward. I know it was you."

Edward grasped at her arm, and she jerked aside. Conversation died at the table, and every face turned in her direction. "You were standing amidst them, buttoning your pants. Did you take your turn upon my mother before you allowed Jaime Stone to strangle her?"

A slurred voice came from the doorway. "He is not man enough to do that."

Katherine turned to see Avery Rudman standing in

the doorway. His sparse hair stood on end and his clothing appeared wrinkled and stained, as though he'd worn them several days. He weaved on his feet as he took a step further into the room.

Matthew rose to stand close to Katherine.

Hampton stepped forward to intercept the inebriated man. Rudman raised a flintlock and pointed it at his chest. The butler came to a halt, his eyes round. Rudman waggled the flintlock, and Hampton backed away.

"You assured me the man was only after Katherine and Hamilton, Edward. There would be no danger to anyone else. I wanted to believe that. I wanted rid of him," Rudman pointed the flintlock at Matthew. Katherine's heart skipped a beat as the man's focus came to bear on her husband. "I knew I would never be able to live up to Jacqueline's memories of you. I just wanted a chance." His bulldog-like features crumpled and tears of self-pity filled his eyes. He wiped them away with his coat sleeve.

"It is not your fault she is dead. It is mine. And his." Rudman poked the flintlock in Edward's direction. "I am going to kill you, Edward then I will end it for myself."

Edward grasped at Katherine's arm and jerked her in front of him. She stumbled, and he looped an arm around her throat holding her back against him. "It was Jacqueline's fault." His voice rose in pitch to a falsetto. "The randy whore could not do as she was told. She would not have been touched had she not continued to chase after him." He threw out an arm to point at Matthew.

Rudman's complexion took on a heated red, and his finger tightened against the trigger.

Matthew lunged against both Katherine and Edward, shoving them off their feet. They tumbled sideways to the floor. The loud report of the flintlock going off rang through the room. Screams and shouts erupted, and the guests, frozen by Avery Rudman's appearance, moved to take cover.

Matthew's weight pressed down on Katherine, and for a moment, she feared he was injured. Edward wiggled in an attempt to crawl from beneath them. Matthew shoved up on one knee. He grabbed Edward by the jacket.

She scrambled from between the two men and

hastened to her feet. Talbot stood against the door, shielding Clarisse with his body. Others peeked from beneath the edge of the table.

Lord Harcourt stood at the door. Two of His Majesty's guards held Rudman against the wall, disarmed. "My apologies, Captain Hamilton. We did not know of his escape, until just now."

His features taut with rage, Matthew frog-marched Edward toward the guards and shoved him forward. The man stumbled and would have fallen had one of the men not caught his arm. "We know you arranged for your brother and his family to be killed, Edward. We know you hired someone to forge a will leaving everything to you. Why would you purposely spread lies to destroy Katherine's reputation? What possible motive would you have for that?"

Edward stared at Matthew, his eyes wild with fear. "You know nothing."

"Yes, we do Lord Leighton," Lord Harcourt motioned for his men in the hallway.

Heavily shackled, Badger shuffled forward between them, his chains clanking noisily. His hair hung in greasy strands down his face. His clothing and boots, smeared with mud and other matter, smelled so bad Katherine's eyes watered.

"Is this the man who accompanied you the night Lord and Lady Leighton and their son John were killed, Badger?"

Badger stuck his face close to Edward's and laughed when the man jerked back with a look of distaste. "Aye, that's the bloke. 'e were so scared 'e couldn't get it up when it were 'is turn on 'er. Nearly wet 'is breeches when the girl came out of the coach and mounted one of the 'orses. 'e should 'ave killed 'er when 'e 'ad 'er under 'is roof. 'e wouldn't be in this mess if 'e 'ad. None of us would."

His beady black eyes settled on Katherine and he winked at her. "Tough little wench. Ye survived Jaime's shot and his special ways. 'e regretted 'e never 'ad a taste of ye before hand, like he did yer mum."

Katherine shivered for there was no regret or compassion in his ferret-like face, only pure evil. Matthew stepped to her side and drew her close.

Lord Harcourt motioned for the men to remove the prisoner. "We will see if we might arrange accommodations for you to spend some time with your accuser, Lord Leighton."

"No-no" Edward protested and began to struggle against the guard's hold. His gaze reached out to Katherine, beseeching her for help.

She turned her face against Matthew's waistcoat and locked away any compassion she might be tempted to feel for Edward.

****

"I do not suppose your aunt and uncle will be eager to have another dinner party for us any time soon," Katherine said as they climbed the stairs to their room some time later after the guests had gone.

Her talent for understatement brought a smile to Matthew's lips and he shook his head. "No. I don't believe so."

"Your hand is trembling," She observed.

"It's just a reaction from having a loaded flintlock pointed at my wife's chest. I thought for certain Avery Rudman had succeeded where Jaime Stone hadn't." His heart seemed to clench every time he thought about it. One brief hesitation and the shot would have struck her, instead of the sideboard. He was suddenly impatient to get her behind a locked door where he could hold her, touch her, feel the life pulsing within her, and draw comfort from it. He scooped her up and carried her down the hall, his long strides eating up the distance.

He kicked the door shut and leaned back against it as he lowered her feet to the ground.

"Whatever is wrong, Matthew?" she asked.

"A man just tried to kill you, and you're being damned calm about it. My insides are still jumping about like a netted fish on a hot deck."

"I am fine, Matthew." Her smile was laced with warmth as she cupped his face and rose on tiptoe to kiss him. He spread his feet to draw her close, welcoming the weight and shape of her against him.

"He shot at you, Katherine."

"He did not mean to shoot me, but Edward." She nibbled his ear lobe sending shivers down his spine, and hot blood racing to other parts of his anatomy.

"You are trying to distract me," he accused.

"Is it working?"

"Yes." She drew back to look up at him.

He shook his head ruefully. "I love you. I've been trying to tell you all day."

Katherine's violet eyes looked deep as a midnight sky. He cupped her cheek, and she held his hand against her face. "You have been showing me what love is since we first met, but I was too blinded by my need for justice to recognize it. By the time I did, it was too late to back away from the course I had chosen. Every time you have been in danger, my insides have jumped about like netted fish on a hot deck as well, until you were safe again." She rubbed her cheek against his bandaged palm. "I will never again risk you, or your love, for any purpose, Matthew. The price is too dear."

"And what of yourself, Katherine? You reached past my grief and showed me how to love again. Every time you've put yourself in harms way—"

She covered his lips with her hand. "Never again, I swear it." She drew his hand downward to cover her heart. "I love you. I will try my best to spare you grief, or worry, in future."

He knew she truly meant it, but knowing her adventurous nature... He loved that part of her, as much as everything else. It was what had drawn him to her in the beginning.

His fingers toyed with the teardrop shaped pearl that rested in the hollow of her throat. It had captured the warmth of her skin and reflected the tone of it, just as he had thought it would. "When I bought this necklace for you, I had something in mind."

"What was that?"

"Seeing what you would look like in it, and nothing else."

A slow smile tilted her lips and she drew his lips down to hers. "Lets find out."

EPILOGUE

Katherine watched from the doorway of the warehouse as Garrett Drake swung down from the hired hackney. He paused to speak to the driver then strode down the cobbled street that ran parallel to the docks, After walking only a short distance, he paused to look at the ships anchored in the harbor. The heavy falling snow powdered the shoulders of his cloak and tricorn..

Lord Harcourt spoke from beside her. "You were right, Katherine. You said it would be impossible for him to stay away."

"Knowing I am truly gone from England, would be very important to him."

A shouted call to action rang out across the water. "Hoist the main sail."

Sing-song answers echoed like a round. The small brigantine began to move down the channel under full canvas. The name Caroline painted in black lettering on her hull was clearly legible. "I'm sorry our departure has had to be delayed again, Matthew." She glanced up at him.

"As the ship clears the bend in the channel, and she is gone from sight, Carson will stay their progress and wait for us. It is important for you and me to see this done."

His understanding brought quick tears to her eyes even as the pressure of his hand against her waist soothed her.

Lord Harcourt turned to instruct the small band of soldiers behind them. As Drake continued to stand and watch the ship, Harcourt motioned to Katherine and Matthew to follow him. He approached the hackney and quickly climbed atop the conveyance to speak with the driver, while Matthew ushered Katherine inside the vehicle.

"You have the drawings?" Harcourt asked as he

joined them inside the cab.

Matthew removed some papers from the inner pocket of his great coat and handed them to him.

Harcourt unfolded them to look at them then shook his head. "Had you not noticed the resemblance, Katherine, we might have never known about Drake's involvement."

"Edward would have eventually incriminated him, had Badger not done so before him." Matthew said taking Katherine's hand in his, and giving it a comforting squeeze.

"Edward did lead us to a house Drake had purchased for Jaime. It would seem, the man felt some responsibility for his son. Perhaps if he had known of his existence while he was still young—but who knows." He gave a shrug. "As much as it has bothered me to arrange it, Badger's willingness to testify to the Drake's involvement with the gang has earned a bid for mercy. Badger will spend some time in prison, but will not see the hangman's noose."

As Drake's voice came from outside the coach, Harcourt grew silent and still.

Drake brushed the snow from the shoulders of his cloak as he swung aboard the conveyance. His eyes widened as he spotted them, and he quickly turned to jump back out the door only to have it slam shut in his face.

"Hello, Mr. Drake," Lord Harcourt spoke and cocked the pistol he held at the same time. "Won't you make yourself comfortable? We have a few things to discuss."

Drake looked over his shoulder at Katherine and Matthew, then turned slowly to take a seat beside the lord. When Harcourt proffered the drawings, Drake set aside his tricorn to accept them. He studied them for a long silent moment. His green gaze, so much like his son's, rose to Katherine's face and a brief smile touched his lips. "You are very gifted, Mrs. Hamilton. You have captured Jaime exactly."

The cold knot of tension eased inside Katherine and her fingers tightened in triumph around Matthew's. "Yes, I believe I've done justice to you both."

Printed in the United States
86682LV00001B/1/A

9 781601 540751